REDWOOD PACK BOX SET 1

CARRIE ANN RYAN

The Redwood Pack
By: Carrie Ann Ryan
© 2016 Carrie Ann Ryan
eBook ISBN: 978-1-943123-48-3
Print ISBN: 978-1-943123-49-0

PRAISE FOR CARRIE ANN RYAN....

"Carrie Ann Ryan knows how to pull your heartstrings and make your pulse pound! Her wonderful Redwood Pack series will draw you in and keep you reading long into the night. I can't wait to see what comes next with the new generation, the Talons. Keep them coming, Carrie Ann!" –Lara Adrian, New York Times bestselling author of CRAVE THE NIGHT

"Carrie Ann Ryan never fails to draw readers in with passion, raw sensuality, and characters that pop off the page. Any book by Carrie Ann is an absolute treat." – New York Times Bestselling Author J. Kenner

"With snarky humor, sizzling love scenes, and brilliant, imaginative worldbuilding, The Dante's Circle series reads as if Carrie Ann Ryan peeked at my personal wish list!" – NYT Bestselling Author, Larissa Ione

"Carrie Ann Ryan writes sexy shifters in a world full of passionate happily-ever-afters." – *New York Times* Bestselling Author Vivian Arend

"Carrie Ann's books are sexy with characters you can't help but love from page one. They are heat and heart blended to perfection." *New York Times* Bestselling Author Jayne Rylon

Carrie Ann Ryan's books are wickedly funny and deliciously hot, with plenty of twists to keep you guessing. They'll keep you up all night!" USA Today Bestselling Author Cari Quinn

"Once again, Carrie Ann Ryan knocks the Dante's Circle series out of the park. The queen of hot, sexy, enthralling paranormal romance, Carrie Ann is an author not to miss!" *New York Times* bestselling Author Marie Harte

AN ALPHA'S PATH

Redwood Pack Book 1

By
Carrie Ann Ryan

AN ALPHA'S PATH

Melanie is a twenty-five year old chemist who has spent all of her adult life slaving at school. With her PhD in hand, she's to start her dream job, but before she does, her friend persuades her to relax and try to live again. A blind date set up through her friends seems like the perfect solution. Melanie can take one night away from the lab and let her inner vixen out on a fixed blind date – a chance to get crazy with a perfect stranger. The gorgeous hunk she's to meet exceeds her wildest dreams – be he is more than what he appears and Melanie's analytical mind goes into overdrive.

Kade, a slightly older werewolf (at over one hundred years), needs a night way from the Pack. Too many responsibilities and one near miss with a potential mate made Kade hide in his work, the only peace he can find. His brother convinces him to meet the sexy woman for a one night of fun. What could it hurt? But when he finds this woman could be his mate, can he convince her to leave her orderly, sane world and be with him and his wolf-half, for life?

CHAPTER ONE

The thundering in Melanie Cross's ears increased as her breath became shallow. Palms sweaty, she bit her lip and nervously tapped her foot, as she took in her surroundings. The lobby looked like a palace. Tall, cream colored pillars and chocolate molding surrounded the opulent sitting area. Gorgeous light fixtures with tear drop crystals hung from the walls and the ceiling, giving the room a soft glow. Warm and inviting. But she didn't want to feel invited. She wanted to leave. Run away and never look back.

What was she thinking? Melanie was a smart, hardworking person. A freshly printed PhD in Nuclear Chemistry and a painstakingly long, nine hundred page, leather bound thesis sat on her desk, proved it. She could accomplish things on her own. Her ideas were acclaimed, and her work referenced numerous times. Any job her heart desired, now hers for the asking. Because of this she was about to bypass the normal post-doc route of working underneath yet another professor. Now she would be an Associate Professor with her own research group at an Ivy League University.

She gained a few close friends over the years, and even though she didn't have an overly active social life – okay she didn't have one to speak of – she thought her life was just peachy.

Yet her friends thought with all of the accomplishments in her educational career she was still uptight. Some even said she was missing her ideal husband. But her closest friend Larissa decided she just needed to get laid.

Mel thought back to when her best friend first told her this crazy idea.

"Really Melanie, when was the last time you got laid? First year? Even earlier? It's ridiculous! You are practically a born-again virgin." Larissa laughed at her own joke and then slid a business card across her newly cleared off lab bench.

"What's this?" A name printed on the card, Jamenson Services, stared back at her. "You're sending me to a gigolo?" She gasped and tried to throw the card away before Larissa quickly swiped it from her hands.

"No. The Jamensons are contractors. The man who owns it is an acquaintance of mine. He built the new green house at my parents. Come on, you need a date and so does he. It is only for one evening, and sex isn't required. But honestly, the way those Jamenson boys are built, you'll be dropping your panties at his command," Larissa lifted one eyebrow and laughed again.

"Oh I don't think so. I'm not that desperate. It's just that I've been so focused on my work that I didn't have time to date a man, let alone look for one." Melanie knew she could've just looked across the lab bench for the last five years to find a date. But really Timmy wasn't at all that worth to look at.

"Honey, you are too rigid. You need one night off before you skip ahead to the next part of your life. Call the number on the card and talk to Jasper. He's the brother of the guy I think would be perfect for you. Do it and get laid." She laughed, pushing the card in Melanie's hand.

SOMEWHERE DEEP DOWN Melanie knew Larissa was right. Melanie didn't throw the card away. She couldn't. Now six weeks later, she found herself sitting in the Hilton Resort in Seattle, about to vomit on the new black Fuck-Me pumps Larissa forced her to wear.

"Miss? Are you okay?"

At the sound of a deep voice, her head shot up to look at a very handsome man. Dark skinned, with piercing eyes, he surveyed her. *Oh my, is this her date?*

"Oh I'm fine. Just getting the nerve to walk into the bar, to get even more nerve to wait for my date." She winced at how fast and squeaky she spoke but really – why was she even here?

"I'm the manager, Lance Morse, let me walk you to the bar, and get you a shot of that nerve." He winked and she smiled him.

Melanie took a deep breath. "Okay." Wow. Surely, anyone could tell she was *Dr.* Melanie Cross, rather than the dumb blonde she seemed to be portraying. *Or not.*

He took her arm and guided her away from where she sat for twenty minutes regretting her decisions. Lance walked her toward the bar, while talking about the various hotel and resort amenities and events. She nodded while he spoke, as she felt the bar beckon her.

"Here we are. Thank you again for coming. If you need anything, feel no hesitation in asking one of my employees to assist you or ask for me by name. Enjoy your evening, Melanie Cross."

She smiled then stopped breathing for a moment. "How..."

"Your friend, Larissa, texted me earlier to be on the lookout for a small, shy blonde by the name of Melanie Cross and you seemed to fit the description. I took a gamble." He smiled.

Before she could respond, he winked again and walked out of the bar leaving her alone.

As she sat down, a Bay Breeze magically appeared in front of her and the bartender winked at her as he walked away. Did all men at this hotel wink? Her phone buzzed as she was just about to get freaked out.

Melanie babe, please relax. Your date should be there soon. Take a nice drink of that concoction and enjoy your evening. Oh and get laid.

Melanie laughed. Larissa possessed a one-track mind. She took a drink when her phone buzzed again.

Just remember to keep an open mind. He really is quite sweet and won't bite. Well, only occasionally. And only if you want him to.

What the hell?

———

KADE JAMENSON STEPPED into the lobby and was immediately assaulted by the delicate honey vanilla scent wafting throughout the room. His muscles clenched and he balled his fists, gaining control.

Mate?

He tried to tone down his edginess, but it felt as though his wolf was trying to claw his way out from the inside.

He spoke to the wolf inside his head, *"It surely smells like a possibility. But we are here for a date with a human. I am not so callous as to stand up a perfectly reasonable date just so I can follow a scent that could lead to disaster. Let me figure out this date first and then I will follow the scent if we have to. We already made the mistake of the wrong mate once; I don't want to do it again."*

Mate!

His wolf was right. He knew the woman who could be his mate wasn't even in the room, yet her scent and the urge to join with another was stronger by far than with Tracy. Kade took a deep breath of the honey vanilla scent and his balls tightened.

Damn. This woman was potentially his mate. How could this happen the night he finally took up his brother Jasper's offer of a blind date?

He quickly texted Jasper to let him know that he needed to break his date or do some major rescheduling and thinking. He couldn't be respectful to this human woman if he was aroused by another scent. It wasn't fair to any party.

His phone buzzed not one minute later with a response.

Kade, don't be an ass. Just go meet Melanie and I am sure you will have your answers.

After that cryptic comment, Kade didn't know what to think. Jasper told him, Melanie was a 5'2" petite blonde who should fit against his 6'2" frame nicely. Those liquid brown eyes that gazed up at him from her photograph, made him want to know what was behind them. That was a first for him. He might have been slightly nervous about the date but he was oh so willing and eager to meet with her. Just remembering her photo made him smile and want to see her in person. He was an Alpha male with no small amount of pride. Hell, he was the Heir to the Redwood Pack, first in line to the throne. Kade took one last deep breath of that honey vanilla scent and squared his shoulders.

He had a date with a pretty blonde.

CHAPTER TWO

Melanie sat at her table and checked her watch. He was only three minutes late. That didn't mean he was going to stand her up. Right? He just wasn't a perpetually early person like her. It wasn't evidence that they weren't compatible.

Compatible? Gawd. She needed another drink. This was just for one night. One night only – if he even showed.

She let out a deep breath and was about to order another drink when she caught sight of an absolutely gorgeous specimen of man.

His body towered over six feet with wide shoulders and a trim waist. The kind of guy displayed on one of those silly romance novel covers. Dark brown, almost black hair, that barely reached his shoulders begged for her hands to tangle in those silky looking strands. A few luscious locks fell into his eyes.

Those eyes.

Deep green eyes set under dark lashes. Pools of jade, swallowing her whole. They were piercing and shifted throughout the room, taking in his surroundings. Yet it felt as though he never let his eyes leave her. *Oh my*. Mel fanned her face before blushing when she realized what she was doing. Damn he was beautiful.

He practically prowled through the room drawing the attention of almost every woman and even some of the men. An almost animalistic wave of seduction ebbed from him.

Damn.

Please, if there was a God, let this be the mysterious Kade Jamenson. *Please.* Larissa didn't give her a picture or description of his looks as she said it would ruin the moment of first meeting. Melanie hadn't agreed when she read that, but if this were Kade she would take back anything bad she ever thought about her best friend.

His nostrils flared as if he were taking in a deep breath, then he smiled a truly feral and triumphant smile as he came to the head of her table.

"Melanie?"

"Kade?"

The both laughed quietly at the sound of them talking at once.

"Would you like to take a seat?" She was the one who spoke first. Well, the alcohol must have gone straight to her head because that never happened with men. Especially drop dead gorgeous men.

He smiled again and sat down gracefully in the seat across from her. She could've melted on the spot under the intensity of his gaze.

"Yes, I am Kade Jamenson. It is good to meet you Melanie Cross." The way her name roughly rasped through his sensuous lips sent shivers through her. "May I order you another drink?"

It took her a moment to drag her eyes from his lips to answer. "No. No, I'm fine at one drink. It seems to have gone straight to my head." She could feel the heat creeping toward her cheeks as she shyly bowed her head. Gawd, why not just tell him you are a light-weight before he takes you up to have wild and steamy sex?

Well, she guessed that didn't sound so horrible. Exciting, but not horrible.

He laughed at her remark. "Sounds reasonable, water it is. Then how about we order something to eat while we talk and get to know one another. I don't know about you but I was nervous as hell before I walked into the bar and saw you across the tables." He shook his head and chuckled under his breath "I know I shouldn't say that because now you think I am some loser, but I can honestly say I'm not nervous anymore. I'm happy I said yes to this date." He smiled at her just as the waiter came to take their order. "Ladies first."

"Um. Okay." She stumbled a bit as she opened her menu. Try as she might, she couldn't get her hands to stop shaking. It's been so long since she's been out. But none of those other dates could have prepared her for the example of sexiness sitting across from her. She sighed inwardly. *He is knock-dead gorgeous.*

Melanie quickly glanced down at the menu and chose the first thing that seemed edible. "I will have the Glazed Apricot Chicken with sautéed green beans and a side salad with balsamic vinaigrette dressing please. Oh, and another glass of water please." The waiter nodded while he took her order and menu before turning his attention to Kade.

"I will have the porterhouse – rare." Kade smiled at himself, as if what he said was funny. "Also a baked potato with the works. Thank you." He gave the waiter his menu. "Would you like to start off with an appetizer, Melanie?" His eyes implored her to do whatever he wanted. She shook her head to rid it of that odd and irritable notion.

"No, I think my dinner will suffice. I suppose you're a meat and potato type of guy since you didn't even bother with a vegetable." She shut her mouth quickly with an audible snap.

"Sorry. That isn't any of my business. Eat what you want. I'm going to shut up now." Her face was so warm that if her cheeks were any redder she would be a tomato.

Kade just threw his head back and laughed loudly, drawing the attention of a few of the nearby tables.

"Don't worry. Say whatever is on your mind. I don't think we need to keep secrets from each other." An odd flash of something passed over his eyes, but he quickly hid it. "But yes, I seem to be a meat and potatoes kind of guy. I'm not a huge fan of rabbit food and tend not to order it if I don't have to. It just seems like such a waste."

"Oh."

Oh yeah. That PhD was really shining through her vocabulary tonight.

"So tell me about yourself, Melanie Cross." He took a drink of the water in front of him and leaned toward her as if he didn't want to miss a thing she was saying. "Jasper told me some things, but that was just facts and figures. I want to know more about you and learn it from you." From the way he looked at her, he must be serious.

"Well, I'm sure you got most of this from your brother, but here it goes. I'm a twenty-five year old single chemist. I just finished my thesis and am on a break before I start my next job. I've spent way too much time behind a lab bench, with my nose in chemical journals to date properly according to my friends. Hence, the seemingly last ditch effort in relationships known as a blind date. So here I am." She spoke so fast that she sounded almost shrill and defensive. But she was terrified of what was supposed to take place that evening – even if according to her friend she didn't have to see his face after tonight. Although, with a face like that, it was unlikely that she would ever forget it.

"So what about you?" She wanted the spotlight off herself as soon as possible. For a woman who could talk in front of four hundred chemistry freshman or seven of the meanest and smartest professors in the field without breaking a sweat, she was slowly going crazy and incomprehensible sitting in front of this one man. One very hot man.

"Well, I'm a contractor and architect outside the Seattle area. I live near my family and we like the woods, and lack of crowds and large population noise. I own a contracting company and mostly build residential and small businesses. Sometimes I do special projects, like you friend's parents' greenhouse. I don't date all that much because I too am busy with work. I was seeing a woman for... a bit before we broke it off." His face didn't reveal anything but she thought she saw an odd expression flicker across his eyes before he blinked it away.

"Was it serious?" She couldn't believe out of all the things he said that was the one thing that popped into her mind. And frankly, did she even want to know? This was a first date for crying out loud.

"It could have been, but it just didn't work out. She is with someone else, and I am free to pursue other... avenues." He kept pausing before some words as if he were trying to decide what to say – as if he were keeping a secret from her. *Hmm...*

"I'm glad, however, that things took this turn because now I'm on a date with a lovely woman." He flashed her a wicked smile right as the waiter brought their entrees.

"Enjoy your meal, Melanie, even though you have more rabbit food than meat."

She laughed, enjoying his odd sense of humor. They quieted while they began to eat.

————

A FEW BITES IN, Kade noticed that Melanie barely touched her food. Nervousness emanated from her skin. Fear even. He, on the other hand, fought his wolf to tone down their hunger for something other than their meal.

The honey vanilla scent sat across from him. His wolf was beyond pleased and ready to jump across the table and mount her.

The man however, was a little more cautious. Relief flooded him when the sweet honey vanilla scent radiated from the beautiful goddess from the photograph. He was on a blind date with his future mate. *How fucking awesome was that?*

His brother and Larissa were either sneaky geniuses or very lucky. They both were scary beyond all recognition sometimes, but amazing nonetheless. He owed the matchmaking duo an apology, but later. First, he had to get to know Melanie and get her upstairs. Even if they didn't have sex tonight and only talked, he would be fine. Because they would have hundreds of years to get to the dirty fun part.

And yes, she was his mate. The mating urge rode him harder than anything he ever felt. Kade was not letting this one get away. He'd do anything in his power to make the blond pixie in front of him want to spend the rest of her soon-to-be-long life with him.

With that goal in place, his wolf subsided a bit.

Don't screw this up. This is the one, Kade.

Kade just smiled at his wolf and brought his attention back to his date.

"Are you done eating? Or would you like some more time?"

She bowed her head again, as a cute and damn sexy blush rose to her cheeks. He wondered if she blushed like that everywhere. She was wearing a sexy black silk and lace number that only accentuated her slightly curvy figure. She was a tiny thing that he knew could fit against him just right.

He could only imagine how she would look with her pale, creamy skin against his darker, bronze skin. Watching her lashes brush her cheeks as she glanced down at her barely touched meal he knew he wanted to kiss any fears or anxiety she carried away.

Mate? I think it's time to go upstairs. Don't you?

He couldn't agree more with his wolf. But he didn't want to rush her. No matter what happened tonight, they would be going upstairs – that was a guarantee. What they did once they arrived however – was up to the woman in front of him.

"You look as if you have the same appetite as me." At the sound of his voice, her head popped up from whatever deep thoughts she was thinking. "What do you say we take a walk around the property?"

"Oh, okay. I guess I am just not that hungry tonight." She smiled sheepishly as she set down her fork and any pretense of enjoying her food.

"Let's go then, the check is taken care of, so we can take our time tonight."

She smiled timidly again and grabbed her wrap and black, beaded bag. He fluidly rose from his seat and offered her his hand.

"Where would you like to walk to?" Kade, again, toned down his wolf and waited for Melanie's reply.

"Our room?"

Her face was still stunning with the shade of beet red it became at her surprising, yet not unwelcome, announcement.

His wolf growled in agreement and preened for attention.

He gave her a smile that promised sinful and wicked deeds.

"That sounds like an outstanding idea, Melanie."

CHAPTER THREE

K ade led her toward the elevator through the atrium, with his hand against the small of her back. The warmth of her delicate body radiated through her thin dress and with his wolf senses, he felt her heart pounding and her breath coming in almost shallow pants. She was aroused, but also succumbing to nerves and fear, the scent wafting from her skin. The need to reassure her pounded through his body, and even though his wolf practically begged to have her, he agreed.

Kade clasped her small, silky soft hand in his larger, more calloused one and entwined their fingers together before giving it a comforting squeeze. Mel smiled up at him and warmth bloomed in his chest. She was so small, so fragile. His.

The elevator chimed and a couple walked out. They exuded sex and drowsiness, and he wasn't the least bit jealous. He was about to be in the same room as his mate.

As the elevator rode up to the twenty-first floor, he tried to make small talk but neither of them was interested. He chuckled under his breath, feeling like a teenager again. Too bad it was almost a hundred years since he was one.

They finally entered their room, aptly named the Dreams Room and closed the door with a resounding click behind them. The room was draped in white and cream silks. There were linens surrounding the open and airy bedroom with candles barely lit where the linens gaped open. The bed was almost bare except for fluffy white pillows and a luscious white comforter. That was good; he didn't want his claws, if they did make an appearance, to destroy too much.

Once they both took in their surroundings, Kade led Melanie toward the center where she abruptly halted and turned around.

Her eyes were huge and she was barely breathing when she spoke hurriedly.

"I changed my mind. I don't think I can do this. I mean it's not you. It's me. Oh hell!" She slapped her hand to her forehead then covered her eyes. Kade bit the inside of his cheek to stop from laughing. She was really too cute with her deep blush and the way she bit into her plump lip.

"I mean, you are great looking. Fabulous in fact. But I'm sure you know that. You must have woman throwing themselves at your feet in droves, but I don't think I can do this. I don't know why I even signed up for this, let alone tell you we should come up to the room." If she continued to talk, she would rationalize herself right out of the room and out of his life. His wolf and he snorted silently. *Yeah, like that's going to happen.*

"Melanie. Calm down. It's okay. We have this room, but nowhere does it say we need to utilize it doing any acrobatics. Well I guess we can try to do cartwheels and those backhand flip spring things that gymnasts do but I don't think that is required either. If you want to talk, we can just do that."

A look mixed of laughter, relief and disappointment ran across her face. Damn, her face was expressive. When they finally did go to bed together, he was going to love watching new emotions run across her face when she came.

It was her disappointment he needed to address first. One giant step and he could crush his body to hers and feast on her until she came. His blood pulsed through his veins, and he held himself still so he wouldn't shake with desire. He had to reassure her that she wasn't the least bit unwanted.

"Now don't look at me like that," Kade's wolf growled at the thought. Fuck, if she gave the okay, he would be on top of her, his cock encased in her pussy in a heartbeat. She was fucking jaw-dropping. "If you were to say 'let's go for it' right now, then I would be there because believe me, you are sexy and I do want you. But I also don't want to do anything that would scare you or that you are not ready for. We can just talk or watch a movie. We can even go for that walk we discussed but opted out of. I am really enjoying getting to know you, and I don't want this night to end just yet."

Kade took a tentative step toward her and removed her wrap and purse to place on the couch in the corner before taking her hand in his.

"I have an idea. Why don't you go take a bath and relax? I promise I won't enter the room - unless you ask for me." A sly smile lifted the corners of his mouth as he kissed her palm. Her skin was warm against his lips. "Once you're done, you can come back out and we can do whatever you want. No pressure." He spread out his hands to convey his easy going attitude and gave her his best innocent expression.

For a moment, she didn't look like she believed his face or his body language, but the words may have made a tiny chink in her armor.

"No pressure? I don't think that will happen. But a bath does sound decadent. It's been awhile since I've taken a long, relaxing soak." Her eyes brightened more and more as the idea took hold.

"Okay then, when you're in there I'm going to order us some snacks and see what they have for movies. We can just veg out and get to know each other some more."

Her answering smile could've blinded some men. "That sounds like a fabulous idea."

She picked up her larger bag that the bellhop brought up earlier and gave him one last smile before heading to the bathroom and shutting the door softly.

Kade took a deep breath of her honey vanilla scent that was more concentrated in the enclosed room and almost shook with anticipation.

He practically glided to the phone to place their orders and smiled to himself. The night may not be exactly how he expected so far, but he wouldn't want to lose a single moment of time with his mate.

———

MELANIE TOOK a deep breath as she gave herself a good look in the mirror. This bathroom may be the greatest and most luxurious thing she'd ever seen, but she barely gave it a second glance.

What the hell was she doing? There was a gorgeous god standing in the room that she practically ran from. What the hell was she doing in here?

All throughout dinner, she couldn't seem to string two coherent sentences together. She resembled a ditzy, shy deer in the headlights. It was no wonder Kade was just fine with not having sex tonight. Oh, he may have said that he wanted her, but he didn't seem to fight for it.

Oh, that was just great. Kade was considerate of her feelings, yet here she was, making him the bad guy. This whole experience made her a wreck. Maybe Mel wasn't experienced with men, but she was experienced with meeting people and communicating with another human being. Tonight was a once in a lifetime opportunity to have wild and passionate sex with a near stranger. And oh yes, just looking at Kade, she knew it would be exactly that. She grew damp just thinking about him, and what wicked things could await her if she would just say yes.

And honestly, what was stopping her? Going through with this would leave her with an amazing and glorious memory. She needed more of those. The need to hear she was beautiful, sexy and wanted overwhelmed her. Mel didn't want to be the "smart" one anymore. She squared her shoulders and looked at herself in the mirror once more.

Oh yes. Once through that door, the needy and long ignored woman in her was going to go out there and tell Kade to fuck her. It was what she wanted – what she needed.

Mel took a steadying breath and changed into more comfortable attire. Comfort wasn't to be found in that slinky dress and Fuck-Me heels. If she were going to make a new memory, she was going to damn well do it in an outfit she liked. Grabbing the door handle with a firm grip, she thought about what was beyond it. The passage led to maybe not her destiny but definitely an amazing night.

CHAPTER FOUR

K ade looked over his shoulder as the bathroom door opened. Melanie changed into a new more comfortable outfit. The top and leggings she put on did little to hide her delicious curves and only increased his desire for her. "Decided against the bath?" Kade's breath became shallow as he watched Melanie practically prowl toward him, even as his eyebrow slightly lifted.

"Uh huh. I also decided that you sounded like a much better way to pass the time and relax me than taking a bath." She smiled a purely seductive grin, though he could still read the hesitancy in her eyes.

He took a steadying breath and nodded. Words seemed to fail him – and the wolf – at the moment.

Kade stepped toward her and brushed his knuckles against her cheek. The responding shiver brought his wolf back to attention.

"We still need to have our first kiss, Mel." Another half step and their bodies brushed, feather light. The anticipation of what was to come proving more erotic than he ever dreamed.

His fingertips traced across her eyebrow and down her cheek before resting on her lips. They were silky and smooth. The tip of her tongue tentatively slipped out to lick his finger, and he moaned.

Leaning forward, he brushed his lips against hers, so lush and ripe he almost came right there. His body melted against hers, losing himself until there was no division between them. Her taste fuzzed his brain, he was slowly losing it. But what the hell, this was his mate, and this was their first kiss.

It was a kiss so sweet and so promising that the sexual tension seemed to hum throughout the room.

He licked the seam of her lips, and she opened for him and moaned. *Dear God, that honey vanilla would kill him.* His other arm came up from behind, and he dug his fingers in her hair in a gentle yet possessive grip. *Mine.*

When they finally broke apart, they were both breathless, and the corner of his mouth lifted.

———

KADE'S ARM wrapped around her as he slowly and methodically ran his hand up and down her back. Shivers of need racked her body. *Oh my, he's amazing.* He led her toward the bed and sat her down gently before joining her. His warmth brushed against her skin through the thin peasant blouse she wore. Another ache ran down her spine, and she took a deep breath and inhaled his scent. Masculine pine and forest invaded her senses, causing her head to swim. She wanted to taste him again. Mel wasn't so hesitant and scared anymore. Well, maybe it was a new scared, but she was anxious to see what came of it.

Kade's hand brushed the underside of her breast and her breath caught. Goosebumps rose in the wake of his hand as it slid down to cup her bottom. She snuggled closer into to him and moved her hand onto his chest in small circles. His heartbeat under her palm increased and his breath quickened. Mel raised her head to look up at him – his pupils dilating in his forest green eyes.

"I'm glad that you decided against the walk." His voice had deepened and taken a rougher edge to it – almost a growl.

The rough tips of his fingers walked against her skin as his hand brushed underneath her shirt. A gasp escaped her, as she felt them splay against her back. Kade lowered his head and captured her lips. His tongue ran the seam of her lips and she parted them. He kissed her fiercely before moving his lips to her chin and then kissing a trail down the center of her chest. His mouth reached her breast and he clamped his lips on her nipple through her shirt. A moan tore from her throat, before she let him strip off her blouse. His tongue delved into her mouth with fevered passion. He undid the front clasp of her bra and her breasts released heavy and ready. Kade went back to her mouth and kissed her deeply. She gasped into his mouth and arched against him. Her nipple pebbled against his touch and she shuddered again.

Kade continued to devour her mouth as he kneaded her breast. She ran her free hand up his chest and neck and dug her fingers into his hair and scalp. He released her mouth and Mel groaned. A soft laugh left his lips before he kissed under her jaw and traced a fiery path down her neck and then back up to nibble on her ear. Her breath came in short pants as she felt his heated breath whisper against her and she moaned.

Her lover moved her body so she lay down, all the while touching her. He rested between her legs and bent down to look directly in her eyes. His pupils were so deep with desire that she could only see a small rim of green. For a moment, she thought they glowed but it must have been a trick of light. She arched against him and ran her foot across his calf. He swallowed hard and bent to capture her lips again, kissing her fully and then lowered to kiss her chin, her neck, and collarbone.

He went back to her breasts, scraping his teeth against the rosy flesh. Mel gasped and moved against him. Kade pulled her nipple through his teeth and suckled before biting down. He released her and then laved the sting. Shudders racked her as he turned his attention to her other nipple and repeated the process. Her desire pooled deep inside her womb and she clenched her legs around Kade trying to ease the ache. A deep masculine chuckle vibrated against her, and he moved downward to kiss her belly slowly. Moving further down, he ran his tongue against the top of her leggings. She moaned and tried to wrap her legs around him but he steadied her. His hands glided up her legs to the waist band and began to pull her leggings down. Mel lifted her bottom to allow him easier access. Kade groaned and pulled them completely off, staying on his knees a moment longer to look his fill up her body as she lay wanton before him. He lowered himself and placed his mouth directly on her pussy through her black, silk panties. Kade breathed in and suckled her clit and she came without his direct touch on her skin. The landscape shattered beneath her eyelids while stars blanketed her vision, and she screamed and moaned. He twisted his hands in the sides of her panties and lowered them slowly down her legs, climbing back quickly and parted her legs wider. He sat back on his haunches to gaze at her. Mel blushed, feeling open and awkward under his scrutiny.

"Your pink flesh is glistening for me, Mel. You are so beautiful when you come and I want to see it again." As he spoke, her muscles relaxed, tension easing from her body. "This bud is waiting for my mouth. Do you want me to suck your clit, Melanie? Do you want me to lick your seam and fill your pussy with my fingers?"

Mel wasn't capable of speaking, so she simply nodded. A satisfied smile spread over his face, and he lowered his head to blow across her. His cool breath dancing against her warmth, made her moan again.

"Damn, I'm going to feast on you until you come, and then I'm going to eat you again. You taste like ripe strawberries ready for plucking. And I'm going to pluck and suck you until I drain you dry of every last juice. Your juices are going to run down my chin and then I am still not going to have my fill of you."

Then he licked her from seam to clit and bit gently down when he reached her nub. Mel practically buckled off the bed and he pressed his arms against her hips to keep her placed where he wanted her. His tongue lapped up her juices, and then she felt him enter one finger insider her. Mel's inner walls clamped down on his finger.

"God, Melanie. You are so tight. I can't wait until I can fill you with my cock and you can milk me. Move on me, ride my hand. Oh Melanie, baby, yeah you like that don't you?" He returned to feast on her and she came again. But he didn't stop this time as she rode her climax and began to feel the next crest on its way. He entered a second, then a third finger, and worked her pussy while his mouth was still savoring and devouring. She looked down to see his dark hair against her pale skin and smiled. He licked her again and then placed a kiss on either side of her thighs before coming up and kissing her.

She tasted herself on his tongue but didn't feel embarrassed. Mel didn't have enough energy to do so. Kade kissed the side of her mouth and then her temple before moving the blankets on top of them. He surrounded her with his body, and she felt his hot and throbbing cock against her hip, and she wondered why he didn't do anything about it.

"I can't even think Kade. Oh my God. I think I lost count of orgasms. But what about you?"

He laughed deeply against her and rubbed his hand against her side.

"I have an idea, why don't we take care of each other at the same time?"

Her gaze widened and she moaned. This man was going to be the death of her. "I have never done that before. Okay."

This new found sensuality in her must be a gift from Kade. She wasn't going to stop it yet. If ever.

He sat up on the bed and knelt before her. Mel did the same and unbuttoned and unzipped his jeans. Her eyes widened when his cock fell into her hands hard and ready.

"You aren't wearing any underwear. Bad boy." She got closer and licked the drop of pre cum at the head.

Kade groaned and forced her on her side. He then twisted her around so her head was at the edge of the bed then laid next to her on her other side.

Mel moaned out loud when he placed his lips directly on her clit. She was already wet and ready for him. He nipped the gentle skin of her inner thigh, then licked up her juices that ran down, escaping her heat.

Mel moaned his name and then placed her lips around his cock. He sucked her clit and worked his tongue in and out of her passage while caressing her ass and gripping her hips. The coarse hair at the base of his cock tickled her lips before she slowly licked her way up his dick to the head. Taking a breath, she put her mouth back on him, swallowed him whole, and rolled her tongue against him. He seemed to like that because he moaned and bit down on her clit in response. In turn, she moaned around his cock in an almost never ending circle of pleasure. She worked him with one hand while digging her other hand into the meaty flesh of his ass. Her throat contracted around his cock as she came. Sucking harder, she gripped him firmer and his balls drew tight.

"I'm about to drop a load down that pretty throat Mel. Are you going to be a good girl and swallow it all?" At her nod with his cock still in her mouth he continued, "Damn, swallow my seed and suck harder, Mel."

When she rubbed her clit against his face, he came in her mouth. She swallowed it all and he screamed her name.

When Kade's still hard cock slipped from her lips, she moaned. *Oh my. How could she already miss his taste?* He lifted her leg and twisted himself so he lay practically on top of her without resting any of his weight on her. *So considerate, her lover.*

———

KADE'S HEAVEN resembled a blond goddess. Her sweet honey taste still flavored his tongue. Mel's soft, sated body lay beneath him, waiting for more. And oh, how he would deliver.

He spread her legs and positioned his cock against the entrance of her heat. Her eyes widened a bit and he kissed her slowly and long-ingly. His wolf was practically howling for him to turn her around and mount her. But the man wanted to see her face when he joined her for the first time.

He wouldn't claim her tonight. Not officially. A bite mark in the curve where her neck met her shoulder began the mating. But he would leave his scent on every square inch of her so no other wolf could come near her without knowing who she belonged to. In turn, her honey vanilla scent already seeped beneath his skin and he never wanted to wash it off. She may not know it yet, but she was doing some claiming of her own. The fact he didn't share with her what he was left him with guilt, but in time she would know the truth. He just hoped she would take it well.

"Wait, Kade. What about a condom?"

Mel's wide eyes forced Kade to stop, sweat dripping down his body. *Shit. How did he explain his way out of this one?*

"Damn, I don't have anything with me. I don't have any diseases, I promise." His voice deepened with barely contained need.

"Me neither. And I'm on birth control."

The thought of Mel pregnant with their young almost sent him over the edge. Their future. Their legacy.

Not that it mattered, since he wouldn't mark her tonight so there would be no pups. Without the mark, they wouldn't be officially mated and therefore no children.

"Are you ready, Melanie?"

She nodded and he slowly entered her. *Fuck.* A soft velvet heat encased him. Kade thought he was going to die from the pleasure of it and he was only partially in. Slowly, he rocked in and out of her pussy before taking the final plunge and sheathed himself to the hilt.

Kade waited and didn't move for a moment while she adjusted to him. This was the first time that he had made love. Yes, he had fucked his share of women throughout his hundred or so years, but this was the first time he was making love with his mate. Bliss.

When she was ready, he slowly pulled out and then leisurely entered her again. She gasped and moaned while he did his best to maintain control. Wanting to take the first time slow, Kade paced himself. Going too fast, too soon might bring out his claws. There would be plenty of time later to go crazy and fuck her brains out. As it was, he had to make sure his eyes didn't glow when he came. Scaring her away wasn't an option.

He made love to her, kissed her and loved her. Murmuring her name against her skin sent shivers down the both of them. His wolf came to the surface as he rode her harder, an outcome that could not be avoided. Kade quickly hid his newly formed claws underneath the mound of pillows. The sounds of fabric ripping were muted by the panting and moaning of their frenzied love making. He tweaked her nipples and then her clit and she came quickly against him. He followed right after her, utterly spent. Lowering himself to the bed, he wrapped his arms tightly around her.

"I don't think I have any more energy." Her voice was deep and raspy. Sexy as hell.

Kade slowly and methodically rubbed circles on her stomach and hip, her soft skin still glowing with their exertion. "We should rest and then I'm going to take you again. How does that sound?" He smiled against her hair when her body shivered against him, even though he had already pulled up the blankets over them both.

"Mmm. Okay. I think I can do that." Her words slurred with sleepiness.

He laughed and they both fell asleep.

He woke thirty minutes later and found himself wrapped around Mel's lush and delicious body. His cock was pressed up against her ass, and he was ready to take her again. Mmm. This was one of the most memorable nights of his life, and he knew that is wasn't quite over yet. His palm was pressed against her stomach and he slid it slowly up to grasp her breast. She gasped and rocked into his hand and against his cock simultaneously.

"Kade." Her voice was hushed and sounded barely awake but he caressed her breast while rocking against her. He licked and nibbled his way up her neck and chin while pinching her nipples. She gasped in surprise when he tweaked them harder and bit the junction between her neck and shoulder, without leaving the mate marking he so desperately wanted to leave.

She buckled against him as he slid his hand down to her pussy and pressed a calloused finger on her clit. "Melanie. You must be so wet for me. I am going to sink my cock into your pussy to make you scream my name again. Does that sound reasonable to you?"

Mel could only nod in response while she came against his hand and he entered her in one stroke, burying himself to the hilt. She screamed his name once more while still riding the peak.

"That's exactly what I wanted, Mel. And now when I do this I am going to play with this little puckered hole back here." He took her juices and spread it on her anus. He slowly played with her and entered just one digit to the knuckle.

"Oh God, Kade! Oh my God! Yes!" At first she tensed at the sudden and unfamiliar intrusion, but then fell back and relaxed so his finger could slide fully in. "Did I hurt you?" He would do his best to never hurt her.

"Oh Kade. Please don't stop. Please." She was gasping and her words were choked but not forced. His soon-to-be-mate looked mused with those rosy cheeks of hers like she had been fucked over and over again. His lover was a vixen and she would be his. He kissed her hard, fucking her mouth with his tongue when he entered her again fiercely. They continued on until they peaked and came crashing down together in a series of pants and gasps. They lay together for a moment before he extricated himself from her and rose to get a warm wash cloth. He cleaned them both up quickly before getting back into bed and pulling her into his arms.

"Get some sleep and we can talk in the morning."

He kissed her brow but heard no response as she was already peacefully asleep. He held her in his arms and whispered into her hair, "and soon baby, you are going to be my wife and my mate. No running. Just hope." He just needed to tell her that. Oh, and the fact that he was a hundred year old werewolf that wanted to bring her unsuspecting into his world. No problem there.

CHAPTER FIVE

Melanie opened her eyes to the early morning sun, pleasantly sore and tired. She blinked once and then again, as images from the previous night assaulted her mind. Kade was so unique and new. He touched and pleasured her in ways she didn't even know could happen outside of the movies. She blushed as a shiver raced down her spine at the thought. His warm, muscular arm draped around her stomach and hips in an almost possessive nature and it made her smile. He was still there. Their lovemaking lasted up through the night and into the early morning, rocking against one another in the throes of ecstasy. During the brief moments between, they spoke of their lives and dreams. Kade was open and honest in most respects. He also seemed to be hiding something from her, but if she were honest with herself, she wasn't surprised. They were only going to be together for one night. Now that night was over. That was the premise of their blind date – there were no promises, no obligations. Now it was morning and even though she could have basked in his warmth forever, she needed to get up and get out of there before she lost anymore of her heart.

And oh how she'd lost it. Kade's actions spoke of kindness, yet he could be aggressive when needed. The man was gorgeous and amazing in bed. And he was also going to walk right out the door without her. Taking part of her with him. She took a steadying breath, slipped from his arm and out of bed, and wrapped the sheet around herself. Kade moaned and scooted closer to her edge of the bed as if missing her. *Wishful thinking.* She leaned down over him, and took in the beauty of his sculpted features, brushing a lock of his dark brown hair from his forehead.

Gawd. Leaving him would kill her. Missing him will be worse.

As she continued to look at him, a tear in the fabric in the corner of her eye made her pause. She narrowed her focus and moved one of the pillows.

Were those claw marks? What the hell?

There were long gashes in the sheets and mattress. Her breath quickened and she took a step away.

"Don't be afraid, Melanie. I can explain." Kade's deep voice was gruff with sleep.

"Explain what Kade? What the hell happened to the mattress?" She took another step away from him.

Kade slowly rose from the bed as if trying not to scare her. Too late, she was becoming pretty damned scared.

"It's going to be okay, Mel. I know I should have told you sooner but I can explain everything." Kade stood to his full height in all his naked glory and said in a calm and collected voice, "I am a werewolf."

Melanie laughed out loud at his announcement, yet even to her own ears it verged on hysterical.

Seriously? Who does this guy think he is? Why not just announce he's a senator or something? That would be more believable.

"Werewolves don't exist."

Larissa's words came back to her in full force and Kade's outrageous statement began to sink in.

Just remember to keep an open mind. He really is quite sweet and won't bite. Well, only occasionally. And only if you want him to.

Wait. Did Larissa know what Kade was? Why didn't she tell her? Pain and hurt exploded through her. Why would her best friend do this?

"You bit me?" Horror skirted up her arms, her neck. What did he do when she was sleeping?

"What?" Alarm and confusion blatant on his features. "No, of course I didn't. I would never do that without your permission."

"So you would bite me? Oh my God." Her chest heaved. He was delusional and she was alone in a room with him.

"Mel, baby, listen to me. I would never –"

"Werewolves aren't real." Yes. Keep saying that. Let him know his delusions were not going to scare her away – too much. She would get him help and then leave his fine ass and be safe. Good plan.

"Then explain the claw marks, Mel. Yes, I am a werewolf. But I wouldn't hurt you. I won't *ever* hurt you. Werewolves do exist and we have for a long time. But I'm just like you, Mel. I breath, I eat, I love. I just happen to turn into a wolf every once and awhile." He gave her a small smile that comforted her slightly but she was still hesitant. She couldn't give into his dementia, could she?

Something from the previous night suddenly came back to her.

"Your eyes. I thought it was just a trick of light, but last night, they glowed didn't they?"

Kade let out the breath he held. "I hoped you didn't catch that. Sometimes they glow when I am aroused or letting the wolf take over. I didn't want to scare you away last night."

"I still don't know if I believe you. Can you show me? Or do you have to wait for a full moon or something?" If all else failed, she was a chemist. A scientist. She needed analytical data. Proof. Melanie didn't know if she wanted him to be able to turn into a wolf right in front of her or for him to say he couldn't and it was just an elaborate hoax.

She pinched herself and it hurt. Nope. Not a dream. Dammit.

"No we don't need the moon to change. We do feel its pull more the fuller it is but I can change anytime. Are you sure you want me to change? I don't want to scare you."

"Too late, Kade." She said wryly. "But I don't want to believe you. Prove it."

"Okay."

Sure, Kade, like anything would come of this.

Standing right before her, his bones contracted and changed, fur sprouting from beneath his skin. He crouched lower and soon there was a slightly larger form of a real wolf with dark brown fur with a strip of white down his nose.

"Shit!" She stumbled back and her legs ran into the couch behind her breaking her fall.

"Oh my God. You are a werewolf. But how? Why? What?" She could barely put rational thoughts together. The science behind such a transformation boggled her mind. How did this happen? What else was out there? This idea completely went against every logical thing she had ever known and learned.

"Kade? Can you hear me? Do you understand me?"

The wolf - Kade – hesitantly approached her while bobbing his head up and down, like a nod.

"Can I touch you?" She raised her arm to put out her hand and Kade came up and let her fingers run in his fur. It was course but with a soft undercoat. She rubbed his head for a few minutes and then sat back against the couch.

Kade went back to the edge of the bed and changed back to human form.

His skin took a slightly sweaty sheen, as if he had been running but other than that he looked the same.

"Does it hurt?"

"Only slightly, but I was born this way so I am used to it. Those who are changed say it hurts more at first. But over time they get used to it and the pain recedes. I can't change too often or I run out of energy though."

"Is it still you when you are a wolf? Did you hear me?"

"I can always hear you and yes it's still me. But sometimes I let the wolf take over so he can run and enjoy the outdoors on the hunt."

"You should have told me."

"I know. But I was just worried that you would run. But there is nothing to be afraid of. Once you meet the others you will see that."

"Others? Wait, what do you mean that I will meet the others? I thought this was just for one night." Her voice was beginning to sound panicked again.

"I want more than one night with you. I want hundreds of years with you, Mel."

"What? How old are you?"

"One hundred and five."

Oh yes. Just state a number like that without emotion. *Gawd.*

"So you are like immortal or something?"

"No, just long lived. And once we're mated, you can be too."

"Mated? Kade, you need to slow down. I feel like I am missing a few things here."

"Sorry, I know I am going about this horribly but I just don't know a good way to explain. Yes, you are my mate. It's a feeling my wolf has and I, as a man, agree. I want us to be able to live long lives together. I know we just met but this is the way of the wolf. It's fate."

The jumbled thoughts swirled in her confused mind. "I thought you were with another woman before. You said it didn't work out. What did you mean?" The idea of fate was foreign to her and he couldn't be telling her everything.

Kade sighed before answering. "Yes, there was a woman before. But no, she wasn't my mate. Not like you. You're different." Mel let out an indigent huff. "When my wolf and I scented Tracy, that was her name, we thought she had the *potential* to be our mate. Fate had other ideas though, because her true mate was another. I'm happy about this, Mel. In fact, I wasn't that upset when I lost her. Not until you, did I know what it meant to find my heart and my other half."

"But how do I know? I'm not a wolf, Kade and I don't know if I want to be one. I don't have a wolfy feeling telling me that you're my mate." She paced around the room trying to collect her thoughts. "I do have feelings for you – I do. More than I should for just meeting you last night. But does that make you my mate and I yours?" She shook her head and blinked away the tears that were forming in her eyes. "I don't know if I want to live forever. I hardly even know you. I was thinking you were just going to leave after last night. This is too much to deal with. I think I need to go." She started toward her bags before Kade stopped her by gently touching her arm. His callused palm still sent shivers down her spine, but she ignored them.

"Don't go Melanie. Please stay." Looking down at his golden bronze

35

skin resting against her paleness brought images from last night into her head. She shook off his hand, along with the memories.

"I can't Kade. This is too much." She quickly got dressed and collected her belongings.

"Then at least let me drive you home or get your number. I know I went about this all wrong, but we are destined for each other. I *want* to be with you. Please." Kade followed her around the room but kept his distance as if trying not to scare her any more than she was.

"You can give me your number but I need some space Kade. I don't know what to do. I just need to get out of here. I'll call you when I can think straight. I promise." Looking into his eyes, she tried to convey how much she wanted him and how honest she was trying to be.

Mel hesitantly walked toward him and stood on her tip-toes to kiss under his chin. His cheek showed the faint shadow of stubble and was rough against her lips. He lowered his head and took her lips in sweet and longing filled kiss.

She broke away before he could become more passionate and convince her to stay because of his body – that wasn't the way to get things done.

Mel took the paper that he had scrawled his number on and went to the door.

"I will call you, Kade. I promise."

She walked out the door and took one last look over her shoulder. Kade looked so lost and forlorn standing naked and alone in the center of the room, but when she looked into his eyes she saw something else. Determination.

CHAPTER SIX

Melanie's heels clicked across the linoleum, echoing in the empty lobby. The teardrop crystals from the lighting fixtures twinkled in the early morning sunlight. She paused, collecting her thoughts. Ironic. She stood by the same chair that she sat in and contemplated if she were making the right decision in going on this date. Now she was back, still struggling with her choices. An empty laugh escaped her. What a mess.

Her emotions ran wild. Fear bounced with happiness at the thought of Kade. A drop-dead gorgeous man wanted her for life, but why? Confusion and doubt settled it, seeping away any happiness. What Mel really wanted to do was run back upstairs, push away all of her emotions, and leap into Kade's arms. Yet, what did it mean to be mated to a werewolf?

Why the hell couldn't he have just been a nice *human* guy? Why was her life so fucked up?

"Melanie? Ms. Cross? Is everything okay?" A familiar deep voice broke her tumultuous thoughts.

The manager who walked her to her table last night stood by her elbow, a concerned expression on his face. Lance. Lance Morse. That's right.

"No. Yes. I'm fine. Just trying to get my bearings." It was then that she remembered what she was wearing – or rather not wearing. Still dressed in her black, lacy mini-dress, wrinkled from its time on the floor and her Fuck-Me pumps, Lance didn't have to guess what she did the night before. Her hand trailed up to her hair. Oh God. She must really look like she was just fucked, plucked, and made over. Heat infused her cheeks as mortification set in.

"Is there anything I can do to help? You took a cab in, correct? Would you like me to call one for you to get home?" Wow, she couldn't believe he remembered how she arrived. But she supposed that this was a nice hotel and the manager must know everything.

"Oh, if it's no trouble. I just want to get out of here quickly." She needed to leave this building before she lost her nerve and went back upstairs to the man who claimed to be her mate. Kade and his delectable body and apparently very sharp teeth.

Lance's gaze sought hers, his brow furrowed. "On second thought, I'm on my way out. Why don't I give you a ride home, save you the cab fare?"

Mel's eyes widened. "Oh, no. A cab will be fine."

The manager placed a warm hand on her arm. "Consider it part of the service. It's really no trouble, you look like you could use a friend to talk to. Let me help."

Too tired, worn and feeling used, she forgot to care about the potential dangers. She nodded. What the hell, she already slept with a stranger. Why not take a ride from another one. Truly risk fate.

After finishing whatever he needed to do, Lance led her to a tan sedan and opened the door for her. Mel slid into the soft leather and released a sigh. She was running from a werewolf. An honest to God werewolf of the paranormal nature. Yep, she was certifiably insane. To top it off, she was in a car with a man she didn't know rattling off her address. She needed a shot of tequila, a deep sleep, and a number for a therapist. In that order.

The ride was quiet if not comfortable. Lance didn't speak, but generally seemed concerned for her well being. She couldn't think about the man she slept with though. Kade, in all his muscular glory, occupied her mind. His number sat in her bag, imploring her to dial. Would she?

"We're here." Lance's voice startled her.

Mel looked up at the small, plain townhouse she called home. Ordinary. Much like herself. This is who she was – not a werewolf's mate.

"Thank you for the ride. Do you want to come in for some tea?" Manners dictated an invitation that tumbled from her mouth before she thought.

A slow smile spread across his face. "That sounds nice."

Inside, Mel started a pot of hot water and took out two clean mugs. "I have Earl Grey and orange zest."

"Orange sounds good. I don't need the caffeine. I've been working all night." He grinned, and for the first time, Mel noticed he was quite handsome and in her house. Alone. What was she thinking again? Oh right, the traumatic experience of a werewolf telling her she was his mate took her rational thoughts and put them in the garbage disposal.

This must be a dream. Why else would the chemistry wiz sleep with a man, and then go home with another. A hysterical laugh burst from her mouth.

"Melanie? Are you okay? No, I know you aren't okay."

Mel kept laughing, tears streaming from her eyes. Why wouldn't this night end?

"Melanie, I have something to tell you. I think you should just sit down."

Lance's calm, serious tone made her laughter cease. *Oh God, what now?* She sat on her couch, hot tea warming her hands.

"I don't know how to say this. But I am just going to say it," Lance nervously spoke.

Mel could only nod.

"Melanie. I'm a werewolf. You are my mate. I know you met Kade, and from the smell of it, you could be his mate too. But I want you to choose me. I know I am not Heir to the Pack, but I could still provide for you. Protect you. I don't want to fight Kade. I want you to choose me."

Lance's pleading eyes were the last thing she saw before she promptly passed out.

———

KADE STOOD naked in the room he shared with Mel for a full ten minutes, watching the closed door, before finally moving. She left.

"Duh, Romeo. You let her go. You didn't follow her. What kind of Alpha-to-be are you?" His wolf growled, and clawed to the surface.

Dammit. He wasn't going to argue with his inner half. Mel had to choose him. He wasn't going to force her and take away her decisions. He did that daily as Pack Heir, making decisions for them. His mate would be different, free. That was what he always dreamed, of a partnership, and he would be damned if he changed his mind now. Mel was a gift from fate and he wanted her by his side.

Kade quickly threw on his clothes from the night before. They held the faint smell of Mel. Honey and vanilla. A shudder passed through him. She would choose him. She had to.

He grabbed his keys and wallet from the dresser and left the room. As he walked through the lobby, he paused. A faded scent of oak and wolf. Someone from his pack – but who? Kade couldn't place it, but it didn't matter. They weren't confined to the den and could go where they pleased. However, the scent was mingled slightly with his favorite honey vanilla.

A growl rose in his throat, but he tempered it. No, it was just a coincidence. It was a large lobby, scents could mix together all the time. Assured that all was well, he left to his car to drive home where he could collect his thoughts and wait for a call. Because if he didn't have hope, there would be no absolution. No reason.

CHAPTER SEVEN

The smell of fresh pencils and wood shavings filled Kade's nose. The grey stroke of lead on paper looked like a series of lines, but together, they would eventually morph into a building – a home. He planned, he designed, he drew. He was an architect. That was his day job and way of earning a living anyway. Though he loved it and needed the feel of fresh paper beneath his fingertips, it was not his only duty. The blood of the Jamsesons ran through his veins and with it the weight of generations of responsibility. He was the Heir. A title placed on him at birth. As the first son of the Alpha, he carried the strength of history and memory. The Alpha's soul was connected to those of his Pack. His father could feel the presence of every one of the Redwoods – old or young. As the Heir, he too could feel their souls, but to a lesser degree at this time. With that connection came power and authority. From a young age, Kade knew that one day the decisions and fate of his entire Pack would rest on his shoulders. And yet, at this moment, not a single wolf mattered to him.

His mate walked out on him.

And he let her.

Why was that again? Oh yeah, his insane idea that his mate deserved a choice – free will. When he first learned about mating,

Kade made his own decision. Whoever his mate, she would chose her own fate – not him. As Heir, he did enough of that for others constantly. Kade refused to do that to his life partner – his wife.

A true Alpha wouldn't have let their mate walk away.

Kade ignored his wolf. Animalistic instincts were the reason he got into most trouble anyway.

"Are you going to tell me what the hell is up with you?" His younger brother, Jasper, didn't startle him. He was a werewolf for fuck's sake, and Jasper's loud footsteps on his front porch alerted Kade to his brother's presence the moment he was there. Though as Beta of the Redwood Pack, Jasper purposely stepped heavily as not to sneak up on him. Their family was close enough, that some things, like warnings before invading their privacy, was just nice.

"I'm fine."

"Sure, that's why you are hiding in your home, scribbling away on your workstation, ignoring my calls. What happened last night?" Jasper sat on the stool next to him. Damn. There was no way he was getting out of this. For no matter the power seeping through his pores, Jasper was just as stubborn and took care of those he loved and vowed to protect.

"I went on a date. It ended. I am back." *Oh, and I found my mate, indulged in the hottest sex of my long lived life and then let the blonde goddess leave me naked, alone in the room. Oh, yeah, not much.*

"Okay. We're getting somewhere." Jasper grinned. Bastard. "How did the date go before it ended?"

"You may have set me up on the date, but that doesn't give you the right to play teenage dream with me, bro. We're not sixteen-year old girls and I didn't go out with the quarterback of the football team. Fuck off."

Jasper clasped his hands together and spoke in a high pitched voice, "Oh but Kade, you must tell me more, tell me more. Like did he have a car?"

Despite his ill mood, Kade burst out laughing. "Dude, you are so not Sandy or a Pink Lady. And you need to watch more TV so you can get more recent pop culture references. *Grease?* Really?"

"I've been busy. Between finishing that complex on the outskirts of

42

town and dealing with the daily needs and wants of the Pack, TV and movies are the last thing on my mind. But you're changing the subject. What happened with Melanie? I can smell her on you, so I know it went at least somewhat well." Jasper's fist punched him on the shoulder, knocking the pencil from his hand. Damn persistent wolf was like a fucking Labrador sometimes, never giving up until he got attention. Jack-ass.

"Fine. We had sex. A lot of sex. Mind your own fucking business."

"I don't need details of that, pervert. I want to know how the actual date was before you went to the sheets. Seriously, I don't match make for a living, bastard. I am the Beta, I take care of my family, my own. And since Tracy, and frankly before Tracy, you have been on your ass doing nothing but work for the Pack or for the company. You needed a break from that, Larissa and I thought Mel and you would be perfect together. At least that was what Larissa thought, I only suggested to her that you needed to get laid. Damn witch wouldn't tell me anything about your girl except give me that picture of her to give to you."

Okay, apparently Jasper was in a talking mood. Rare, and decidedly annoying. Fuck.

Kade let out an exasperated sigh. Jasper wasn't going to let this go. "The date went great actually. Melanie is smart, gorgeous, attentive and innocent. We ate, I talked, we went to the hotel room that you guys so graciously reserved for us. That's it."

Jasper merely lifted a dark eyebrow.

"I'm not talking about the sex." *The really mind blowing, wolf howling sex.*

His brother snorted. "What happened after the sex, moron?"

More sex. And then some cuddling and some talking. And then some more sex. He really needed to get his mind off of that. But it was so good, the way her face would blush when she came, calling his name. The feel of her wet heat clenching around his cock. And that's enough of that.

"Shewasmymate."

"Huh?"

"Melanie is my mate." There the words were out. And yet, no relief came. Just shared misery.

Suddenly Kade was airborne as Jasper pulled him into a deep, brotherly hug.

"Damn. Larissa knew what she was talking about. Your mate? That's awesome!" Jasper's smile was so contagious, it almost broke Kade's gruff exterior. Then, just as quickly as his brother's exuberance appeared, it was gone. "Wait, if you found your mate, then why are you here alone, looking like someone kicked your puppy? Is it because she is human? Because if you let her go because you don't think she is good enough for the Heir of the Redwood pack, I'm going to kick your fucking ass."

"Do you really think I'm that much of a pompous, entitled jerk?" Kade's muscles, flexed. Dumbass little brother thought it was okay to come in to *his* home and thrash him? Oh, he would show him who was Heir – Alpha in training.

"Well, look what happened with Tracy," Jasper's eyes widened as he spoke her name. Oh yeah, brother, you screwed up.

"This wasn't anything like what happened with her – and you know it. Don't fucking bring that clusterfuck of a situation up again." Anger raged through his system. This was not the same thing at all. He didn't want Tracy, and she left. Kade truly craved Melanie, and she left. See? No similarities.

I don't understand you. How could you let our mate leave us?

Again, Kade ignored his wolf. He would probably regret that later on their hunt. But he wasn't in the mood to justify his decisions.

"I'm sorry, Kade. I know Tracy is in her own realm of selfishness. I'll quit coming to my own conclusions. What happened with Melanie last night?" To his credit, Jasper actually looked contrite and generally interested.

Kade sighed. Jasper was his Beta, he relied on his brother more than any of his others. He should be able to tell him anything, rely on him for advice. That didn't make it any easier.

"Melanie and I did, um, complete part of the mating." Heat crawled up his neck. Yep, he was officially a teenage pup.

Jasper merely gave him a goofy grin. Ass.

"Well, you know." Kade took a deep breath, he was the fucking Heir. *Use big words dumbass.*

"We made love, our souls began the process of joining. But I didn't mark her, I wouldn't do that without her permission."

"Of course, Kade. You never mark your mate without a full understanding of mating. That's the first rule of it. Go on."

"I know you've never felt the urge of mating once you catch their scent," a shadow passed over Jasper's eyes, but Kade continued, "damn, it took almost all of my control not to shift. I couldn't use my full strength because she is so fragile, so my energy had to go somewhere, at some point my claws shifted. I was just so intense. I couldn't stop myself."

"Did you hurt her?" Jasper's voice was calm over a dark tone.

"No! No. I didn't. I have more control than that. But I did tear up the sheets and Mel noticed. I couldn't lie to her Jasper. I woke up and she's freaking out about the rips in the linens and I told her everything."

"Everything?"

"I blurted out like an idiot that 'I'm a werewolf.'"

"You didn't."

"In those exact words. I didn't lead up to it or try to make her feel better. Fuck. What was I thinking? Telling a human woman, my other half, that I'm a fucking werewolf? No wonder she laughed and thought I was crazy."

"Kade, what else did you do? Because I have a feeling this isn't the end."

"I proved it."

"How did you prove it Kade?" Jasper's voice had a nervous edge to it.

"I changed."

Jasper burst to his feet. "Are you fucking kidding me Kade? You change into a mangy wolf in front of her and you wonder why she isn't by your side?"

"I'm not mangy. I'm a fucking awesome wolf with a full coat." *Yeah, good comeback Kade.*

"So not the point, oh mighty Heir."

"Fine. I turned, she freaked. I turned back, she freaked some more.

45

Then I told her my age and we were mates and we will be together for our long lives."

If Jasper's mouth hung open any wider, it would literally hit the floor.

"Don't say it, I know I didn't act with the most sense or grace."

"Kade, brother, you didn't act with *any* sense or grace. What the hell were you thinking? Let's get past the whole 'I turned into my wolf in front of a human and told them all of my secrets' thing, which by the way is against almost every code you know and uphold as Heir, thing. What happened when you told her this?"

"Well, she told me I was crazy and then she said she was crazy too. Then she let me give her my number and she said she would call, before she left the room."

"Damn."

"I'm pretty sure I lost my brain somewhere during the night though. I'm not a kid, Jasper. I know how to have a decent conversation, but I just don't know. Mel's honey vanilla scent turns me in knots."

"Honey vanilla?"

"Not the point, Jasper."

"What? It's the first substantial thing you have said about her. What are you going to do?"

Kade sighed. What would he do? She left him and he let her.

You'll wait for her and welcome her. It's fate, Kade. She will come.

Kade smiled at his wolf's basic idea of a nonbasic concept.

"I'm going to wait for her, Jasper. She will come to me – she has to. Its fate. I'm going to do all I can to make our home here for her though, in the meantime. When she does come, it will be to a place she can fit in and be happy. That's the least I can do."

"That's a great idea Kade. But why don't you go for her?"

"I can't. I promised myself as Heir and especially when I'm Alpha, I would not force my will and law on my mate. Melanie needs to make her own decision."

"If that's what you think is best."

"It has to be Jasper, it just has to." Because if she didn't call him, he would be lost.

CHAPTER EIGHT

Melanie's head throbbed. Her eyes slowly cracked open to see her living room ceiling. Was that a cob-web? She should really get up there to clean that. Wait. Why was she lying on the couch?

Oh yeah, her mental breakdown and the fact that werewolves apparently bred like bunnies.

"Thank God, you're awake."

Mel stiffened. Lance. Another self-proclaimed werewolf. He was still there. For the love of God, please don't try and prove it the same way Kade did. Don't panic. Just slowly get up and find a weapon – or call the police.

"Melanie? I won't hurt you. You're safe with me. I promise."

The crazy man – no, beast thing – said he wouldn't hurt her? And just how exactly was she to believe that? Yeah, silence seemed to be the best thing at this moment.

A cold, wet trickle trailed down her neck. Oh gawd. Was it blood? Did he decapitate her while she slept? *Okay Melanie, get yourself together. You wouldn't be breathing and talking to yourself if he took your head.* Unless he made her a zombie. Wait, were there zombies? A shudder ran through her.

A hand shot out and messed with something on her head. *Please, don't kill me.*

"Oh, are you cold? The ice I put on your cut is melting."

Oh thank God, not blood. Just melted ice.

"When you passed out, you hit your head on the table. You're going to have a rather large bump on your hairline, but I think you'll be fine." Lance's voice carried a thread of worry and care. Dammit, apparently werewolves are thoughtful.

"Please don't touch me." See? That was nice and calm.

Lance's face fell and he stood back. He looked like a kicked puppy. Mel snorted. Sometimes she cracked herself up.

"If that's what you want, Melanie. I'm sorry for blurting everything out like that. I'm just nervous." Mel gave him a good look. He did look cute, but in a best friend sort of way. Nothing like Kade.

Kade.

Her mouth salivated and her womb clenched as memories of the night before flooded her mind. They shared the best sex of her life, and then he ruined it by coming out as a monster of the night.

Lance's nostrils flared as a shudder racked his body.

Oh shit. Don't animals have a keen sense of smell? That's what she remembered from reading that romance novel Larissa gave her. Well, this was embarrassing.

"It's okay Lance, really. Just tell me what's going on. Why do you think I'm your," she swallowed hard, "mate?"

"You smell."

"Excuse me?" Well, just when she thought the guy was cute. She was gonna kick his ass.

"No. No, that's not what I mean. You smell perfect. Like honey. I swear." If Lance backtracked any farther he would be out of the house. Well, that sounded like a good idea.

"Lance..."

"My wolf scented you and that is how I know we are mates. At least the potential to be one..."

Now why did this conversation sound familiar?

"Lance, stop. I've already heard this from Kade."

"Kade. Right. About that, I know he thinks you can be his mate too. I mean, I..." Lance's ears blushed red.

An uneasy feeling settled in her stomach. "How did you know that exactly, Lance?"

"Um, well, I walked by your room this morning and heard your fight. I didn't mean to intrude, it's just werewolf senses, ya know."

Oh, she was beginning to.

"Lance, I don't think I'm your mate. And frankly, don't you think it's a bit rude to tell me this the morning after I find Kade?" She really just needed this guy to leave so she could think about Kade. Gawd, she already missed him. Yearned for him.

"I know it's regrettable that you already slept with the pup, but he didn't mark you so, things can be circumvented."

Egotistical bastard, wait... "Pup?"

"Kade's about fifty years younger than me, a boy in comparison. If you chose me you could have a man."

And that was it.

"Lance, you need to leave. Now. Thank you for the ride and the possible concussion, but you need to go."

"Melanie."

"Go."

The man backpedaled, practically running from her home.

What a night. She finds the perfect man, sleeps with him and then he informs her he's a werewolf. Then another man helps her and says the same thing. Two mates. She needed a drink and a friend. Mel walked to the phone to call Larissa. It was her fault she was in this mess, and she could get her out of it.

"KADE AND LANCE? You're one fucking lucky lady!" Larissa squealed before wrapping her arms around Mel.

"Didn't you listen to anything I said? They're werewolves. Kade changed right in front of me."

"So?" A genuine look of confusion crossed her friend's face.

"What do you mean 'so'? Are you telling me you knew they were wolves? That you know of this whole other world and didn't tell me?"

Mel knew her voice shrieked, bordered on hysteria, but she didn't care. Seriously, this was too much to deal with.

"Mel, stop acting like a drama queen. I swear you've been spending way too much time with your nose in the hydrocarbons to look at anything else. Yes, I knew. I'm a witch."

Mel's head began to throb, her vision growing dim. No. She shook her head. One fainting spell was enough for the day. This wasn't the 1800s for Newton's sake.

"A witch. Like toil and trouble and smoking cauldrons type of witch?" Too late, Mel realized she might have offended her best friend. Crap. Maybe she was Wiccan.

Larissa merely laughed. "Is Hocus Pocus the only taste of witch-craft you've seen? Don't get me wrong, I love Bette Midler, but that's not what I am. I do have magic, but I'm also more in tune to the Earth. Mel, hon, there's a lot out there that you've never seen, but it's time to grow up, but on your big girl panties and open your eyes."

"What I need is a drink." *Maybe a whole lot of drinks. Like a barrel.*

"I brought the whiskey for your morning tea. Don't worry, babe, I know you. But after I give you a smidge, we need to talk."

"Fine."

Larissa prepared the tea while Mel sat and closed her eyes. Now that Lance was gone, the enormity of her situation began to sink in. She left Kade in the room so she could think. Did she want to change her life and be a werewolf's mate? Did she truly believe everything in front of her eyes?

"Mel," Larissa's stern tone pulled her from her worries. "You need to call Kade. You need to tell him what Lance said." A cautious look passed over her face. "Mel, this situation is more dire than you think. This is not only about you and your decisions. If you can't make a choice, they'll be forced to fight."

"A fight? Over me? That's fucking idiotic. If I don't want either of them, then they need to fucking walk away. Be a man."

"Mel, they aren't men. They're werewolves. There's something else you need to know." Mel wasn't sure she wanted to hear this. "Neil's one too."

"You're mated to a werewolf?" And just when she thought this day couldn't get any stranger. *Yep, the wolves were definitely multiplying in full force.*

"Yep. And I'm in a constant state of bliss."

"So that's how you know the Jamensons?" Things were starting to click in place.

"Yes, the Jamensons are the ruling family. Kade, is the Heir, first in line to be Alpha."

Mel knew the power running through his veins, felt it when he pounded into her. The strength in his hands when he gripped her tightly, yet the control in his almost gentle touch.

"So he's the big cheese. What does this have to do with your dire circumstances? Why do they have to fight?"

"It's tradition. The thing is Mel, Kade's already been through this before."

"Tracy."

Larissa quirked a brow. "I see he's told you a bit. Well, then I'll make this the unedited version. That bitch Tracy, dangled her perky breasts in front of Kade and his best friend, Grant. Then she claimed innocence and confusion, letting the men fight for her. That woman sure does love attention. Well, Kade really didn't want her – not like I'm sure he wants you. I can tell these things, sense them. But he's the Heir, so he had to fight. So he did, partially. Most of us suspect he gave up so Grant could have her. Good riddance. Fate must be a real temperamental bitch since Kade seems to be in the same predicament. That is, if you can't make up your mind." Larissa leaned forward, daring Mel to do just that.

"Why do I have to make up my mind? When I said yes to this overnight date, I said yes to dinner and maybe sex. Not a life altering wolfy fight."

"I didn't think to put it in the fine print, sue me."

"Fuck you."

"No, I think that's Kade's – or Lance's – job." Larissa didn't smile, but pushed the cordless phone toward her. "If you don't have the guts to call him, call Jasper. Here's his number."

"Larissa, I still don't know why they need to fight. I'm human, not a wolf. This isn't my problem."

"Melanie Cross. Stop being a selfish ass. It's time you grew up and took your nose out of your precious theories and science. This is affecting lives. Plural. Get over yourself."

Angered and a bit hurt, Mel glared at her so called best friend. "Larissa..."

Larissa held up a hand, cutting off her response. "Call him."

CHAPTER NINE

K ade stood back and smiled. Pride swelled as he dusted off the last of the eraser shavings. Finished. He spent the morning and most of the afternoon designing a preliminary sketch for the add-on to his home. A present for Mel. His home currently was a bachelor's nest, with heavy, chunky furniture and dark colors. The three-bedroom cottage most likely contained enough space, but Kade wanted to add more to it — to make it *theirs* not *his*.

Shit, since when did he become such a sentimental pup? The strength of his mating urge must be detrimental to the brain. If only his Mel would walk through the door. That would make everything better.

Yes, so you can mount her and mark her. Perfect.

Kade snorted at his wolf. Yeah, life didn't quite work that way. But his wolf could always hope.

The door crashed open, signal of Jasper's arrival. Tension and worry evident on his brother's features. This couldn't be good news.

"What is it?" Fear for his family, Pack, *Melanie* left a bitter taste on his tongue.

"You're not going to believe this."

"Tell me." Kade took a step toward him, urging him to continue.

"I need you calm, Kade. You can't go all Alpha and tear shit up."

Frustrated and nervous, he flipped Jasper off. "Fucking tell me."

"Melanie called," Jasper held out a hand before Kade could respond. "Like I said, Melanie called me. I don't know why she didn't call you directly, other than the fact she feared your reaction."

"What do you mean my reaction? Fucking get on with it."

"Seems you weren't the only wolf Melanie met last night."

Scents of oak and wolf flooded his memory. *Fuck.* Why didn't he follow up on the trail, rather than believing everything was okay? As Heir, he never left things to chance – except with Mel. *Fuck.* His wolf clawed to the surface, anger coursed through his veins.

"Who?" One word. One question grunted, pulled from his throat.

"Lance Morse. A low level wolf who manages the hotel you two stayed at. When Larissa and I booked your room, we didn't think anything of it. I'm sorry, Kade."

"Did he touch her?"

"No, I don't think so. Melanie is fine, Kade. But he took her home." Kade growled. *That fucking wolf thought he could care for his mate?*

"Kade, Melanie could be Lance's mate too."

Rage swept through his system. Blood pounded in his ears as Kade let out a gut-wrenching howl.

Not again.

He thought he was done with this indecision and fighting shit when he gave up Tracy. Was fate cruel enough to repeat his pain? Apparently so. *Damn!*

A hand on his shoulder brought comfort.

"Kade," Jasper's voice pulled him to the present. "We'll do what we can, but Mel doesn't know what to do. I don't think she wants this." Jasper sighed, pity in his eyes. "You know what must be done."

Yes. He knew. It was a familiar and acidic concept. If there were two potential mates, she would have to choose. If she couldn't – he would fight. Again.

And, fuck he would fight. Kade's wolf was already in love with her. The man was well on the way of following head over feet behind him. He and Mel shared a connection, even if she chose to deny it. The

54

circle where he would fight for his heart called to him. He was the Heir, he would do what was right – what was just.

"Call the circle, Jasper. Lance and I will meet at the center. The victor will hold Mel's heart." It would be him. His wolf whimpered and growled. It had to be him.

———

MEL WATCHED as the trees passed in a blur. That's how her life in the past two days felt anyway. One event or person caught for a moment before falling into shadows – leaving but a memory.

A snort escaped her. Apparently, meeting two werewolves claiming to be her mate and breaking open her world to the paranormal let her poetic juices flow. All aboard the crazy train.

"So, where are we going? Or is this more cloak and dagger, secret society stuff?" Larissa wouldn't tell her. Her supposed best friend merely threw her into the passenger seat of her car and drove. She didn't even ask. Pushy witch.

"We're on our way to the Redwood den. It's deep in the forest." Well, Kade did say he lived on the outskirts of Seattle. "The Pack's lived there for over a millennia. It is deeply entrenched in Pack magic and history. So, don't be an arrogant ass and fuck it up." Larissa didn't let her gaze off the road, but her tone indicated a raised brow and no nonsense. Stern witch.

"I don't want them to fight over me. I just want to go to work and forget all of this." Even as she said it, pain ebbed through her. She knew she couldn't – no, wouldn't – forget Kade. His very essence imprinted on her soul. But was one night worth giving up everything she worked so hard for? How could one man – no, one werewolf – be enough for that? Kade's world eluded with violence. Hell, they were on their way to watch two grown men fight for the right to claim her. How Neolithic was that?

"I swear to all that is magic, Melanie Cross. This isn't about your closed minded human rules. This is something far greater than you – tradition. You don't want to choose between Kade and Lance? Fine. But then they have to fight in the Pack circle. Get over it." Apparently,

Larissa crossed the threshold of being nice and understanding and entered the world of bitchiness. If Mel wasn't so confused, she could start to really like this side of her best friend.

"I sound like a sulky teenager, don't I?"

"You're more angsty than Edward Cullen on a sunny day."

Their laughter filled the car, releasing the ball of nervousness that churned in her stomach during the ride. No matter what she did, there would be a fight. Resigned, Mel took a deep breath.

A non-descript wooden arch signaled their arrival to the den. Larissa drove a bit further, nodding at the guards at the entrance. After a mile or so of dirt road, they finally stopped in front of what looked like a visitor center.

Really? What would be in there? *Please* feed the wolves?

A tall, built man opened the front door, walking toward their car. He looked slightly taller than Kade, with darker hair. But there was no mistaking the similar features and the fact he possessed the same jade eyes.

Oh, how she missed those eyes.

"That's Jasper, Kade's brother." Larissa's voice made her blink. Those Jamenson parents sure do breed sexy men.

Mel shook herself, bringing her attention to the striking woman following Jasper. Long blue-black hair fell past her shoulders and blunt bangs enhanced her features. This woman was easily the most beautiful woman she had ever seen. Again, her eyes reminded Mel of Kade. Damn, their genetics were a medical marvel.

Larissa opened her door and Mel followed suit. The cold mountain air tickled her nose. Inhaling, she sighed. The air smelled cleaner – crisper.

"Larissa, it's good to see you again." Jasper bent down and kissed her friend's cheek before turning to her. "Melanie, it's good to finally meet you." He smiled a sad smile. "I wish it were under better circumstances, but it doesn't make it any less true." Kade's brother lifted her hand to his lips, lightly brushing it. Though Jasper was very attractive, Mel felt no flutters of arousal. Apparently, Kade ruined her for others. *Damn wolf.*

"This is my sister Cailin." Jasper nodded toward the beauty, but the woman didn't acknowledge her.

"Cailin." One word on a growl and his sister bent her head, though Mel still saw a trace of defiance in her eyes.

Really? Bowing in submission? This is why she didn't want to be a part of this. She would belittle herself for no one. Enough of that happened during grad school, she was through.

"Ignore my sister. She's in a mood."

"Our brother is about to fight – maybe to the death – because this little blonde human refuses to make a decision. Excuse me if I don't welcome her with open arms." A viscous scowl turned her porcelain face into a menacing landscape of beauty.

"Excuse me? I'm sorry if I'm more enlightened than you, but I don't see a reason to fight over me."

"Oh, in that we agree." Cailin smirked.

"Okay, you may be a bitch – in every sense of the word – but don't fuck with me little girl." Who did she think she was?

"Stop it. Both of you." Jasper's voice commanded them both to obey. Surprisingly, Mel did.

"Let's just get this over with."

Jasper sighed. "Before we head to the circle you need to know a few things. Yes, they will meet in the circle over the right to mate with you. That is our custom – our ways. Please do not disrespect us and voice your detrimental opinions in our place of worship." He looked her in the eyes and Mel felt the beginnings of shame sweep over her. *Damn.*

"Kade and Lance will fight in the circle until one gives up – or one dies."

Mel's heart clenched. "To the death?" A whisper.

"Yes, Mel. To the death." Jasper's tone held no argument. "Are you sure you cannot choose?"

No words came. Lance wasn't an option. Not one bit. But was Kade? She wasn't ready to decide. How could she?

She could only shake her head.

Jasper let out a sigh before continuing. "You cannot interfere. You will watch and then you will let the winner come to you. Once they do – that is up to the two of you."

"I don't have to go with them do I?" Not that she didn't want Kade, but was this binding?"

"It's your choice once the circle is set and a victor emerges." Jasper checked his watch, "It's time to go."

Mel's heart raced as they walked toward the grassy circle surrounded by weathered stones. She didn't want to watch this. How could this be happening?

A glance across the circle took her breath away. Kade. He stood bare chested, muscles gleaming, and barefoot. His hair blew loosely in the wind, touching his shoulders. Just under three days passed and yet she missed him. She fell a little bit in love with him the night they shared together, but she didn't know if that was worth giving everything up. Losing her humanity. There wasn't enough time to think. Everything was happening too fast.

Her lover walked toward them on steady steps. For a man about to fight for his life, there was not a hint of nervousness. His face was blank of emotion except the slight sadness in his eyes. Was it sadness for her? Or the upcoming match?

"Kade." Nothing else mattered. The words she tried to string together in the car to say to him were gone. Though she didn't know her future, she wanted him to bend down and press his lips to hers.

Kade merely quirked the side of his mouth in a sad smile before lifting his hand to her face. He brushed her brow, trailing down to her cheek. His warm, calloused fingertip sent shivers through her.

But he didn't kiss her.

Too quickly his warmth left her. Did he not want her? Mel glanced down at his clenched fists and released a sigh. He wasn't as unemotional as he tried to show.

What was wrong with her? Her tumbling and confusing thoughts gave her a headache and hurt her stomach. Whatever happened here tonight would set the course of things to come. Now she only needed to make up her analytical mind. She needed more data, more time. But her heart screamed at her.

She was making the wrong choice.

CHAPTER TEN

K ade inhaled the mountain air threaded with the anticipation of the gathering crowd. An eerily familiar chill crept up his spine. *Damn, how could I be doing this again? What did I do to deserve this?*

He didn't know if he was speaking to God or his wolf, but neither answered. It appeared no matter what, he would be alone in this fight, and maybe for the rest of his life.

Despite his mind telling him not to, he risked a glance at Mel. *Damn*. It wasn't his imagination. Even with the worried scowl on her face, she still looked amazing. Her long blonde hair flowed in the wind, whipping about her face in small gusts. His hands fisted as he fought the urge to go over to her and brush a lock behind her ear.

Dammit, he was doing this for her. For them. Doubt clouded his mind. Did she even want him? Or was she like Tracy? Desiring another man, but without the backbone to say no to the Heir of the Pack.

Kade shook his head, dispelling the inner fears assailing his mind. He needed to focus. Lance stepped into the circle, a smirk of confidence on his face, yet fear in his eyes. *Huh?* Lance was a low-level Pack member. There was no way Kade could lose to him. That explained the fear, yet why the smirk?

"Kade." Lance's deep voice echoed through the circle and the noise of the Pack hushed.

"Lance."

"Men," his father's voice cut through their rising tension. "You're both here in this place of magic to battle, man against man, flesh against flesh, for the right to mate Melanie Cross." His father turned his head toward Mel, forcing Kade to do the same. She stood wide-eyed, frozen.

"Melanie Cross, do you acknowledge either of these men? Do you choose and stop this fight?" His father's voice boomed toward the crowd.

She shook her head, and Kade's heart plummeted. It didn't occur to him until right then that he was actually hoping she would choose him. What did he expect? One night and she would fall madly in love with him? It didn't matter that that's what happened to him.

Kade looked into Mel's eyes. Fear, yet pleading radiating from them. Without blinking, he turned from her toward his opponent. The smirk didn't leave.

"Why are you smiling?" Curiosity pulled the words from him.

"You've lost before pup, and she never said no to me. Why would she want the politics that come with your job? With me, she has more options."

Uncertainty attacked him. Dammit.

"Watch your back Lance. I will fight with everything I have. Mel's worth fighting for. Remember the power I hold that comes with my 'job'. Don't fuck with me." Kade growled the last part, wiping the smirk off the jackass's face. Good.

"Men, stand ready at the center. And begin when I tell you." Sadness threaded his father's voice. No father wanted to see their son, especially their first-born, fight, maybe to the death, for a mate – twice.

Kade planted his feet, the soil smooth against his bare skin. Clad in only an old pair of faded jeans, his mobility was the greatest it could be without being naked. Much as he would like to walk around nude in front of Mel, the others may frown upon that. Plus the whole dangly bit issue during a fight – not a good idea.

Lance stood four feet across from him, mimicking Kade's stance. Though all werewolves were required to go through fight training as adolescents, not all Pack members were adequate in it. Kade knew every single wolf in his pack. Because he was Heir, he also felt each of their souls. Lance wasn't a fighter; he was a schmoozer, a prick.

Kick his hairy ass.

Ah, nice to see his wolf didn't leave him completely alone. Kade inhaled, letting his wolf rise to the surface just a bit. A warm golden glow appeared on the ground in front of him. Good, his eyes were lit, time to get this shit over with.

"Now," the Alpha commanded.

Lance jumped first, attacking with his right, leaving his left flank open. Amateur. He ducked and sank his fist into his opponent's side. The other wolf howled in pain but rolled with it, before kicking at Kade. He moved to the side, narrowly escaping the blow and spun to punch Lance in the face. Bones crunched under his fist as Lance's nose broke. Again, the other wolf screamed but didn't quit.

They fought, scraped, and hit, neither backing down. Kade risked a look at Mel. Her hands were in front of her, balled together with tension. Her eyes were wide with panic yet she was still beautiful. His.

He wasn't surprised when the punch hit him square in the jaw as his attention was focused elsewhere. Pain radiated through his cheekbone and lower mouth as his teeth crashed together. *Fuck.* Kade spun and returned the blow. Lance's head snapped back, the blood oozing from his lip mixing with the congealed blood from his nose.

Kade needed to end this. Mel was his. Not this fucking wolf who couldn't even fight to protect her. His wolf snorted and clawed in agreement. *Good.* He growled, letting his Heir power radiate. Lance blanched. *Fucking wolf better fear him.* Kade punched with his right, flesh in to Lance's cheek, breaking the bone. Then punched with his left, ribs bruising underneath his fist. Lance gasped, a green hue flowing over his skin, before falling to the ground.

Though a fight to death might be expected, Kade needed a yield. He would not kill another man in front of Mel. Fear already wafted from her skin, and he didn't want to add to it. Kade knelt by the fallen wolf, the crowd's cheers silenced. He placed his palm on Lance's neck, cutting off most of his air-flow.

"Back down, Lance. You cannot win this. I refuse to kill you in front of her."

Recognition flashed in his eyes. *Yeah buddy, I love her and I could kill you. Give up.*

Lance lifted his chin, bearing what little neck he could. It was over.

The crowd cheered. Their Heir won. Victorious. But Kade knew it wasn't over. He may have won the battle, but he would not force his Mate. No matter the traditions.

The audience quieted as Kade walked toward Mel. His heart pounded in his ears. This was by far scarier than the fight he just left. He loved her. What if she said no? What would he do if she left?

Kade stood in front of her. The sweet honey vanilla smell masked by her fear and pain.

"Mel?"

THE BRUTALITY of the fight left Mel speechless. This was not humane. No, this was barbaric, animalistic. Her fault. Before Kade walked into the circle to fight, she knew she was making the wrong choice. Why did she let them fight? Why didn't she love Kade enough to leave everything behind she has known and worked for?

Even as she thought about it, she knew the answer. While she attended school, choices were made for her, paths laid and followed without resistance. Yet, now she held the decision. The power to follow her own life, her own path. No one could take that from her. She'd known Kade for less than a week. Spoke to him for less than a day. If he had merely given her time to decide before, the outcome may have been different. But not now. Confusion racked her brain. Time wasn't an option, so the decision would break her heart. Already, she felt numb.

"Kade," her voice broke. "I..."

"Leave us." Startled, Mel looked around. The crowd dispersed quickly and quietly. Some still held curiosity, but most looked upon

Kade with pity. Whether it be for her humanity or they knew her answer, she didn't know.

Drawing on the little courage she had left, she spoke, "Kade, I can't." Pain flashed in his eyes, but he didn't speak. "This isn't my life. I can't give up everything for a man I don't know. Kade, we don't know each other. You may have a wolf to guide you, but I only have my experiences."

No one spoke for what seemed like an eternity. Then Kade bent down and brushed a lock of her hair behind her ear. Her breath hitched as he leaned further to touch his lips to hers. His hand still in her hair, he pulled her to him, kissing her with a desperation she thought was only hers. Their tongues clashed, lips hungry and eager. Finally, Kade released her.

"If that is your decision, I will let you go. I love you, Melanie Cross." He lifted his arm as if to touch her once more, but let it fall.

With one last look, he pleaded with her, but she didn't know what to do. He left the circle, taking her heart with him.

CHAPTER ELEVEN

K ade sat on his porch, a beer in his hand. Though his metabolism would burn off the effects quickly – he needed to feel nothing. Numb. Anything to get his mind off the fact that he was mateless after meeting two potentials. Mateless after two meetings in the circle. Mel left him.

You let her leave, you fool. Why didn't you tie her up and keep her here. I'm sure there's something you could've done to pass the time while she makes the right decision.

Kade snorted at his wolf's attitude. Though an image of Mel tied naked to his bed-posts flooded his mind. *Fuck.* He shook his head. She left. That delicious fantasy would never happen.

Footsteps sounded on his driveway, altering Kade to an unwelcome guest.

"Hello Kade, you look like shit." The sickly sweet voice pinched his nerve endings.

Tracy.

Tall and curvy, her body lent itself to many pup's wet dreams. Long chocolate brown hair flowed to her ass, hours of work evident in its perfection. His body didn't react. She wasn't Mel.

"What are you doing here? Shouldn't you be with your mate,

Grant?" Fuck, that sounded jealous. No, he wasn't jealous of Grant. One look at Mel and Kade knew – Tracy wasn't for him. No, he was jealous of what Tracy and Grant shared. What he lost when he let Mel walk away.

"That's not a very nice greeting to someone you loved now is it?" She batted her eyes and pursed her lips. Typical, she needed something. What, he didn't care. He just hoped she would leave so he could wallow in misery with his beer in peace. Was that too much to ask?

"I never loved you, Tracy, you know that. I thought we could have something because of our wolves, but you didn't want me either." Pain made him honest and slightly bitter, but who the fuck cared.

Tracy huffed. "Fine, Kade. Be an ass. But you are the fucking Heir of this Pack and you need to act like it. It was bad enough you were going to mate that human, but then you *let* her leave? I'm glad I picked Grant. You're nothing."

A growl slipped from his lips and she cowered in fear. Tracy's wolf possessed almost no strength, yet she was a bitch. Kade, however, didn't give a shit. He wouldn't move from his perch for anyone but the blonde who left him.

"Leave Tracy."

"No Kade, I won't. I'm sorry for saying that, but I need help."

"Go."

"But its Grant, he lost his job and..."

"Go."

"Kade." Her whiny voice pleaded. Kade wanted to throw up.

"Tracy, I don't care about you and Grant. If you have a problem, go see Jasper. That's his job. But leave me the fuck alone. You wanted Grant? You have him."

"And you have nothing." Tracy's sneer only confirmed his own shortcomings. It wasn't anything new.

"Goodbye, Tracy."

"I'm glad that human left you. You aren't even worthyof that piece of shit."

Kade leapt off the porch and had Tracy on the ground, gasping for breath before she could blink.

"You may call me names but you will not dishonor Melanie. She is mine."

"But..." He pressed down harder on her windpipe.

"I love her, Tracy. You will respect her."

Her eyes widened and she nodded before Kade released her. She scrambled up, not bothering to wipe the dirt from her dress and ran.

You chose the right woman, Kade. Tracy isn't worth anything. Mel will come back. She will see reason.

Kade let out a pathetic half-laugh. No, Mel made her choice. Kade was just the one who had to live with it.

———

BEN AND JERRY'S Karmal Sutra ice cream was manna. The creamy caramel and chocolate fudge ice creams surrounded a thick column of caramel goodness. Mel sighed in ecstasy as she let another spoonful melt on her tongue, the flavors cascading in an almost orgasmic symphony.

And this was as good as it got. Ice cream and the Discovery Channel on a Saturday night. No men or sex for her. She was the fucking idiot who walked away from her mate and left him. Now she faced four hundred freshman three days a week teaching them general chemistry, though they could care less. When she wasn't banging her head against the chalk board explaining once again that energy of light is inversely, not directly, proportional to it wavelength, she was again stuck behind a lab bench. With her new title she now called the shots but she still didn't have a passion for it. She really didn't give a crap about the radioactive nuclides and alkali metals in different silicates and soils. She'd lost her passion. No, not lost, she'd left her passion with Kade.

Her door opened without an announcement and Larissa strode in, an angry look on her face. After the match, and her dismissal of Kade, Larissa drove her home in a silence that scared the shit out of her. Her best friend wouldn't even look at her, nor speak. When they arrived at her home, Larissa sat there, a sad look on her face and waited wordlessly for Mel to leave. That was the last time she saw her and it'd been almost a month. Mel braced herself – this wouldn't be good.

"You pathetic human. You are sitting here eating fucking ice cream and watching the god damn TV? What the hell is your problem?"

"Larissa..."

"Shut up, I'm not done yet. You left the perfect man for you because you didn't know him? Why couldn't you have just talked to him? Is that such a foreign concept? For such a smart girl, you sure do make the worst decisions."

Shame flooded her. She knew she made the wrong decision, but how could she go back to him? She left and walked away. He didn't want her back. Why would he?

"I know you're miserable. I can feel it pulsating from you. Why are you still here?" Larissa sat down on the couch in an inelegant plop, exhaustion, and clear bewilderment on her face.

Mel broke down in gut wrenching sobs. She knew she was an idiot, but she couldn't go back.

"Oh baby." Larissa moved to her side and enveloped her in her arms. Warm scents of apple pie and earth filled her nose. Mel dug deeper, salty tears running down her face, staining her best friend's shirt.

"Shh, it's okay. We can fix this." Her witch crooned in her ear, comforting her.

"I don't think I can, Larissa. I think I screwed up bad."

"Don't worry, just cry it out. We'll figure out something."

"But what if he doesn't want me?" Deep down that was her biggest fear. And if Mel were honest with herself, that was her fear all along. She lied to herself when she said it was about her job, her life. No, fear ruled her and said Kade would change is his mind and let her go. So she let him go first. Or worse, he would do the honorable thing and stick with her, but resent her through their long lives.

"Oh baby, he wants you. He's just as miserable, if not more, as you."

"Really?" Okay, now she was happy that he shared her misery. *Wow. Pathetic, much?*

"He's your mate."

Yes, he was.

CHAPTER TWELVE

She never called. A month passed and his mate didn't call. Kade knew he should have followed or begged her. But he couldn't. He kept to his own promise as Heir to not influence or force his will on his mate.

The past month clearly won for the hardest of his life. His wolf barely spoke to him and was grouchy as hell. In turn Kade acted like an ass to anyone who came within five feet of him.

His father, the Alpha of the pack, told him to get his shit together and stop moping about a woman. *Nice. Great parenting skills there.*

He threw himself into his work and designed his mate a home. Their home. She would come back. She had to. Once she came, he would start building so they could have a future together. If he lost that hope and let the stray thought of her not calling enter his head, he didn't know what he would do. Maybe go lone wolf, because he wasn't sure his Pack would tolerate his mood much longer. His heart ached for Mel. He could barely eat, and sleep was a far off concept.

The sound of a foot on a broken tree branch brought him out of his reverie and he turned to the source, ready to attack.

Honey and vanilla teased his senses.

Mel.

She stood in front of him, in light worn jeans and dark green sweater. His wolf howled in celebration.

"Melanie." A gasp along his breath. *Why?*

"I'm so sorry Kade," her eyes filled with tears and he fought the urge to wipe them. "I needed more time, but I shouldn't have left the way I did."

The uncomfortable silence grew heavy with tension.

"Why are you here?"

Oh good job ass. Why aren't you welcoming her with open arms?

"I called yesterday. Your father answered and told me where you were. He also told me you were acting like a shithead and I needed to come fix it. I think it was an order." She smiled wryly at him and he laughed at her.

"My father knew you were coming? What the hell? Why didn't he say anything?" He needed to kick his father's ass once his brain turned back from mush.

"I think he wanted it to be a surprise. Don't be mad at him. I am sorry it took so long for me to get my act together and not be an idiot. I'm sorry I left. I'm sorry you even fought. Lance was never an option Kade." Hope swelled. She wanted him, not that douche bag.

"I was so lost and confused at first and by the time I got my thoughts into something similar to a coherent pattern, I had so much planning to do."

"Planning?" he really needed to work on those one word sentences.

"Planning." She smiled and continued. "I had to quit my job and find a teaching position I liked near here. I know that I won't be able to stay there too long because I won't be aging and that might become suspicious but I still want to work for awhile. Of course if I become pregnant that might be another matter. Oh and will I give birth to puppies? Because frankly that scares the shit out of me." She smiled again and Kade lost it. His mate was moving here and talking of bearing his young. *Heaven.*

He couldn't wait any longer. He grabbed her and crushed his mouth to hers. He almost forgot her taste of sweet ecstasy. Her tongue fought for control against his as she rocked her body against him.

After however long they stood there tasting and touching each other, they finally broke apart gasping for breath.

"You're here. You are really here."

"Uh huh." She smiled brightly and his heart melted again.

"I love you Melanie. I am so glad you came. I made a house for you. Well not a full house, just the plans, but if you want to change everything let me know. I would do anything for you, my Melanie." He held her against him and breathed in her sweet scent.

"I love you too, Kade. I am sorry it took so long for me to get here. But I'm not leaving. I want you too much and I want to see your world. Teach me everything."

"My pleasure, mate, I will teach you anything you desire." He smiled wickedly and carried her off to his room. Melanie was here, with him. Their future together would intertwine, walking the same path. It was about time.

———

KADE CRADLED her to his chest, the feel of his heartbeat against her cheek brought her home. No amount of job security or teaching could replace this.

"I love you Kade." She knew she already said it, but it needed repeating.

"I know."

Mel slapped his arm.

"Really? 'I know?' Who do you think you are? Harrison Ford?"

"Oh God, my mate makes *Star Wars* jokes. I think I just fell a little more in love with you." Kade set her on his bed – their bed.

Mel gulped. "I talked to Larissa about mating and she told me a bit." Kade looked down at her expectantly while stripping them both of their clothes. "I want you to mark me."

His eyes glowed as he growled. "That can be arranged." A guttural sound. His hands shifted, sliding up her bare skin sending goose bumps down her body. The cotton sheets below her cooled her overheated body, as he kissed her lips, then along her jaw down to her neck. She braced herself for the bite, but Kade lifted his head.

"Are you sure you want this?" Oh, how she loved this man, this wolf. Even now, he gave her options.

"Yes. With everything I have."

Kade moaned before kissing her, his tongue playing with hers. She fought for breath as his mouth trailed long her neck again, and gasped has his calloused fingertips brushed and pinched her nipples. He licked the crease where her neck met her shoulder and she shivered. Anticipation crawled through her. She felt his teeth elongate before they punctured her shoulder. The tension of her skin ebbed as his teeth slid into her skin.

Mel braced for the pain, yet it soon passed as a soft flow of love and sex flooded her. *Holy shit.* Kade's bite pulsated through her body, pinching her nipples and clenching her pussy. As he bit and growled, her climax neared. Kade bit harder once more and her control broke. Spasms of need and glorious warmth cascaded as she came. *Fuck, and he didn't even touch her down there.*

"Mine." One word. Yet full of possessive meaning.

Her mate removed his fangs as they slid back to their normal self.

"Yours." Her voice deepened into a raspy tone.

Still wet and swollen from her orgasm, the head of Kade's cock brushed her folds and she shuddered.

"I want you Melanie."

"Now. Please."

Kade, propped up on his forearms above her, kissed her softly. Gazes locked, he entered her in one quick thrust. She groaned as her walls clamped down on him. He practically whimpered, then reared back and slammed into her.

Each thrust brought her closer to completion as she lay underneath her mate. He reached down and drew circles around her clit and she shattered, him following soon behind.

"I love you Melanie."

"I love you Kade."

Though her path may be radically different than what she planned, here in Kade's arms, Melanie found her true destiny. Forever.

A TASTE FOR A MATE

Redwood Pack Book 2

By
Carrie Ann Ryan

A TASTE FOR A MATE

Jasper Jamenson's only responsibility to being the Beta of the Redwood Pack, second son of the Alpha, is to protect the Pack from themselves and the human world. After a century of selfless service, his brother's new found mating forced him into taking a good look into his life. He isn't sure he wants a mate, but fate may have other ideas.

Willow Delton is a skinny, bakery owner – the type most woman love to hate. Being without family, she finds herself alone to the Greek god with green eyes who saunters into her bakery every morning. Her desire to follow him, to be with him, overrides every rational sense she possessed.

Jasper and Willow are drawn together, despite every nuisance that works against them. But evil beyond even Jasper's supernatural compensation will make war against him, by going after the only thing in his eternal life he desires – Willow. Is Willow's heart enough to overcome Jasper's soul to save her life? A fight he cannot win, but to save her life – he must.

PROLOGUE

S mells of sulfur and ash permeated the Circle as the rhythmic beating of drums mixed with growls and murmurs. Voices elevated as Taiko drums increased in tempo, matching the heartbeats of the Pack around Corbin.

A blond male in low-slung jeans howled as he eyed the bare breasts of the woman next to him. The man beside him gave a sharp growl while beating his chest. Corbin stood outside the mass of people and felt the rising tension creep up his arms. *Nice.*

Corbin was the Alpha's only son and Heir. His people shouted for him, begging for his presence. The Pack must make a sacrifice, but he would rather play with his new project. His last one endured only a few short days. What a waste of soft flesh.

A scream ripped from the throat of a young woman behind him. Corbin inhaled her fear and smiled. The sickly, metallic taste felt heavy on his tongue. An aphrodisiac for a wolf like him. Flesh slapping flesh in painful bursts silenced her. Corbin tilted his head toward the crowd and it parted. Their rumblings of conversation quieted as their Alpha's presence commanded their upmost attention.

Following his father, Corbin entered the Circle, not bothering to look at whom he passed. These lowlifes of the Pack meant nothing to him. He stopped beside his father in the center and looked around. They were manic with frantic energy, eager to see the outcome of their sacrifice. He lifted his chin to signal the entrance of their main entertainment.

Four men walked from between groups of boulders, carrying two wooden planks. Chains circled the flat boards to encase two young, frightened women. The pale haired one made no sound and remained unmoving, her eyes wide and vacant. The other, this one with raven hair, struggled, moaned, then screamed for freedom. The men dropped their captives in an inelegant heap. But really, these girls didn't deserve much more.

He looked down at the dark-haired one who continued to fight her bonds. How dare this bitch have the audacity to fight? Didn't she know it was useless? Fighting only showed her disregard for her betters – for him. Corbin's hand came down across her face. His sharp strike reverberated through the air. But as he raised his fist to permanently shut her up, his father called him.

"No, Corbin, let your sister be for now. For her regrettable uselessness and her inability to submit, she will be the demon's bribe to do with as he wishes." His father curled his lip and snorted before he quickly masked his features.

The slut deserved what she got.

Gesturing to the other woman, who had long since given in to her fate, his father spat on the ground. "Your cousin, on the other hand, will do what is needed. Like a good bitch. She will be sacrificed first for the calling."

Raising his fist, he yelled to his Pack. The answering call vibrated through the forest, and the steady beat of the drums intensified.

The Pack's desire to conquer crawled along Corbin's skin, tickling his nerves. Inhaling, he savored it. *Ah, it's almost time.*

Walking toward him, his father spoke again. "You still have one sister left once this is done, and you'll still have your plaything." He growled a laugh as Corbin turned his head to the right and looked into the field past the group of his followers at his younger sister.

Ellie's brown hair lay lank on her shoulders and dirt smudges adorned her face, her bloodied lip only now healing from his earlier play. She could have been so much more, been by his side in a position of power. But alas, she didn't share his views. Unmoving, she watched the proceeding with a fire in her eyes that belied her submission. She would not be easily quieted, and Corbin relished it.

"Use this." His father handed him a silver dagger with red rubies on its hilt. "It's been bespelled by a witch and only needs the blood of a living sacrifice to tear the veil and bring forth our demon."

Corbin smiled and took the blade, running his finger along the sharp edge, careful not to cut himself and destroy the magic. He looked down at his captives on their boards and smiled. *Oh, this will be fun.*

Corbin brushed the pale hair out of his cousin's eyes before bending down over her bruised face to whisper in her ear. "You will be a good girl now and accept your honor. Through you, we will finally conquer the Redwood Pack. You are doing us a service; remember that."

A final whimper left her swollen lips before he straightened to his full height and plunged the dagger into her chest. No sound escaped as the frail light in her eyes faded to darkness.

"Take our bounty, our blood. We give freely, this magic of death. Sacrifice meets endless faith. Cross the veil. Meet your summoners."

His father's voice echoed through the forest again as the blood of Corbin's cousin drenched the dirt floor of their sacred Circle nestled in the forest. Lightning arched across the cloudless sky, and fire erupted in a ring, surrounding the Pack. Growls and yells grew louder as the smell of death and sulfur increased. The dark scents of ash and sulfur seeped into his pores. Invigorating. The thumping energy of the dark magic mingled with the loud resonance of the drums, as a flash of bright lighting scattered across the tree line causing the Pack to jump.

The drums stopped and voices hushed as a lone man appeared through a gap in the bodies. Not a man – no. Dressed in a fine black suit, he was dangerously beautiful with a face smooth like granite. Only the red irises of his eyes gave away the fact he was not of this world. No, not man, but a demon. Their demon.

———

CAYM TOOK clean and precise steps into the Circle from the forest where he'd broken through the veil between Earth and Hell, and arched a brow at their offerings. The Alpha's daughter was indeed a fine specimen and a decent bounty. But he wouldn't have expected anything less. If this Pack wanted his power to aid in their quest, true sacrifice was the only option. The eager faces of the Pack stared at him with need. Their scent of tension and anticipation washed over him. Yes, this Pack would do. His lips quirked into a smile.

Ah werewolves, still lower class and ill-bred. Caym would enjoy killing this raven-haired wolf before he killed his way through the others. Walking through the veil on the tails of death released him into this world. He'd be forced into aiding this Pack – but he would have his freedom and taste the blood he so desired.

"Demon!" A tall man with caramel skin and dark hair bellowed. Power radiated off him in waves.

Ah, the Alpha of the little wolf Pack.

"We call on you to aid us in our time of need to destroy the Redwood Pack and claim our rightful, dominant place," the other man continued, and Caym fought the urge to roll his eyes. "We offer you the most prized female as your bounty. Do with her as you wish."

The Alpha's arrogant face could not hide the blatant fear in his eyes. Yes, he was wise to be fearful of him; after all, demons were relegated to Hell for a reason. And Caym was among the worst.

Struggling against her chains, her bronzed flesh bloodied and bruised, the dark-haired female enticed him. He smiled.

With a nod at the Alpha and the werewolf beside him, Caym strolled toward his gift. He traced his finger down her cheek, loving the feel of her blood pulsating against his skin. She jerked way from his touch, so he pressed harder.

He loved it when they fought.

He trailed his fingers down, resting them on her breasts. Her eyes widened before he dug his claws into her flesh to feel the beat of her heart. Her blood pooled around his hand, the warmth spreading along his cool skin. Delicious. The girl's final scream set his blood to boil and filled his cock.

Holding her warm beating heart above her now lifeless form, he smiled. Caym lifted it over his head before letting out a mighty roar.

Death by his hands. The sweetest of sacrifices.

"A deal with the Devil indeed." Caym spoke clearly, eager to find his next victim, no matter where it came from. "I accept." He gave his best, almost civilized, smile. If his cruelty showed through it, how was he to blame? He'd tried.

CHAPTER ONE

The scent of cinnamon and sugar danced on the air as Willow Delton heaved opened the heavy oven door to remove her prized cinnamon rolls. The plump, buttery pastries were baked to perfection, and she set them on the counter to cool. The only thing missing was her thick and creamy frosting, but that would have to wait.

Willow stood back and stared around her commercial grade kitchen. She'd started her bakery from scratch, and it had grown into a successful, albeit small, business. Incredible, really. She'd never thought the day would arrive when she finally had a place to call her own. She was right where she wanted to be. Her favorite part of the day was being able to meet one-on-one with her customers. She loved the looks on their faces when they bit into her temptations, that look of ecstasy not seen on this side of the bedroom door that flashed across their eyes.

Of course, that particular look as the result of a man was long absent from Willow's face. Too excruciatingly long.

She stood back and closed her eyes, conjuring the memory of her mystery man's face. The image that filled her mind made her forget the lack of human contact. The thought of his deep, husky voice tickled her spine whenever he spoke. Green eyes caught her in his web with only a glance. She'd fallen for a stranger and didn't even know his name. He'd come into her store every morning and ordered a cinnamon roll and coffee with only a few words. Then he 'd pay cash before lifting up the corner of his mouth in a semblance of a smile and walking out of her store. Was it strange she worried he'd keep walking and never return?

A bell's tinkle pulled Willow from her reverie and self-pity. As she turned to greet her customer, her heart leapt to her throat. Him. Her mysterious fantasy man. As she tried to regain her senses, she took all of him in. He had to be one of the tallest men she'd ever seen, easily over six and a half feet. The tight black T-shirt he wore hugged his biceps and cut into his muscular physique, while his broad shoulders stretched and strained the seams. His body tapered down to a narrow waist and hips as they met his thighs. His long legs she wanted to grip, encased in worn jeans lead to work boots. Hmm, construction perhaps? She glanced back up his body to his striking face.

He wasn't beautiful, but he did have a face most women would dream about. A strong jaw and cheekbones gave him an aura of strength, the kind of strength that would be protective. His hair was midnight black and long enough to brush his shoulders, however, today, a band held it back, showcasing his face more. He studied her, his green eyes calm and calculating. Willow let out a surprised gasp at the sexual heat radiating from him. Could she possibly be imagining things?

———

JASPER JAMENSON FOUGHT himself as he walked into the bakery that morning. This would be the seventh week in a row he'd come here, every day but Sunday. And that was only because the damn store was closed. As good as the cinnamon rolls were, and they were little tastes of heaven, it was the woman behind the counter that brought him there every morning.

Following a particularly bad night in the forest on a hunt, Jasper had been pissed and hungry. Another wolf had tried to play a dominant game, forcing Jasper to hurt him. The stench of the other's defeat had remained on him, only angering Jasper that much more. The scent of the morning's freshly baked goods pulled him through the quaint and welcoming door, and the slender goddess who served him brought thoughts of a different form of servicing to mind.

Slightly above average in height – he would guess about five foot seven – she was the perfect height to settle against his body. For someone who owned and operated a bakery, she was as skinny as a rail. However, if he looked close enough he could see the telltale signs possible of curves. And with just a little bit of his help and pampering she would gain some well-needed cushion. No matter what, she'd look amazing underneath him. Her long, light brown hair curled in a bun on the top of her head. His fingers ached to pull out the pins and watch it tumble down her back. Hazel eyes sought him and begged for his protection. Damn, he was willing.

Her look made the wolf within him perk up and growl.

"Mate? I want her". His wolf paced beneath the surface of his skin, calculating the best way to quickly claim their mate.

What his wolf spoke of was a possibility. There were only a few women in the world through time that carried the scent to signal the potential mating. Unlike his brother Kade, who had met two women recently that carried the scent, Jasper had never in his one-hundred and three years come across a woman who brought forth the mating urge. However, if all encounters were like this one, Jasper didn't know how others walked away. The urge rode him hard and he fought his wolf for control if only for a moment, something that hadn't happened since he was a pup.

He mentally spoke to his wolf. *"We are not ready for a mate. And a human no less. She knows nothing of us. If, and that is a big if, we chose her to be our mate, we will have to go slowly into this. I don't want us to scare her. But she is beautiful, no"*

His wolf growled in response.

"Do you want to scare her away? Let's get to know her first, see if she is a good match, other than that incredible cinnamon scent. I'll talk to Adam and find out everything I can about her. I am the Beta; I cannot put my Pack in jeopardy."

God, he really sucked at this. This time he needed to put on his big wolf panties and actually ask her out.

"Then we could mark her."

He snorted at his wolf. Yeah, that was taking it slow.

Jasper shook himself from his inner thoughts and looked into those hazel eyes. The spot of flour on her cheek begged for his hand to brush it way. He fought the urge. No need to freak her out. Her chest moved slowly, her small breasts rising and falling. The cinnamon scent of her filled his nostrils and he took a deep breath, the aroma going straight to his cock. The slight gasp that escaped from her kissable lips almost broke his control, and he fisted his hands to regain it.

"Good morning." His voice lowered an octave and became a growl. He cleared his throat and started again. "I come here every morning and I don't think I ever gave you my name. Let me rectify that." He closed the distance between them so only the counter separated them. "I'm Jasper Jamenson. It's a pleasure to meet you." He held out his hand in hopes of touching her skin.

Willow blinked up at him and seemed at a loss for words. Her lips opened slightly, begging him to lean down and taste her.

"Uh... yeah... I'm Willow Delton." She shook her head, gave him a small smile and placed her slender hand in his. He'd been right – her skin was incredibly soft and made him want to take a bite.

"Yes, I know, you own this place." He gave her hand a squeeze and released her.

"So, Jasper, do you want your usual?" The sound of his name on her lips hardened his cock. Without waiting for him to respond, she turned back to her work-table to ice her cinnamon rolls.

"Sounds good." He watched as her hands moved swiftly and confidently across the baking sheets. "What time do you get off?"

"Smooth, Romeo. Why don't you just ask her to bend over the work table for you?"

Ignoring his wolf Jasper continued, "I thought that we could grab a bite to eat tonight and go see to the arts fest they have running in town."

Oh dear Lord. Why didn't he ease into this?

"Oh, are you asking me out on a date?" She wrinkled her brow and looked utterly confused at the prospect.

"Yes, I am. I've been in here for over a month every morning, and as much as I love your food, I had an ulterior motive."

Surprise flashed across her face before her eyes lit up with excitement. "I've never been to the arts fest in town. I didn't want to go by myself and didn't have anyone to go with me." Her mouth snapped shut at her revealing statement.

Laughing quietly, he shook his head. "So what time do you get off?"

"You really need to stop putting it like that; it gives me ideas." Again, he ignored his wolf's sarcasm.

"I close at four and should be done cleaning up by five. It's only me here today so it's going to take me an hour to close."

"What do you say I come back at six and we go to dinner from here?"

Her smile almost blinded him as she nodded before taking off her apron. "Okay. Sounds good. Here's your breakfast." She handed him his black coffee and a small brown bag with a pink logo.

Taking everything from her hands, he set them down along with the cash to pay for it. Giving into temptation, he leaned over the counter to brush the flour from her cheek.

She jumped and a flash of alarm raced across her face.

Chuckling under his breath, he reassured her. "Just some flour. I'll see you at six, Willow." He grabbed his breakfast and walked to the door, taking one last look behind him at the woman who was his mate. He was one lucky bastard.

Whistling a jaunty tune, he walked toward his Jeep, unconcerned and happy while leaving his mate to do her work. The hairs on the back of his neck lifted, and his wolf came to attention. The street was empty but for a few people; nothing looked out of place. Jasper took a deep breath but didn't detect another presence. With one last look toward his slender brunette, he shrugged off the uneasy feeling and continued to his Jeep.

CHAPTER TWO

The man of Willow's dreams walked out the door but this time was coming back for her. She had a date with Jasper. Her heart pound in her ears, and she felt like jumping up and down like a teenager. She bit her lip, holding back a squeal. Probably not the best time to do that.

Jasper – the name suited him. Unique, yet strong. Closing her eyes to savor the feel of his presence, she tried to recall every word he'd said, every move he' made. The warmth from his fingertips still tingled against her cheek. She took a deep breath of his lingering male scent and steadied herself before opening her eyes. An older couple stood staring at her with their lips pursed and brows furrowed. She must have been completely out of it not to hear the bell.

"I'm so sorry. I'm just having one of those days. What can I get for you? I have fresh cinnamon rolls for you if you like." She couldn't wipe the grin off her face and helped them to begin her day.

Breakfast and lunch flew by. Cleaning the few tables inside her shop, she hummed to herself as she thought about the night to come. She had a date. The small mountain town they lived in had a decent selection of potential matches. But from what she's observed, they were players or married. Sometimes both. Not until Jasper walked into her bakery, had she noticed a man. And oh, did she notice.

Suddenly the hair on her arms stood on end and she tensed. Someone was in the bakery. Why the hell hadn't she heard that damn bell? She turned quickly and bit off a gasp. A large man stood almost directly behind her, blocking her path. He glared down at her with a malicious curl to his lips. Tension and danger ebbed from him.

Letting this man know he scared her would be a mistake.

"Can I help you? I'm about to close, but I still have a few baked goods that are fresh and good to go." *Subtle, Willow. Let's try not to let the scary man know he is terrifying, shall we?* At least her voice didn't shake.

The stranger hadn't moved or spoken a word. He was at least as tall as Jasper and had the same hair color, but the similarities stopped there. Where Jasper was handsome in his masculine looks, this man was anything but. His hard face sported a nose that might have been broken, but never set. His lips gave an almost perpetual snarl. He was beefy, muscular, and downright scary. With his presence, any happiness and confidence Willow had gained that day evaporated.

"Let me just go behind the counter—" *Where access to the back door is.* "—and I can help you with whatever you need." Her voice started to crack, and she walked quickly, trying to get away from him.

Just as she reached the counter, his hand shot out and grasped her upper arm in a painful grip.

"What are you – ?"

He shook her hard, her body whipping around like a rag doll, and ended her sentence before he pulled her toward him.

"You smell just like him. He shouldn't have done that. If he really cared for you he wouldn't have marked his scent then left you all alone." His breath was rancid and crawled against her ear as he growled at her.

What is he talking about?

"Please let me go. I don't know what you're talking about."

She punched him in the gut. Years of living in foster homes taught her quite a bit. He grabbed her hip and rubbed himself on her while licking her ear. Gagging, she twisted and tried to scratch him. He only pulled her closer and rocked his erection against her.

As she opened her mouth to scream, he let go of her arm and closed his hand over her mouth.

"Nuh uh, little girl. No screaming or I will make you suffer longer before I kill you. You are a pretty thing, though a little skinny for my taste. Not enough tit to grab onto, but you'll do. That fucker thinks he can claim you for his mate? Fuck him. You are going to be mine, at least for a little while before we tear you to pieces." He smiled and lifted his hand from her mouth to give her a bruising kiss.

She resisted, but he held her head to him by pulling her hair and rocked again. His erection brushed her, and she shuddered. Tears streamed down her face as she whimpered in pain.

Just then, the back door slammed open and another stranger came barreling in. The man wasn't as tall as her assailant, but he looked similar, except for the jagged scar running along his face.

"Shit, Isaac, stop fucking around. If the Redwoods know we're on their territory they'll tear our throats out. Not to mention it reeks of the Beta in here. Once he finds out, there'll be hell to pay. Just get the bitch in the car and don't fuck with her. She's the Alpha's first. Once Hector gets a taste, you can have her. Assuming there is anything left."

"Fuck you, Reggie. I can do whatever I damn well please with this tasty piece."

The man named Reggie glowered at Isaac. "Get the fuck in the car, dude. I'll gut you if I have to." Isaac buckled under an unknown force and Willow gasped.

Oh my God. What's going on? What is that?

Was it a Taser? No. She didn't see one.

Oh God. What was happening?

As he shifted again, Willow tried to break free.

"No, pet, I don't think so." His dry tongue licked the side of her face. Bile rose in her throat.

Oh God, she didn't want to die.

"You're coming with us. And when that fucking Beta Jasper gets wind we have you, then we can kill him too." Reggie strolled across the room toward the two of them.

The fist came at her face too fast to register until she felt a painful explosion against her cheek.

The last thing she remembered was wondering where they were taking her and what did Jasper, her dream man, have to do with it?

CHAPTER THREE

"You look so cute dressed up. Willow isn't going to know what hit her." Melanie, Kade's mate, bounced around Jasper's living room helping him to choose his clothes for his date with Willow.

A growl sounded behind him, and Jasper laughed out loud.

Yep, his older brother was a tad bit possessive.

"Hey, man, it's the truth." Jasper ducked when a pillow from his couch flew by his head.

"Oh stop being a baby, Kade." Mel's eyes danced. "He's handsome, and he's going on his first date with his mate. There's no reason to be jealous. In fact, the better he looks, the more likely he is to come home with his mate. Once he's all marked and mated, it'll be one less male you have to growl at." Mel sauntered up to Kade and whispered in his ear. Whatever she said must have been good because Kade's eyes darkened as he took his wife's mouth. A smidge of jealousy settled in Jasper's stomach. Hopefully, he was about to do the same with Willow.

After a few minutes of them going at it, Jasper threw a pillow at them. "Seriously, you two need to get a room, and not one in my house." He grinned and tucked his black button-down shirt into his new dark jeans. Jasper also had on his favorite black boots and kept his hair down. Whenever he refrained from his typical ponytail and left his shoulder-length hair loose and half-dried after a shower, the scent of Willow's interest increased. He wanted to keep that up.

"Fine, fine. But I don't want to hear anything when I do the same to you and Willow once she gets here." Kade slapped his back in brotherly love, and Mel gave him a comforting hug before leaving him alone with his nervous thoughts.

He shouldn't be nervous. Willow was his mate. Fate had designed them for each other. Though there were others that had the potential to be his mate, Willow was it for him. Her cinnamon scent had seeped into his soul. She was his.

"We will take care of her every need and pleasure her beyond comprehension. No problem."

Jasper snorted at his wolf. "You really need to stop saying shit like that. She's human. This is going to be hard enough seeing how I have never mated before, and I don't want to fuck this up. But add on the fact that I'm opening her eyes to a world of supernaturals from her nightmares... Yeah, this could go poorly." That was the last thing either of them needed.

His younger brother, Adam, strode through the door without knocking, as all of his family was known to do. Over a hundred years of being together had dissolved most boundaries. "Jasper man, you really need to stop talking to yourself. And don't worry. Just be yourself and everything will work out. On second thought, just be me."

"I was just talking to my wolf. I don't like talking in my head all the time. I look like a nutter, rather than just sounding like one." As a werewolf, he shared a body with a wolf spirit much older than he. And if he asked this wolf, much wiser, too. The man was more dominant and chose when to shift, but the wolf always had an opinion. When he was in wolf form, he sometimes let his wolf take charge on a hunt, but Jasper was always present.

Jasper took a drink of water from the pitcher in the fridge and flipped Adam off. "And fuck you. You keep your dumbass away from my mate."

And if he touched her, then Adam would pay. Maybe he'd make him watch *From Justin to Kelly* then put Icy Hot on his balls.

Adam laughed and took a glass of water for himself. Adam was only about an inch shorter than him, and other than Adam's shorter hair, they could pass for twins.

"You don't need to worry about that. I know when someone's staked his claim. But I do need a favor from you." Adam straightened when he spoke as an Enforcer, rather than his brother.

"What's up?" Jasper fell into his role of Beta, though thoughts of Willow were not far from his mind.

"One of the adolescents took a stroll through the woods near Main Street, where Willow's bakery is, and thought he smelled something. It could be nothing, but I need to check it out. I figured since you were going down there anyway, I'd catch a ride with you and then wolf it back to search for scents."

Jasper's body went on alert. His heart beat in his ears. "When did you hear this? Why the fuck did you wait until now to come and get me? My scent is all over that bakery. If some lone wolf goes near Willow, they're just going to think she's meat. I haven't claimed her yet." Jasper could feel his wolf prowl, ready to attack the dangers surrounding his mate.

"Calm down. I just heard about it before I walked here. We can go together to check out the threat. But as I said, the pup wasn't sure what he smelled. He wasn't sure if it was a wolf or not. But seeing how it's close to Willow's, I thought we should go."

Jasper grabbed his keys and had left the house before Adam had time to take another breath. He needed to check on her. If anyone came near her or even sniffed her, he'd kick some ass.

"Let me drive, man," Adam said as he reached the driveway. "I don't want you to take us off the road. You're a little edgy now."

Jasper tossed him the keys and climbed into the passenger seat of his Jeep.

THE SMELL of other wolves reached his nose before his eyes registered the front door ripped off its hinges. He jumped from the Jeep before it stopped, with Adam following close behind. Jasper entered the bakery and took in the scene. Broken chairs lay on their sides among wooden splinters and gouges on the floor. Glass shards littered the carpet, creating a landscape of destruction.

"Mate?"

His wolf clawed to the surface, begging to be let out. The need to find her and demand retribution rode Jasper hard. Fuck. He'd kill anyone who dared lay a hand on her.

Jasper took a deep breath. There wasn't any blood. Thank God she wasn't bleeding. She could still be injured, but it was a good sign there wasn't blood. Two wolves had been there. Their scent lingered. But they weren't lone wolves. No, worse. They were from his Pack's rivals – the Central Pack.

His soul fractured as his heart clenched. His blood boiled and his temples throbbed. He slammed his fist into the wall and growled in agony. He was too late.

"Where is she, Adam? Why the fuck did they take her? How the hell did the Centrals get in our territory and take my mate?" He breathed heavily and paced throughout the chaos.

"I don't know, Jasper, but believe me, we're going to find her then kill any wolf that touched her." Adam had lost a mate years before when a rival attacked her. Jasper knew he would do anything to save Willow.

Adam was already on the phone with their father and brothers while Jasper searched for any clue. The Centrals were ruthless, and their leader, Hector Reyes, was a sadistic bastard who believed in the superiority of wolves over humans and witches. There were rumors he'd killed his wife when she tried to protect their daughter from being sold.

Adam closed his phone and caught Jasper's attention." North and Reed on are their way. Mom and Dad are going to stay behind with Cailin, Mel, Kade, and Maddox, as well as the stronger of the Pack's wolves to protect the territory in case this is just the first assault. The four of us will go to Central territory to retrieve her."

Jasper should have thought more for Willow's safety. He should have put plans to protect her in place. He hadn't even marked her. He'd already failed his mate. Once he saved her, and he would, he'd make sure he never failed her again. No matter what.

"They're going to be here soon," Adam said. "We need to get outside. Are you ready? We're about to violate the treaty by entering their territory without permission."

Like he gave a shit. He paced the length of the room, his muscles twitching with anxiety and aggression. Barely suppressing the urge to pound another fist into the nearest wall, he said, "They came here and kidnapped her. I have no idea if she's alive or dead. We aren't fully mated; she doesn't carry my mark. I can't feel her in here!" He slapped his fist to his chest above his heart.

A stormy look flashed across Adam's face, and Jasper immediately regretted his tirade.

"I'm sorry, Adam, I wasn't thinking about Anna. I'm so sorry."

"It's okay, Jasper. I, above all, know what you are feeling now. But this will be different. We're stronger now. We will find her." Adam gave him a rough hug before he left the shop. The sound of a car outside signaled the arrival of his brothers. Time to kick ass and find his mate.

CHAPTER FOUR

A slam of a car door woke Willow.

Where am I? What happened?

Head pounding, her thoughts collided then slowly coalesced. The scratchy surface of a torn fabric rubbed against Willow's bound wrists behind her back. She craned her neck to the side and discovered faded upholstery. She was in the backseat of a car. *Well, at least I'm not in the trunk.* Sarcasm aside, terror churned in her belly. An unwelcome friend in a dire situation.

Why couldn't she be the kick ass heroine of one of those newer, cheesy romance novels? She could take the knife tucked in her boot, free herself, and kill anyone in her path. Okay, maybe not kill, but seriously maim nonetheless.

Willow inwardly winced. Damn, she was officially going crazy. Who were those men that had taken her? Isaac and Reggie. That's right. What did they want with her? She was just a bakery owner with no family to speak of.

Jasper.

They'd tossed his name about before they knocked her out. But why? What did he have to do with it?

The car door opened abruptly, the sound of the metal grinding against metal piercing Willow's ears. Her breath stopped, fear taking over.

"She's awake." A man – no Isaac – spoke to people she couldn't see before leaning in the car. He reached beneath her to pull Willow out by her tied hands. The rope dug into her flesh, and she felt the faint trickle of warm liquid down her hands. Oh God, they'd broken the skin. A whimper escaped her, as Isaac pulled her to his chest.

"You smell sweet. We're going to have fun with you." Like in her shop, his breath assaulted her face. Distress trailed up her chest, seeping into her bones. *Don't let this man be the last face I see, please.*

He pulled her, not at all struggling with her weight, toward a drab gray building.

A wolf walked out the door, leading her down a dimly lit hall.

They keep wild animals here?

The wolf growled, then its body rippled. Its bones crunches and muscles tore, finally reshaping into a naked man.

"Hello, Willow. I'm Hector, the Alpha, leader of the Centrals. And I'm going to be the last thing you see." He smiled.

Willow screamed as he backhanded her, throwing her into the wall. At the sound of the man called Hector's laughter, she fell into blessed darkness with some last conscious thoughts.

Werewolves are real.

And they are going to kill me.

BRACING HERSELF, Willow cracked open only her right eye because her left one had been swollen shut and took in her surroundings. Water trickled down the aging stone walls and dripped against concrete floors. A draft from the small crack under the door cooled the room and froze Willow's bones. She was locked in a basement or cellar of some sort with no windows and only a steel door as a way out.

The handcuffs currently digging into her wrists and ankles deterred any thought of moving. Hector had knocked her out cold with his fist, and she hadn't woken until they dropped her on the cold floor, naked and chained with a collar around her throat. The lack of an ache between her thighs was a blessing as she knew she'd escaped being raped – for now.

After trying to stay awake for what seemed like hours, she drifted in and out of consciousness until hands tugged at her chains, jostling her awake again.

"Get up," a gravelly voice ordered. "Time to speak to the Alpha."

What was an Alpha? Why couldn't she sleep? Her eyes felt heavy and exhaustion pulled at her, but she couldn't rest. Oh God, she didn't want to see the werewolves again.

Trying to conserve the last of her dwindling energy, she let them drag to a room on one of the upper floors.

"Ah, my pet. I'm happy to see you here. I'm Corbin, the Alpha's son." He smiled a cruel smile and Willow curled up into a ball. His hands rubbed along her arms and legs, trailing her stomach and breasts.

She fought the urge to shudder.

Oh God. This isn't happening.

"Little human, do you know why we took you?" Another voice spoke and Corbin lifted his hands.

Willow lifted her head, following the sound of the voice to meet the eyes of their Alpha.

Little human? Oh God. It wasn't a nightmare.

Although something inside told her to lower her eyes in submission, she refused to give him the satisfaction. Most likely of Hispanic ancestry, he looked to be about thirty-five with tan skin and mangy brown hair. His eyes were such a deep black they sent shivers down her body. Dressed in slacks and an expensive button down shirt, he didn't look like the gang leader she'd thought him to be. He looked more like a muscular business man on his way to a lunch meeting.

The slap across her face echoed through the room and forced her to whimper.

"Lower your eyes, bitch! You are not fit to be in my presence, let alone to look into my eyes. You're lucky I don't kill you on the spot. But then that would be putting an end to my fun, wouldn't it? No, little human, you're going to be my toy to play with before we kill you. Then your Jasper is going to know who is master won't he?" No longer did he sound the angry leader, he sounded like a malicious, sadistic man. Bile rose in her throat as her fear almost overpowered her. He gave her a menacing snarl then tugged at the chain on her collar to pull her toward him.

"Would you like to see what is going to kill you?"

He nodded toward to the man who'd abducted her, Isaac, who began to strip. Long scars trailed down his body and Willow tried to turn away. Hector tugged at her chain again and forced her to watch. Isaac bent at the waist and knelt. Willow gasped as the sounds of bones breaking and shaping resounded throughout the room and hair sprouted through his skin down his arms and torso. The bones on his face angled and lengthened to resemble a snout. His body heaved and twisted as he completed the change. Where Isaac had stood as a man, now an enormous golden eyed, black wolf hunched. The wolf threw back his head and howled, sending shivers down her spine and goose bumps along her arms.

Willow screamed.

Screamed and screamed while trying to scramble way. The leader only pulled on the chain harder.

"You will die by his claws and teeth. You will be begging for death before he is through with you, little woman."

He tugged on the collar again, cutting off her breath. *Dear God, please save me.* As she fell to floor with black spots dancing across her vision, the wolf crawled on top of her. Drool dripped down her body. She reached out, trying to reach for an escape that wasn't to be found and blessedly passed out.

WILLOW SHOT UP and winced as pain lanced through her body. Memories of what had transpired flooded her mind. She was locked in a den of werewolves. The monsters of her nightmares were real and on other side of the door ready to kill her after they – she gulped – played. Willow had always thought she was stronger than most, but even this was too much for her.

Tears wet her cheeks as she begged God for a chance. Please God, let Jasper find her and save her. She was alone in a cold, dark room with no chance of escape. Sorrow enveloped her. *Please, Jasper. Come.*

Jasper.

The Alpha had taken her because he had a feud with her mystery man. What had he done to deserve that wrath? What did she even know of him? What little she'd overheard during her stay led her to believe that he, too, was a werewolf. But he'd been near her for weeks and never hurt her. Why would that cruel man take her to hurt him?

When Jasper came, he'd be answering her questions.

If he came for her.

Willow took a deep breath and flinched at the pain in her ribs. Damn. They were probably broken. She needed a doctor.

Finally closing her eyes, she calmed herself and curled into a ball. Suddenly the door broke away from its hinges and flew across the room. She gasped in terror.

"Willow." Her name was a growl but relief flooded through her.

Jasper.

He came.

"Willow. Oh baby. Let me get you unchained." Jasper knelt down and brushed his hand against the bruises on her face. Unwillingly, she flinched, and he froze. Cursing under his breath, he growled again before reaching for her chains.

The sound of metal crunching and grating hurt her ears, but Jasper removed the cuffs from her wrists and ankles. Her skin prickled, and pain shot up her arm as the blood flowed freely again. She moaned and bit her lip.

"I know it hurts Wil, but let me get this collar off you and then I'll take you home. I'm so sorry baby, I..." He choked off the last words as tears fell from his eyes.

He was crying for her? He couldn't be all that bad for a werewolf.

"I'm going to put my shirt around you and then pick you up. It's going to hurt, Wil, so brace yourself." His eyes, still glassy from unshed tears, gazed into hers.

Jasper laid his shirt over her, tucking it around her. Pain shot through her body as he gently, oh so gently, cradled her nearly clad body to his chest. His lips caressed her forehead, and he took a ragged breath.

"Let's go home, baby. Reed, go start the car and, North, I want you in the back with us to check her when we head out. Adam, make sure you stay behind us and watch our backs."

Willow finally noticed the three men that joined them in her cell. Even in the dark, she could tell they were Jasper's brothers. The same green eyes filled with looks of pure anger stared back at her. The one called Reed was much skinnier with sandy blond hair. He nodded once and lowered his gaze before jogging out of the room.

From the corner of her eye she recognized Adam. He'd come into her shop with Jasper a couple of mornings, but he'd kept his distance, much like he was doing now. Willow strained her neck to see the last brother, North, who also looked like Jasper but with less muscles and dark blond hair. He seemed to be checking her body for injuries from across the room, and with each surveying glance, the anger in his eyes intensified. Though deep down she knew the anger wasn't directed at her, she still shuddered and buried her face into Jasper's chest. He smelled of forest and man, yet underneath, there was another scent – wolf.

Jasper held her closer and rubbed his cheek across the top of her head. She could feel the beat of his heart against her cheek, and as his breathing slowed, so did hers. Jasper would protect her. She had to believe that.

"I'm taking you home, Wil." When he took a step toward the door, she winced, and he froze.

"Did I hurt you? What can I do?"

She shook her head and shivered. It hurt all over, but being in his arms was worth it. He hadn't told her how he'd got here, and she didn't want to face what was out there.

Jasper's grip tightened for only a fraction of a second before it loosened. "They aren't out there, Wil. They were gone when we got here. I think they knew we were coming and left you here for dead." They both winced at the truth of the statement. "We can talk more once I get you home, baby. Okay?" She nodded against his chest as he followed North to Jasper's Jeep, Adam close behind.

Willow had almost fallen asleep in Jasper's arms when they stopped suddenly. Jasper's growl vibrated against her cheek. She looked up, and her heart stopped. They were surrounded by wolves and men – at least thirty bodies. Panic crawled up from her toes as she opened her mouth to scream. Only Jasper's voice prevented her.

"Don't make a sound. They can hear even your heartbeat. I will protect you. We all will."

A cackle of the most grotesque sort swept through the surrounding forest.

"I wouldn't be so sure, Beta. You will not live past the hour." The deep voice surrounded them, but Willow couldn't see who it came from.

Jasper growled again and North moved to cover them. She could hear Adam's heavy breathing behind them through her haze of pain and knew he must have moved closer as well. The pounding in her head and the men around them took all her concentration.

The Alpha stepped forward to glare at the three of them.

"I have a proposition for you." Hector, took another step toward them, smiling. "As much as I want to kill you and drink the marrow from your bones, this human scrap has entertained me. She is untainted and unclaimed. You give her to me and I will let your wolves go. For now. I have plans for this little human." His smile was cruel, and Willow almost vomited with fear.

Would Jasper give her to them? In doing so, he'd save himself and his brothers. He hardly knew her and had only asked her out. They hadn't even kissed or been on a date. She was nothing to him, and his brothers' lives were on the line. She knew the choice he would have to make and she didn't want to make it any harder for him or herself.

She tried to wiggle down from his arms to let them live. Jasper's hold tightened a moment before letting her go. Blood rushed from her head and her heart shattered.

He let her go.

She was to be the sacrifice. Holding in a whimper from the pain of standing and a broken heart, she tried to keep herself steady. Jasper held onto her shoulder and when she tried to take a step away from him, he brought her closer to his chest.

She needed to get away from him. Death hunted for her, but she couldn't look at him, for he would see the betrayal she felt.

Stop being ridiculous.

Choosing his family was the right choice. Betrayal shouldn't be a consideration.

"I see." Jasper's voice lowered to a rougher edge. Willow dared a glance over her shoulder and gasped at his face. She'd been right, he was a werewolf. His upper canines had elongated, and a ring of gold had formed around the forest green of his eyes. But she wasn't afraid of him. Not this wolf.

Jasper growled under his breath, and she flinched. "Then I guess I must claim her now."

Before she could register the shock of his comment, Jasper tugged her to his chest and bit down on the curve of her shoulder where it met her neck. When his teeth punctured her flesh, she felt and heard a distinctive pop, before pain shot through her system. The bite deepened, and he held on, growling all the while. Willow's knees gave out, and she would have collapsed to the ground if not for Jasper's hands holding her up. He rocked against her and she felt his rock hard erection against her ass.

He's tearing into my flesh and getting off on this?

Panic flooded her.

But then a curious tingling swept over her. Peace and sex. Like honey, the feeling flowed through her blood and body to her head and breasts, then down to her stomach and womb before tickling her toes. Gasping, she held on to Jasper for stability as she came against him in front of thirty angry wolves and his brothers.

Her juices flowed down her legs as the men surrounding her flared their nostrils in excitement. Some broke formation to rub the evidence of their arousal, awakening her from her sexual fog.

Jasper released her shoulder, licked the wound, then nuzzled her cheek. Heat climbed her face as she became of aware of what had just happened. Jasper had bit her, and she'd orgasmed. *What the hell?*

A roar of pure rage and hatred echoed through the mountains.

"Fucking Beta! You think that just because you're a Jamenson you can defy me? You fucking claimed her? I'll kill you. But first I'll take that bitch, rape her and beat her in front of you!" Hector screamed, spitting out his words in pure fury. He opened his mouth to condemn them again, but was suddenly flying through the air after being smacked by the front of Jasper's Jeep. The crunch of gravel beneath the tires was the only warning they'd had.

The Jeep skidded to a halt in front of them. Adam threw himself into the front while North grabbed Willow by the arms, ignoring her wounds, and jumped into the back. Jasper followed close behind. He'd barely landed in the seat before Reed drove off into the forest like a maniac.

"Fuck!" Reed roared as he drove on. "He had you mark her? In front of them? Fuck, man! Fuck!" Reed's knuckles whitened against the wheel as he drove. He looked in the mirror and cocked his head. "The wolves aren't following us. I don't know what's going on, but it's like they're stuck there. Is some unseen force holding the other wolves back? Why would they do that? That wasn't wolf or witch magic, man, but I don't fucking know what it was. That was something deep. We gotta tell Dad."

What were they talking about? First werewolves and now magic. Her head spun.

Jasper pulled her off North and laid her across his lap. His warmth swept through her, seeping into her bones. She curled into his body, his arms cradling her.

Reed panted and talked fast as the adrenaline sped through his system. Willow reached over the seat and touched his arm. Startled, he swerved off the road, before righting himself and looking toward her.

"Thank you for coming back." Her voice was raw, and it hurt to move, but it needed to be said.

"Yeah, man, thanks." North nodded toward Reed and began to examine her, though it was difficult as she still lay across Jasper's lap. His pokes and prods made her wince and moan. With every flinch, Jasper's growls grew louder, and his arms tightened.

"And thank you North and Adam. It's nice to see you. Well, not nice, but..." She was rambling and she knew it. She looked up at her savior and tried to hide her heart. He couldn't know how deeply she felt for him. "Thank you, Jasper." She choked off a sob, and his hold tightened almost painfully.

"I need to breathe." She tried to smile, but she knew it came out like a grimace.

His hold loosened immediately, and he rubbed his hand against her ass. "Sorry." His voice roughened. The anger in his eyes hurt her already wrecked heart. That bite had meant something, and they'd forced him into it. She didn't know what the future held, but Jasper had been coerced into doing something he didn't want and he would only resent her for it.

"I think she has some broken ribs, Jasper," North said. "But other than the bruising and a few cuts, I don't think there's anything else broken. I won't know until we get back to the den and my equipment." North stopped touching her and immediately Jasper's shoulders relaxed.

They rode for over an hour before Jasper finally broke the silence.

"We're almost at the den, Reed and Adam, you both need to tell the Pack what happened. North, Willow and I will join you at your clinic, and you will check her for deeper injuries." His brothers nodded in agreement. Willow was surprised they didn't question Jasper's demands.

I wonder what that means.

Willow burrowed into Jasper's side. He may have been angry with her, but cold had leached into her bones, and only Jasper's intense body heat could warm her.

With one decision, the world opened up and tried to swallow her whole. She'd said yes to Jasper's invitation and the bad men came. The things that went bump in the night had captured her and almost killed her. Their rescue had provided safety for her through their power. For now she was going to the wolf's den, where the monsters lived. Her heart may be broken and the man she barely knew and had fallen for might resent her, but he was her savior. She'd cling to that and his warmth for as long as she could.

CHAPTER FIVE

J asper looked out the Jeep's window, his gaze on the passing trees. The Redwood Pack's den lay in a valley where two mountains converged deep within the forest. It was Jasper's home, his oasis. Protected on three sides by nature, the Den reflected a symbol of strength and longevity. Something he desperately fought to preserve in his role as Beta. When the battle between demons and werewolves had ended over a thousand years before, the first of Jasper's ancestors settled in the forest, mistakenly thinking the ancient large trees redwoods. The misinterpretation had given them their moniker and had long since been a token of humor within the Pack.

Jasper took a deep breath, watching the scenery in a blur. Trees and greenery filled the den. Wildflowers burst with color among the bushes and gardens surrounding some homes and landmarks. Homes were spread about and hidden below the canopy to allow individual privacy. In the center of town, brick buildings and small shops rose up from the expansive gardens. In the northern plain, large rock formations created the circle where meetings and dominance battles commenced. The first spiritual and magical settling of the Pack struck ground here. The pull of his family and Pack tugged on Jasper's heart – he was home. And his mate was by his side. Happiness swept through him.

Willow fell asleep before they arrived at the gates. The magical barrier that hid the den from outsiders slid over them as they passed through, their Pack connection acting like a key in a lock. It humbled him that she felt safe enough to fall asleep in his arms. But she probably wouldn't be sleeping if she knew what was forced on them. On her. Crawling through the underbelly of their fucked up world was not the best way to be introduced to ones future. His prior glee subsided a bit.

Jasper didn't know what was worse, the shattered and broken look on her face when she thought he would let her die or the pain that encompassed her when he bit her shoulder. The sensation of binding his wolf to her through the bite had nearly made him come at the same time as Willow had. Only the danger surrounding them stopped him. They were only bound through the mark, and their mating was incomplete. They still needed to consummate the relationship by him spilling his seed in her womb before their souls joined eternally.

The circumstances had stripped her choice. Now she was forever bound to him. He'd wanted to subtly coax her into his life and into his bed. That was no longer an option. They'd have to make love soon or the mating urge would take over his body and make him uncontrollably violent and nearly rabid. As it was, it rode him hard, and only the bruises on her face and heart stopped him. Never would he touch her again without her acceptance. Painfully, Jasper would wait and try his best to help her heal her and understand his world before taking that next step. He just hoped it didn't take too long.

His wolf snorted in agreement.

The gravel crunched beneath the tires as Reed pulled up to North's clinic. The one-story ranch home was one of the newer buildings in the den, but still had a rustic feel. Jasper carried his mate, cradled in his arms, inside and laid her down on the soft examining table. North followed silently behind them and bent over his patient. Jasper's wolf growled and bristled at his brother's nearness to his mate.

His wolf prowled to the surface. "*We marked our mate and need to finish it. Your brother is too close to her. His scent must not mingle with hers. That is our right and privilege."*

North merely lifted a brow but continued his work. All werewolves talked to their wolves, whether spoken aloud or not. North bandaged the bite on her shoulder, though with the enzyme in Jasper's saliva it would soon heal and not leave a scar.

The image of the bite was not what marked her; rather the bite allowed his scent to completely permeate in her skin her forever. Unlike before in the bakery when his scent merely touched her skin, now it was in her pores and in her cells. She would forever be his, and once she marked his shoulder, the same would be true of him.

Because she was human, his wolf only mated one-sided. When and if she transitioned and marked him, their wolves would be fully joined, as it was only his wolf was mated. As a man and woman, it would take the act of making love for their souls to bind. Werewolves were cohesive and volatile symbioses of two beings. It made sense that their mating would require two steps to complete.

"She has two broken ribs but no other internal injuries." North's voice pulled him from his thoughts. "I'm going to bind them now, but because of the mate mark, she should be healed within the next two days or so. The bruising and small cuts should be gone by then too. Other than being sore, I think she's going to be fine."

North removed his gloves and shook his head. "Physically anyway. I can only imagine how she is going to be mentally and emotionally. I know this isn't how you wanted to mate her, but like it or not, she is here, and she's yours. Do you know what you are going to do about it?" His voice held sympathy but none of the pity Jasper had been afraid would fall upon Willow.

Jasper took a breath and tried to release the anger building within. "She's mine. There's no question of that. I'll do whatever it takes for her to accept me and our world. Our Pack is important, and I'll protect it with my life, but now I have Willow and I need to protect her too." He let out a deep breath and walked toward her. Tracing the edge of her cheek with his finger, he felt the heat from healing, and he knew she would wake soon with questions.

"I'm going to take her home and get her cleaned. Hopefully by the time she wakes up, I'll have better answers for her." He gently picked her up and carried her to the door North held open for them.

"I don't envy you that conversation, bro. Dad most likely knows what happened. Be prepared for his visit, as well as Mom's. Dad's going to want to make sure you're all right and meet the mate you've chosen – not to mention the Central Pack needs to be taken care of. Mom will want to pamper Willow so they'll be in your hair." North's lips curled into a smirk, and he let them leave with a nod.

"Thanks, bro."

"Good luck."

———

WILLOW'S EYES FLUTTERED OPEN. Jasper knelt above her. His gaze roamed her body, though not in a salacious way. Probably checking her injuries. Her eyes met his, and she felt as if she'd come home. Pain radiated in her head as she shook the idea of him loving her from her mind. He'd been forced into protecting her, being with her.

They were in a bedroom that held a large wooden king-sized bed of a deep color and matching furniture. The walls and carpet were a warm honey that looked like they would wrap around her and soothe her to sleep.

The room was clean with only a few pictures of what she guessed were his family and a few hand-carved wooden animals and figurines. The room felt like it welcomed her home and again, she suppressed the feeling.

"Hey." Her voice sounded raspy and not at all like hers.

He blinked then brushed the tip of his finger against her brow. Her body shivered, and he pulled away.

"I don't know how to make this up to you, Wil. I have so much to tell you, but first, since you're awake, let's clean you up." Jasper stood and held out his hand. He helped her from the bed before leading her slowly to the bathroom.

He gently pulled off her shirt and paused. His chest rose and he growled, then shook his head. His hand fisted and he turned to start a warm bath. She stood there in his large and comfortable bathroom naked and vulnerable, but Jasper would never hurt her. For all of the new revelations and supernatural events she'd experienced in the past day, she trusted Jasper. Though it hadn't been the most romantic of circumstances, he'd held her naked in his arms not more than a few hours before. There was no need for modesty at this point.

"Let me help you." His hands were rough and calloused as he touched her hip and led her into the bath. The water steamed hot and stung her aching skin but after a moment, began relieving the soreness. She moaned as she knelt in the water, and the hand on her hip tightened.

"This feels good. Thank you, Jasper."

"That's nice to hear, Wil. I would put in some Epson salts to help, but I want to make sure we clean off this dirt and grime first." He held a washcloth in his hand and lathered it with soap. The scent of sandalwood tickled her nose. She grinned at the smell. Jasper's smell.

He cleaned her body with gentle care and no words. The cloth brushed over her nipples, and she looked up, but he didn't stop, nor did he stop when he delved between her legs slowly and leisurely, washing her in her most intimate place. Though he touched her in a way no other man had in a long time, he didn't make it sexual, merely cleaned the night away from her skin.

He turned on the hot water again and rinsed her body then washed her hair. Once clean, he lifted her from the bath and patted her dry with a soft, fluffy towel. Her muscles felt weak, heavy. He put one of his shirts over her head, lifted her to his chest, and carried her to the bed.

Jasper finally spoke again as he laid her down. "I know you have many questions, but you need to rest. When you wake up, I'll answer anything you ask. I know this is not what you wanted, but we'll work it out. Just to warn you, my parents will be here soon, and they'll want to talk to you, so gain any energy you can from sleep, my Willow." He kissed her cheek and was about to lift himself from her when she placed her hand on his cheek.

"I trust you, Jasper. Thank you for coming for me." Her voice sounded calm, but firm. She couldn't have him thinking it was his fault, he was the one who was stuck with her.

Blinking once, he nodded and kissed her palm. He seemed to struggle with something before lowering his mouth to hers. His lips were soft and wet as he deepened the kiss. She gasped and opened her mouth to him before biting softly on his bottom lip. He growled and pulled away.

Panting heavily, he shook and stood straight. "Rest well, Willow. I'll be here if you need me." He turned quickly and strode out of the room, taking her heart with him.

WILLOW WOKE up to the sound of voices in the hall. Before investigating, she slowly studied the room. She was still alone. She closed her eyes again, then reached her arms above her head and winced in pain.

Yep, still hurts.

Rolling her head around her shoulders, she stretched as best she could, trying to soothe some of her aches and pains. Someone had laid out sweats on the edge of the bed when she slept. She hauled herself up and put them on. Once in the bathroom, she got the first look of herself in the mirror and gasped.

Her eye was already black and blue, but oddly enough, the swelling seemed to have gone down. There were cuts and scrapes along her cheek and hairline, but the blood had been washed away by Jasper the night before. Lowering the neck of Jasper's shirt, she removed the bandage. She saw bruising around her throat in the shape of the collar placed around her neck and the impression of Jasper's bite that had saved her gave her shivers. The stark contrast between the heavy, dark purple bruising and the paleness of her skin scared her. The image in the mirror was not that of the baker and loner of the day before, but the survivor thrown into a new world. A world that scared her. But not Jasper. Only the thought of losing him did that.

The voices from outside the bedroom grew louder and she steadied herself to find them. She slowly walked to a large living area of dark brown and tan masculine furniture, the wood decorated with carvings. The room was mostly sparse except for Jasper and two others who looked to be his siblings.

Immediately they stopped talking. The topic of conversation must have been her. Jasper stood and took a step toward her. Before she could comprehend the worried look on his face, it cleared to a blank expression.

"Willow, did you sleep well?" Jasper stood before her and caressed her bruised cheek with his knuckles.

His touch left her mind in tangles, but she nodded. Her gaze wandered to the two quiet people who rose to their feet behind Jasper.

Jasper noticed the object of her gaze and smiled. "Wil, these are my parents, Edward and Patricia, most call her Pat though." He took her hand and linked their fingers before leading her to the young looking couple before her.

Jasper's mother was warmth and love personified. It practically radiated through her pores. She looked to be about five feet tall, and soft, motherly curves made her welcoming. Light brown hair with natural, almost blonde highlights and warm brown eyes only accentuated her beaming smile.

Jasper's father was a tall man, though not as tall as Jasper. With broad shoulders and similar build, he reminded her of his son. His hair was dark brown, lighter than Jasper's. His gaze rested on her, sizing her up and taking measure.

A soft growl broke the silence.

Jasper.

"Dad, Mom, this is my mate, Willow Delton." At the word mate, Willow stiffened. He'd called her that before, but she wasn't prepared for the casual ease at with which the word left his lips.

What exactly did that mean? Had he claimed her like an animal? Did he even want her?

"Hello, Willow Delton, it is good to meet the mate of my second son. I'm sure you have as many questions about us as we have of you. Please sit down." Edward's deep voice held no room for objection and waved her toward the couch.

"Dad, don't grill her."

"Oh, Jasper honey, we won't do that. We just want to get to know her, and I am sure, after last night, she has many questions. I mean she was just introduced to our world and none too nicely." Pat, smiled and took Willow's other hand in hers as Jasper sat beside her, close enough that their thighs touched and she felt the heat of him.

At Pat's comment, silence swept through the room. Willow didn't think she could take another strained and awkward silence, so she stepped up to the paranormal plate.

"So, I guess you guys are werewolves. I'm guessing shaving is a bitch." Her mouth shut with an audible snap as heat crept up her neck into her cheeks. What on earth had possessed her to say that? *Good job Willow. Tell the very big werewolves, who could snap you like the twig you're named after, that they have a hairy problem.*

Jasper's boom of laughter vibrated though the room, and her tense shoulders relaxed. Pat too laughed, and the lines around Edwards's eyes crinkled in amusement.

"Yes, we're werewolves, but I have no problem shaving in the morning." Again, Edward almost cracked a smile, and Willow knew she'd taken a huge leap toward acceptance with this man.

Edward sobered before he continued. "There is much you need to know, and I'm sure Jasper can tell you some, but I'll begin. We are the Redwood Pack, and once Jasper completes the mating you, too, will be part of us." Willow's brow furrowed and she shot Jasper what she knew must be a confused look, but he only scowled at his father.

Wait. Completes the mating? Like sex? Oh, geez.

"We've been a Pack for over a millennium and I've been Alpha for over two hundred years." Her eyes widened at his age and the fact that he looked damn good for it. "There are many other positions in the Pack, and you'll learn them over time; however, I'm in charge. It is my first duty to express my deep sorrow and regret that you've been pulled into this world without your permission. However, since the choice was taken from you, we must move forward.

"Our lives are deeply entrenched in secrecy and now yours will be as well. All you know will have to be left soon, and you must come with us for your safety. We know you only have few connections to the human world, but even those must be severed." Willow was startled at the amount of information they possessed concerning her.

"I understand. At least I think I do. But what about my bakery?" It was the only thing she had to call her own and to show her accomplishments in life. Without it, she had nothing.

Edward shook his head. "For now I think it must remain closed, at least for your safety. In the future we can discuss your reopening, but we can't say as of yet. Your safety as Jasper's mate is more important to us."

Willow took a deep breath and resisted the urge to cry as pain radiated through her heart. She nodded but couldn't speak. Jasper squeezed her in comfort, and the tightness in her chest eased.

"I know, Willow, this is a lot to take in now, but it'll be okay. We will protect you. You also need to decide whether or not you want to change, as it is your choice and privilege as Jasper's mate." *Change? Like into a werewolf?* Again, Willow took a deep breath to process that bit of terrifying information.

The idea of werewolves still scared the crap out of her, she'd never seriously thought they could exist and now she was surrounded by them, having a real conversation. She wasn't even sure she'd wanted a man, but she had one – who was a bit more than a man. And they offered her a choice of becoming one...

Her mind spun and she rubbed her temples.

Edward leaned over the coffee table and patted her hand reassuringly. "There will be many people who want to meet with you, most of them family, and we will be having a Pack meeting soon to discuss what happened out in the woods. But, I welcome you to our family, Willow Delton."

Edward stood and nodded. Pat got up and gave her a warm and soft hug, careful of the bruises. "Welcome to the family my dear. We may have many sons, but I only have one daughter by birth and one by mating. I'm honored to call you my own, dear." She gave Willow a smile with watery eyes and left the house with her husband.

Still sitting, Willow thought about everything that had changed. Even with the preternatural energy that exuded from him, Jasper was a calming presence beside her and she knew, no matter how he might resent their bond, she would cherish and take care of him as long as she could.

CHAPTER SIX

The door clicked softly as it closed behind his parents and not for the first time since he'd met Willow, Jasper was at a loss for words and action.

"What can I do, Willow?"

"I've only seen wolves when they tried to kill me." She wrung her hands together and bit her lip.

Jasper winced.

"Can you change into one? I mean, can you show me your wolf?"

He exhaled. This was something he could do. "Are you sure I won't scare you anymore than you already are?"

She shook her head. "I don't think that could happen. But I need to see you. You're good and not evil and if I see you as a wolf, that might help. You know."

He nodded and stripped off his shirt.

Her eyes widened and he blushed like a school girl. "Oh, I need to get naked to be a wolf. I don't want to tear my clothes. Wolves don't really care about nudity. I mean, we don't walk around the den naked or anything, but when we change we don't get embarrassed. But I can go stand behind the couch or something."

She blinked then matched his blush. "No, you can stay where you are. I need to get used to it right?"

He grinned then stripped off his pants. He heard her gasp at his lack of underwear, but he didn't react. He couldn't. He only prayed his cock wouldn't stand at attention before he could change.

He stood straight, then looked directly in her eyes. She stared back, careful not to look below his chin and he smiled.

God, she is too cute.

Jasper pulled on his magic and let the change sweep over him. His bones broke then realigned, but he only felt a twinge of pain. He'd been changing into a wolf since he was three and was used to it. Fur sprouted along his skin and his face elongated into a muzzle.

Soon he stood as a black wolf on four paws, frozen under Willow's stare.

She stood, unblinking.

Shit. Was this too much? Did he lose her already?

Finally she blinked. "Jasper?"

He tried to nod, then sat. She took a step toward him and held out her hand. He lifted his head so her palm rested on top. She backed up, then shook her head and sank her hand into his fur. He leaned into her touch, loving the way her soft hands wound through his fur.

"You're so soft."

Jasper leaned closer and relished her touch.

"You're such a beautiful wolf, Jasper."

Jasper leaned back then shifted back into a man. He knelt naked next to her body and she laughed.

"That's so cool."

He chuckled. "That's better than being scared, I guess."

"Definitely."

Jasper put his clothes back on and tried not to think about her small hands roaming his body. Again, he found himself at a loss for words.

Jasper's mind sprang into gear with the sound of her stomach growling. He jumped up. "How about breakfast?"

The rosy color that highlighted her cheeks at the sound of her stomach made her look damned cute.

"I'm starving. I haven't eaten since before I started work." She bit her lip as her eyes grew cloudy.

Damn. Life could change so quickly from one moment to the next.

"But let me cook. I mean I don't want to intrude on your home and take over. It's just that I love cooking, and I do it every morning to open the shop or on Sundays just for me." She gave him a small smile, and the wolf inside him, normally a ferocious male, melted. They both would do anything for her, and Jasper knew the decadent taste of her cooking well enough not to hold her back.

"If you are up to it, Wil. I love your food, but I don't want you to feel like you need to do anything for me. Ever. Especially if you are still feeling sore and achy." When she just grinned and nodded, he took her by the hand and led her to his kitchen.

Slightly over hundred years old, he'd lived in his house nearly as long. He'd updated it over the years to keep up with the times. He was still working on parts of it, and now that he had a mate, he knew they would need to expand with more space so she'd feel comfortable and there would be enough room for their pups.

The kitchen had been the first job he touched. He'd created a wide-open space with enough room for his large family to occupy. There were stainless steel appliances with dark wood cabinets and grey stone countertops. Masculine, even with the large island, but still homey to him and it melded with the forest outside.

Jasper led Willow to the large two-door refrigerator and opened it to reveal fairly stocked shelves. He didn't entertain or cook often, but when he did, he preferred a good, hardy meal.

"Is there anything you're interested in? I have everything you could possibly need for breakfast. At least I hope. I know you have more expertise in that area than I do."

Dear God. He was rambling like a teenager. Except for that one glorious kiss when he'd put her to bed, they'd barely touched. He knew many things about her, but she didn't know that much about him. That would have to change – and soon. She may have been forced into his world, but he would do his damndest to make her feel included and part of their Pack.

Willow studied his offerings like an artist would study a blank canvas before painting. In a matter of moments, he knew she'd cataloged his food and would come up with a perfect and delicious meal. Glancing up at him with a sly smile, she took out eggs, cheese, and veggies and set them on the island. With her second trip, she grabbed bacon, potatoes, and oranges.

He would have offered to help, and the man his mother raised begged him to, but he didn't want to interrupt her thought process. He loved the way she glided around the kitchen as if she'd been here all along. Even with the bruises, she was still gloriously beautiful and he knew through the mate mark she would heal any injuries quicker than a normal human. It was a one-time only perk of the bite and she wouldn't heal fast with other injuries until she changed.

If she changed.

"Do you think you can make orange juice and coffee?" Willow's soft request brought Jasper out of his thoughts. "I can do the rest, but I don't want to take over your kitchen completely."

"I can do that." He walked over to the cabinet and pulled out fresh gourmet coffee beans and put them in the grinder. Soon the smell of freshly ground coffee filled the air. He quickly set the automatic coffee maker to percolate and began slicing and squeezing oranges.

Willow moved around his kitchen with ease as she made breakfast. She broke the eggs against the side of the bowl before whisking them. He followed her hands as she moved quickly. The sound of fatty bacon popping and sizzling echoed in the kitchen, and she went back to the cutting board to slice onions and mushrooms for her omelets.

When he wasn't looking, she'd diced potatoes for homemade hash browns that were now browning on the stovetop. Already his mouth salivated at the thought of such a gourmet meal.

Like a magician, Willow prepared light and fluffy omelets bursting at the seams with bacon, spinach, mushrooms, and feta and ricotta cheeses. On the each plate, she put three slices of bacon and still sizzling hash browns before he had time to put their drinks in mugs and glasses.

Thank God he was a werewolf because his arteries would be screaming if he was a normal human at his age.

Taking the plates from her hands, he set them on the table next to the drinks. Before she could protest, he took her face between his hands and placed a feathery light kiss to her lips. He lifted his head from hers, looked into her eyes, and gave her a smile.

"Thank you for breakfast. This has got to be the best meal I have ever seen made in this kitchen. I can't wait to see what you come up with here in the future."

At his startling reminder of their mating and future, her eyes widened and her lips parted. Jasper took this as another invitation to kiss her plump lips again. So he did.

When he pulled away, he smiled and said, "Let's eat."

Because if he didn't eat food, he'd want to indulge in her. And ravishing her against the kitchen table might not be the best way to slowly introduce her to this whole mating thing.

Willow bent over the table and set her plate down, her firm ass right near his crotch.

Jasper groaned. Yeah, this might be harder than he thought.

———

JASPER AND WILLOW walked the short distance to meet his family. Rather than worrying about all the questions still unanswered, she took in the scenery. Tall trees Jasper assured her were not redwoods surrounded them, and he told her the story of how his Pack had been was misnamed. Walking along the undergrowth over the worn paths, she felt as if she were in another world without city life. She snorted.

Yep, that pretty much covered it.

Though she'd been there less than a day, she'd already fallen head over feet in love with the den, and was well on her way to falling in love with the man beside her. If they gave her a chance, she'd feel right at home and never leave. A desire and need swept through her – the need to have a family, a home. She'd do anything she could to make this fairytale land hers.

Soon they reached another home with light beige paint and chocolate trim. Ivy crawled up the side, reminding her of an English cottage.

Willow took a deep breath to steady herself and she felt Jasper lightly squeeze her hand. She glanced up at him and froze.

His pupils were so large she could barely see the green rim. Though strength and honor shown through, she knew he'd do anything to protect her, even from his family. Something lurked in his gaze she couldn't quite grasp. That thought and reassurance staggered her.

Did he truly want her?

But before she could fully comprehend his look, the front door opened, and a beautiful blonde woman stepped out to greet them. Shorter than Willow, but curvier. She had a pert nose and large blue eyes, along with an ivory complexion and a welcoming smile.

Willow relaxed slightly.

"You must be Willow. I am so happy to meet you, even under these circumstances." Willow was immediately wrapped in a warm hug that wasn't too tight on her still sore ribs.

"Willow, this is Melanie, my sister-in-law," Jasper said.

"Let's get you in the house. You must need to sit down and rest." Melanie released Willow and took her hand to lead her inside. Willow gave Jasper an almost desperate glance over her shoulder, but he stared blankly before following them inside the home. Whatever look and feeling that passed between them before Melanie interrupted, was so far gone it was like it never happened. The achy feeling in her chest was no longer just from the pain of a few broken ribs.

Damn it. Why did Mel have to walk out of the house right at that moment? What was Jasper thinking? What did that look mean? Her arms tingled and her heart sped. God, she was in high school again, falling for the cute quarterback. But this time, did the object of her affection return her feelings?

Walking inside the house, she noted it was on the verge of melding two personalities. She could tell it had started out as a vastly masculine bachelor home. There were dark contrasts of deep greens and browns spread throughout the house, along with architectural drawings that looked to be hand-drawn.

From what she remembered from the rumors around town surrounding the sexy Jamenson family, Kade, Melanie's husband, was the part-owner of their family contracting and construction company. Kade served architect, while Jasper was the second owner and main contractor. It was well known he liked to go in and work with his hands and get dirty when it came to wood-working. The hand carved figurines and other decorations around Jasper's home came to mind, and she almost gasped aloud at the immense talent he possessed.

Those hands could work wonders with wood. Wonder if they could work other places, too.

Shaking her head to return to the present, she took another step to fully enter the living room and immediately froze at the group of drool worthy model-like male flesh in the room.

The Jamenson brothers stood in front of her, and Willow didn't know what alter their parents had prayed to, but they'd all been blessed in good looks and build. Most gave her small smiles that she returned but one sat in the corner with a glare on his scarred face. A shudder went through her before Jasper placed his hand on the small of her back. Warmth spread through her, and she calmed.

Jasper's deep voice broke through the silence. "This is my mate, Willow. Willow, this is my family. You have already met Reed, Adam, and North." He nodded his toward each of them, and they returned the gesture while giving fuller smiles to her.

She raised her hand at a sad attempt at a wave before letting it fall. Talk about awkward. What could she say to the men who'd seen her naked and chained to a stone wall before saving her life then had witnessed the best orgasm of her life? Hallmark didn't make a card for that.

"You've just met Melanie, and this is her mate Kade, also my partner at the company," Jasper continued.

She looked up at the brother named Kade and saw a man who looked closer to Jasper in looks than the others. His hair was slightly lighter than Jasper's jet black, but darker than the rest of the brothers. They shared the same piercing green eyes and honey tan skin. He was also built and tall, but not as tall as Jasper. If anything she was sure Jasper was the biggest of the bunch. Good thing she liked big.

Kade came up to her with his hand extended and she placed her hand in his firm grip.

"I'm very happy that Jasper finally has someone to share his life with. I'm just sorry it had to occur this way. Melanie and I were lucky enough to meet relatively unscathed." He released her and put his arm around his mate's shoulder in a sign of pure love and contentment.

Again, Jasper growled at his brother and Willow ached that he was stuck with her. Dammit, she really needed to get over herself and show him that she was worth it. Maybe tomorrow.

She smiled and nodded at him. Words stopped in her throat and she found herself unable to speak again. For supposedly being such a smart person, she wasn't doing too hot at this moment.

Jasper squeezed the side of her hip and turned her to the scarred man the corner. "Maddox, this is my mate. Behave. Willow, this is Maddox. Pay no attention to him."

Maddox stood to his full height, which was about five inches shorter than Jasper's six foot six, and stuck his hands in his pockets as if he were afraid to touch her. He had dark blond hair, and other than the long scar that ran down the side of his right cheek from eye to chin, he looked familiar. She'd seen this face before. North.

"Twins." Her voice only a whisper, but the wolves heard.

"Yep." Maddox gave her a sad quirk of his lips. "But I am the pretty one." He sat back down without another word and folded his arms across his chest. Sadness slid across his eyes.

Why would he be sad?

"It's nice to meet all of you." Her voice finally returned but she was too overwhelmed meeting his family to say anything more.

"Don't forget me."

A sultry voice came from behind them, and Willow turned to see the most beautiful woman she'd ever laid eyes on. She was about five foot five and fit but skinny. She had a lighter version of Jasper's green eyes and straight black hair, that was so black it was almost blue.

"Now that you've met the brothers, I guess it's time to meet the sister." Jasper's sister glided across the room like a dancer and gave Willow a strong hug.

"It's good to have more women here. I can only take so much testosterone."

"Cailin, I was getting to it. You weren't here yet." Jasper gave his sister an exasperated look and nodded toward her. "Willow, this brat is my annoying baby sister Cailin. Beware, she may look nice now, but she bites." Jasper tossed them both a playful look before the room erupted with laughter.

"Dude, I would keep one eye open tonight. Cailin is likely to gut you for that remark." Someone – it sounded like Reed –warned Jasper.

"Let's take a seat, and ignore Reed." Jasper's face sobered before he continued. "We're here so I can tell you a little bit more about being a werewolf, what my family's Pack positions are and answer any other questions you may have."

Willow just nodded and urged Jasper to continue. This was one of the moments she'd been waiting for.

She was in a new place, filled with new people. Now, she has a new family, but knew nothing about them. The glimpse of a nice little life that could come her way if she stayed with Jasper would be nice. But she was still terrified.

She was Jasper's mate. Right? But he didn't really want her. There were a million things to both dread and look forward to, but first she needed some answers. And at this moment, he was offering some. She had dozens of questions, but no idea where to start or stop. She needed to shut up and listen. Her mind spun and she blinked at Jasper's concerned face.

"Okay, werewolves can be born and made. Most wolves are born. Turning someone is beyond painful. It takes a bite and almost true death for it to occur. And even then, sometimes the change doesn't take, and they die anyway. Hence the reason we don't do it often."

She didn't know if she wanted to be a werewolf just yet, but a little pain wasn't going to keep her from him. Okay, he said a lot of pain. But that still couldn't stop her if she set her mind to it.

Jasper held her hand and goose bumps spread over her arms. Her body flared with a subtle arousal and she blushed. This overwhelming need for him shouldn't be happening so soon. But ever since that bite, she couldn't stop wanting him. Thinking about their future. Crazy, but real.

"Our wolves live within. They're another being we try to work cohesively with. However, at a young age, we must learn to take control over them. They're more primitive and in more tune with nature than our human selves. Unlike what the media portrays, we don't need the moon to shift, but during the full moon, our wolves are more of a presence, and we do feel the call toward it. At that time, our Pack likes to go for hunts as a group. The full moon pulls us together as a Pack and allows our wolves in control, if only for a short while."

"So all of you turn into wolves?" She asked.

Jasper smiled and a lock of hair fell into his eyes. Oh how she wanted to brush it out of his face. But she didn't want to come on too strong.

"Yes, all of us do."

"Can your wolves talk?"

"They talk to us in our heads." He grinned and she wanted to kiss him. "It's like having another person inside your head sometimes and gets annoying, but you get used to it."

"That's really weird. Do you talk out loud?"

He laughed, his brothers joining in. "Sometimes. But mostly we just respond in our heads."

"So your wolf is its own being."

"Yes, and much older than us. Like an old soul."

"Really?" How awesome was that?

"Really." He smiled and brushed her cheek with the back of his hand. Warmth tingled throughout her body and she struggled not to jump on his lap.

Where was this coming from?

"As for the positions in the Pack," Jasper continued. "It can be a little more complicated. What I am about to tell you goes no farther than this room. Not all in the Pack know every part of every position, and not all Packs have our, for lack of a better word, magic. But since you're my mate, you have the right to know all of this."

There was that word again. *Mate.*

"First there is the Alpha, the leader." Jasper continued. "Our father. The Alpha can feel every single one of his Pack's souls. Some bonds are stronger than others, like those with his family, but no matter what the relationship, he can feel them, and the Pack is comforted by that. Also as the Alpha, he leads the Pack and makes the decisions. We're not a democracy, and there's no council of elders who decides things. Our elders are our knowledge holders, not our masters. If the Alpha is corrupt, then someone can challenge for his seat, but it would take a strong wolf to take down our father. As it is, I am not sure anyone other than one of his sons could do it, and I don't think we would.

"The Alpha's sons hold most of the other positions. Only three are by birth, however. The others are gifts sent by the magic of the wolf that blesses them with their gifts." Maddox snorted at this statement, but Jasper ignored him. "Our generation, however, is the first to be missing one of the positions gifted to us, but that just means we haven't found that person yet.

"Back to the positions. The Alpha's first son is also an Alpha wolf in terms of his strength. He is called the Heir, and in our case that title falls to Kade. He too can feel the Pack, but not to the degree that our father can. As he ages and gets closer to taking over the Pack as true Alpha, the strength of the bond and his responsibilities with increase. Our father can either die to give Kade the new position or step down in the future when he reaches a certain age, but as Dad is only around two-hundred and fifty and Kade is only a hundred-and-five, he still has time."

Willow's jaw dropped, and Jasper smiled.

He looked damned sexy for his age.

But what if she didn't change? So she'd grow old and die while Jasper stayed young? A shiver crept through her. She couldn't live with that.

Jasper chuckled. "I guess I forgot to tell you. As werewolves, we age very slowly. We are not immortal, but we are harder to kill. I think the oldest wolf we have at the moment is about one thousand, but she is very secretive about her age. This is one of the reasons mates choose the change to werewolves. It would be a sad existence to watch your love grow old and frail and not be able to do anything about it."

No one spoke at that depressing thought. At that moment, Willow decided that, no matter what Jasper thought, she would change. She would be by his side and take care of him and be his mate. He may resent her, but she would take the lifetimes they had together to make it up to him.

"Right." Jasper cleared his throat before continuing. "Next in line is the second son, me. At a hundred and three, I'm the Beta of the Pack.

I take care of the daily tedious duties around the Pack and my main job is to ensure our existence remains a secret. I will keep my job until Kade's second son comes of age and is prepared to take over. As Mel and Kade have only recently been mated and have no children, yet, I will be Beta for a while."

"But what about if Kade doesn't have a second son? Will you always be Beta?" She asked.

"If they don't have a second son, then I'll always be Beta. If I die, then the second son of the oldest Jamenson will be Beta. No matter what, the power will stay in our family line. We just have to hope that we have a lot of sons."

"That sounds a bit sexist."

Jasper laughed. "Believe me, I know. But I didn't make it up. Maybe as time change, fate will change the way the power forms. But so far the Jamensons have been, shall we say productive."

The others in the room laughed.

"What do you mean?"

"I mean that we all have many kids, so there usually isn't a problem."

"Oh." She felt a blush rise up in her cheeks.

This was all so much to take in. Power and hierarchy so different from her own. Her head hurt.

"The third son, Adam – who's one hundred– is the Enforcer. His job is inner Pack discipline and protecting the Pack from outside forces. Though we all do the latter, he is in charge of most of it daily. Thankfully Adam is one tough son of a bitch and is good at his job." Adam gave them both a half smile and shook his head.

"There's also the Omega. This position is not relegated to only the Alpha's family, however, Maddox was lucky enough to be called on."

This time Maddox didn't quirk his lips or snort.

"At ninety-six, he can feel all of the emotions of the Pack."

"But how is that different than the Alpha, Heir or you?"

"The rest of us can only feel that they are there. We don't know if they what they are feeling – emotionally or physically. But Maddox can feel *all* the emotions. Some stronger than others and he can never fully turn them off or ignore them. Touch seems to strengthen the bond so give him space. It's also his duty to the Pack to help with these emotions, but as anyone knows, help is sometimes not easy or welcome."

Maddox sat in his corner with a blank face and his arms folded against his chest. Only his eyes gave away the torture and emotions he must feel. Willow inwardly winced at the everything he must have been feeling.

"Maddox," she asked, "how can you stand all of it?"

"I have to." He answered. "All the happiness, pain, every type of emotion is multiplied. You get used to it." He shrugged and she didn't believe him.

Again the room grew silent before Jasper continued.

"Last is our Healer. Their job is to heal physical wounds. They can fix most small wounds and, with only immense power, can heal stronger ones. Right now that place is vacant as our father lost his brothers in the last war. We are unsure why we don't have one, but I can only guess that someone will come to our Pack with the ability, maybe as one of our mates."

Well, she sure wasn't the healer. She could barely put on a Band-Aid.

"I thought North would be your Healer?" She asked.

"He's a medically trained doctor, but doesn't have the magic. And he can't feel the physical wounds that the Healer can."

Willow's eyes widened. "The Healer can feel *all* wounds?"

"Not the actual pain, but they can tell they're hurt."

"Those are the major Pack positions. But each of us do our parts. Mom is the Alpha female and aids Dad. She's unlike Alphas most that though in that she looks like a good little housewife, but she can eliminate threats with the best of us and helps make all of Dad's decisions. They're a fully functioning working pair."

He gave Mel a smile, "Mel is a chemist who has a job outside the den, but she's working on upgrading our archaic attitudes and helping around the Pack." The men all snorted. "But one day she will take over Mom's job, and I'm sure she is opinionated enough that Kade won't revert to the old ways." Mel laughed out loud and everyone in the room joined her.

Oh, she already liked Mel.

"Too true, man. Too true." Kade leaned in gave his mate a full-on-the-mouth kiss that seemed inappropriate outside the bedroom, but didn't seem to faze the wolves.

Willow shrugged. Apparently, wolves were a little more physical and open. As long as Jasper did the same to her, she would be just dandy with that. A blush crept up her cheeks and she lowered her eyes Maddox arched his eyebrow toward her.

Darn emotions. No hiding from wolves.

"Reed is ninety-eight, an artist, and draws our Pack history. He says he doesn't do much, but we need it, and it helps the cubs learn to shift. North, as you know, is our Pack doctor. Without him I don't know what our Pack would do."

Both brothers looked uncomfortable with Jasper's praise.

"And me, Jasper? What do I do?" Cailin's voice grew soft and seemed so sad.

"You, my dear sister, at twenty-three and the Alpha's only daughter, can be whatever you want to be."

Cailin snorted. "Seriously? I'm not even allowed out of the den. I'm stuck here as the 'precious princess'. No, thank you." She turned toward Willow. "I use herbs to make medicine for North and I also make music. But I *will* find a way to be useful to the Pack, rather than just falling into a good marriage because I have the ability to breed pups."

Pups? Yeah, Jasper needed to explain that one.

Japer let out a small growl. "You will mate who you want, when you want. Dad's not like some of the other older wolves out there who see you for political gain."

Cailin didn't respond, but looked unconvinced.

Willow didn't envy her. Though the thought of having such a large family seemed amazing, the whole overprotectiveness thing was a bit much.

"Well then." Mel said, breaking the tension. "Kade and I made an early dinner. Let's eat and get to know Willow. Shall we?" Mel pulled Cailin to her feet and dragged her to the kitchen. The rest of them followed.

Jasper and Willow sat alone in the room, her thoughts going in a million directions.

"Thank you, Jasper."

"For what? Scaring you?"

"No, for telling me the truth. For not keeping secrets. I know we have a lot more to talk about but thank you for sharing with me what you did." Boldly she reached up and pressed her lips to his in a sweet kiss.

Willow could almost feel the future with this man, this wolf. Now she only needed to make sure he felt the same way.

CHAPTER SEVEN

Later that evening, her heart beating loudly in her ears, Willow clung to Jasper's hand as he led her to the Pack circle. The Alpha planned to introduce her to the Pack and discuss her kidnapping and its ramifications with the Central Pack. Located in a valley filled with tall trees and grass, the meeting place nestled between two rock faces. Raised edges formed stadium seating in the rock worn smooth over time, and Willow was surprised they actually were comfortable. In the center lay a flat grassy plane surrounded by mud and dirt, like an archaic football field. The pulse of Pack energy coming from the circle and the weight of boundless magic and decisions over centuries danced over her skin.

"So is everyone going to be in wolf or human form?" Willow asked.

Okay, that was a stupid question. But she hated silence.

Jasper laughed. "Human form. As much as we love our wolf ones, it's kinda hard to talk to each other on four feet."

Willow laughed. "Oh, but how do you communicate when you are a wolf?"

"Instinct. We follow each other or move our heads to indicate where we want to go. It isn't like we have philosophical discussions when we're hunting. I know some myths say we can talk telepathically, and though that would be cool as hell, we don't."

"So, no mind readers. Good to know."

"Well, not that I know of anyway. But it could happen I guess. Maybe it comes after mating." Jasper smiled.

"Really? What am I thinking now?" Willow teased.

"That I look good in this shirt?" Jasper laughed.

Willow widened her eyes. "Wow. I can't believe it. You caught me."

They laughed, and Jasper held her close to his side. "Really? I'll have to wear this more often."

He leaned down and brushed his lips on her hair. Heat radiated over her skin. Thank God he couldn't actually read her mind right now. She'd die of mortification.

As they stepped into the circle to sit with his family, Willow felt the eyes of dozens of wolves in human form home in on her and Jasper. Some looked wary of a new face; others were mildly curious. Some of the men stared at her appreciably before inhaling deeply froze. Their eyes widened and their jaws dropped. She didn't know what that meant, but she burrowed into Jasper's side nonetheless. He let go of her hand and wrapped a possessive arm around her. Her rapid heart-beat immediately calmed as a feeling of peace swept over her.

When Jasper moved, the anger and disbelief from some of the women in the circle crawled over her skin. They glared, curling their lips, then scoffed. One woman snarled and looked at Willow as if she were a bug in need of being wiped from the windshield. Jasper's arm tightened around her, and he bent down to whisper in her ear.

His warm breath tickled her neck, and she shivered as he spoke. "That's Camille. She's let her desire to be my mate known, but she doesn't have the potential, nor does she make my wolf want her. Even if she did, she's too shrewd to be worth it. I will always protect you, but be wary of her. She's a bitch in every sense of the word." She felt his lips brush against her temple before he straightened and led them to their places.

People milled about until Edward took his place at the stone alter. His loud booming voice echoed throughout the circle, as if magic aided it.

"Settle, Pack."

With two words, the sounds of rustling and subtle chatter dissipated. The power of his voice as an Alpha swept over her, and a feeling of belonging settling in. Was it because of the mate mark? Or something more?

"We're here tonight for two purposes," Edward said. "To welcome our new Pack member, my son's mate, Willow Delton Jamenson." The new name startled her, and she looked at Jasper for a clue, but he merely shook his head and mouthed "Later."

"We are also here to discuss the reasons for which she's entered the Pack and what must be done to strengthen our resolve and protect our future."

The wolves murmured their welcome to her and some even smiled in her direction. She smiled back and tried not to look like an idiot with her still bruised and cut face. Jasper tightened his arm around her.

God, she was falling in love with this man! Tears welled in her eyes, but she held them back. She would not cry in front of his Pack.

"Jasper's mate will be an asset to our Pack, and I am truly honored to have her as part of our family." His normally harsh stare warmed when he turned toward her with a quirk of his lips. The warmth disappeared in a flash, as he turned again to address the circle.

"However, in order for her to join us, my sons had to rescue her first. The Central Pack kidnapped her from her place of business against her will." Edward's eyes glowed with anger as the tension level of the Pack members in the circle rose.

Chaos erupted as the Alpha relayed the events of her kidnapping. Wolves shouted and growled on her behalf. Willow looked at the faces, angry and seething. Anger for her. She was touched. Their willingness to retaliate because of her mistreatment humbled her. When her gaze reached Camille, the woman had the nerve to smirk. She sighed.

Oh well, guess she couldn't please everyone.

"Settle down Pack." The growling stopped immediately when Edward's voice rose above the crowd. "My sons have already been back to the location, but found it empty. They have abandoned that part of the territory line but have violated our treaty by stepping foot on our land. We will find them and take them down, but we must protect our Pack!"

"Wait!" Willow's voice broke through the noise and all eyes turned to her. "Do we have to attack right away? I mean can't we make sure everyone else is safe first?" She plopped down next to Jasper and rubbed her forehead.

Stupid! Why did she have to say anything?

"Yeah? Why risk our Pack for her?" Camille said, the words spewing from her mouth like raw sewage.

Willow's belly tightened with knots. This woman scared her.

"You will watch your tongue, Camille, before I take it from you," Jasper growled. His eyes glowed to a bright gold, blazing in his anger.

Camille immediately lowered her gaze, but still had a smirk on her face.

"Willow, we will protect the Pack, but these cruelties cannot go unchallenged. We are a strong Pack, and we protect our own." Edward's voice signaled the end of that line of the conversation, and he continued to discuss how they would retaliate.

Flushed with embarrassment, Willow sat silent for the rest of the meeting, wondering what Jasper thought of her after that little outburst. She really had to try harder at keeping her mouth shut.

Jasper leaned over and whispered, "It's okay, Willow, you just don't know Pack protocol yet. It takes time, but I will always fight for you. No matter what." He kissed her temple and pulled her firmly against him.

WHEN THE MEETING ENDED, Jasper led her back to his house. Something crunched on the gravel, and Willow paused.

When she looked up, she saw the man who'd given her that lewd look in the Circle. Geez, he gave her the creeps. He smiled at her, and she fought the urge to vomit.

"Franklin, remove yourself from our path. I don't have the patience for you tonight." Jasper's voice cooled, and he moved her behind him.

"*Tsk tsk,* Jasper. You missed something, didn't you? I only saw the mark against her shoulder, but the mating isn't complete, is it? What, couldn't take her for a ride yet? Your cock broken?"

Willow didn't even see Jasper move before his fist connected with Franklin's face and the other wolf was on the ground.

"Poor move, Beta. You need to finish that bitch, or I'll take her. Watch your back."

Jasper ignored him and picked Willow up and carried her to his home. Movement over his shoulder drew her gaze to Adam and Maddox carelessly lifting Franklin and leading him back to the circle.

He set her down in the foyer while he closed the door behind him.

"Jasper? What did he mean the mating wasn't complete? What's going on?" Her heart beat faster.

This was all too much. Did he have to bite her again? Mate her in public or something? Like in those romance novels? She hardly knew him, but she didn't want to lose him.

"He meant we've only completed part of the mating. I have to spill my seed in your womb to bind our human halves. The mate mark only claims you as my wolf's mate." Jasper's face darkened and he looked angry at the prospect.

"Oh." What else was there to say? His wolf and had the situation forced him into biting her. Now he didn't want to finish claiming her? He didn't want to make love to her. Coldness crept from her heart into her veins. The loss for something she hadn't even known she craved ached in her chest. For all her affirming and promising she would make Jasper see she was worth it, he deliberately held more of himself back to prove he didn't want her. It hurt.

Willow had been thrown from home to home her whole life. She had no family and meeting the Jamensons had already brightened her life. No stupid mating rule could tear her away. Not now. She straightened her shoulders and prayed she didn't make a fool of herself.

"Well then. I guess we can change that can't we?" She looked up into his deep green eyes. Heat radiated from him, warming her body in an intimate caress.

"You want to finish the mating?" Jasper's voice deepened to an animalistic growl. His nostrils flared as he took deep breaths.

"Please," she whispered.

He took the space between them in two steps and crushed his mouth to hers.

CHAPTER EIGHT

The flavor of his mate's mouth was a masterpiece of sugar and heat exploding on his taste buds. Jasper delved his tongue into Willow's mouth hard and fast, teeth clashing against teeth. He held her face in his hands, then held her hair back in a firm grip. Lifting his lips from hers, he framed the side of her face with his other hand, careful of her bruises.

"You're so beautiful." His words were a whispered growl that sent shivers down his mate's slender body.

The wolf inside him prowled and preened, eager to finish the mating and mount to completion. The man wanted to fuck her hard against the wall and then twice more against the counter and bed just because he could. But first he had to shake away the doubt he'd seen clouding her eyes throughout the day.

"Willow, I chose you. Do you understand that? I came to you and asked you to be with me. If not for them taking you from me, I still would have chosen you. I choose you." He held her against him, pleading with his eyes and baring his soul.

Willow's eyes widened but before she could speak, Jasper kissed her again, a soft caress against her lips.

"I know you didn't ask for this, but I will do everything in my power as a man, as Beta of this Pack, as your mate, to be worthy of you. I never want to see the fear and pain in your eyes again. I want to see the light and sweetness that I have begun to fall in love with every day for the rest of my days." Jasper's heartbeat reverberated in his ears, and he and his wolf waited for her response. He could feel Willow's pulse quicken underneath his fingertips as they rested on her silky skin.

He watched as her throat worked as she tried to speak. "I thought..." She hiccupped a sob and Jasper's grip tightened, "I thought you were forced." She swallowed hard, and tears spilled down her cheeks. "I already promised myself I would do what I could to be worthy of you." Jasper kissed her tears as she sobbed, trailing them to her lips in a hard and demanding kiss.

They both stepped back and took a deep breath.

"It's me who's not worthy of you," he rasped.

"I choose you, too," she whispered.

At her words, his wolf howled in approval as he took her sweet ass in his hands and lifted her against the wall. Her eyes closed, and her dark lashes lay against her milky white skin intensifying her beauty. Kneading her ass, he kissed her again, running his tongue against the seam of her lips, reveling in the softness of them. Moving from her mouth, he nibbled her chin and licked and suckled her neck to behind her ear. She shivered as her heat ground against his rigid length.

Growling, he bit harder on her mate mark and watched the shock of ecstasy wash across her face. He'd heard the mark was an erogenous zone and filed that tid bit of knowledge for later. Lifting his face from her neck as her hand roamed his body, he searched for a place to take her.

"I'm going to fuck you hard and fast this first time, then I'm going to take you nice and slow so I can savor you." Her answering moan and shudder was the only response he needed.

When they'd first came home, they entered the house through the garage and the nearest flat surface was his woodworking table. That would have to do.

Carrying her with her legs wrapped around his, while still kissing and kneading her, proved more difficult that he would have imagined.

For his advanced age, he acted like a pup. If she didn't stop rubbing against his cock like that, he was gonna blow in his pants before he even got to feel her heat wrapped around him.

Still holding her with one arm, he used the other to viciously swipe away the odds and ends on the table. A loud crashing sound echoed in the room, followed by Willow's giggle. He bit into her plump lip.

"You think that's funny, do you? Am I going to have to punish you for making fun of me?" He smiled to show he was only joking. Her pupils dilated with arousal, and he growled in approval. Laying her on the table like a pagan sacrifice, he admired her hair spread like a chestnut halo about her head. Her cheeks blushed and her eyes bright, she'd never looked sexier.

He removed her shoes and swept his hands up her legs slowly, stopping every so often to squeeze and rub. Her breath quickened, and his heart pounded. He trailed his fingers along her inner thigh, purposely missing her core. She moaned. And when he reached her button fly, she held her breath. His wolf tried to claw to the surface, too eager to care about control, but Jasper held back. He wanted to take his time and make her feel comfortable. To feel loved.

He popped each button on her fly, released her jeans from her waist, and slid them down her legs. He froze.

Damn. She wasn't wearing any underwear.

Fuck. Him.

Blushing furiously, Willow tried to cover herself, but he stopped grabbed her wrist and held it above her head.

"I didn't have any clean, and that isn't something you can borrow, you know?" She looked so innocent, and he wanted to eat her up. Everywhere.

"I would say that's something I have to fix, but I like you bare. Tomorrow, though, I'll get you anything you need. I promise, but right now... Damn, I love your pussy."

Light brown curls, slightly groomed, covered her mound. Jasper growled with lust. He didn't want a little girl with just skin. He wanted a woman who could produce his pups and take all of his cock.

Tracing his fingers around her outer lips, he followed the trail of curls to her center. He dipped one finger to the knuckle. Wet heat clenched around him. Damn. He removed his finger and licked it.

Jesus. She tasted of cinnamon and sugar everywhere. He sat her up and ripped off her shirt and stiffened at her naked breasts. Put new bra on the shopping list. Her nipples hardened under his gaze.

Scratch that. No bra. Ever.

Dusky pink nipples puckered in the cold air of his work room. Small breasts that could easily fit in his hands. He sucked on her lips again because he couldn't resist her taste and trailed down her neck to her nipples. He latched on to her right breast where he sucked and bit until she thrashed against him. He brushed his fingers down her stomach, and he thrust two fingers hard and fast into her. Gasping, she came against his hand at the first thrust and screamed his name.

Jasper released her breast and licked her collar bone. "That's it, Willow. Ride it, baby." He crooked his fingers to ride on her G-spot as she rode the wave of her orgasm.

As she lay boneless on the table, Jasper quickly removed his clothes and lifted her legs to his shoulders. Damn, he loved a flexible woman. His Willow was perfect for him. He brushed her clit with his tip.

"Watch me, Willow. Watch me take you. Feel my cock fill you, then feel my seed as our souls merge." Too entranced to find words, she merely nodded. He gripped her waist to secure her to the table and entered her to the hilt in one thrust. She screamed, and he froze.

"Wil? Did I hurt you? Am I too rough? You're just so tight. I don't want to hurt you." Though it ached not to move, he knew she was still tender from her orgasm.

His mate shook her head before answering. "No. No. It feels so good, Jasper. It's just been so long, and you're so big."

Jasper chuckled. "Well, we could have worse problems, I guess. Are you ready for me to move?"

At her nod, he swiftly withdrew before slamming back home. Her breasts jiggled with the force. He did it again and again, each time aiming deeper until she was almost convulsing around him. Her wet heat was so tight around his cock that, when his balls drew up, he knew he wouldn't last much longer. He flicked her clit until her eyes glassed over and her body shuddered in release.

He howled as his seed spilled into her womb and he felt the final mating bond lock into place. Willow's soul and happiness wrapped around his in a tight and loving embrace. A look of awe crossed her face.

Thank God he wasn't the only one feeling this.

He'd thought he'd known what mating meant, but now he realized he didn't have a damn clue. It was so much more than saying they were bound. Her very essence flowed within him, her love for him radiating from every poor. Still inside her, he leaned over her, and wrapped his arms around her body, refusing to relinquish the connection.

"I can feel you," Willows whispered. Tears fell to down her cheeks, and he kissed her softly on the lips, pouring all his love into that one kiss.

"I can feel you too. I love you. Willow."

Sighing, she kissed him fully back. "I love you too, Jasper."

Tears fell to her shoulder, and he knew they must be his. The Beta of the Redwood Pack, the fiercest Pack of them all, was crying about his mate and he didn't feel at all bad about it.

CHAPTER NINE

It was time. They gathered in North's basement, nervous with fear and anticipation. The harsh sterile smell of a medical room attacked his wolf senses, heightening the tension in the room. White walls, bare of personal touches, closed in like prison bars.

Tonight Melanie was officially becoming part of the Pack. She'd become a werewolf. It would be a brutal process that required near death. Though Jasper had helped in many changes throughout his years, he didn't know if he could stomach this particular one. Since meeting her, Melanie had become a sister to him. Watching her go through the change might take a part of his soul with her.

Looking at his mate, his heart clenched. Her chestnut hair was pulled back from her face, enhancing her soft beauty. Willow desired to be changed as well, but would she after witnessing this? That morning he'd woken up wrapped around his warm mate. The feel of her heart beat against his chest in sync with his own made both the wolf and the man want to howl for joy. She and he were tired from their initial mating and then twice more in the middle of the night.

His wolf brushed the surface of his mind. "*It was about time we mated her. I can feel her soul with ours. Once she is changed I know she will be a beautiful wolf.*"

He could only agree with his wolf. But he fought the very idea. All of the happiness that Jasper had gained from Willow the night before sucked from him like a vacuum. Scared beyond what he liked to admit, he tried to prepare himself for what was to come.

Muscles aching from their hard and fast gymnastics the night before, Jasper stretched his body before coming to Kade's side. His brother bent over Melanie, whispering reassurances and words of peace in her ear, though from the looks of it, Melanie was the calmer of the two.

Strapped down to a table with cords and wires covering her to take her vitals, she looked nervous, but at an odd form peace. Her chest moved with her deep breaths and Kade rubbed her arms and stomach before placing a gentle kiss on her lips. Jasper could hear a faintly whispered "I love you" before Kade backed away from her.

"Mel, I know this will hurt, but we can't give you drugs. It'll interfere with the change and may cause adverse reactions." North's voice was calm, though he didn't mention the actual reactions, as those were too grotesque.

Pulling Kade back to the corner of the room, Jasper took a good look at his family. Though not all of them were needed for the change to take place, they came to show support for both Melanie and Kade in their time of need. He truly loved his family.

Willow stood behind Mel's head, holding her hand and wiping her brow. As if she could feel him looking at her, she looked up into his eyes, giving him a small smile. Heart aching for her, he smiled back. Maddox stood beside her, holding Mel's other hand, murmuring comforting words, using his gift to calm her emotions.

Reed, Adam, and he held Kade back in a corner. The bite and mauling of his mate to induce the change would be painful for not only her but would cause Kade's wolf to go ballistic and want to kill anyone who would hurt his mate. With as much power that ran in Kade's veins, it would take the three of them to hold him back when he and his wolf were enraged. They asked Kade to back out of the room, knowing full well it was a lost cause. Kade refused to part with his mate. If things went wrong, he needed to be near her.

Again Jasper thought of Willow and the fact she'd expressed

interest in changing. Though their lifetimes varied dramatically, he didn't know if he could risk her dying now rather than dying in only a few short decades. A hurdle to be jumped later.

Cailin and his mom were aiding North with his medical preparations and would act as nurses if the need arose.

The clicking of claws on the linoleum brought silence to the room. A large and magnificent gray wolf entered. The sight of his father in his wolf form always urged Jasper to bow his head. Though Jasper was a strong wolf, the immense power and pride emanating from their Alpha was a force to be respected.

Putting one paw in front of another, his father prowled farther in the room. Jasper watched as Mel's eyes widened before she continued taking shallow breaths. Kade growled and whimpered while pushing at the three holding him back.

"Shh, it will be over soon." Jasper's whispered words were empty placations even to his own ears.

Before he could blink, his father charged and pounced on the table. Teeth pierced Mel's shoulder, the shoulder opposite Kade's mate mark. Kade's wolf came to the surface, claws erupting from his fingertips. His brother tried to claw and bite his way through the barrier of strong werewolves. Jasper planted his feet and held on to him with his gaze still on Mel and Wil.

Mel screamed in agony but kept her attention on Willow. The bite in her shoulder was not that of a mate mark, but a brutal assault that forced the change by adding the enzyme to her blood. For the greatest chance of a conversion occurring, the Alpha had to be the one to bring her over. His father released Mel's shoulder only to bite and tear into the flesh of her chest and stomach. Blood seeped into the crisp white sheets she lay across, a crimson splash of color against the stark contrast of sterility. Ripping into her side with his teeth and claws, his father continued to bring Mel near death. Her body convulsed and thrashed, fighting the chains and ropes holding her down. She screamed and cried, the sound piercing his heart, before finally passing out from the pain. Still, his father didn't quit, for she needed to be as close to death as possible to ensure the change, one bite wasn't enough.

Tears running down his cheeks, Kade screamed and growled,

putting his full Heir's powers into fighting his brothers to get to his mate. Adam pulled his arm back and punched Kade directly in the face, crashing his head into the wall. Reed bent down and shouldered him in the stomach with a grunt, keeping him pinned. Jasper put his elbow against Kade's throat and the other across his chest. However much pain the brothers inflicted on him, Jasper knew the pain from seeing his mate in distress and practically dying in front of him would be worse.

Jasper looked across the room at Maddox and blink. His younger brother paled to a deathly white. His teeth digging into his lip, cutting into the flesh. He shook, his hand still gripping Mel's as he took her pain.

How the hell did he do it?

Finally, after what felt like hours later, his father backed from Melanie's seemingly lifeless body before changing back into a man. His mother quickly left her daughter-in-law's side and put a robe around her pale husband. For all the Alpha in his father, he still looked shaken. It must have been agony for his father to inflict his son's mate with that type of pain. Jasper didn't envy him.

Things moved quickly. North and Cailin expertly took Mel's vitals before cleaning her and wrapping her in cool cloth infused with herbs that would aide in healing her wounds. All the while, Willow and Maddox continued to hold Mel's hands and whisper to her motionless body.

He prayed the change took. Prayed another old soul and spirit of a wolf found its way into Mel's body and blended together in perfect harmony. The enzyme may force the change to start – but it took a magic power beyond their touch for it to stay.

Jasper looked around the room and froze. Every single person wept. The strongest family of wolves in the known world broke down, weeping for their own. The salty taste of his own tears reminded him of the night before when Willow and he had finally mated. The memory proved to be bitter sweet at this drastic difference in situation.

Watching the pain and sorrow in his mate's face he knew he couldn't let her change. Though he would love to live his long life with her, he didn't know if he could see her harmed as Melanie had been. Taking a deep breath while still holding his brother back, he vowed that he would do all in his power to keep her from changing.

Once Melanie's vitals calmed, Kade did as well. Pushing past his brothers, he knelt at his unconscious mate's side and wept. Praying the change had taken hold, the family silently left room to give the pair a moment of peace.

As soon as they were upstairs, Willow rushed into Jasper's arms, clinging to him for support. With only a nod to his brothers, he picked up his mate and carried her home so that they could try to remember that they were alive and possessed each other.

———

WILLOW RUBBED her nose against Jasper's neck, inhaling his woodsy wolf and man scent. He smelled like home. Curling into his body, she let herself relax. Though she tried to be stoic and strong for Melanie, she'd been as frightened as when the Central Pack had taken her. Watching Edward tear into her new friend's body had taken all of Willow's inner strength not to run from the room. Knowing Jasper was there to cling to later was the only thing that kept her calm.

Jasper didn't let her go as they entered his, no their, home. Closing the door behind him he strode toward the bedroom and set her feet on the floor while dragging his hands up the sides of her body to cradle her face.

"I love you, baby. I don't think I can live without you." Warm breath tickled her lips as he whispered his devotion.

"I love you, too." Her heart ached for him, and she needed him inside her – now.

He brushed his lips softly against hers. Jasper dropped his hands from her face and gently pushed her down until she lay on the bed. He took off her leggings and top leaving her bare before him. Willow's breath hitched. His pupils grew until only a small rim of forest green remained, a ring of gold glowed around the green. Kneeling before her, he took her legs and spread them so she was completely open to his gaze. The corner of his mouth quirked when he looked at her pussy. His nostrils flared, taking in her scent.

"I haven't even touched you yet and you're already glistening for me." His voice lowered, rough as if it was hard for him to speak. Taking her knees in his hands, he abruptly pulled her toward him so her ass lay at the edge of the bed and her cunt directly in his face. He gave a wicked smile before leaning over and licking her from puckered hole to the top of her mound with his wide tongue. Her hips bucked from the bed, but he quickly placed his palms on her pelvic bone to keep her secure. Looking up at her, he licked the juices from his lips, and his eyes glowed gold.

Before she could gain the energy to speak, he suckled her clit. Rubbing her mound against his nose, she moaned and tried to twist her body. It was too much; he sucked and sucked while moving his tongue quickly against her clit. He trailed one palm down to cup her ass as he squeezed the globe and growled against her pussy. The rumbling of his growl caused her clit to tingle and her pussy to clench. Removing the hand from her ass, he took two fingers and circled her opening before entering her quickly. Curling his fingers, he rubbed her G-spot at the same time he bit down on her clit. Stars shattered behind her eyelids as she screamed his name until her throat was raw.

Even as she began to come down from her high, Jasper didn't relent. Rubbing her from the inside out and kissing her sweet center, he forced her to her peak again before she cascaded down.

"Oh my God." Her voice deepened with lust, her throat sore from screaming. *He is going to kill me with pleasure.*

"Call me Jasper." He laughed against her thighs at his lame joke before crawling up her body to lie next to her. Palming her breast in his rough hand, he tweaked her nipple, making her moan again.

"No more, baby. I need a moment." An idea came to her, and she gave him a sultry smile. "Don't move." He gave her a curious look but remained where he was.

As quickly as she could, she scooted down so she knelt on the bed between his legs. Raising an eyebrow in her direction, he knit his fingers behind his head and laid back as if he knew what she was about to do.

His cock was long and wide, with a slight curve to the right. That explained why he'd hit all of the perfect spots last night. *And it's all mine.* Giggling to herself, she took his cock in her hand and pumped it twice to watch the drop of pre-cum bead on the tip. Smiling again, she leaned down and licked it up. It tasted salty, yet sweet and still full of Jasper's forest taste.

Before he could stop her, she opened her mouth wide and relaxed her throat to take him fully into her mouth. When her lips reached the coarse hair at the base, she swallowed, allowing the back of the throat to squeeze the tip of his cock.

"Fuck! I didn't know you could do that! Fuck!" Out of the corner of her eyes, she saw one of his hands fisted in the comforter, and the other grabbed her hair in a tight almost painful grip. She made him fight for control. Nice. Moving back up his cock, she rolled her tongue until she released him with an audible pop.

Willow did this over and over again while rolling his balls in her palm before he gripped her hair tighter and pulled her off him.

"Damn, I was about to blow down your throat. It's too much." He panted and looked pained, his face strained. He gripped her hips and flipped their positions, digging her into the bed.

"But that was what I wanted to do." She stuck out her lower lip and pouted.

"But I want to come in your sweet pussy ,baby, with you wrapped around me."

Oh. When he put it that way...

Shivers danced down her spine, and she reached up to kiss him.

He knelt above her, their fingers entwined, before looking directly in her eyes. Slowing without blinking, he entered her. It was the perfect moment. Poignant and full of love. She could hear the catch in his breath and knew he would love her forever.

Slowly, he slid into her with two soft thrusts before slowly exiting her warmth then slamming back into her. He repeated this over and over until she was panting and moaning and begging for release, but they never broke eye contact.

Finally they groaned and came together before collapsing in a heap of tangled arms and sweat. Jasper leaned over and kissed her, murmuring his love before falling into a deep sleep. It had been an emotional day. That was for sure.

Willow, still encased in his arms, stayed awake a bit longer. The look of determination on his face after Melanie's attempt at the conversion had not been lost on her. He wasn't going to let her change. She was sure of it. Closing her eyes, she prayed for guidance, knowing the pain would be terrible, but the outcome of forever with Jasper would be worth it. She would do anything for him and to be with him. Whatever it took, she would be a werewolf. Be his werewolf. She would be a Jamenson in truth. Now she would have to convince Jasper. *No problem there.*

CHAPTER TEN

I ncorporating one's self into a Pack of werewolves should come easy to anyone. Right? A snort escaped Willow before she could stop it. Though she had a leg up on others in meeting new people because of her past, she still was at a loss in some respects.

Her parents had died in a car crash when she was a little girl. She'd been sleeping in the back seat when a drunk driver hit them head on. Willow could still smell the scent of burned hair and blood. Could still hear the crunch of metal against metal. She could barely remember what they looked like.

Jasper helped alleviate that. His face and touch sent her to her dreams at night.

But what did she have to give back? Was she even worth it?

A twenty-four-year-old college dropout, she possessed little options in providing a true help to the Pack. She'd been relegated to being surrounded by a protection detail that would keep her from outside harm while Jasper's keen eye was elsewhere. Willow was learning the art of being a Pack member. Laughter rumbled in her chest at the irony.

"What's so funny?" Reed, her new brother-in-law, current body-guard, and Pack artist asked. With a paintbrush in his hand, another brush behind his ear, and numerous splotches of colors from his current project, he looked like the typical struggling artisan. Lanky, with the build of a swimmer, his body held power and strength to fight any attack, though, anyone who faced him might laugh at the red smear on the tip of his nose.

"Nothing, just thinking. Here, let me get that." She reached for a clean towel behind him before rubbing his nose with it. They both collapsed in laughter as the red merely spread across his face and the towel.

"Great job, Wil. Before I may have looked like Rudolph; now I look like a clown bent on revenge." Gasping for breath, Willow dampened the cloth with more water, but Reed held her wrist.

"Please stop before I fully resemble a tomato." He took the towel from her hands and wiped his face the best he could. Honestly, it may have been too late for the tomato. She laughed again.

God, it felt so good to be with people who considered her family, even if they'd only known her for a short while. After surviving the car accident that took the lives of her parents at the age of six, Willow had bounced from foster home to foster home until she finally graduated high school. With the lack of connections to the human world, Reed and Adam told her she was a perfect candidate for entering the Pack, though, according to Jasper, that had no bearing on their mating. Either way, the warmth seeping through their mating bond shook off any doubt of his choice.

Thoughts and questions assailed her, and she didn't know whom to ask, but Reed seemed the most open.

"Can I ask you something, Reed?" Willow bit into her lip.

"Sure, Wil, what's up?" Reed cocked his head. He'd cleaned most of the red from his face, but a pink hue remained on his skin.

"Well, I would ask Jasper, but I don't want him to get the wrong idea. I mean, I love him, it's just..." She hung her head. Damn, this was harder to put into words than she'd thought. She stepped back, and her legs hit a stool, forcing her to take a seat.

"Now you're starting to worry me. Tell me what's going on." Reed knelt in front of her, taking her hand in his. Though he didn't possess the emotional magic Maddox did, nor the bond she shared with Jasper,

Reed's touch cemented her in the present and gave her the courage to ask.

"Tell me about mating." The words tumbled from her mouth before she lost the nerve. "I know Jasper is my mate; I feel it here." She laid her hand on her heart, the beat pressing into her palm reminding her she was alive and connected to Jasper. "But I don't understand why others say Jasper had a choice. What don't I know?" Pain radiated through her chest at the thought of losing Jasper. That couldn't happen.

Reed furrowed his brow. "Jasper didn't explain it to you?" He shook his head. "I don't think I'm the right person to tell you. That is something between you and Jasper."

She gripped his hand harder, a lifeline to the unknown. "If I ask him, he'll think I question our bond, that I don't want him. That isn't how I feel, but I don't know anything about the Pack." Frustrated, she ground her teeth. "Just tell me. I won't leave him. I can't leave him. But I need to know." Her brother-in-law let out a breath. "Fine. But if Jasper tries to kick my ass, I blame you." A slight quirk of his lips softened his threat.

"Fate decides who's our perfect companion, who can connect our souls and complete our future. However, with the lifespan of a werewolf, fate's been kind. There are people out there with the potential to be our mate. We need only find them and mate them."

There were others? What she shared with Jasper wasn't unique? He could have another mate? Her heart clenched as thoughts swirled her mind, leaving her nauseated.

"Stop that, Willow. That's not what I meant. Jasper chose you. You are the ideal mate for him. Anyone else he could've mated wouldn't be perfect."

She shook her heat vigorously. "No, he didn't choose me. He was forced into it. Don't you understand?" Fear crept up her spine and she blinked away tears. Reed griped her chin, forcing her gaze back to his.

"Look at me. Jasper chose you. He chose you the moment he walked into your bakery all those months ago. He just wanted to take things slow. You can blame him for going at a snail's pace if you'd like." Reed gave a small laugh before continuing. "Just because fate allows us the option of different mates, it is truly difficult to find the one perfect mate. Jasper and you are mates. He marked you so cannot choose another while you live. And frankly, why would he? I see the way you two look at each other. And, Willow, honey, remember that we can hear great distances. Your home isn't exactly sound proof." A wicked smile crossed his lips as heat scalded her cheeks.

"Oh." Yeah, that sounded intelligent. She wrote a mental note to ask Jasper for some heavy drapes to dampen the sound from their bedroom. And their living room. And the kitchen...

"At least we know you two completed, right?" Reed laughed at his own joke as mortification set in. The Jamensons were a little too close for comfort sometimes.

"But I haven't marked him. What does that mean?"

Reed frowned. "That means you could leave him if you wanted. It would hurt the both of you like hell, but it could happen."

Oh.

"But I would never do that."

His face softened. "I know that, Wil."

"But seriously, Jasper and you are two halves of a whole. Believe me. Did Jasper tell you about Kade?" Her face must have revealed her confusion because Reed continued. "Before Kade met Melanie, he'd found another potential mate in Tracy. His wolf felt an ability to connect with her, and because she was a werewolf, he thought she would be a decent choice. However, Kade wasn't the only one who felt a connection to Tracy. "

Reed shook his head and took a deep breath. "His best friend, Grant, sensed it too." Anger flashed across his face and he stopped talking.

Bewilderment settled in. Every time she spoke with a Pack member she learned something that blew away her expectations of normal.

"Two mates? What did Tracy do?" she asked.

"Tracy wanted them both and refused to choose, forcing Kade and Grant to fight for the right to mate her."

Alarm traveled up her spine. "What do you mean fight for her?" No way. Fighting like cavemen for a woman?

155

"They fought in the circle as men. Fist against fist. Flesh against flesh. But Kade's heart wasn't in it, so he conceded." With a shrug, Reed looked as if he didn't care Tracy wasn't his sister-in-law.

"But that's barbaric!"

"Willow, we aren't human. We're werewolves." He lifted an eyebrow. "You have taken everything we have thrown at you amazingly well, but is that because you still don't believe?" Concern was evident on his face with something else. Pity?

"I'm trying, Reed." Frustration engulfed her. Dammit, this was so new to her, wasn't she allowed a moment to be unsure?

"Don't feel sorry for Kade. It was because of the whole incident he met Melanie. After the circle he needed a night to himself, so we set him up on a blind date. As fate would have it, Melanie was his date and his mate." Reed laughed at his rhyme.

Willow rolled her eyes. Gah, even concerning serious topics, men could still act like they were twelve.

"So it worked out for Kade because there was a backup for him? Is it always like that?" The woman from the circle came to her mind – Camille. Willow pushed away jealous thoughts. Jasper was hers.

Again, Reed's face was so open the sorrow that swept his face broke her heart. "Not always. Not for Adam. Not for Anna." The sound of the woman's name across his lips brought an ache to her chest, though she couldn't place why.

Reed took a steadying breath before continuing. "Adam was on a hunt when Anna was taken from their home. Before we could find her, she'd been raped and beaten. She was also pregnant with their first young." Tears ran down his cheeks, and Reed's voice broke. Poor Anna. Poor Adam.

"Maddox is the Omega, Willow. He could feel every painful blow Anna felt. Everything done to her, and been helpless to stop it. By the time we could get to her, Maddox was in a catatonic shock. There was nothing we could do. She was gone." Reed choked on his words. "There was no back up for him. He still feels her loss. We all do."

She couldn't take it anymore. Willow opened her arms and held Reed. This was Pack. Comforting one another, staying strong. This was something she could do.

Reed kissed the top of her head and stepped back. "Jasper would kill me if he came in and saw me in your arms. I happen to value my life." Their laughed quickly dissipated the tension.

"You are going to make some woman very happy one day Reed." His open heart and good nature would be a gift to anyone.

"Or man." He winked as Willow stared in shock.

"Man?" Well, that was unexpected.

"I'm open to either – or both. As long as there is a bond I'm happy." Reed smiled.

Huh, that was a nice way to look at it.

"Well then, good for you." They laughed together again as Reed picked up his forgotten paintbrush.

CHAPTER ELEVEN

Willow finally settled into life at the den. Being pulled forcefully from her normal routine and thrust into the world of the paranormal seemed to work for her. When the Central Pack abducted her, the bakery had been destroyed beyond repair. When they first saw the damage, they'd thought it was merely a few chairs and decorations. But Reggie and Isaac were thorough.

Bastards.

Her ovens and stoneware, gone or broken. Everything wasted. Willow's heart clenched at her broken dream. It wasn't fair. What had she done to deserve this? Everything she'd worked for was gone.

Jasper's response to the destruction was simple. Start fresh. They would use this horrible event to combine their lives and build together. Willow may have lost part of her life with the loss of her bakery, but her mate incorporated her into his life. That was more important than a few lost cinnamon rolls.

As it was, her talents in the kitchen weren't going to waste. Every morning she'd cook for him and her various new family members who "accidentally" showed up unexpectedly. That was something she was getting used to. Nothing like being bent over their kitchen table with a good morning from Jasper as a hungry werewolf walks through the door. Talk about embarrassing.

Her bakery might be closed but not her desire to feed people. It was amazing how well Jasper knew her after only such a short time. The center of the Den housed many small shops and provided goods for the needs and wants of the Pack. But there wasn't a place to eat that didn't involve going to someone's home. Here Willow could find her place, though she wasn't a werewolf – yet.

No matter how successful she'd thought she was before, the love radiating from Jasper and his family truly made her happy.

Willow took a deep breath and inhaled the mountain air. The crisp scent tugged at her heart and invigorated her bones.

"I love the air here. I mean I know it's only like twelve miles or so from where I lived before, but it just seems so much cleaner here." She breathed again and closed her eyes.

"I think you are sensing the magic in our air."

Willow opened her eyes at Reed's statement.

"Huh?" In the circle she'd thought she'd felt something, but smelling magic? That was a bit too weird for her.

"We're high up in the mountains in the most beautiful forest in the Americas, if not the world, so yes, the air is clean. But what makes it cling to your soul is the Pack magic inherent in everything we do. I know you aren't a werewolf, but you're connected through your bond with Jasper. You will be a little more open to feeling these things than an average human." Reed smiled and led her to a vacant building.

A familiar warmth spread though her heart and she smiled at the gorgeous specimen of man walking toward her.

"Jasper." His name was a reverent whisper. She couldn't help it.

Before she knew what she was doing, the smell of forest and mate surrounded her as she ran to him and Jasper clutched her tightly to his chest. His heart beat soundly against her cheek. Home.

"Mmm, it has been too long since I have seen you, my Willow." His lips were a light brush of sensual taste against hers.

"It's only been since this morning, Jasper." Smiling, she took his parted lips as an invitation, melding her tongue to his.

A discreet cough behind them reminded her of Reed's presence.

"Not that that wasn't hot, but really, I thought we came here for a reason." Reed's smile belied his sarcasm.

"Guess we did. Come, let me show you." Jasper kissed her brow and took her hand.

He grinned mischievously, and she smiled. He was up to something. What could he be planning with an old abandoned building?

"Jasper? It's an empty building. I mean, it's a nice one, but what are we doing here?"

"I know you've been putting on a brave face with losing your bakery. Wil, baby, that place was your dream. The product of your hard work and love. I know I can never replace that for you, but I can help us move on together. "This place? It's yours." Jasper opened his arms pointing to the barren walls and open space.

"What?" Her pulse quickened. Hers?

"Wil, you've been cooking and baking for Pack members for the four weeks you've been here and asked for nothing in return. The Pack and I recognize your passion for what you do, and we want to show you how much we love you. Open a bakery here, or do what you want with it. I know you want to contribute, and this is how you can do it. The Pack wants you – I want you." Jasper's jade eyes begged her to take the chance, to be part of his Pack in more than name.

"Mine? I mean..." She choked on a sob as the rush of love and acceptance swept through her. They wanted her. They respected what she had to offer.

"Yours."

"Oh, Jasper, I love you. Thank you." She jumped into his arms and wrapped her legs around his waist.

"Still here, guys." Reed's voice startled her as Jasper laughed. "But really, Willow, we all want you to feel like you belong. And once you decide exactly what you are going to do, let me know. These grey and lonely walls are begging for a mural and my hands are itching to comply."

Again, her heart almost burst with joy and love as she slid down Jasper's body to plant her feet.

"What a pretty picture. The lovebirds and the twink." A vicious snarl and cruel words brought their celebration to a screeching halt.

Camille. God, that woman was a bitch in every sense of the word. Beside the female wolf, Fredrick glared like the bully he was. Ever since the circle, those two had been inseparable and, frankly, annoying as hell. They just couldn't seem to get over whatever grudge they held. It felt like high school all over again.

"Camille, you really need to get over yourself and lose the attitude. It does nothing for your complexion," Reed said.

Camille shot a venomous look at Reed before sauntering toward Jasper.

"I see you've bought your helpless plaything a new store. What's next? This little human will never be part of us, Jasper. What were you thinking when you mated this piece of trash? She will never be like us. I can't believe you chose her when you could have had me, a real were-wolf. Not something that needs to be changed in order to fit in."

Camille's toxic rant disgusted Willow. She knew there were some in the Pack that valued pure lines and magic by birth, but it had never been thrown in her face before.

Jasper growled. "Shut your fucking mouth. You overstep your bounds, Camille. Go back to your little home with your goon and leave my family alone. You are lucky I have honor and don't hit women. But Fredrick, I would run if I were you, I don't have any qualms where you are concerned." His voice was laced with ice.

"I know my place, oh mighty Beta." Camille sneered. "But your human better learn hers." With one last poisonous glare, she stormed out of Willow's new bakery with Fredrick hot on her tail.

"You need to be careful of that one, Jasper. I don't think that is the last we'll be hearing of her." Reed's warning came as no surprise to Willow.

"I know. I know. I have been lax in my Beta responsibilities, I think. It's my job to deal with rumblings of unease." Jasper's voice still held anger, but a bit of sadness as well. What did Camille mean to him? Her pain must have shown on her face because Jasper bent to kiss her lips.

"I never loved her. I don't even like her. She is nothing to me. I'm just sad this is what Camille has become." Jasper shook his head as if to organize his thoughts. "Let's go home. We can celebrate there." He gave a wicked smile, and Willow's pussy clenched. Oh, she wanted to celebrate now.

"On that note, I'm going to Adam's to warn him about the duo of doom. Have fun." With a wave and a smile, Reed left, and they were alone.

"Quickly, I need you." Jasper threw her over his shoulder and ran home. Some days she could really get used to his caveman antics.

By the time they reached their home, Willow panted with need. "What do you do to me?"

"I think the better question is, what am I going to do to you." Jasper's eyes darkened as he growled against her ear, the breath trailing down her neck pulsating against her. "I want you."

"Take me. Please."

Jasper wrapped her hair around his fist and kissed her with bruising force. He unsnapped her jeans and had them down around her ankles before she could blink. She gasped as his fingers twisted the sides of her thong and tore it from her body.

He kissed and nibbled her neck around the fading mate mark before lifting his head and turning her around, bending her over the couch. The rasp of a zipper and rustle of jeans sent shivers over her spine. He danced his fingers across her thighs, before he finally brushed against her clit. She bucked against him, aroused and ready.

"You're wet for me. Do you want me?" He licked her ear and nibbled her lobe.

She moaned and nodded, unable to speak.

Jasper entered her to the hilt in one quick thrust. Stars shattered behind her lids. He barely touched her, and she came. God, she loved this bond. This man. He quickly withdrew before he pistoned into her again and again. The sound of his balls slapping her ass as his thighs rammed hers increased her pulse and desire. With one hand still holding her hair in a firm grip, his other hand crawled up her chest, twisting and pinching her nipples, causing her pussy to tighten around his thick shaft.

He shifted before he plunged into her again, his cock rubbing against her womb. Willow began to ride the crest again, closer and closer to orgasm. His stiffened and released a shout that echoed off the walls as he came, filling her. His seed warmed her. The sound of his release brought her to completion as she cried out his name. After that, their heavy breathing was the only sound in the quiet room.

"I love you, Jasper."

"I love you too." He pulled back and picked her up, before carrying her into their bedroom.

"Where are we going?"

"You didn't think we were done celebrating did you?" Seeing the grin full of promise on his face, she exhaled a happy sigh.

Oh, how she loved celebrating.

———

THE WOOD beneath his hands felt warm as he carved the banisters for Willow's bakery. He loved working with wood, making this come to life. This was for Willow, his Willow.

"You done fondling that wood?" Reed laughed.

"At least I have something to fondle," Jasper quipped.

"Dude, that's low."

"How is the painting coming?" Reed was painting a mural on one of the walls, and Jasper was in awe of his little brother's talent.

"Almost done. I hope she'll like it."

"I'm sure she will; she loves your work."

"I hope so. She needs something nice, ya know?" Reed smiled.

"Considering she's my mate, I do. I love making her smile."

The door opened and Camille walked in.

Dammit, he hated that woman.

She prowled across the room and ran a well-manicured fingernail down his chest.

"Hello, Jasper," she purred.

"Remove your finger before I remove it for you," he growled.

She stuck out her bottom lip and pouted. But she removed her finger.

"You used to like my touch."

"No, I tolerated it to scratch an itch." He knew he sounded like an ass, but being nice wouldn't get through her thick skull.

"Ouch, Beta has claws." She snarled.

"Camille, what do you want? You don't want me. I sure as hell don't want you."

"I just wanted to see your little mate's new digs. Don't fault me."

He glared at her, not believing her at all.

"I'm the Beta of our Pack. You need to remember the fact that I help lead our people. You do nothing but belittle them." He let out a small glimpse of his power, anger at her pettiness through the past years seeping through. The depth of the strength curling out from his chest to his fingertips, filling the room with its presence, thickening the air.

Her eyes widened, and she buckled under the power, going to her knees in submission.

"Go, Camille. Do not come in here again. Do not bother my mate or my family. Go away. Tell your little goon Fredrick, too. Do you understand me?"

She whimpered and nodded, backing away on her hands and knees, through the door Reed held open.

"Shit, Jasper. Nice show of power. You almost got me to submit." Reed quirked a brow.

Jasper shrugged. "I didn't use it all. I just wanted her out. She's been bothering me for years and being a bitch to everyone. I've been so preoccupied that I haven't been a good Beta. I shouldn't have let her get away with it for so long."

"You know she's not done yet, don't you?" Reed asked.

"I know. Camille will never learn. But she has to know that I won't lie back and take it."

"Good to know."

"Now get back to painting. I want to make this place look amazing for my Willow."

Reed nodded and went back to work.

Jasper smoothed the wood in his palm and got back to what he was good at, what he loved, for the woman he loved.

CHAPTER TWELVE

T he smell of fresh paint and wood shavings tickled Willow's
nose. The tangy scent of male sweat on glistening bodies
mixed with the sweet and sugary chocolate aroma from the
brownies she'd baked that morning. A luscious and sinful combination
if there ever was one.

The marble countertop was cool to the touch as she ran her hand
along the smooth edge. The deep, ruby-red velvet inlay of the picture
board above the glass panels clung to her fingers. Burgundy and chocolate colored ribbons adorned it, begging for pictures and memories to
surface and be known. To be immortalized.

Sounds of hammer pounding nails and a saw slicing into two-by-
fours filled her ears, keeping the latent fear at bay. She felt ghostly
hands gliding and gripping her arms, forcing her immobile...

No, no, that was over. She was safe. The sounds of metal yielding
and arching as the final oven was moved brought her back.

She let out a sigh. *This is mine. Made for me.*

The Jamensons were on the last day of construction for her new
bakery in the Den. Everyone had worked together to put in the last
sets of shelves and decorations, while Reed focused solely on his mural.
Broad brush strokes and minute details covered the large expanse.

Dark bold colors of chocolate, cherry and a lighter cream interplayed and entwined to create a masterpiece of lines and shapes. An abstract painting that expressed love and warmth. Beautiful.

Today was also an anniversary of sorts. Four months before, the Central Pack had abducted her from her previous bakery, changing her life forever. Though it frustrated Jasper to no end, her Pack, because they were hers now, had not retaliated against their enemy. During another Pack circle, in which they discussed when and how they would attack, Camille and Fredrick stated that due to the fact Willow was not Pack at the time of her kidnapping, the Redwood Pack could not and should not go after the Centrals. It was against the code and laws of their history and it gave the Centrals a weapon to hurt them. The fury on Jasper's face when they told him caused Willow to shudder. It took every ounce of her strength to stand up to him and say enough was enough. They would not enter the Central's land on a wave of revenge. They'd hold their own.

Though the imprisonment threaded her nightmares, the outcome of her mating with Jasper could not be ignored. Thanks to Hector and Corbin, really. Willow snorted and looked around her new shop.

Tan walls with brown trim that reminded her of chocolate chip cookies were lightened by large windows in the front of her store. Soon, white curtains with brown stripes would accentuate the curve of the windows and pull in the color of the room. Large photos in dark brown, wooden frames hung on the walls. Each picture was of a family member, infusing her bakery with love. Tables and chairs with white and brown tablecloths dotted the floor in front, leaving a walkway to the counter, which would showcase her treats and delicacies.

Her family built this. For her. This was her home. Tears clouded her eyes, but Willow held them back. This was a time for happiness. No crying allowed.

A growl sounded behind her and she turned. Mel sat on the ground with a snarl on her face, and Willow broke out laughing.

"It's not funny." The frustrated look on Melanie's face was priceless. "This stupid curtain rod broke in my hands. I guess I don't know my own strength." With a shrug, she threw the bent pieces of metal away and picked up another.

Melanie's strength and shorter temper had arrived after her first shift two nights prior. Apparently, she'd transformed amazingly well and fit into the life of a werewolf nicely. A sense of jealousy swept through Willow, but she shook it off.

No.

It will happen. Jasper will ask me to change and join the Pack fully.

At least, that's what she told herself.

"What did I say about your stress levels, baby?" Kade's soft growl announced his presence. Mel fell into his open arms with a sigh. "And you really shouldn't be in here with Reed and his paint." His brows furrowed as he brushed a lock of hair from his mate's face.

She suddenly wanted Jasper near her.

Curiosity overcame her and she interrupted the loving couple's moment. "Are the fumes too much for your new senses?"

A slow smile spread over Kade's face.

Okay, she was missing something.

"Kade needs to watch his mouth, but I guess the wolf is out of the bag." Melanie beamed a smile. "We're pregnant."

The shouts of glee and congratulations from the Jamenson family were so loud Willow was sure her new picture frames would vibrate right off the walls.

A baby.

Tears glistened on Pat's face. Edward, in typical Alpha fashion, choked back his emotion. Cailin screeched and threw herself into Kade's arms. Reed gave a laugh and knelt to place a gentle kiss on Mel's still-flat belly, cooing sweet nothings. North pushed their artist brother out of the way.

"Congratulations, my sister wolf." North then proceeded to take her pulse at the wrist, instructing her to 'keep the excitement level to a minimum.' Apparently, he couldn't resist playing doctor even for a moment.

Kade was hugged and roughly slapped on the back as Mel was gently and reverently held and kissed. However, Reed didn't seem to get the "be cautious around the pregnant lady" memo and spun her around the store.

"Get your hands off my woman." Kade's growl only made Reed and Mel laugh harder.

Mel's contagious laughter died slowly as Adam stepped toward her. Willow saw misery flash in his eyes before he blanked his expression, holding Mel in a bone-crushing hug. Pain for her brother-in-law shot through her heart as she remembered that Adam had lost not only his mate but his child.

Jesus. She couldn't even comprehend what he felt right now.

As she shook her head to cast away those saddening thoughts, movement caught her eye. Maddox stood alone in the shadows, the light from the window illuminating his face. Willow sucked in a breath. *His eyes.* Gold radiated and pulsed from his unblinking gaze. Though wolves' eyes glowed during passion and anger, this, she felt, was different. Eerie. She took a step closer, and it hit her. Emotion. A tingling sensation like a thousand fingertips dancing across her skin made her shiver. Maddox was an empath. The empath of the Pack. The feelings of happiness and glee emanating from his family must be overwhelming and spilling from him. With a quirk of his lips, Maddox gave a nod of his head, finally closing his eyes.

Arms wrapped around her from behind, and she sank into Jasper's embrace. Warmth seeped through his touch as Willow watched Kade kiss his mate.

"I want that." Jasper's breath danced along her neck as he spoke closely to her ear. His arm slid down her front, his palm caressing her stomach. Butterflies fluttered within, and she smiled. She'd been wrong before; *this* was home. Four months. Only four months of being his mate, and she already wanted – no, needed – to bear his young.

"Me too." All thoughts of nervousness and trepidation toward the change fled her mind as Jasper bit into the flesh of her earlobe.

"With all of the practicing we've been doing, I think it's only a matter of time. Don't you?"

"Uh huh." Rational thoughts and real words had apparently escaped her.

"Wanna go practice some more?" His deep, throaty laugh vibrated down her spine and she turned in his hold, wrapping her arms around his neck.

"I think that can be arranged." She smiled at him, watching the love radiate from his eyes. She was at peace in his arms, in her bakery, in their home.

Please, never let this end.

"YOU REALLY MET ON A BLIND DATE?" Willow asked.

"Yep. Odd right?" Melanie laughed.

The two of them sat in Kade and Mel's house, drinking hot chocolate and eating cookies that Willow had baked the night before. The other woman glowed. Pregnancy suited her.

"My friend, Larissa, who's a witch mated into the Pack, set me up with Kade. They all thought we'd get along and have fun. But they had no idea we were mates." Mel explained.

"Fate's tricky like that."

"I didn't believe in fate at the time. I mean, how could I? I'm a chemist. Analytically speaking, fate, mates, and werewolves shouldn't exist. But here we are." Mel shrugged.

"I take it you didn't react well."

"I was horrible. I left then let Kade fight for me." Mel teared up, and Willow pulled her into a hug. "Sorry, hormones. I should have listened to my heart, but instead I let my brain make all my decisions. I hurt him and myself. I'm just lucky he took me back."

"Mel, of course he took you back. You didn't do anything wrong. You're allowed to take time and think."

Mel let out a breath. "But Kade's going to be Alpha. That means I'm going to be the lead female of this Pack someday. I just don't know if I can gain their respect."

Willow took the other woman's hand. "They already do, Mel. I see the way people come to you for advice. The way they ask you for help with school and other things. Mel, they look up to you. You have their respect. You're going to make a great Alpha female."

Mel sniffed and waved her hand in front of her face. "Thanks, Wil. I hope so. I have the attitude for it, according to Kade." They both laughed. "But enough crying, you came over here for something, right?"

Yep, Mel would be a great Alpha. There was no hiding anything from her.

"I want to change," Willow blurted. "I want to be a wolf. But I don't know how to convince Jasper."

Mel's eyes widened. "I take it Jasper doesn't want that."

"I don't know. He doesn't say anything when I bring it up."

The other woman sighed. "No one can order him to let you. But you do have your own power. If you truly want to, we can make it happen. But you need to find out exactly why he's acting like this. I know Jasper; he's a nice guy and doesn't do anything without a reason."

"I know. I'm just scared."

"Wil, maybe he is too."

Willow sighed. What was she going to do?

CHAPTER THIRTEEN

J asper sat in his parents' living room, dread filling his belly. Fear crawled up his back, wrapping its spindly fingers around his throat, choking him. The thoughts and actions he'd tried to repress had caught up with him.

The Centrals wanted Willow back.

Well, that was too damn bad. There was no way they were getting a paw near her. Determination settled on him like a second skin. He took a deep breath, inhaling the familiar scent of his mother's sirloin stew and his father's pipe smoke that was failing miserably at being masked by a wood fire. No doubt his mother would be in the room soon to scold her husband lovingly on his infraction. Jasper smiled at his parents' relationship. It was what he wanted with Willow. What he needed.

Watching Kade go through the turmoil of two circles and fighting for Tracy, then Melanie, yet rising from the ashes with Melanie by his side, brought feelings of jealousy to Jasper. Before this, Jasper had done his duty. He'd cared for his Pack had been at their beck and call. If a Pack member needed a job, a shoulder to cry on, someone to talk to, Jasper was there. Even calls in the middle of the night used to be the norm. And he'd been okay with it. He laughed with others, helped

Reed play practical jokes on their brothers. Yet something had always felt missing. Willow.

And now Hector Reyes and his sadistic bastard of a son, Corbin, were trying to destroy his world and seize his mate.

His wolf growled and clawed to the surface.

"They will not take her. We can protect her. Though, there is a way to make her stronger."

Jasper ignored his wolf, anger spearing his consciousness. Dammit, he couldn't lose her. He couldn't, no wouldn't, let her become a wolf. It was too dangerous. Melanie had been lucky, she survived the change. It wasn't a guarantee. Maybe one in ten wolves actually survived the change. That's why most didn't even try. Fate usually mated wolves to other wolves – not humans. What would he do if Willow died trying to become like him? He loved her the way she was.

He was strong. Dammit, he was the fucking Beta of the Redwood Pack, the third strongest wolf, behind Kade and his father, of the most powerful Pack of the Americas, if not the world. She would be safe with him. He could protect and keep her in his life.

Already, he was making adjustments to their home. Adding touches here and there that excited Willow. It was her place too. He'd bought cooper-bottom pans and other kitchen goodies that made her eyes light up. Together, they'd bought pillows and decorations so their home didn't look so masculine. The need to show her she belonged ran deep. Not only had he built the bakery for her with his own two hands, he was creating a space for the two of them.

His father's voice interrupted his thoughts. "Jasper, are you listening to me?"

"Sorry, Dad." He took another deep breath to calm his nerves, focusing his attention on his Alpha. "What were you saying?"

His father gave him a pointed look before speaking. "Adam's received information that the Centrals demand Willow. They say she was theirs and we didn't have a right to enter their territory and take her. Regardless that she's your mate, they have a point. We did trespass on their territory. But it doesn't matter. She's your mate and they kidnapped her. There are rumors they will cross our border and attempt to take her unless we give her up."

Anger burned in Jasper's veins.

Adam rubbed his jaw before speaking. "Jasper, it gets worse. Corbin is telling others that Willow was his potential mate and he hadn't had the chance to mark her before you showed up. He is saying that you stole her from him without fighting in the circle. He demands reparations."

Jasper shot to his feet in a blind rage. "He thinks to take my mate? My Willow? That barbarous fuck thinks he can speak those vile lies and live?" Blood rushed in his ears, his heart pounding. He clenched his fists, as panic and fear seeped beneath his fury threatening to suffocate him.

"Calm down, son." The Alpha's voice swept over his outrage, soothing his ache. "We know you won't let Corbin take her. He has no claim. We won't allow it." His father's voice was stern and held the power of an ageless force. Pack. Japer drew in the magic of home, calming himself.

This was what it meant to be Pack. To take in the power surrounding him and bring him home. To calm the wolf and his emotions in order to think rationally. He didn't know how lone wolves did it.

Silent throughout the discussion, Kade rubbed his temples, a sign of frustration and deep thinking. "There is something more. Something darker. Willow was not a potential mate for Corbin. As evil as he is, Corbin could not have allowed her to be hurt as she was if it were true. That means this obviously false statement must be a shroud for their real intentions."

"Magic." Adam's answer brought a flicker of a memory, something that Jasper should know. But what was it?

"They were stuck." At his brothers' and father's obvious confused looks, Jasper continued. "The wolves at the Central's compound where we found Willow. Adam, don't you remember what Reed said? They were stuck. They didn't follow us, as if a magical barrier held them in place. It was magic; I'm sure of it."

"But what type of magic could do this?" Adam asked. "What are the Centrals hiding?"

"Could they be working with the witches?" Kade asked.

Jasper shook his head. "I don't think so. The magic felt different. Oily. Almost sliding against my skin. I almost forgot that. I was too worried for Willow and getting us out of there at that point."

"I've never heard of magic like that." His dad added. "But I am relatively young. We may need to ask the elders." Again his father's voice calmed his worries. It felt good to be with family.

"Magic should not taste tainted," Adam said with a deep growl. "Witches are in tune with the Earth, and are part of it. Witch magic should feel earthy like freshly dug soil, floral like just bloomed flowers, fresh like the wind brushing your face, warm like the sun dancing across your skin, or cool like sliding your hands across clean and clear water. That is magic. Not slick and oily."

Sometimes his brother surprised him with how much he knew about others' culture, though as the Enforcer of the Pack, it was his job not only to protect them from the outside world but to understand the outside world as well.

"Witch magic is hereditary," Adam continued. "In most cases they heal or do good. There are few that are truly powerful."

"The magic that is inherent in the Pack is different as well," his father interrupted. "It provides proof of strength and family." Jasper nodded, urging his father to continue the story he knew well, told to him as a young pup.

"Though it is legend, it is said that werewolves were formed from the Moon Goddess. Saddened by the atrocities of man and the weakening of their souls, the Moon Goddess stepped down from her ivory crescent throne and walked among the dense forests and rivers.

"There she found a hunter deep in the brush, searching for his next kill. The Goddess knew this man must eat and provide for his family, but she was disheartened at the depravity of the souls she watched over. The act of free will was not unknown to her, so she stood back and waited for the decisions the hunter made.

"A rustling of leaves alerted them both to an approaching beast. The hunter took aim with his bow and struck a gray wolf, injuring it but not killing the animal. He walked over to his prey, leaning over it, as the Moon Goddess drew nearer to the two, thoughts of redemption wafting through her.

"Startled by the Goddess presence, the hunter bowed yet stood protective over his kill. The Goddess told him that man needed to understand the connection between Earth and man. The man, confused, was unprepared for the magic pulsating and shocking through his system when the Goddess bent and touched her palm to his heart and the wolf's.

"That night, she created the first werewolf. Not man, nor beast, but a blending of the two. Man would dominate and walk the world, yet the wolf would remain internal forever, always challenging man's wants and desires. During times of the full moon, the Moon Goddess's pull is immense, non-tactile entity and man will change into the beast he hunted and killed, running through the forest of Earth on four paws rather than two feet. In times of great stress and need, man can choose to be wolf.

"The magic that the Moon Goddess placed on us that night in the forest still runs through our veins. It is earthy and good. Though we are human, we do carry within us a savage and uncivilized element that drives us. Our magic connects us, and it is not evil." Jasper's Alpha closed his eyes, bowing his head.

"If the Centrals are using magic, it's not from a wolf. It is their human selves that harbor evil, not their inner magic," Kade said. As the Heir of the Pack, he most understood his wolf.

"So you're telling me what we felt was not from witches, and we know it was not werewolf magic. So what was it?" Jasper's question silenced the room.

What had the Centrals unleashed?

Jasper's muscles clenched at the thought. After reviewing everything they knew, it seemed their enemies were touching something unknown and dangerous. Even though it may only be a ploy, they still wanted his mate. His Willow.

"I won't let them take her, no matter what evil they uncover." Jasper's growl was low, seething. He was edgy, the skin rippling on his forearms. His need to hunt was urgent, yet he wouldn't leave Wil alone, unprotected. His palms itched as the necessity to build something, to create with his hands took hold. If he couldn't kill his enemies now, he would expunge his energy somehow.

"Of course, Jasper. Willow is safe with us." Kade stood and walked over then kneeled before him. "I vow to protect your mate with all I have in me." The magic of his words snapped in place within Jasper. For Kade to vow this, while his own mate was pregnant, touched him deeply.

A binding vow and agreement through their wolves. They'd go to the grave to protect Willow and fight by his side.

"I, too, vow." Adam took Kade's place, and again, the magic washed over him.

"I vow, son, to protect your mate, my daughter."

"Dad, what if this is a ruse? What then? What do they want from us?" Jasper asked, needed to ask the obvious question.

Edward sighed. "I don't know. Maybe power? They're the second ranked Pack in the Americas below us. It's the only thing I can think of."

"Then we need to stop them. No matter what." Jasper growled.

If only it were that easy.

CHAPTER FOURTEEN

"Honesty, Wil, the smells emanating from this basket are killing me. Can't we stop and eat before we go to the circle?" Jasper's plea and boyish grin not only made Willow laugh but surprised her.

For the past few days, Jasper's demeanor bordered on distant, if not cold. At first, she'd thought it was something she'd done, but his attitude wasn't unique. The entire Jamenson family was on edge. Tension floated on the air, thickening as time passed. Something was coming. Willow didn't know what, but she kept on alert.

"If you want to explain to a group of hungry wolves where their food went, go for it. But I'm not Little Red Riding Hood on the way to grandmother's house. I will not ask 'What big teeth you have' and give you my food."

Standing next to her, Jasper kissed the top of her head and held her close. "You know it's not food I want, my Willow," he murmured in her ear, sending goose bumps down her arms.

"You know we don't have time for that."

"That's not what you said this morning when you took me in hand to teach me a lesson about laundry." He quirked a brow, and Willow blushed. *Damn him.*

"It isn't my fault that you refuse to sort your laundry. For a wolf who is over a hundred years old, I'd think you'd actually know how to do it yourself."

Jasper tickled her side, and she almost lost her basket.

"Hey, watch the food, baby. You do realize that if you'd just let me hold the damn thing, we wouldn't have this problem." At her defiant look he continued, "And I do know how to sort laundry. I just don't sort it into twelve different piles. Lights and darks work well for me."

Willow loved this playful side of him. She'd missed it this past week.

"Are we really going to start this conversation again? I mean really, it's laundry. And if I remember clearly, you got your way. I sort, you do the folding." Her teeth bit into her lip as she thought back to exactly how they came to that arrangement.

The smug look on his face indicated his thoughts were on the same path. *Men.*

"What can I say? This whole domestic bliss thing kinda fits."

"That's what you say now, but once I start having you do dishes, you're gonna run in fear."

"I don't run in fear from anyone. And I've been doing my own dishes since before you were born. Just –" Jasper's stopped and flared his nostrils.

Willow stopped behind him, her gaze on the woods surrounding them.

"Jasper, what–"

He held his finger to his lips and she shut up. *What's going on?*

"Willow, I want you to run back to the house and lock the doors," he said, his voice low, angry, and laced with fear.

"Jasper, no. I'm not going to leave you." Fear may have a hold on her, but she wouldn't leave his side for anything. Not while he was alone.

He cursed under his breath, and glared. Gone was his joyful expression from earlier. The cold brutality of his Beta power settled in over his face like a stern mask.

"Now." His voice low, threaded with anxiety.

"Jasper, I can help."

"I can't focus on you and whatever is out there. I need you to go. Now."

Fear crept up her spine; danger lurked around the corner. She rose to her tip-toes and brushed his lips in a gentle kiss.

"Be safe." *Please, I can't lose you.*

"Run, Willow. I love you."

"I love you, too."

The basket fell from her hands, the contents spilling to the ground, as Willow ran toward their home. Her chest burned from exhaustion as she climbed the hill. A howl split into the night, causing her to panic.

How far had they walked?

The hair on her arm prickled her skin and she stopped. Something was out there. In front of her, blocking her path? Or behind her?

Damn it, she didn't want to be the dumb chick in the horror movie who ran into a trap. Why had she left Jasper?

Something tugged on her brain, and she looked toward where the path led to the forest. Why did she want to go in there? She bit her lip and took a step closer to the darkness. Another howl echoed in the air, and she took another step. She needed to see what was past the line of trees. Some sort of magnetism drew her in, clouding her thoughts. Every time she tried to back away she only moved farther in.

Fear crawled up her spine, but she kept moving.

Great, now she really *was* the dumb chick who dies first in the horror movie.

Despite her uneasiness, Willow moved into dense forest, leaves rustling against her cheek and sides, as she walked. The large trees rose up toward the sky, reaching for the light, as worshipers would their god. The canopy stopped the light almost fully in some places, making it hard to see. Damn it, she really missed Jasper.

Dead leaves crunched under her feet as she ventured farther. The thick trees muted the outside noises, creating a tomb like feeling. A large lump on the forest floor stood out against the fading light. Willow squinted her eyes, praying they would adjust to the darkness. In times like these, she wished she were a werewolf. The disparity on the ground didn't move as she walked toward it, holding her breath.

A twig dug into her knee as she knelt down beside it. Finally, her eyes adjusted so she could get a good look. And screamed.

———

THE SOIL SIFTED between his paws as Jasper sniffed the ground. He shouldn't have sent Willow off. Why had he done that? He shook his head, trying to clear out the cloudiness. Something dug into his brain, not letting him think.

When he'd first inhaled that tangy scent with Willow, he needed to get distance from her. Like in a trance, he yelled at her to leave him and not stay by his side where he could protect her. No, he had told her to run away alone, with no help. A command that he in his normal thinking self, he would never have made. Something urged him to let her go off on her own with a threat around them and run the opposite direction. When she ran, he'd shifted, bones rearranging, muscles tearing, and after that Jasper had followed the tangy scent into the forest, away from his mate. He howled at the power suppressing his mind

"Magic."

Finally. His wolf hadn't spoken to him since he'd begun his walk with Willow. Someone had laid a magical trap for him and her, and they'd walked right into it. Damn it. He howled again, a pain=filled howl. Why the hell would someone try to trap them?

As a wolf, his senses were sharper, more attuned to the Earth. Though before he'd felt the need to be in this part of the territory, he knew now that nothing would be found here. He'd been duped, and so had his wolf. By magic.

A scream pierced the silence. *Willow.*

On four paws, he ran through the overgrowth of the natural forest, not caring that branches tugged at his fur. His mate's scream sent dread through him. Once he found her, oh and he would, he would kill the sick fuck that separated them.

Maddox might be the one who would kill quickly and effectively to avoid feeling the pain and fear. But, like Adam, Jasper would torture. Before he gutted them, they would suffer.

His heart thudded in his ears as he followed their mate-bond to his

Willow. Thank God they'd completed the connections so he could always find her, barring outside forces.

Willow screamed again just as he jumped over a rotted log. She stood over a lifeless body, her face pale in shock. Her brown hair fell lank in her face, over her wide, frightened eyes. When she caught sight of his wolf, she visibly exhaled in relief. Jasper lowered his head and pulled his magic to turn back into a man. Though it hurt slightly, his age dampened the pain of transformation.

Naked, he knelt and took Willow into his arms. Her body felt cool against his overheated, sweat-slick chest.

"Shh, Wil, it's okay. I'm here." But he almost hadn't been. Some outside force had pulled at them, edging them apart, trying to put chinks in their armor.

"Jasper." A soft whisper. "Why did I leave? Why did I come here?"

"I don't know exactly. But we'll find out." And those responsible would pay.

With Willow still in his arms, her breath still raspy against his chest, he finally looked down at the corpse at their feet.

A woman's body lay perfectly on the floor, her hands clasped on her chest reminiscent of Snow White in the fairy tale. If it hadn't been for the bruising, cuts, and blood, she would almost look peaceful. Light brown hair surrounded a pale, gray face with glassy, hazel eyes. Willow's eyes.

Cold dread gripped its icy fingers around his heart as the implications of the body sank ink. A message. And not very subtle.

"Jasper, she looks like me."

"Come on baby, let's get out of here." He stood up, unmindful of his nudity, and tried to walk Willow away from the sight he thought would haunt her nightmares. He knew they would haunt his.

"Wait." She grabbed his hand in a surprisingly firm grip. "There's a note."

Jasper pushed her behind him. She'd seen enough already tonight. He knelt toward the body, trying not to look at the face that so closely resembled his love that his heart hurt, and carefully took the note from her hands.

Keep yours close.

Three words. Three simple words and Jasper's wolf clawed to the surface to protect their Willow. Fire ran through his veins, and he had the courage to do what he should have done in the beginning. He bent over the woman and inhaled her scent. A soft floral over crushed stone. Talon Pack. They resided on the other side of the Central Pack in Montana and were their allies and friends. The Talons were low in the power rankings of the Packs but protective of their own. How they hell had the Centrals taken her and brought her here?

Fuck.

"Let's go home. I need to call my father and brothers."

A nod.

Damn it. He knew it wasn't over. The family had just talked about it. Vows were spoken. Yet, somewhere deep down, he'd prayed it wouldn't come to this.

War.

CHAPTER FIFTEEN

Back at the house, Jasper paced in their living room. The Centrals had a lot of nerve. Coming onto his land and bringing a fucking witch with them. Not that he had a prejudice against witches. Far from it. He trusted them with his Pack's protection, healing, and in some cases, friendship. But the fact that they would align themselves with their rivals and use tainted magic left a bitter taste on his tongue.

"That reminds me, that tangy smell from the forest. Why was it different?"

Jasper cocked his head at his wolf's question. Yes, not a pure witch's scent. But what? Unlike in some folk-lore, there was no such thing as black or white magic. A witch's magic came from their soul and the earth and smelled of earthly things. The sickly sweet smell shadowing the forest just an hour ago was not of earth. Hector and Corbin were meddling with something deeper than normal magic.

The dark entity from the night of his marking Willow came to mind. Who was he? His instincts told him that whoever the ally the Centrals had found, it was not of this world. Something new. Tainted. Something to fear.

Jasper took a deep, ragged breath. Whatever deals their enemies had made, not all were revealed. An unknown magical entity aided the

Centrals, bent on taking his mate, though Jasper had a feeling that wasn't their prime objective. No, they wanted something else. Desiring Willow was just a cover, a distraction. And a damn good one.

"Jasper."

He stopped pacing and looked at Willow. Her pulse beat rapidly, moving against the slick sheen of sweat on her neck. Eyes bright, she blinked, yet her fear remained. Tonight was not the first time she'd seen a dead body. No, her parents' held that honor. The accident that claimed their lives had also ripped her innocence away. The wet road and the inebriated driver combined in an interplay of dilapidated metal and glass had forced his Willow into foster homes and away from their comfort.

Now, because of Jasper's mark and his *forced* mark, she'd lost some of the inherent innocence of being human.

"Do not blame yourself, Jasper. The blame belongs solely on the Centrals' shoulders. Willow is yours. Ours."

Jasper desperately wanted to believe his wolf so he could take Willow in his arms and tell her he loved her. Tell her everything would be okay. But he couldn't. Words escaped him.

"Jasper."

The confusion in her voice brought him out of his thoughts.

"Yes, Willow?" God, how he loved her. He would do anything to protect her. Even from the things she didn't know could hurt her.

"When we were out there, something took me from you. I didn't want to leave, to run. But I did. Why?"

"Whatever killed that girl had a form of magic I've never seen. You didn't run away they took you." That thought scared the shit out of him.

"I felt so helpless out there. I don't want to feel that way anymore."

Her gaze rested on him, pleading for his help. His heart broke for her. No, he didn't want that either.

"I need to change, Jasper. I need to become one of you. It's the only way."

Logically, he knew she was right. However, the prideful male in him resented the inclination. He clenched his fists as his wolf clawed to the surface. Anger for those who stole her safety made him see red.

"Jasper. Watch your words."

He ignored his wolf. "It's too dangerous. You saw what my father did to Melanie. He almost killed her. I don't want you to go through that. The pain of the change is excruciating. And even after the biting and tearing of your flesh, there is no guarantee you will even be a wolf. You could die. I won't risk that."

"But isn't it worth a try?"

"And once you do," He couldn't listen to her words. If he did, she could be hurt. There was nothing more important to him than her health and safety. He continued as if she hadn't spoken "And once you do, you'd have to deal with the fact that you've lost your humanity. You'd be a wolf. An animal."

"Don't say that. I don't think of you as one. I love you."

He gave a joyless laugh at her declaration.

"I may walk on two legs, but I have urges just like any animal. I could kill you at a moment's notice if I didn't control myself. I don't want you to deal with that."

"That wouldn't be an issue if I was a wolf just like you. I could hold my own."

"But then you would be forced to control your strength with others. To deal with that inner pain."

"So you would rather me die of old age, while you remain young?"

"I would rather have you safe but for a few decades then dead at my father's hand."

Her mouth gaped open and her eyes welled. But her tears didn't fall.

What the fuck was he doing? Why was he picking a fight with her? Yes, these thoughts were not new. But he could've spoken rationally with her. Now he was cutting her down because some sick fuck had scared him with the images of losing her.

"Fix this. You hurt her."

His wolf, again, spoke true.

"I can't believe you just said that." Willow's voice held a trace of pain, but that slight pain was overshadowed by her anger.

He opened his mouth to speak, but she held up her hand.

"All this time I thought you would change your mind. I sat back patiently waiting for you to realize that, if I didn't change, I would die. Leaving you alone. Reed told me to wait, that you would come around. And I stupidly believed him."

She'd spoken to her brother about this? His thoughts jumbled as he panted in anger.

Willow heaved a breath and continued, "I don't understand you, Jasper. You say you love me, yet you don't want to be with me forever? If you love me so much, why can't you give me the tools for me to protect myself?"

"Are you saying I'm not strong enough to protect you?"

"Oh, you stupid wolf! That's not what I'm saying at all. And you know it."

Damn it, he didn't want to fight with her. What the fuck? The Centrals didn't want his Willow. No, they wanted to hurt his Pack. This whole mess lay on his shoulders. If he hadn't been so brazen as to take a human mate and hadn't failed to protect her in the first place, this never would have happened.

"I never should have walked into that bakery," he whispered. "I never should have chosen you. This shouldn't have happened."

He knew he whispered his pain at his failures at protecting his mate, yet he didn't know Willow had heard until he looked up and saw her face.

Pain. Utter betrayal. Hurt crossed her face as the first tear fell down her pale cheek.

"Dammit, Jasper. She doesn't know what you mean."

"Willow, that's not—"

Again, she held up a hand and shook her head.

"I see." No emotion. No more tears.

The love of his life simply blinked twice then walked out the door. Out of his life.

———

THE DOOR CLOSED QUIETLY BEHIND her as Willow walked to the end of the patio. A cool breeze chilled her bare arms, yet she couldn't feel it.

I never should have walked into that bakery. I never should have chosen you. This shouldn't have happened.

Throat too dry to swallow, she shook head, begging for rational thoughts. Those words. How could he have said that? Daunting pain cascaded through her body as a chasm opened in her heart. A fog settled over her as she slowly stepped off the porch to the path leading away from their home. No, his home. Confusion and loss swallowed her whole in a pain that fractured her heart, pulsating down her arm, tingling her fingers. It was like when a limb fell asleep, but she couldn't move for fear, if she did, she'd lose feeling forever.

Jasper didn't want her.

Willow walked to a bench at the end of the path and sat down slowly. What would she do now? All her life she'd been alone, struggling to find connections. Had she tried too hard? Made something out of nothing? Jasper had come into her bakery and asked her out on a single date. He didn't ask to have her shackled to him. He didn't even want her around long enough to be his true mate. He would wait for her to die off then find a mate he actually wanted. Her mark was simply a pity bite so she didn't have to die in the hands of Corbin and his cronies.

How was she going to get home? Did she even have a home? How was she going to live without him? A chill of loneliness spread over her. She couldn't breathe. Everything was gone. Destroyed. Sobs locked in her throat, but her tears wouldn't fall.

Willow sprang from the bench and blindly ran into the forest. Away from the pain and loss that Jasper brought with him. It wasn't smart or safe, but who cared? She just needed a minute to breathe. Then she'd leave and move on. She wouldn't wallow. That wouldn't solve anything. After a few minutes she stopped, her breath coming in ragged pants.

A branch cracked, shattering the illusion of safety and silence around her. Willow went on alert. Dammit, why had she just left leave like that? She looked over her shoulder as a shadow passed. She opened her mouth to scream, but a hand came behind her and closed over her mouth.

She felt a painful prick in her arm, and as her mind became fuzzy, she realized the prick had been a needle injecting something into her bloodstream. She fought to keep her eyes open, praying she would see her attacker.

"Shh, Willow. You'll be taken care of."

That voice. She knew that voice, yet she couldn't pull her thoughts together. The person behind her lifted her up and carried her deeper in to the forest. She tried to scream again as she struggled against the oncoming blackness but could find no energy to make a sound.

Jasper wouldn't come for her this time.

CHAPTER SIXTEEN

Willow opened her eyes and, for the second time in her life, woke in a strange room. She blinked, her eyes straining against the bright overhead lights. Memories of a voice and a needle flooded her mind. Not again.

Unlike her last kidnapping – *geez that sounds pathetic* – she wasn't locked away, chained in a dungeon. No, this time she lay across a magnificent king-sized bed, sinking into the lush mattress and surrounded by down pillows and comforters. All in all, quite a different arrangement.

Dark colors filled the room. A deep royal blue antique finish layered the walls with a textured design that soothed yet made her feel closed in. Heavy, gray drapes covered the large windows blocking all natural light, but the overhead light illuminated the room in an eerie glow. Cherry furniture carved with plump cherubs stood in place around her. The gaze from the cherubs' little eyes bore down on her, their presence sucking in the stale air, suffocating her.

Crap, why was she lying there, thinking about the decorations in the room and creepy accessories? Apparently, being taken hostage numerous times had taken a toll on her brain. She needed to get out of here. She tried to swallow, but the cotton taste in her mouth caused her tongue to stick to the roof of her mouth.

"Water?"

At the sound of the voice so near her. Willow screamed.

"Oh no, precious, you mustn't do that."

The cruel man who'd held her chains the last time, Corbin, smiled. He walked to the side of the bed with a glass of water in his hand, the coolness of the glass condensing the water droplets in the stifling humidity of the room. He set the glass on the table and sat on the bed next to her. She wanted to scream again, but she wouldn't. Because he could kill her at any moment, she didn't need to antagonize him.

"Here, my darling, drink up. We can't have you dying of thirst, can we?" He smirked and she cringed.

She didn't want to *die* at all. And why the hell was he acting so nice? This sickly pleasant Corbin worried her more than the yelling man she'd met before. Though her hands were free, his reflexes were far faster than hers even when she was at her best. No, attacking him here without a plan would not be wise. Dammit, she wished Jasper were here.

Great. Why did she have to think about him? He didn't even want her anymore. How pathetic could she get?

He placed the glass to her closed lips. What if he drugged her?

"I've already drugged you. I'm not in the mood to do more at the moment. Drink." His voice carried a lethal edge, sending shivers down her spine.

She opened her mouth, letting the cool liquid slide down her achy throat. She gulped as he tipped the glass more, forcing her to finish it all. Fear pooled in her stomach. No matter her thoughts, Corbin held the control, the power. Even a simple task such as drinking would be on his terms. Not hers. Willow forced herself not to cry. Even a single tear would allow the monster a victory over her that she couldn't allow. She only prayed that his mood wouldn't change until she found a way out. Bile rose in her throat at what he could do when she lost conciseness, or what would happen if she didn't.

Oh God, I just want to go home.

A sob choked her as she remembered she had no home.

"Oh don't cry, my pet." Corbin took a cloth napkin and dabbed the corner of her mouth and eyes. "Nothing good comes of crying. And I haven't done anything to warrant your begging for redemption yet."

She bit her lip and forced herself not to cry out.

Corbin slowly slid his hand down her neck, across the bite Jasper had left the night before, then down her arm, to rest on her stomach. That's when she realized sometime during her captivity, they'd changed her into a soft cotton, low-cut blue dress. She shuddered at the thought of Corbin's hands on her bare skin. He bunched the fabric in his fist and leaned over her.

His nostrils flared as he spat, "You smell like that bastard. I'm going to have great joy in replacing that." He smiled again, and she closed her eyes, afraid of his wrath.

The feel of his fingers on her knee as he brushed her skin made her stomach revolt. *Oh God, I don't want him to touch me.* Memories of her last time with him and the feel of his hands assailed her. In those few short months with Jasper, she hadn't forgotten Corbin liked playing with her. Those instances of vulnerability and the inability to protect herself still haunted her. She didn't want any new horrors added to her already shaky past.

"You never should've left. You can't imagine all the pain that went into getting you here again. Well, I suppose you will know the pain soon enough, won't you?" Corbin tilted his head and laughed. Her stomach almost heaved to spew the remnants of her lunch.

Willow took a deep breath and thought on what he said. How had he accomplished entering Redwood land to take her? Had he had help? The familiar voice before the needle prick came to mind. Who'd attacked her? She tried to think, but something fogged her mind. Dammit, it was right there but faded out of her reach. Could it have been magic? She didn't know enough about witches and other paranormals to really make a guess. Ignorance of the unknown grated on her.

"Honestly, Willow. You need to pay attention." Corbin gripped her chin, forcing her gaze to his. "That's better, my sweet. Now, why did you leave me? We were just getting to fun part when that bastard pup took you from me. You were a naughty girl, letting him bite you like that in front of my Pack and his brothers. *Tsk tsk.* I think I could do something with that vixen you hide." He leaned over and brushed his lips against hers. Tears leaked from her eyes as she tried not to pull away, afraid he'd do worse than kiss her if she did.

Corbin licked her tears and moaned. "Fearful tears. One of my favorites. Now that Jasper tossed you to the curb, I can take you. At least until I get tired of you. But if you're a good girl, that can be a long, long while."

How did he know that? Jasper, please come for me.

Dammit, she couldn't just sit here and take this. As quickly as she could, she clawed her hand against his face and scratched him with her nails. *Thank God for her new manicure, courtesy of Cailin.* While he howled in surprise, she kneed him in the groin and jumped off the bed, the door in sight.

Hands wrapped around her waist and threw her in to the wall. Stars and swirls shattered behind her eyelids as the side of her head slammed into the wall. Corbin's fingers dug into her arm, pain ricocheting from his firm grip. He pulled her to his chest, inhaling her scent, before throwing her down to the bed.

Willow screamed, frantically trying to run for her life through her dazed mindset. Her attacker slapped her hard across the face, splitting her lip. He took her arms and legs, chaining them to the bed with a built-in harness. His ease at the task almost made her vomit.

"I told you not to fight. I'm going to enjoy teaching you how to obey." His voice revolted her and caused a nasty shiver to slide down her body.

"Corbin!" Hector's voice bellowed in the room. "Get off her. You can play later. We have things to discuss first."

Willow sighed in relief when Corbin stood and walked to stand behind Hector as the other man walked into the room. She tensed again when she looked up and saw she was now in a room with two men who could rip her to shreds in a second and a third who felt familiar.

The man had dark hair and dark eyes, and he tilted his head and stared at her. If he hadn't looked like he could kill her and enjoy doing it, she thought he could pass for a wicked angel. But there was nothing angelic about the man when he smiled at her.

Oh God, he's worse than Corbin. Darker.

When she took a deep breath to gather her courage for what was to come, she detected a hint of sulfur on the air. What the hell had the Centrals done?

"Willow, child. I'm glad you could be with us today." Hector smiled at her, and she scoffed? Really?

She must have spoken out loud because his smile slipped just a bit. Though he didn't resonate a true evil quality, as Corbin and the other man did, Hector still carried a ruthless power that curled out from his pores.

He sat on the bed, taking the seat Corbin had vacated. He leaned over her and brushed the hair from her face.

"What do you want?" Her voice sounded rusty, pained.

Hector smiled a sad smile and whispered, "Darling, you're just a tool. A necessity. Something to be used and discarded when the time comes."

She needed Jasper. No matter what happened between the two of them, she still loved him. He would come. He had to.

"You should've just stayed with us," Hector said. "But now we have to deal with you. It's no offense to you, darling. But business is business. Power is power." His eyes glowed when he said it. His wolf must be rising to the surface. She prayed he held control.

"Why are you doing this?" Tears ran down her cheeks, pooling on the sides of her face and into the pillow.

Hector sighed as if he regretted even talking to her. But if she kept talking, that would give her more time to plan her escape. If she could. Plus any information he gave could prove useful. At least she hoped.

"The Redwoods have too much power." His chest heaved as he passionately spewed his diatribe. "They think they are superior, but they are nothing. Weak. Pathetic. It should be me. My Pack. Those fucking Redwoods took too much from me. Bastards."

"The fucking arrogant assholes blend into the humans, thinking them equals. That is a disgrace to who we are, what we can do. We are werewolves; yet they don't relish their strength. No, they just dictate what the other Packs can do. Well, that will be no more. Soon, the

Redwoods will understand exactly who they are messing with and who will be their master."

All three men laughed. They were crazy. Utterly insane. And they held her captive.

"Nobody understands my brilliance except my son. But they will."

This couldn't be going anywhere good.

"You see, my wife thought she'd go against me. She took our daughters and tried to run to those Redwoods. She underestimated me, but don't worry, I took care of her. And just to make sure she knew her last act wouldn't go punished with merely her death, I made sure she knew one of her daughters would die for the greater good."

Holy shit. He'd killed his own wife and daughter for his psychotic plan? She needed to get the hell out of here.

"Corbin is strong and will walk beside me as we kill the other Packs. All of them. He will help me rule."

Willow looked over at the crazy man's son and saw an odd smile on his face. He was hiding something, but she had no clue what, but something other than the craziness was going on in this family. Maybe she could use it. She inwardly sighed. Yeah, right. What could she do? She was alone. No Jasper. Any self-defense moves he'd taught her wouldn't work against werewolves. Why hadn't she changed already? Resentment and anger over Jasper's betrayal rose up again, but she stamped it down. This was not the time to reminisce over a lost love.

"And because of the generous sacrifice of my daughter, I now have my ally, Caym." He turned and swept his arm out, bringing their attention to the dark angel in the room.

"Caym is a demon, bound to me and my purpose. I may have had to kill my niece and daughter to accomplish this, but it's no matter. I have another daughter if needed. And with the aid of Caym, and the other demons he will bring forth, we can kill the Redwoods and rule. And once I am the Master Alpha of all the Packs, I will kill the humans or use them as slave labor, finally bringing them down to their rightful place."

The depth and depravity of his plans sickened her. If not for her own survival, she needed to get out and tell someone what she'd been told.

"Why are you telling me this?" She knew her voice couldn't hid her fear, as she choked out the words.

Hector smirked at her and patted her bound hand.

"Because, dear, you will die soon."

That's what she thought he'd say. She wasn't ready to die. Not by a long shot. Her heart sped and she clenched her fists.

"I will slowly and painfully beat you until I am satisfied. Then I will give you to Corbin, who will peel the skin from your body. Finally, we will leave you for dead. There will be no escape, he will not be able to save you and you can't stop us. Who, my dear, could you tell then?"

Willow finally lost her battle with her nerves, screamed.

CHAPTER SEVENTEEN

The door closed had with a click, and Jasper stood on the other side, numb. She'd left. Fuck. That wasn't what he'd meant to say. He only meant to prove to her that it was his fault, not hers. That the Centrals wanted her because he chose her. Not because he didn't want her. That was the furthest thing from the truth. He loved Willow more than breath, yet when the words tumbled from his lips, he hadn't thought of the ramifications. Holy hell. What had he done?

Unable to deal with the feelings that overwhelmed him, Jasper sat and stared into space, thinking of all that had gone wrong and all the ways he'd failed her. Finally, after what seemed like hours, he felt the nudge of his wolf, so strong it was almost impossible to ignore.

"You broke our mate's heart, then let her walk out of this house. Go out there and fix it, or you aren't the Beta I thought you were."

His wolf's disappointed tone cut deep. Shit, he needed to get to her.

Jasper shifted his feet to the door and opened it, praying she'd merely walked to the patio to compose herself and might be sitting there still. When he found it empty, Jasper's heart sank just a little bit more. He inhaled, finding that sweet cinnamon scent, and followed it down the path. He trailed it until he came upon a bench. The scent was concentrated in that spot, as if she'd sat there for a while. Curious and getting more worried, Jasper again walked along the path until he found her scent once more, this time hovering near the entrance to the forest.

What the hell had she been thinking walking into the dense brush right after they'd found that body?

"She wasn't thinking, dumbass. You destroyed her."

His heart raced as he agreed with this wolf. He quickly jogged into the forest, hoping she would be there. *Please God, let her be there.* Finally, after what felt like too long a trek, he found a flattened part of the undergrowth where she must have sat down. But where had she gone?

A shift in the breeze and another murky wolf's scent carried on the wind. Along with that was a tangy sweet scent. Fuck. The scents weren't strong, rather a muted replica of their former selves. They surrounded the place where Willow rested, yet no trail left the spot, as if something magical had swept it away.

Oh God.

They'd taken her.

Again.

Jasper fell to his knees, pain ricocheting from his heart down his body. He howled in agony. Bile rose to his throat as he fought the urge to vomit.

He'd failed. Again. Tears streaked his face as anger burned through his veins. Those fuckers would pay.

His wolf howled, slamming into Jasper's body, begging for release. Claws erupted from his fingertips, as he fought for control. He couldn't shift. Not now. He needed to be human to find her. To get help. His muscles and tendons stretched along his back as his bones began to break. Jasper inhaled, struggling for control.

"Not now." His voice sounded guttural. Fuck, his facial bones were already reconstructing themselves.

He closed his eyes and pulled on the power within. The urge to change subsided, as the power washed over his body, soothing his wolf.

Thank God.

He reached into his pocket and pulled out his phone. His fingers shook as he dialed Adam's number. As the enforcer, Adam would know what to do, rather than run in half-cocked without a plan. Jasper's mind was too muddled and pained to formulate one.

The phone rang twice before Adam finally answered.

"Hello?" Adam's voice sounded slurred from sleep.

"Adam, they took her. Come to the forest outside our home." His voice broke at the end, pain and hurt again radiating throughout his body.

Adam growled. "Fuck. I'm on my way. Don't move" The connection ended with a click, and Jasper put away his phone.

He sat on the spot where Willow had lain, tears dropping onto the dead leaves. They needed to find her, save her before the Centrals did to her what they did to that Talon wolf.

What would he do when he found her? Not if, but when. How could she ever forgive him for letting her be kidnapped? What could he do?

"Jasper." Adam's voice startled him.

Shit, he needed to get his mind off the unknown and find Willow.

"What happened?"

"We fought, and she left."

Adam's eyes darkened. "I see. Fought about what?"

"She wants to go through the transformation. But I said it was too risky. I couldn't lose her."

His brother's voice deepened. "Go on."

Jasper gulped. "Then I said I shouldn't have gone into her bakery. Because I did, she was in danger. I know I'm an idiot. I didn't mean it the way it sounded."

Adam's fist connected with his jaw, almost breaking the bone. Caught off guard, he couldn't keep his balance and he flung backwards, his head slamming into the ground.

"What the fuck?" Jasper snarled.

"Let me get this straight. You told your mate she wasn't good enough to be a wolf."

Jasper opened his mouth to defend himself, but Adam leaned down and punched him again.

"I'm not done yet. After you said it was okay that she'd die long before you did, you then told her you never should have been with her in the first place. Did I miss anything?" Adam's chest rose and fell in heavy pants.

"That is not exactly how it happened, nor was it my intent." But coming from Adam's lips, he was surprised Willow hadn't stabbed him before walking out the door. He sounded like an ass. A cruel and uncaring ass.

"You won't be hearing any argument from me."

"Fuck your intent. Don't you know how lucky you are? You have a mate. And you let her walk out of the house after you practically ripped her heart out. I would kill you myself if it wouldn't upset Mom."

"I know what I said doesn't make sense. But don't you see? It was my fault she got hurt in the first place."

"You egotistical bastard. No, it wasn't. That fucking lunatic Hector and his equally crazy son, Corbin, are the ones at fault for putting her in danger. Not you."

"Fine. But if I let her change—"

"Let her? You fucking idiot. You don't *let* your mate do anything. She's her own person. If she wants to change into a wolf, and it sounds like she does, she probably only wanted your approval because she loves you and wants to make you happy."

Dammit. His heart hurt. Why was he such an idiot?

"But the shift is dangerous. I couldn't risk losing her." The last of his arguments sounded lame and unworthy even to his own ears.

"So you would let her die?"

"I didn't want her to be killed from the change."

"But you would rather lose your mate than have her by your side into your years?"

"Adam, you above all, know what it's like to lose a mate. I didn't want lose her." As soon as the words left his lips, he wanted to take them back.

His younger brother slammed into his body, forcing him back to the ground. Adam straddled his body, fists flying. Jasper put his arms in front of his face to protect himself, but didn't hit back. He deserved it.

Adam hit and clawed, screaming in agony. Jasper had always known there was pain and anger just beneath the surface of his brother, but he'd never seen the immense brutality of it. Why the hell had he brought up Adam's dead mate?

Finally, Adam lifted off of him, breathing heavily, and stood. Blood marred his knuckles, and Jasper knew his own face and arms wouldn't look much better.

"You will *never* bring up Anna again. You don't have the right. I lost *everything* because of those bastards, and yet I stood back and didn't retaliate because of my loyalty to this Pack. You let your mate walk out of your home without a fight because you were an ass and you hurt her. You are nothing. You don't deserve the power and station you wield nor do you deserve Willow. You better pray she is still alive. Because if anything has happened to her, I will kill you myself." Adam held out a hand. When Jasper gripped it, Adam hauled him to his feet.

"I will help you find her and bring her back. Not for you, but for her. With all that has happened in her life, she deserves happiness. Not a mate who would hold her back, for fear of his loss. And you will not force her to be with you. If she doesn't want you after this, because it is clear she left with a purpose, I will take care of her."

Jasper's wolf rose to the surface at the thought of his brother being with his mate.

His voice deepened to an almost growl. "You don't touch her."

"I don't want her sexually, you ass. But I will protect her like you should have. I don't want another mate. I've already been through that; I won't go through it again." Sadness and utter exhaustion covered Adam's features.

"Adam, I love her. She's everything to me."

"Then prove it. Once we find her, let her change. You both deserve it."

"I know that now."

"But you better do something to prove you deserve her. I won't let you hurt her again."

Reed came out of the darkness, anger evident on his features. "What the fuck are you two doing? You think fighting like a couple of asshats will solve anything?"

"Adam and I just needed to have a heart-to-heart. We're going."

"Good, because as the two of you waste time, the Centrals have your mate and you know it. Let's get going."

They ran to Reed's truck. As Jasper tried not to think about what could be happening to his Willow at this very moment. He prayed to God that his stupid, callous mistake didn't cost her her life.

———

WILLOW'S BREATH came in shallow pants, waiting for Corbin's next move. After Hector's announcement of her eminent death, the prodigal son quickly removed her chains and carried her outside to a grass circle. The layout of stones reminded her somewhat of the Pack circle in the Redwood den. The pulsating magic of centuries of tradition she felt within the other circle calmed her. This one, however, held a sickly and fearful bitter after taste that made her skin crawl.

Her head lulling to the side, she blinked then stared down at the field below her. They had chained her to a wooden table in the center of the circle and angled it so she could see her surroundings. A blessing or a curse, she didn't know. The ground beneath her held a rusty hue, rather than the natural chestnut and tawny soil on the outskirts of the circle. Bile tried to worm its way up her throat as she tried to suppress the thoughts about what might have caused the dirty crimson overlay.

Another difference was, unlike the Redwood's circle, other than the three men corralling her, no others were present to bear witness to her torture. Her shame. Resigned to her fate, she prayed for quick death. Contrary to the Central's beliefs, Jasper wouldn't come for her. He'd told her he didn't want her, and she'd left. With every sneer and cruel promise from Hector and Corbin, Willow lost just a little bit more of who she was and what hope she could have held. A sense of loss and confusion enveloped her. No one would save her – not even herself.

Corbin's hand struck Willow's face. Hard. Pain shot through her cheek and jaw, as her eyes watered. She screamed, her voice breaking as she choked. She tried to squirm away, but the chains bit into her skin. After what seemed like hours, though it could only have been minutes from what Willow knew, Hector gave Corbin permission to begin his fun. She'd never thought she would miss the demented Alpha's crushing blows and slaps, but his son's ruthless and menacing smirk while he yielded his own punishment seeped into her soul and chipped away at her sanity. A fast end would surely be coming soon, right?

Hector stood in the center of the circle with an odd smile on his face. The demon, Caym, stood off to the side, also with a smile on his face. Though she could barely see it, as he continually looked off in the distance, his gaze on the outskirts of the circle. Like he waited for something, or someone, to come and interrupt their play at any moment. Her head hurt, and her thoughts had jumbled together. She closed her eyes, not aware of the others anymore.

The night had long since faded into the daylight hours. The cloudy overcast sky cast a sepia tone over the field, resembling an old picture. She tried to imagine she was just an observer, not a participant in this nightmare. A cool breeze brushed her skin, as Willow tried to forget where she was and focus on something else. Something more pleasant then the grueling pain inflicted by a lunatic werewolves. Colorful, yet dead leaves fell to the ground in a gust of wind. Wasn't it an odd twist of fate that as leaves poetically withered and died their very essence would help create the pure beauty and elegance of the flora to come in the future? Would that happen to her when Corbin finally grew tired of his games? No, that wouldn't happen. She was just a human. A dying one.

"Willow, you aren't paying attention." Corbin's voice grated on her already frayed nerves, his anger oozing out in each syllable.

Corbin slapped her again. It hurt, yet the numbness from a constant attack settled over her. *Ah, sweet release.*

The light glistened on the tip of a knife he pulled out of his tool kit. Yes, the man actually had a tool kit for these special occasions. God help her. Her heart beat in a staccato pattern in her ear as he leaned over her body and smiled.

White, hot pain flashed in her side as he cut a shallow slice in her abdomen. He did it twice more as she screamed and cried. Corbin laughed and licked her blood from the knife. He moved his arms and the tip of his knife rested on her cheek. Willow froze in fear.

"I'm going to show that bastard pup you belong to me, if only for a little while." With a flick of his wrist, he dug the blade into her cheek. Salty tears pooled and down her face, mingling with her warm blood on her wind-cooled skin. If by some miraculous reason she survived this, she knew that final cut would scar her face for life.

Corbin stood, raising the knife above his head, and she flinched. He abruptly stopped lowering his arm. Instead of stabbing her, he threw back his head and laughed.

"Oh thank you for your fear. I relish in it."

He moved again, thrusting the knife toward her. She closed her eyes, ready for death.

The dull thunk of the blade embedding into the wooden table filled her ears.

Fucker keeps playing games.

He took her chin in his hand and forced her gaze to the knife buried to the hilt.

"That could have been you, my sweet. But I have been kind thus far." Corbin grinned with hooded eyes. "Not anymore."

Oh God.

He leaned over her head and strapped it to the table at an odd angle. "I won't bite you. No, you don't deserve the blessed gift that comes of my bite. But I will show you what it is like to marvel in the presence of a true wolf.

"You will never become a wolf. I will leave you here to die. And Jasper will come to find your rotting corpse. Too late to find the one he loved and lost."

"Jasper won't come for me." Her voice sounded rusty. She prayed Jasper would be safe from this tyrannical kingdom.

Corbin slapped her again and his palm connected with her cut. Though it stung a bit, she blessedly could hardly feel a thing.

"Oh, the fucker will. Believe me. Already they are on their way, though they have met our roadblocks. But those they fight are only our lower powered wolves that need to be culled. Once they get through that hurdle, he will be here."

God no. Please let him be lying.

"Even if Jasper doesn't love you, in truth, his wolf thinks you're his mate. Oh, Jasper will be forced, again, to try and save you, even if a whore like you doesn't deserve it. But his time he'll be too late."

Not Jasper. Corbin could do what he wished with her, but Jasper had to be safe.

"Now that I've secured your head to the table, if you close your eyes at all, I will prolong your suffering. Do you want that? No? I didn't think so."

He stood back and stripped himself of his clothing. Corbin howled then began the process of turning into his wolf. Willow watched as his muscles flexed and tore, and his bones broke and reformed. Fur sprouted from under his skin covering his body. His facial features lengthened; a muzzle and long canines dominated his face. Soon a midnight black wolf with chocolate brown paws stood beside her. She looked deep into his full black eyes. That's why they looked odd. Every other wolf she'd seen had a gold rim surrounding their normal eye color. Corbin's were a deep black, as if to swallow her soul along with killing her body.

Her breath hitched, and her pulse sped, beating in her ears. No tears fell from her eyes. She would not beg for her life. This cruel abomination of man was not worth it.

Corbin leapt toward her.

It really was a magnificent jump.

Claws ripped into her flesh, in a delayed reaction, she felt no pain. Caym moved into her field of vision and crooked a corner of his mouth into a grotesquely beautiful smile. A scream tore from her throat and the large tears in her flesh finally registered to her brain. He dug into her legs, stomach, arms. These weren't superficial cuts. She'd die. Soon.

Only her face, with the large cut from before, remained safe from his wrath. Excruciating agony filled her as she kept her eyes open. If she closed them, he would take longer. She didn't think she could last must longer anyway. Blood pooled around her body as black spots formed in her vision.

Jasper. I'm sorry. I never should've left. Forgive me.

Finally, his growls ceased as blessed darkness pulled her toward peace.

. . .

THE GROUND DUG into Willow's back. The air cool against her skin. A voice whispered in her ear. Willow didn't want to wake up. Why couldn't they leave her alone?

"Willow, wake up. You need to swallow this, it will help with the pain and aid with your healing. Please, wake up."

Willow opened her eyes and focused on the blurry image in front of her. Dark eyes and dark hair over smooth light mocha skin. Familiar. But who was she? Was she an angel? What happened? Why couldn't they leave her alone? She was dead.

She opened her mouth to speak but pain erupted in her head.

"Shh, don't try to speak. I'm Ellie, Corbin's sister. I'm here to help." She gave a sad smile and brushed the hair from Willow's face. "Please, drink." The woman named Ellie tipped the cup to her parched lips and forced a revolting, pickled liquid down her throat.

As soon as it hit her stomach, warmth radiated through her system and her blinding pain subsided.

Ellie set to removing some of her bindings and cleaned up some of the blood. How on earth was this kind and gentle woman related to those sadistic bastards? Tears streaked down the young woman's face as she pressed a cool cloth to Willow's cheek.

"I'm so sorry."

"Not your fault. Thank you." It hurt to speak, but whatever was in that cup had helped.

"Help is coming for you, Willow."

Willow just smiled and shook her head.

Ellie smiled back and kissed her forehead.

Finally, she fell back into a deep sleep. Maybe Ellie was right. Maybe Jasper would come after all.

CHAPTER EIGHTEEN

J asper tightened his jaw as his teeth sank into fur and flesh. He twisted his neck in a quick jerk, and the sound of his opponent's spine cracking in pieces echoed off the trees. The rust colored wolf grew limp, and he released him. The dead wolf fell to the ground among his compatriots. Foolish weak wolves thought they could fight against some of the top of the Redwood Pack.

When they'd first come upon the clearing, a group of fourteen low-ranking Centrals prowled among the trees on the outskirts of the forest, blocking their path. Jasper and his brothers calmly got out of the truck, as calm as they could be with tension and fury running through their veins, and changed into their wolves. As their animal counterparts, they bit, clawed, and attacked their way through the interfering wolves. With each strike, Jasper could only think of Willow. Was he too late? Would he reach her in time? What would he find when he got there?

Each minute that passed added another rock to the pile in his churning stomach of nerves. He called on his inner power and quickly shifted back to human, his brothers soon following.

"Shit, that was too easy." Reed was barely out of breath, as they all grabbed their clothing littered around the truck.

"I know. They were only a distraction. A delay." Anger burned in his veins. Those fuckers deserved their death. He wouldn't waste a moment of pity on their lifeless corpses. Hector and his son had his mate at this very moment. Nothing was more important that finding her. Saving her.

A lock of his hair brushed the back of his neck as the wind shifted. Something familiar tugged on his sense. Jasper inhaled. A faint trace of cinnamon.

Willow.

He threw back his head and howled, running through the trees, following the fading scent like a lifeline. He heard the gentle crunch of leaves behind him. His brothers followed, flanking him and protecting against unseen forces.

The familiar sickly sweet and tangy scent from before overlaid Willow's intoxicating cinnamon scent. Though it confirmed the connection between the Centrals and the murder of the Talon girl, Jasper could only think of running toward his Wil. Tree branches and stones cut his bare feet and arms as he hurried through the brush, keeping an eye on his surroundings.

"*Find her.*"

Jasper didn't need his wolf's simply phrased demand to keep going. He could only pray she was alive. Only pray that she wasn't hurt. Too badly. The rumors concerning the Central Pack scared the shit out of him if they proved true with his Willow.

A branch scraped his cheek. Warm droplets of blood ran down his chin. He broke into the clearing.

Oh my God.

Willow lay prostrate on a wooden table, like a ruthless sacrifice to a god he would never know. A bloodied angel. Her brown hair flowed in the wind, giving her stilled body a ghostly movement.

Dark crimson pools fringed the table holding her. Burnt orange and yellow leaves adhered to the sticky substance in a cruel collage of pain and hatred. Chains lay on the ground, not attached to her. Someone had released her, but he couldn't think about that now. The dead grass of the circle looked like a wasteland of Pack culture and tradition, lacking the very essence of goodness and solidarity that made his Pack whole. No other sounds, breaths, and life signs remained, other than that of his brothers and, hopefully, his mate.

"Willow!"

A gut-wrenching scream ripped from his throat and he forced his leaden limbs to action, running to her side. Blood pounded in his ears. The sound of Reed's shout of disbelief and Adam's cry of pain reached him. But Jasper couldn't focus on them.

He knelt by her side, tears streaking his face. Blood spattered almost every inch of her body. How on earth could one small human lose that much and still live? One large knife wound split her cheek. Slices and gashes covered her skin. Bile rose to this throat at the hint of muscles and organs though some of the deeper cuts.

Her chest rose and fell, slowly, raggedly. He exhaled in relief.

She was alive.

Thank God.

Careful not to touch anything that might hurt her, though it didn't look like that could be avoided, he caressed the clean side of her face. The coolness of her skin brought him out of his reverie.

"Willow." Though he meant his voice to carry and wake her, it came out on only a whisper.

"You must change her, Jasper." Adam's voice was a void of emotion.

Not an option.

"I can't, Adam. Do you know what I would have to do? I can't hurt her any more than she already is. My wolf won't allow it." As it was, his wolf whimpered, struggling not to curl next to its mate and pray.

"Jasper, we can't do it. We don't have that kind of power. Only you, Kade, and Dad do." Reed's voice broke.

"It has to be you, Jasper. You need to be the one who changes her. Only you can save her." Adam's voice held no pity in his voice, only strength of acceptance.

Sobs wracked his body as he gained the courage to do what must be done.

God, I promise that I will leave her alone or do whatever she needs, but please, let her be okay. Don't let my foolish mistake of careless words and not being able to protect her take her life. Please.

He took a steadying breath and stood to strip out of his clothes.

His brothers gave him an encouraging nod, and Jasper called his power, to change into his wolf. It took precious energy from him every time he forced the change, but only his determination to save his mate gave him the strength.

When he changed, he padded to his mate's side and licked her face, whimpering at her wounds. He couldn't be the man during this, so he let his wolf come to the surface, relishing the power and animalistic sense of cohesiveness. Almost like watching through a haze, he sobbed and nuzzled Willow.

Around him, Adam and Reed checked the perimeter, then knelt to hold Willow down, just in case by some twist of fate, she moved or struggled during the transformation. He huffed out a breath, nuzzled her one more time, then bit the fleshly part her arm.

A rush of pain through their shallow bond and a trickle of blood.

This was not a hunt and his final catch of his prey. No, this was his mate. He released her arm and bit into her shoulder, growling in fury. This shouldn't be him. But it was his penance. Only a small piece of it. She was in this situation because of him. Though with each bite and tear a small piece of him died, it would not be enough. Nothing he did would compensate for the fact she lay practically dead due to his words.

He bit again and again and, with each bite, released more of the enzyme that made them who they were. He prayed it took. Just a small about of the enzyme wouldn't do. It had to take.

A shaking hand on his back stopped him.

"That should be enough, Jasper," Reed choked.

With tear-filled eyes, Adam knelt and placed Jasper's jacket over her still form. Thank God he used his and not Adam's. Though he might not deserve it, the possessiveness of his wolf wouldn't allow another male to scent her. His brother knelt and carefully picked her up, holding her to his chest like fine china.

Jasper used his remaining energy to change back to human and tugged on his clothes, weariness dissolving into his bones. He walked toward Adam, hands outstretched for his mate.

Adam softly growled and shook his head, while Reed tried to step between them. What the fuck?

"Adam, now is not the time to push my buttons. Hand her to me. I need her." Need was such a weak word compared to what he felt.

His wolf growled in agreement.

"You must earn her trust back, Jasper. Do you really think you deserve to hold her?" His brother's chest heaved in growing anger.

What the hell? Did Adam really think it was okay to hold his mate hostage? He might have made the worst mistake of his life letting her walk out of their home, but Jasper needed her by his side.

"Adam, give me my mate. My wolf needs her to calm. And let's not forget that another spirit is melding itself to her right as we speak. She needs me. I need her. She's my everything."

Adam begrudgingly sighed then gently placed Willow into the cradle of Jasper's arms. Her cool weight settled on him like a long lost limb. Rightness. He brought her closer, inhaling her cinnamon scent. Their heartbeats synching into their familiar steady and living rhythm.

"When she wakes up, she gets a choice. This is not your decision," Adam growled.

Jasper nodded, without taking his eyes off her. Oh, he would give her the choice he should have from the beginning. But he would use every ounce of himself to prove his worth. His love.

Not a word left their lips on the trip back to the truck. Careful not to jar her injuries, yet hesitant to linger any longer in enemy territory, Jasper walked softly, whispering words of faith and hope to her.

As soon as they reached their home, North burst from the front door, his serious doctor face on. Thank God for his brother's medical skills. He might not be the true Healer of the Pack, but his hands held mercy and a healing power of their own.

Jasper held off his brother, in too much pain to let go of Willow even for the walk up the steps. His father and Kade stood in his living room, anxious and grieved expressions on their faces.

A muffled scream brought his attention to the bedroom doorway. His mother stood with one hand clasped over her mouth, the other on her chest.

"She's alive, Mom."

She nodded then walked hesitantly toward Willow.

"Someone has begun the healing process."

"I know. I scented a potion of some sort on her when we got there. I don't even want to think about what she looked like before."

"Jasper," North whispered, "we need to get her to the bedroom so I can make sure she's healing okay. I can already tell that some things are already healing, as some of these cuts have become smaller in the last two minutes, but I need to examine her."

Jasper walked past his family, into the bedroom and placed her in the center of the bed, watching as her wounds sealed. It had taken. *She'd change at the next moon. Thank God.* If only he'd have said okay to the transformation before. There was no doubt in his mind what she'd gone through far surpassed any pain and agony she would have endured in a sterile change, such as Mel's.

And it was his fault.

North and his mother set to work, cleaning off the blood, dirt, and gore while checking her vitals. Not needed, and feeling deservingly unwanted, Jasper walked back to the living room.

"She's going to be okay." Though his voice broke, he did not cry. Not now. He had to be strong for her, even though inside he was crumbling.

"I don't know how you did it, bro," Kade wondered aloud. "I could barely handle being in the same room when Dad changed Mel. How could you do that to Willow?"

"I had to, Kade. There was no one else. What else could I do? But, yes, I will have to live with the fact that, not only did I cause her to be there, I had to be the one who changed her." Shudders racked his body, remembering the taste of her blood on his tongue. *Never again.*

"I hope, son, that it will be enough power." His father's voice wrapped around him like an old blanket. "After going through so many changes and then having only a Beta to force the change, it will be tricky."

"It has to be enough." There was no other choice.

"Though she's healing now, there's no guarantee she will wake up. Or that she will survive the first change." Reed's statement was an unwelcome reminder of the tenuous nature of their race.

He left the room and returned to the bedroom while they discussed the ramifications of the Central's attack and what must be done. Though it was also his job, he couldn't focus on it. His sole reason for living lay prone on their bed, struggling to live.

North sat in a chair beside the bed, watching the rise and fall of her chest. Next to him, on the nightstand, the wooden angel figurine Jasper had made for Willow, stood vigil, her oak palms in prayer. He'd made it for her as a present, but had yet to give it to her. His mother scurried around the room, cleaning up the blood-soaked sheets and cloths, a determined look on her face. His mother was no wilting flower. No, royal werewolf blood ran through her veins, her pride in her heritage evident in the way she held her head high and had raised her family. It had also shown in how she took care of her Pack.

Jasper knelt on the floor next to Willow, taking in her gaunt features. Even pale, with the new scar on her cheek, beauty emanated from her skin, her soul. He closed his eyes and prayed.

Dear Lord, please let her live. Let her survive the change. She doesn't deserve anything that has happened to her. She gave up everything to be part of this Pack. Don't let her give her life as well. She can hate me with every fiber of her being, as long as she wakes. I'll do anything for her, even walk away. But, please, save her.

With a final thanks for her survival, Jasper opened his eyes and leaned over her to kiss her scarred cheek. Yes, no matter what, he would show her what she meant to him. To the Pack. He only hoped she could forgive him. Because he would never forgive himself.

CHAPTER NINETEEN

The lingering smell of sandalwood tickled Willow's nose. She inhaled, letting the familiar and, for some reason, loving scent, bring her closer to the surface of the deep pool she swam in. Floating higher and higher, she basked in the soothing warmth, wrapping around her like an old friend.

"Wake up, Willow. Open your eyes. It's time to begin."

Who was that?

The soft feminine voice didn't sound like anyone she knew. Wait, who did she know? Where was she?

Questions formed and tumbled in her mind, cooling the surrounding warmth as she tried to make sense of what was happening.

The sounds of footsteps on the lush carpet mingled with the crunching of grass beneath a person's foot. The bending of a blade of grass underneath a paw sounded crisp and clean. So near. A door opened to a home, followed by more footsteps.

Behind the intense sandalwood came the strong scent of freshly ground coffee, fatty bacon sizzling in a pan, the creamy scent of home-made pancakes with fresh whipped cream and berries. The sharp citrus smell of squeezed orange juice overpowered her scenes as she caught a whiff of wood shavings.

Why could she hear and smell all of this? What was going on?

Willow steadied herself and cracked open her eyes. Blinding light flooded her eyes, and she quickly closed them. A throaty moan escaped her lips, as she repeated the painful process again.

Was this bright light heaven?

Was she truly dead?

A figure sat beside where she lay. She squinted to clarify the image. Adam.

Disappointment swelled. Why had she thought Jasper would be next to her when she woke? *If* she woke. Obviously, she was nothing to him. Adam being here proved that.

"Willow?" Her brother-in-law's voice was barely a whisper, as though shocked to see her alive. At least that was what she thought, though it could be about what she looked like. Because if she looked like how she felt, then a pile of dirty laundry and rocks would be a step up right about now.

She tried to swallow, but her throat was too dry.

Adam placed a cup of cool water on her lips and she drank greedily. The gesture was so different from when Corbin had done the same when he held her captive, nearly drowning her in the process. It wasn't, however, the same as if Jasper had done it.

"Jasper?"

Dammit. She hadn't wanted to say that. Didn't want to show the world how much he still meant to her.

Adam smiled.

"He's sleeping on the couch. Took all I had in me to force him to sleep. He's been by your side for the four days you've been out. Watching you breathe, making sure you were as comfortable as possible."

"Four days?" How bad was she if she'd been out for *four* days?

"Yeah, Wil. You were down for the count." He smiled again and looked relived. "Thank God you're awake now."

"Who was the woman? You only mentioned you and Jasper in the house, but I heard a woman's voice telling me to wake up. Who was here?"

He looked confused. "It's only been me and Jasper for three days,

Wil. We didn't want to overwhelm you. We wanted to give you time to wake up, to heal. No woman has been here."

"*I'm your wolf, dear. Get used to me.*"

Holy crap.

"I'm a werewolf."

Adam smiled a sad smile, nodding. "Yes, Wil. That you are."

"Willow."

The sound of Jasper's awe-filled, raspy voice in the doorway forced her to turn toward him.

It looked as if he hadn't slept in days. Tired lines circled his haunted eyes. Was it because he'd seen what happened to her? Had he missed her?

Jasper looked guilty and sad, but every time she felt the burn in her chest from taking too deep a breath, her body ached. Old tears streaked his face and she knew she would forgive him for his words – eventually. He wasn't the one who'd gutted her. No, that had been those sadistic bastards Corbin and Hector. She tried to remember exactly what had happened, but only fuzzy memoires came to the surface.

She wanted him to come to her and hold her until she felt better. To make her feel whole again and help with her overwhelming senses. But then, she also wanted to kick his ass and throw him out of the room. Her dumbass male thought it was okay to think it was all about him and his choices?

Bastard.

Well, it was too late now, wasn't it? The wolf that whispered to her to love Jasper proved Jasper had been wrong and she could survive the bite. She *had* survived the bite. The contradicting thoughts and desires were no help to her already muddled brain.

Jasper stood in the doorway, hesitant to walk into the room. She could smell the worry and hope wafting off his skin. *Weird.* He clenched his fists, rocking on the balls of his feet, as though he were ready to spring into the room at a moment's notice. His worn jeans clung to his legs, and a wrinkled T-shirt stretched tight across his muscles brought a need to her she didn't want to think about.

Mate.

Was this what he dealt with every day? Why he was also so primal toward her during their lovemaking?

Not sure what I think about that.

"What happened, Jasper?" If he wasn't going to step into the room, well then she needed some answers.

He opened his mouth to speak, but Adam cut him off.

"What do you remember, Willow?"

Images flashed through her mind. A dark bedroom, then a wooden table. A cold glint of metal. Warm blood seeping from her pores. Slicing pain racking her body. Flashes of agony. Ghostly feelings that would never fade.

An inhuman whine escaped from her throat. She closed her eyes to try and block out the memories.

"Everything will be okay, Willow. Together, we are strong. And our mate is here."

She didn't want to rely on her mate. Look where that got her. Stupid new wolf didn't know anything. And frankly, she wasn't sure if Jasper even wanted her to be with him to begin with.

Her body ached when she tried to move, and a sharp pain stabbed in her side. Adam quickly put his hand on her arm to settle her. She whimpered again at the feel of his touch. No, this wasn't right. He wasn't hers and not what she needed.

Jasper growled from the doorway and rushed to her side. As soon as he neared, his mere presence calmed her wolf. *Idiot wolf. She wasn't supposed to feel for the man who didn't really love her.* If the damn thing had been a cat, she surely would've purred in contentment. *Annoying.*

Adam raised an eyebrow and released her arm, backing away slowly. He gave a nod to them both, and then retreated from the room, closing the door softly behind him. But from what she could tell from her newly enhanced senses, a closed door wouldn't stop him from listening in. However, the green eyes assessing her every feature put all thoughts of Adam out of her mind.

Jasper slid onto the bed, careful not to jar her body and cause her pain. How frustrating. He wasn't supposed to be nice and cautious of her well-being. He was supposed to hate her. How else would she have ended up in this situation?

"Willow, baby. I'm so sorry."

Tears filled her eyes. His admission didn't change the fact that she hurt. Everywhere.

"I didn't mean what I said," Jasper whispered. "I only meant that because you knew me, the Centrals wanted you. Not that *I* didn't want you."

Warmth filled her chest. Could she believe him? What if he changed his mind? Again. Could she really be that girl who waited for her husband, without something of her own? She didn't want to be worthless, depending on others, lacking a purpose.

"This was all my fault, Willow. I shouldn't have denied you your choices. I love you. I'm so happy that you're my mate and we are bound. But I wish the circumstances were different. That's what I could have said. Not mumbled my displeasure at others."

Hope cascaded through her, but she ignored it. She wasn't ready to trust him yet.

"I wanted you, Jasper. I've wanted you since you walked through my bakery door asking for cinnamon rolls." Her voice lowered, unsure.

"And I'm an idiot. You deserve a lifetime of happiness and are going to make a beautiful wolf. I shouldn't have let my fears step in the way of what you mean to me. I'm so sorry."

Tears fell down his cheeks, splashing the bedspread.

"I'm so sorry you got hurt and almost killed because of me."

Though he held some of the guilt on his shoulders, she couldn't allow him to carry it all.

"Jasper, it isn't your fault. I shouldn't have left the house and walked outside in the dark with a killer on the loose. Why don't you just slap a 'kill the dumb chick' sign on my forehead?"

"You weren't thinking clearly because of what I said. Don't take the blame for that."

"Fine, but that means you can't either. I can blame you for saying what you said, but not for me getting kidnapped and almost killed. No, that wasn't you. That was the Centrals. They were the ones who tortured me. Not you. I got hurt because those men are sadistic wolves who thrive on the pain and powerless feelings of others. They got someone to take me from my home." Her voice trembled.

A familiar, yet unrecognizable face flashed in her mind and a sharp pain radiated in her temples.

"What do you mean? Who took you? Do you remember?" Jasper's voice rose slightly.

Just as quickly as it came, the image faded away. *Damn.*

"I can't remember exactly. But something's there. I know it." Frustration clawed at her as she tried to latch onto a memory.

"Take your time. It will come to you."

She sighed. If only it would come now, rather than later. That way she could put it behind her.

"I want you to know that you can do anything you want once you get better. I'll do anything you want. You just need to heal."

What the hell was he talking about? Where was her strong-willed mate? Did he really feel that bad? She missed his Beta attitude.

"I don't want to do anything else. Stop blaming yourself."

He sighed. "Just get healthy."

"I guess I have a long time to be healthy now."

Jasper let out a watery laugh and leaned over to brush his lips lightly against hers. Her wolf howled at the contact. What an odd feeling, having another spirit sharing her space, feeling her moods and touches. She did agree with her wolf that his lips were soft and brought a needy feeling in her.

When he lifted his lips after the brief sweet kiss, his eyes widened. A slow smile crept over his face.

"I think my wolf likes yours. This could be interesting, watching them preen for each other."

Oh yes, very interesting.

"I forgive you, Jasper."

He stopped moving, and his smile fell from his face.

"Willow, don't you need more time?"

She smiled. "Shut up, Jasper. I forgive you. We need to move on, and I need your help. Kiss me again." She liked this more assertive side of hers. Maybe this werewolf thing won't be too bad.

"See, I told you I'm pretty awesome. You'll see the magnitude of my greatness."

Willow smiled at her wolf's cute attitude. It would take some getting used to, but totally do-able.

Jasper smiled and kissed her again. His lips parted and her tongue darted into his mouth. That sandalwood scent enveloped her, wrapping her in a cocoon. His sweet taste burst on her taste buds. *Dear God, did Jasper always taste this orgasmic?* She loved being a wolf. She tried to reach for him to urge him to continue, but he pulled back and kissed her forehead.

"You need your rest and I don't want you to overexert yourself. I'll be here when you wake up." He smiled, and she fell for him again. He left the room, closing the door as quietly as Adam had.

Yes, she loved him and forgave him. But that niggling feeling wouldn't go away. Could she trust him? She just didn't know.

"That's a foolish way to look at it. He's our mate."

Her wolf was too young to know what she was talking about.

"Hey I may be new to you, but that doesn't mean I'm young."

Huh?

"You're tired. I'll tell you all about spirits and the Moon Goddess later. But you can trust Jasper."

She so wanted to believe that. But she'd followed her heart blindly before and look at the pain it caused. No, it would take time and action rather than faith to find a new balance in their relationship.

———

JASPER WALKED BACK into the room twenty minutes later to check on her. Willow lay under to covers, sleeping soundly with a small smile on her face. The cuts and bruises had healed fully the day before, but she would still be sore. Too sore for his comfort. And what would come tonight wouldn't help her soreness. Because tonight the full moon rose high in the sky, the first time she would change – if she could change without dying in the process. He quickly buried those useless thoughts. They would only bring more pain, more grief.

Though werewolves didn't need the full moon to change, their initial change always occurred on their first full moon. Whether they were changed as adults or sometime after their third birthday, the moon would call. And those with strong enough bodies would answer.

Jasper sat on a chair next to the bed. In his hands, he held a piece of fine oak, smooth and ready to be molded. An outline of a female wolf began to take shape. He took his carving knife, slowly adding details and intricacies of what she could look like as a wolf. Once Willow changed, he would add an exact likeness. The wood felt warm in his hands. Heavy. Substantial. Something he had the power to change and control. Though the grains of wood would voice their desires, Jasper's expert hands could form what he wanted. What he needed. Not the case for the woman in front of him.

Her cinnamon scent filled his nostrils, calming him. She was safe. At least for the moment. Her scent now held traces of wolf, hidden among her original scent. It was sexy as hell. Once she changed, the scent would only intensify.

He'd almost lost her.

Blissful relief spread through him at that one word: almost.

Her wolf would be beautiful. He could already sense her spirit. The new wolf felt strong and would be able to carry Willow through anything. Already a strong woman, her new addition would only increase her power. And if she allowed him by her side, she could face anything. He would be damn sure she had the defenses to do so.

The choice would be hers, though he didn't know what he would do if she walked away. And God forbid if she found another male. When Adam had touched her earlier, flames burst through his skin and seeped into his bones. He thought he would jump across the room and punch his little brother square in the face, but he fought the urge. When she'd whimpered at that touch, he'd almost torn Adam's arm from his body.

He would stand by and let her walk away from him if that was her choice. It needed to be her choice, though it would tear him to pieces and destroy his soul to do so. He knew she said she'd forgiven him, but he'd seen something in her eyes when she said it.

She might forgive him, but she didn't trust him.

He would do anything to regain that trust.

CHAPTER TWENTY

Willow took a deep breath and gripped the wooden dresser to hide her shaking fingers. Her body was still sore, but she was still surprised at the lack of bruises covering her skin. This new healing ability was sure something. A light caught her eyes in the reflection, and she jumped.

Gold.

A werewolf. A mere human no more. And tonight she'd find out if she could handle the change. She closed her eyes, not wanting to look at the reminder that her life as she knew it was forever changed. Over.

Now she'd walk on four legs under the moonlight and howl to their goddess. Hunt for prey and open her senses. She stood naked in front of the mirror, trying to calm her nerves before her first hunt. Her first change. The full moon called to her, tugged at her bones, seeped in her pores, her blood.

Jasper said it would hurt. He wouldn't lie to her. Not now. But he qualified it with sad eyes and said it wouldn't be as bad as what she already went through. Not nearly as bad.

She shuddered.

Thank God.

She put her arms through one of Jasper's soft flannel shirts and buttoned it up. They'd be naked before the shift but didn't want to walk about in her birthday suit just yet. And, if she were honest with herself, she wanted to envelop herself in her mate's scent.

She held the long sleeves up to her nose and inhaled.

Oh, how she missed him.

"He will protect you tonight, Willow. Always. Forgive him."

It was still so weird to hear another person, albeit a wolf, sharing her mind. But, she didn't know if she could fully agree with her wolf – yet. Time would tell.

"Are you ready to go, Wil?" Jasper cautiously walked toward her.

Clad in only sweat pants, his bare chest begged for her hands. But she shook it off. Too soon. Way too soon.

She nodded, not knowing what else to say. Fear choked her. Why was she so afraid? She wanted this. Besides, she'd been through worse. But this time was different. She was going to change into a being that gave people nightmares. She loved Jasper's wolf. The feel of his fur against her skin, his warm body leaning against hers as he panted from exertion from his runs.

She could do this. This was her destiny.

She squared her shoulders and took his hand. He jumped at the contact and gave her a small smile.

Jesus, he looked so guilty. So pained. He hadn't hurt her physically, just emotionally. And even then, she knew why he'd said it. He was just a stupid male, not the sadistic bastard Corbin was.

"Come on, let's get wolfy." She smiled.

Jasper cut off a laugh and shook his head. "Okay then."

He led her toward the backyard facing the alcove of trees. The wind brushed her hair, ticking her nose. It would only be the two of them tonight. She didn't need the Alpha, as it was Jasper, not Edward, who bit her enough times to bring on the change and call to her wolf spirit. She only needed to be by his side and call forth her wolf under her first full moon. They would meet up with the others for the rest of the hunt after she changed. If she changed.

A shudder ran through her. She was so scared, yet Jasper was her rock. He showed no fear and helped her. But she knew inside it must be different, that he felt the same fear she did.

He turned her around to face him once they reached the center of their yard. He slowly unbuttoned her shirt, and she let out a gasp.

Oh my.

His calloused fingertips brushed against her skin as the moonlight danced upon it. She inhaled the clean, crisp mountain air that mingled with Jasper's sandalwood scent.

Home.

Yes, that is what this felt like. What could be wrong with this? Though it may not seem right, and not inherent to nature, she knew the change was right for her. Inherent to her being. No amount of pain would take her away from this. This was hers.

Soon she stood naked in the moonlight and her skin began to itch, like something was coming or missing. She didn't know, but she knew her wolf would tell her.

"Willow, babe? I will hold on to you during your first shift." She relaxed slightly at Jasper's words. "You will change in my arms, and I won't let you go until you are a wolf. Then I will shift beside you. Okay?"

She nodded then the first burst of pain racked her body and she let out a whimper.

"Shh." Jasper pulled her in his arms, resting her head on his naked chest.

Another whimper turned to a scream as pain shot down her body.

"It will be okay Willow. It's only natural".

"Natural? Really?" She said to her wolf.

Jasper merely lifted a brow at her nonsensical words, and a blush covered her naked body.

"You'll get used to talking to your wolf. I do it all the time." He gave her a small smile.

Sharp pinpricks of pain danced along her spine, and she bowed into his arms. He pulled her closer to his chest and she inhaled his scent and relaxed. Jasper lowered them to the ground, cradling her in his arms, and kissed her deeply. Their tongues clashed and mated, bringing Willow's thoughts to him and his sensual taste, rather than concentrating on the pain racking her body.

Wow, love that type of distraction.

Jasper pulled his lips away and whispered, "I will be here. Always."

She smiled then screamed as her bones broke and her muscles tore. Oh, God. How did Jasper do this daily?

Tears ran down her cheeks and her body molded and reformed. Fur sprouted along her skin, and her facial muscles went numb then cracked and reformed. Her vision blurred, then came back crisper. Clearer. She screamed once more as her body made its final painful alteration, and she ended on a howl. She bent her head and looked at her paws. Paws?

She was a wolf.

Holy crap.

"Wow, you've got to be the most beautiful wolf I've ever seen," Jasper rasped.

If a wolf could blush, she was sure she'd be doing it at the moment. But instead, she just rolled her eyes. That seemed like a universal trait to tell a man he was full of it.

He laughed and pet her fur. Her fur. How crazy. She leaned into his touch, loving the way his hands felt on her over-heated skin beneath her pelt. An odd sensation for sure, but totally amazing.

She rolled her neck, needing some room to get used to her knew body, and Jasper released her. She maneuvered herself to stand on all four paws, loving the way the grass felt between her claws. Jasper stood and smiled down on her. Cautiously, she walked toward him.

Well, at least she tried.

One back paw collided with a front paw, and she landed face first in the dirt, a collage of legs and fur.

She looked up at her mate holding back a laugh.

This is so *not funny.*

Okay, maybe a little. But he didn't have to laugh about it.

"Baby, you'll get used to it. I promise." Jasper chuckled.

Willow tilted her head. *Really?*

"Hey, I was a pup when I learned to walk on four paws. I'm sure I ate dirt a few times. You should ask North about the time he learned. I swear, for a doctor who now has such great reflexes, as a kid, he had horrible balance issues. But really, Willow, let your wolf come forward. She'll teach you what you need to know."

"I'll help, don't worry. You'll have control, but I will aide you."

Willow relaxed with both their encouragements. At least she didn't feel completely alone in this.

Jasper took off his sweats, and he stood gloriously naked, his erection jutting out.

He gave a small, sheepish smile. "Sorry, you were naked. I couldn't help it."

What did he have to be sorry about? She only wished she were human so she could jump his bones.

She panted at the thought.

Her wolf laughed. *"You can do that later. Enjoy your hunt. And no, we don't do the nasty in our wolf forms. Some lines you just don't cross."*

Willow let out a grunt that sounded like a laugh.

She watched as her mate turned to a magnificent black wolf, and came at her, nipping playfully at her legs and flank. He licked her muzzle and she bent into him, inhaling his scent.

"Sexy wolf."

Willow totally agreed with her wolf.

Jasper nudged her, and Willow let go of her control. Her wolf sprang forward in her mind, and her body followed suit. She ran through the forest, the grass and dirt crunching beneath the pads of her paws. Low-lying branches brushed her flank, but she leapt out of their way and over fallen logs at a fast pace. She quickened as she went up a hill, stopping once she reached the top. Jasper came to a stop behind her, and she howled at the moon, knowing full well she was fitting into a stereotype. But why the hell not?

Jasper joined her in her howl, his deep baritone blending with her softer pitch. Together their music was a melody of unity, passion, and love.

Her mate.

For always.

LATER, still in wolf form, Jasper and Willow ran through the forest to meet up with the others. The overwhelming scents of other wolves assaulted her nose and she shook her muzzle. It was still so weird to get used to seeing so many werewolves in one place, snuggling, exploring, and yipping. Like a family. A large hairy one.

A big gray wolf entered the clearing, and the slight growls and yips quieted. She recognized this wolf. Edward.

Their Alpha.

Her Alpha.

Without knowing why she did it, other than it was an inherent part of her, a calling, she lowered her body in submission, tilting her head to bare her throat to Edward.

The Alpha padded toward her and locked his jaw around her throat, using a light pressure to show her who was in charge. Her wolf relaxed as a sense of being – of rightness – settled over her.

She was Pack in truth.

Home.

Edward released her and howled. The surrounding wolves joined in. Jasper nudged her flank, and then licked the spots where Edward's scent lingered, effectively staking his claim as well. Though the human in her might still be cautious toward him, her wolf felt comforted by his gesture and leaned into his touch. Jasper lifted his head and howled with his family, Willow joining in soon after.

As if an unheard signal went off, the wolves began their hunt. The younger pups, adorable on their new legs and soft fur, stayed close to their mothers, as their fathers ran off with the men to hunt. Though it might have seemed barbaric to her, she felt the ancient customs of men providing for their family was comforting to her wolf. When she saw a smaller wolf dart off with the larger ones, Willow almost laughed. Cailin joined the men, hunting her prey. Those poor men.

The thumping of small feet reached her ears.

A rabbit.

A juicy, mouthwatering rabbit.

Her wolf perked up, and she was off, running after the sound, using the instincts she didn't know she possessed. Another small wolf ran by her side.

Mel.

Together, the two women, now sisters, gave chase. Willow

hunkered down up wind, and waited, Mel doing the same by her side. The large rabbit hopped into a clear view, and Willow nudged Mel.

Mel nodded. Then pounced.

Willow was still new at this, but this was Mel's third time on the hunt.

Together they killed their dinner and sat, tongues wagging, at their good fortune.

If wolves could laugh, she was sure Jasper was doing so when he walked to her side, Kade right behind him walking toward Mel. He dropped another, larger, rabbit by her feet and used his muzzle to scoot it toward her.

Aww. How sweet. He got me a meal.

Too bad she was a strong female werewolf and could provide for herself. But it was the thought that counted.

Wow, times sure have changed.

She bit into the rabbit and grimaced. Her wolf liked it, but geez. This was like the Easter bunny or something.

Just imagine it's a chocolate-filled one. Yeah that will work. Not.

After the four of them ate, Kade licked Mel's face then nodded toward them, gesturing toward the woods. Jasper gave a small growl, and the other couple ran back into the forest, leaving her and Jasper alone in the clearing.

She stretched her mouth in a wide yawn, though she wasn't that tired. Jasper nipped her side then covered her smaller body to protect her while she changed back.

Once human, she sat naked on the grass, under the trees, feeling invigorated.

Jasper changed back to human, and she panted with need. He crooked a brow and opened his mouth to speak, but she grabbed his cock and pulled him closer instead.

"Jesus, Willow," he grunted.

He crushed his mouth to hers, his taste bursting on his tongue. She growled into his mouth, licking his tongue and nipping at his lips. Blood pumping, she couldn't get enough of him. She needed him. Now.

He thrust into her fist, growling. She moaned when he squeezed her rear, pulling her closer.

Jasper pulled away, fire and caring in his eyes. "We should get back to our clothes. I don't want you to get sick. You just got well."

Damn her mate and his seeing to her needs. She needed this first.

Willow shook her head. "After." She didn't know if this brazen part of herself was due to her wolf or the fact that Jasper was the sexiest man she'd ever seen, but she didn't care. She wanted him inside her. Soon.

Jasper groaned. "No complaints from me." He thrust his cock into her closed hand, increasing the friction, and moved his hand to play with her lower lips, soaking him.

"Jesus," she rasped as he inserted two fingers into her, curling them to rub on her most sensitive spot.

"You like that? You did so well today, baby. You were such a fucking fantastic wolf. You deserve a reward." The wicked gleam in his eyes almost made her come on the spot.

He pulled out of her reach and kissed her once more, before turning her.

"Seeing you as your wolf put a thought in my mind." He put her on all fours, her knees sinking into the wet soil.

She screamed when he licked her seam all the way to her clit. He grabbed both cheeks and spread her. The cool breeze felt like heaven against her overheated sensitive flesh. Jasper growled then buried his face, sucking and nibbling her.

She buckled and leaned back, urging him to go deeper.

His tongue darted in and out, then he bit down on her clit. She called his name, and before her mind could clear from the earth shattering orgasm, Jasper mounted her in one stroke.

He filled her completely, body and soul. He reared back and thrust again, his balls slapping her swollen pussy as he did it again. Together, they healed. Their souls combining, their bond tightening. Whatever had happened in the past was just that – the past. Everything was forgiven and they were ready to move forward.

He gripped her hips with a bruising force and swiveled his hips, hitting her just right. One more stroke and they came together in a connection of bliss.

Jasper pulled out of her, turned her to her back, then kissed her deeply.

"I love you," he whispered.

"I love you, too."

He lifted her up, a playful and dangerous glee in his eyes, and wrapped her legs around his hips, placing her back against the tree. The bark dug into her skin, the pain feeling soft and good.

Jasper smiled then entered her. Hard. Her core, already swollen and wet, clenched around him. He smiled and stopped where he was. He released one hand to brush the hair from her face, a smile on his lips.

This was perfection.

This was her mate.

Jasper reared back and slowly entered her again, rotating his hips to brush her clit. His strokes stayed steady and purposeful, but they never broke eye contact. Finally, she blinked and smiled.

"Let me mark you," she whispered.

Unsurpassed pleasure flashed over his face. "Make me yours."

She leaned forward, her fangs elongated, and bit into the soft spot where his shoulder met his neck. They came together with his shout as she pressed down harder, marking him as his mate.

Forever.

CHAPTER TWENTY-ONE

"Okay, what about this one?" Jasper laughed as he placed it near her lips.

Willow sat on the counter, her legs spread, his body between them. He'd blindfolded her with a silk tie and kissed her gently while he did it.

"Um, a cucumber?" She giggled.

Lord, his mate was too cute for her own good.

"What the hell does a cucumber smell like?"

"Well, like a cucumber. And green." She smiled and he leaned over to kiss her soft lips.

"Baby, I hate to be the one to tell you this, but green doesn't smell. Even to a werewolf."

"Hey, don't take away my fun. If I say it smells green, it smells green." She stuck out her lip like Marilyn Monroe, giving Jasper the urge to bite it.

Knowing he couldn't distract their lessons with sex – though it did sound like a fantastic idea, if he did say so himself – he just laughed instead.

"Hey, shut it. Don't laugh at me. Cucumber green smells green. Was I right?"

"Yes, yes. It was a cucumber. Your nose is amazing. You are were-wolf perfect. But you are weird, but that's why I love you."

"Well, Jasper, you're the one teaching me. What did you expect?"

Oh, that was it.

He grabbed her waist, tickling her. Willow wiggled, trying to get away, laughing. They were in the kitchen, teaching her the ability to home in on a scent. Through the past week, he'd slowly taught her what it meant to be a werewolf. She wouldn't be in top form for a while yet, but she was improving remarkably. But it didn't surprise him. She was his mate after all.

The door opened behind them, but he continued his torture on Willow. He'd heard Adam coming up the steps; no doubt Willow did as well. But, geez, at some point his family would have to learn to knock.

"Whew, thank God you two are dressed. I so didn't need to see that. Again." Adam laughed.

He felt her blood rush to the surface as it lay against his skin. Yeah, that time on the kitchen table had really embarrassed her, but damn, it had been totally worth it.

Willow jumped off the counter, removed her blindfold, and jumped into Adam's arms in a huge hug. She was like that with all his family. At first it made him jealous as hell, but now he loved it. It meant she felt at home with him and his life, that she felt comfortable enough to be herself. She and Adam were closer than the rest, forming a friendship over her kidnapping and his loss of Anna. He felt a twinge of jealousy at it, but shook it off. Willow hadn't left him yet, and he hoped she never would. She said she'd forgiven him and they were closer than ever. But did she really trust him?

"Um, are you sure I wasn't interrupting?" Adam asked, a brow raised and bent down.

The blindfold dangling on his finger caused both men to laugh.

"Hey." Willow playfully hit both of them. "It's not what it looks like. We were just practicing."

They laughed harder.

If Willow blushed any harder, she'd be Santa red.

"I meant," she began smoothly, "we were practicing with scents."

Jasper tugged her close and kissed the crown of her head. "It's fine, baby. We were just joking. But, Adam, was there a particular reason you were here? Or just to show your ugly face?"

"Ouch, man. That hurt. I brought some papers and deeds for you that need your John Hancock."

Ahh, the joys of being a Beta. Jasper sighed. He loved his work, taking care of and protecting his Pack, but the paperwork in this modern society was a bitch. And frankly, he'd hoped Adam was here with news from the Centrals. But that never seemed to be the case. The bastards had gone underground. There wasn't a trace of Hector or Corbin. Anger coursed his veins and he clenched his jaw.

Warm lips caressed his chin. "Hey, stop scowling."

Jasper nipped at her fingers and growled. "Sorry."

"Hey, I can leave if you want."

Crap, forgot Adam was still there.

Jasper cleared his throat. "No, stay. Really, we were just hanging out. Promise."

Adam shrugged.

"Please?" Willow asked. "I made Greek salad, baba ganoush, and chocolate baklava. And I brought fresh bread from the bakery on my way home."

Adam groaned. "Sounds amazing. But, where's the meat?"

Jasper laughed. That's what he was thinking.

Willow let out a laugh. "You could get over it, Adam. Jasper is getting used to all the veggies."

Jasper put on what he thought was his best smile. "Sure. I love veggies."

He grunted when she elbowed him in the gut.

"Liar." She smiled.

"Caught me."

"That's why I also made lamb, so shut it. Both of you." She glided back to the kitchen and Jasper watched her walk. He loved to watch those hips sway from side to side.

"Dude, you're drooling," Adam teased.

"Damn straight."

. . .

AFTER DINNER they laid on the couch, Willow snug in Jasper's arms and Adam on the other end, his feet on the table.

"I want to watch a movie. One we all like."

Jasper smiled. The three of them never could decide on one, and Willow usually got to pick whatever suited her fancy.

Yep, still love her. Every bit of her.

"Okay," Adam said. "Which one?"

"Grease?" Jasper asked.

Adam smacked him upside the head. "Dude, what is your fixation with that movie?"

He rubbed the back of his head. "Hey, that hurt. And I like Bad Sandy."

All three of them laughed at his odd choice for a movie.

"Really?" Willow asked once they could breathe again. "I could wear the leather pants if you want?"

Jasper groaned.

"Hey, not now. Not here." Adam waved his hands. "Let me watch the movie first. Then you two can go play 'You're the one that I want' with blindfolds and leather pants. But leave me out of it."

Jasper hugged them both close to him and laughed.

Oh, how he loved his family.

IT WAS funny how two little pink lines could cause a brain aneurism.

Okay, maybe not that as bad as that. But it could still change a person's life dramatically.

Oh, hell.

Willow was pregnant.

How did that happen?

She blushed when she thought about just exactly how that happened. Yeah, no condoms and mate marking proved fertile. Just ask Pat or Mel. Or now her.

She'd just gotten used to the whole werewolf thing. And that came after the whole being Jasper's mate thing. How was she supposed to be a mom on top of that?

Her head throbbed as the idea of sudden responsibly threatened to choke her. What if the Centrals wanted her baby? Her breaths came in pants as she began to hyperventilate.

Jasper knocked at the door, his sandalwood scent partially masked by worry.

"Willow, baby, what's wrong? I can feel your unease from the other side of the house."

She took a deep breath and tried to calm herself. Tried to tell him she was okay. But no words came out. Okay, apparently she wasn't okay. Her vision blackened. Okay, she *really* wasn't.

"Willow? I'm coming in."

A nod was her only response, though he couldn't see it through the closed, unlocked door. What was the point of locking a door in a house with a werewolf. They could get in anywhere they wanted. And apparently their sperm could do the same thing. Her poor unsuspecting egg. Why did the sex have to be so good?

Jasper walked into their master bath and took one look at her huddled on the ground. He switched his gaze to stare at the stick in her hand.

"Are we?" His voice cracked.

She could only nod. Like a dam bursting, tears flooded eyes and overfilled her eyes, spilling onto her cheeks.

Was he happy? Was she? Wasn't she supposed to be?

Damn it. She hated the fact that she feared the Centrals so much that they were ruining this for her.

Jasper stood still, his face expressionless.

Tears continued their trail down her face, soaking her shirt.

Her mate's face cracked in a huge smile. "A baby? Us?"

She nodded again. Okay, seriously? Why couldn't she speak?

Jasper walked toward her, studying her face, and his smile vanished.

"Wait, what's wrong. Are you sick? Is something wrong with the baby?" He pulled her in to his arms, hugging her, then pushed her back. "Wait, is that bad? Should I not touch you? I need to call North. Or Mom. Or the elders. Yeah. They'll know what to do."

His innocent and clearly panicked expression, along with his practically incoherent ramblings, washed away her own craziness. She let out a relived laugh.

"No, I'm fine. Really. No need to call in the cavalry. But you can call them over to tell them our news, later, if you want." She kissed him softly, and he relaxed against her.

"Willow, then, what was wrong? Why did you look so sad at the thought of being pregnant? I thought for a minute you didn't want it. I know it was fast, but it's okay. *I'm* happy."

She shook her head. "I was just worried. I'm sorry I freaked out."

Jasper angled his head. "You're allowed to freak out. I think it comes with the hormones. But, baby, wolves have babies all the time. Is it the shifting? Look at Mel, she shifts while she's pregnant. It's natural."

Willow nodded. She already knew about the shifting and pregnancy. That wasn't new, but having it confirmed still came as a relief.

"But what about the Centrals?" There she'd said it. Voiced her concerns.

He let out a growl.

"Never again, Willow. I won't let them her hurt you." He put his hand on her still-flat stomach, cradling her. "Or our baby."

Though she desperately wanted to believe him, she still had a lingering ounce of doubt. They'd taken her before. Broken the Redwoods' wards and trespassed on their lands. The Redwoods might be powerful, but the true evil the Centrals possessed crossed boundaries good couldn't and wouldn't cross. Would Hector and his Pack to it again? Take her or her child?

Willow put her hand over Jasper's. "I hope so."

She leaned into his hold, sitting on the bathroom floor, and vowed she wasn't weak anymore. No one would harm her child. And if they tried, she'd kill them. Slowly.

Yes, it was good to be a werewolf.

A WOMAN'S scream filled the room. The hairs on the back of Jasper's neck rose and he cursed.

Dear God, what the hell is going on in there?

Jasper watched as Kade paced the room, waiting for Mel to give birth. She'd gone into labor in the middle of the night, and ten hours later, she was just now getting to the pushing.

How on Earth did women do it?

They'd sent most of the family home due to responsibilities and necessity of sleep, so Jasper was left alone with the soon-to-be-father, who currently was pacing a hole into the carpet.

"Why do I have to be out here?" Kade growled, pulling at his hair. "My mate is hurting in there. And I am stuck out here like a pup in the dog house. What did I do?"

Jasper laughed then felt a bit ill at the thought of Willow going through the same thing.

"Kade, you were just in there, remember? But Cailin threw you out."

Kade snarled. "Well, she's just the baby. What does she know? She had no right to do that."

"Dude, you were yelling at North to give her drugs, though you know wolves can't have them. I know she was in pain, but she was getting through it. You were the one freaking out. You threatened anyone who came near her. Cailin had every right to do what she did."

"Mel wanted me there. She needs me," Kade whined.

Poor guy. It must be brutal to know your mate is on the other side of the door in pain, but couldn't do a damn thing about it. Jasper did his best not to think of Willow lying on the bed, screaming in pain in just a few short months. At least one of the two of them in this room had to be sane.

"Mel was just being nice, Kade. In fact, I'm surprised she didn't kick your ass."

Kade blushed and stopped pacing. "Well..."

Jasper laughed. "Yes?"

"She might have threatened me with various acids that could dissolve bones and hide the bodies."

Jasper laughed, his side aching. Damn, he loved the chemist side of his sister-in-law.

Kade joined in his laughter. "But that may not have been because I was – as Cailin accused – hovering. It might have been because she blames me for putting her there."

Jasper sobered. "She'll be okay, Kade. Stop worrying. Women have been doing this for thousands of years."

Kade gave a bitter laugh. "Sure, remind be to say that when Willow is in this situation in about seven months."

Jasper shuddered. "Don't get me wrong, I am so happy that we're having a baby. But the whole pain thing is just too much. I don't know how they do it."

The sound of a baby crying froze both men in their tracks.

"That's why," Jasper rasped. "That's why they do it"

Their mother opened the door, a huge smile on her face and tears in her eyes. "Come on, Kade, come inside and meet your son."

"Finn," Kade whispered.

Pat nodded. "That is what Melanie said. Thank you so much for making me a grandmother."

She kissed him and gave him a fierce hug. Kade's cheeks were drenched with tears, and he walked through the door with a dazed expression on his face. Willow passed the new father on his way in.

She, too, was crying, and Jasper opened his arms. She slid against his side, and he hugged her close, inhaling her cinnamon scent.

Willow took a deep breath and sniffed. "We need to tell your father and brothers. I know Mel didn't want everyone here when they had duties, but they need to know."

Jasper kissed the top of her head. "We will, don't rush. Just let me hold you for a sec." He had an image of himself holding his son or daughter to his chest, and his body filled with warmth. He couldn't wait. It was something worth fighting for.

———

WILLOW WIPED down the remaining flour on the counter from the last batch of cinnamon rolls. She laughed at the familiar sensation. She'd been doing the same thing at a different bakery, but now things were so different. She wasn't alone anymore. She had a growing family.

She did what she loved and was with a man she loved even more. And together they'd created a new life. A baby.

Something bad had to happen soon, right? Isn't that how it always happened?

She shook off that depressing though.t. No use concentrating on something that might never come to pass.

Willow took out the now cooled sugar cookies from the shelf and started to frost them. She laughed at the little bunnies and deer forms. Wolves sure loved them in any form. The fact that it didn't bother her told her maybe she was starting to get a complex. She shrugged. Poor Bambi and Thumper.

Oh well, they tasted delicious, both in sugar and on the bone.

The bell rang over the door, but she didn't look around to see who it was right away. Reed was watching outside, and she knew it was safe. But the overwhelming potpourri scent invaded her nose, making her want to puke.

Camille.

"Well, Willow. It's nice to see you've gotten everything you deserve."

Her throaty voice set Willow's teeth on edge and made her want to throw something. Preferably something sharp and pointy. With poison.

Willow set her piping tube down and smiled.

"Camille, it's so nice to see you."

Right. Maybe in a vat of hot oil. Yes, that would be a nice way to see her.

Camille smiled, resembling a viper with sharp teeth.

"I just came here to show my support and tell you there are no hard feelings, despite what you may hear about me. I'm so happy everything worked out with you and Jasper, your wolf...your baby. I hope you'll call me if you ever need help with...it."

Willow's stomach clenched at the thought of that smile and what lay behind it. Like hell that woman would go anywhere near her unborn child. She forced herself not to put a hand on her belly, protecting her young. She wouldn't show weakness.

"Thank you." She spoke though gritted teeth.

That woman was a bitch. A menace. She spent her time trailing behind the Jamenson men, trying to find a mate. Nipping on whatever bits of scraps people left for her. And these days, it seemed that Fredrick was the only one leaving anything around for her.

Camille sighed. "I just came into see if anything caught my fancy. But I don't see anything that suits my taste. You know how it is."

Bitch. Stuck up eats-too-many-sweets-as-it-is,-bitch.

Willow raised a brow. "Well then, I'm sure you know the way out."

Damn, she really loved this new wolfy fierce side of hers.

Anger flashed over Camille's face, but the woman wouldn't get what she wanted. No, Willow wouldn't reach across the counter and smack a bitch.

Camille nodded then walked out the open door. She stopped once she reached the outside and glanced over her shoulder. Pain shot through Willow's head and Camille was gone.

Flashes of hands, a deep voice mingling with a higher one.

Willow gasped.

It was them.

Fredrick and Camille.

Oh my God.

They were the ones who'd kidnapped her and given her to the Centrals like a sack of flour to be traded. They were the traitors. Bile rose in Willow's throat. How could they go against the Pack? Hurt them like that?

Willow dropped the towel from her hand and ran.

Reed grabbed her arm and pulled her close as she made it out the door. She'd forgotten she wasn't alone, that her brother-in-law was there to protect her.

"Wait. Willow, what's wrong? What did Camille do?" Reed demanded.

"It was them..." She choked, too angry to cry.

"What? Who? Who was them? Tell me what's wrong."

She took a deep breath, trying to clear her thoughts. "I remember now. That night. The night with the dead girl. It was Camille and Fredrick. They took me. They helped the Centrals."

Reed's face turned to stone. He didn't ask how or why she suddenly knew but took out his phone and called Jasper.

Willow mentally slapped herself.

Why didn't she think to call? Her brain was too jumbled.

She heard Jasper growl and shout at the news.

Reed closed the phone and tugged on her arm. "Come on. Let's get you home. Jasper's waiting."

A howl split the air, followed by dozens more.

Slick oily magic filled the air, choking her.

Reed cursed. "We're under attack."

She was too late. She'd remembered too late. Camille and Fredrick had betrayed the Pack. Again. She only prayed she hadn't realized too late to save her family, her Pack, her home.

CHAPTER TWENTY-TWO

Jasper bent to pick up the phone he'd thrown against the wall in anger. He'd always known Camille was a slimy bitch and Fredrick a dumbass goon, but he'd never thought they would stoop to the level of betraying the Pack. Shouldn't he have felt something? Noticed something? Shouldn't Maddox have felt their cruel brevity through their emotions?

He shook his head. There was no use thinking about the what-ifs and whys. They'd fucked up. They'd let parasites, leaches, into their home, their Den, and his mate suffered for it. Jasper swallowed the lump of guilt in his throat. They'd kidnapped her. Stuck her with a needle and threw her at the feet of the depraved and soulless Centrals. They'd cut her, stripped her of her dignity, and forced him to bite and tear her flesh to make her a wolf.

Not all the Centrals though. There was one. The girl who'd helped Willow with that herb concoction. He would be forever grateful to whoever that was, for she'd saved his mate's life. But now Jasper would have to take a life, or give the responsibility to one in his family. Fredrick and Camille had to die. They needed to pay for their crimes and their sins.

He only hoped it hurt like hell.

A howl in the not too far distance stopped Jasper in his tracks.

What the hell?

A dozen more followed.

Dear God. We're under attack.

Heart pounding in his chest, he quickly dialed Adam. As the Enforcer, Adam would have information.

"What the hell is going on?" Jasper demanded.

"Our Den has been breached. The Centrals are coming!" Adam yelled.

Jasper could hear growling and fighting over the line. *Shit.*

"Jasper, they killed the sentries."

Fuck.

"Dammit, it won't end there." A howl again, this time closer to his home and familiar. "Did you hear that?"

"Yeah, it's Maddox. He's getting the families to the bunkers. I have Mom, Cailin, Mel, and Finn. And Dad is out protecting our people, along with the rest of the enforcers and our brothers."

"Good, we've prepared for this. Protect the weaker, kill the invaders. We can do it."

"Jasper, they knew exactly how to get past our shields. We've been betrayed."

He let out a painful breath. "Willow remembered. Camille and Fredrick. They're working with the Centrals."

Adam cursed. "Get out there. I'll take the circle; you get to the south side." His brother sighed. "Jasper, school was in session. I don't know if they got all the kids out or not."

"I'll check. I'll get everyone to safety."

"Take care of yourself."

"You too." They both hung up.

Jasper tucked the phone in his pocket and ran out the door. Damn it, he wanted to get to Willow. To make sure she was safe and inhale that sweet cinnamon scent. They were a pair, connected. He needed her and the child she carried more than breath. But Reed was with her. His little brother was strong and could protect her. And if he were honest with himself, Willow could take care of herself. That didn't mean she had to.

He jumped off the steps, his feet hitting the pavement of the side-walk, and ran toward the howls. His Pack was in trouble, and he intended to save them – and kick the Central's ass. Though he didn't have proof it was them yet, there was no doubt in his mind who would be ballsy enough to encroach on their turf.

The Centrals would pay for what they've done.

He ran into the forest and the trees reached out and scratched his face, but he didn't care, his sole intent to find anyone who needed his help. In the distance, he saw a fallen man. He inhaled, catching the scent. Dammit, he was a Redwood. Jasper ran to the lifeless form and searched for a pulse.

There wasn't one.

A scream of fury ripped from his throat. Another life wasted because the bastards wanted power they didn't have the right or the soul to possess. His wolf rose to the surface, trying to take over, but Jasper set his teeth and remained in control. Though he wanted to go on a rampage and kill anything that crossed his path, it would do no good if he hurt someone he knew and cared about.

Another scent drifted on the breeze.

A Central.

And either an arrogant bastard who didn't care he was standing upwind or a fucking idiot. Jasper didn't care. He'd kill the fuckwit and show who actually held the power and strength.

"Change. You can take him as a wolf. Easy."

Jasper shook his head. No, he needed to be on two feet and totally in control. He needed to feel the pulse of the enemy fade beneath his fingertips. And for more practical reasons, he needed to be able to answer the phone in case someone called him for help – like Willow. It was hard to do that with paws, and despite what some people thought, werewolves were not telepathic.

Jasper crouched behind a tree, waiting for the ignorant fucker to walk his way. The brute of a man walked heavy-footed through the brush, not caring who heard him.

How much of an idiot was this guy?

Jasper inhaled again, trying to determine if the man might be leading him into a trap. No, the guy was alone. And a moron. He almost felt bad for the guy.

Within a breath, Jasper's arm shot out, and he twisted the Central's neck with a calming snapping sound. The other wolf lay dead at his feet, and he shook his head. Too easy. But worth it. He never liked killing for the sake of killing, but those who dared come on his land deserved what they got.

Jasper left both of the dead man where they lay. He would come back and deal with the bodies when he could. No matter which side, no one deserved to rot on the ground. Each deserved a proper burial. He ran through the forest, getting closer to the southern end where a large population lived, as well as where the school was. It chilled his blood to think of what he might come upon, but he continued on.

A group of five young wolves in their animal forms – not Redwoods – came out of the bushes, anger and an unhealthy glee in their eyes. Five on one, not great odds, but doable. The largest one jumped, teeth bared, and attacked. Jasper held out an arm and ducked, ripping the wolf by the scruff as he pivoted. The wolf yelped and tried to turn and bite, but Jasper growled and snapped its neck. He threw it at the four remaining wolves and snarled.

Two of them started forward and aimed at his legs.

Cheap bastards.

He faked left, then rolled to the right, letting the wolves run past then come back for him. He grabbed the knife from his boot and dug into both of their flanks, one right after other. They collapsed onto each other, and Jasper finished them quickly. There were only a few Centrals he actually wanted to see suffer these nameless faces were not them. The last two wolves, seeing their compatriots fall, growled but did not attack him. Jasper growled back and rushed them. The wolves jumped, and Jasper grabbed them both, throwing them into a tree. He heard the distinct sound of bones breaking, but didn't know the damage. He raced to them both and killed them quickly.

Panting and tired, he wiped his knives on his jeans and left them the bodies behind. It took a lot of energy to fight like that in human form, but he was Beta; he could do it. But he needed to find his Pack and find out what exactly was going on. He needed to find Willow. Now.

He finally made it to the southern end and stopped, his mouth dropping. Utter devastation. Homes and business burned. People screaming. Children crying. What had the Centrals done? And why didn't the Redwoods have the power to stop it?

Jasper continued toward the melee, fisting his hands. The smoke from the fires stung his nose and his anger increased. Why would they do this? What possible reason was there to kill women and children?

A small cry from behind a bench made Jasper freeze.

"Hey," Jasper whispered, using his most calm, soothing voice. "Come out. I'm safe. Smell me. I'm Jasper, the Beta. I'll get you where you need to be."

A small girl, around the age of five crawled out. Jasper picked her up and she snuggled under his chin, crying.

"Shh, darling. Come on. Let's get you to a safe house. Okay?" As Jasper wiped away some of the smudges on her cheeks, he finally recognized her. Larissa and Neil's oldest daughter. He tried not to think about what it meant that she was out here alone. And not with her parents, Kade and Melanie's best friends. "Gina, it's okay. I'll get you home."

At the mention of her name, she relaxed and stopped crying. "Okay, Mr. Jasper."

Jasper held her closer and ran to Larissa and Neil's home, praying someone was there.

"Gina!" Larissa ran out the door, hunting blade in hand, toward her daughter.

"Mommy!" Gina wiggled down from Jasper and jumped into her mother's arms. Larissa caught her with one hand, the other still carrying the blade, protecting them both. Nothing like seeing a witch mother and werewolf mate in action.

"Jasper, thank God. I couldn't get to the school. I have the neighbors in our basement, and I'm setting wards. I can still feel Neil, and he called a while ago saying he's with your father. Thank you so much."

"It's no problem; get inside and be safe."

Larissa smiled and kissed Jasper's cheek. "You too. Kill them."

"Yes, ma'am."

Jasper ran off and helped others along the road find protection, fighting off invading wolves as he did. Where were all these guys coming from? And where the hell was Willow?

———

MORE SCREAMS REACHED Willow's ears, and she held tighter to Reed's hand. Though they had planned to run to her home and stash her there, she couldn't stomach leaving so many people in danger. Together, she and Reed had gotten most of the weaker wolves around them to safety and were herding the rest of them to a bunker. Thank God the Redwoods had plans for so many types of emergencies, because, in all the commotion, she wasn't sure she'd be able to do it herself.

"Willow, we need to go. Jasper will kill me if anything happens to you or the baby. And frankly I like you too." Reed gave a nervous smile and pulled her down the road.

As they reached a corner, four wolves sprang out of the bushes. She inhaled, and that sickly oil scent invaded her nose.

Centrals.

Reed quickly went to work on the closest three, dodging blows and giving some of his own. But the last wolf only had eyes for her. She set her feet and braced for the wolf to launch. Adam and Jasper were teaching her self-defense, and she was stronger by far than when she was a human, but she was still learning and not nearly as good as Reed. The wolf growled and tried to bite her. She pivoted and kicked it in the face with all her strength. It collapsed at her feet, but was still breathing.

Reed came back from the three dead wolves – *go Reed* – and finished the last one for her.

"You shouldn't have to kill if you don't have to," Reed growled.

Relief coursed through her, and they ran toward her home. Where was Jasper? She needed him. Not to protect her, per se, but to be by her side. To know he was safe and away from Corbin and Camille. She held her stomach, her palm resting were her child lay, and prayed that Jasper would be safe.

A rustling of trees, a putrid scent, and a wolf jumped out of nowhere. Pain seared her arm, as sharp teeth nipped at her flesh. She growled and swiped at the wolf, anger making her wolf come to the surface. Reed snapped the other wolf's neck and kicked it for good measure.

"Shit, Willow. I couldn't smell that one coming until you did. There's too much in the air, too much magic, it's hindering my senses. Fuck. Are you okay? Let me see. How bad is it?" Reed was worried.

Willow took a deep breath. "I'm fine. It's not deep. Let's get out of here." She struggled to contain her wolf, who wanted to go out and kill something. But the human in her wasn't ready for that.

"Little Willow is bleeding again. How ironic."

A voice from the darkness caused the hair on the back of her neck to rise and nausea to roll in her stomach.

The demon walked toward them, a cruel smile on his lips.

Her heart stopped. He was faster than them. Stronger in all magic. What could she and Reed do?

"Willow." Reed smiled a sad smile. "Run."

The demon tilted his head and laughed. "One will do. Run away, little Willow. Go to your mate. Well, that is, if there is anything left of him after Camille is through with him."

No. He was lying. He had to be. That's what demons did. Jasper was fine. Right?

"Willow. Go."

"No, Reed." Tears fell. Between the stress and her hormones, she couldn't hold them back.

"Find Jasper. I'll be fine." The look on Reed's face told her he didn't believe that any more than she did.

Reed pushed her, and she ran. Ran to her mate and away from her brother by marriage. She'd be back. She'd get Jasper, and they'd save Reed. That was what was going to happen. He wouldn't fall. No. He'd be fine, just like he said.

She ran into the forest, and though she'd past her line of vision. She was still close enough to hear the demon's laugh and Reed's pain filled scream.

Close enough for the scent of Reed's blood to reach her nose.

Willow opened her mouth and screamed for help. For Jasper. For anyone. Just for someone to come with the strength to make this go away and take vengeance. To save Reed – if there was anything left to save.

CHAPTER TWENTY-THREE

illow's scream for help reached Jasper's ears, and his body twitched with horror. Was she hurt? He ran toward her screams, praying he wouldn't find her helpless and in pain. He cleared a fallen log and came up behind her.

"Willow!"

"Oh, Jasper."

She jumped into his embrace, her tears soaking his shirt. He squeezed her hard, making sure she was real and not a dream. She crushed her mouth to his, kissing him with all her might. He inhaled her scent, grateful for the sweet cinnamon smell, until he smelled the tangy scent of blood lingering beneath.

"You're hurt," he rasped.

"I'm fine. Really. It's just a scrape."

Jasper shook his head. "No, you're bleeding."

"I'm fine. I'll heal. But Jasper," she choked out. "I think they killed Reed."

He froze. "What? What did you say?"

"The demon. He killed him. Or at least hurt him badly. The demon came for us and Reed told me to run. I didn't want to, Jasper. I almost didn't." She took a deep breath. "But the demon said you were in trouble, but you aren't." She choked up again and shook her head.

"Breathe, baby. Tell me what happened."

"I left. I left him there. I ran to come for you. Reed pushed me away. And then I heard the demon laugh and Reed scream. That's when I called for help and ran back to him. I couldn't let Reed die like that. But he wasn't there, Jasper. He's gone."

Willow broke down, and he held her close.

Jesus. Reed. His baby brother. Gone? Had the demon killed him? Or just taken him? And if he did, why? Jasper shuddered. And if the bastard took his brother, what would he do to him? Would Reed even want to live after something like that?

"Willow, it's not your fault. You did the right thing. You protected our baby. Reed can take care of himself. I'm sure he's okay." Even to his own ears, it sounded like a lie. But he didn't like the alternative. It wasn't an option.

"Jasper, what about the Pack? The children? Is everyone safe?"

"I know most are but not all. But we need to get out of the forest and find the others. I don't think we lost too many, but losing just one is one too many." Jasper clenched his teeth as rage fought with the sorrow inside him.

"We lost some? Who?"

"I don't know, baby."

He went stone cold. He wouldn't cry because it wouldn't accomplish anything, but he held Willow close. The pain at losing so many at the hands of evil felt as though it would crush him, but he couldn't let it. He had to be strong for Willow, for his Pack.

Someone stepped on a branch behind him, and he went on alert, covering Willow. Jasper inhaled and growled at the intruder. The soon to be dead intruder.

Fredrick.

"Took you long enough to remember, bitch. But it's okay. Your Pack will die soon, and I will be in the power at the side of greatness, rather than below the feet of you shits." Fredrick growled.

"How could you to that to your Pack? You were part of us? How could you betray us?" Jasper asked.

"Easy, you are nothing. Worth nothing."

Jasper shook his head. All this for power? For not being part of the Jamensons? Pack hierarchy was blood, driven by instinct, not by choice. Fredrick had been born low on the totem pole but not looked down upon because of it. As a pup, they'd cherished him because he was a gift – like all children. But as a man, he was barely tolerated but because of his attitude, not because of his low status in the Pack.

The betrayal to the Pack alone warranted the other man's death. But because he'd a hand in hurting Willow, no, Fredrick would die by his hand. Now.

Fredrick pulled out a knife and lunged. Jasper pushed Willow to the ground and she crawled for cover under a log, protecting her stomach. Jasper ducked under the blade and rammed his shoulder into the other man's gut. Fredrick grunted and bent over, dropping the blade. *Damned stupid werewolf.*

Jasper elbowed the man in the jaw, forcing Fredrick to the ground. Jasper straddled him, dropping his own knife, and pummeled the other man's face and chest with his fists. He shouted and took out his rage for the loss of Reed, hurting Willow, the dead wolf in the forest, Gina's tears. Everything. He pounded and pounded until his fists were bloodied.

"Jasper, stop. He's dead. Baby. Stop." Willow brushed his arm with her fingers.

He dropped his hands and rested his face on her stomach, inhaling her scent. The bastard was dead by his own hands, but he didn't feel any better. Didn't know if he ever would.

"Wow. So barbaric." They turned toward the sound of the voice Camille laughed and clapped, starting the pair. "Wait until you meet my little demon friend."

Jasper growled and lifted off the dead man, preparing to leap at the bitch and kill. But before he could launch himself toward the woman who tried to ruin his life, Jasper flew through the air, Willow right beside him. An unseen force threw them across the path to the ground. He grunted on impact and reached out for Willow.

What the hell?

He pulled her close and covered her with his body, praying that she and the baby were okay.

Jasper heard laughter, and the previously unseen force stepped from the trees.

"Oh, you can't protect your mate for too long. But go on trying. It amuses me," the demon crooned.

"You should have picked me, Jasper," Camille said. "I would have been better than the trash you are laying on." She pulled a gun from behind her back, raised it, and pulled the trigger.

Hot, searing pain burst through his arm, but nowhere else. It hurt like hell, but could have been worse. He did his best to cover Willow more.

"Jasper, you're hurt," she whispered.

"I'm okay."

Camille laughed again. "Not for long. I'm going with my Corbin. A man with real power, not someone who begs for his daddy's love."

Jasper pulled on his Beta powers and took a deep breath. "Camille. You are cut off. Pack no more. Shunned."

He could feel the tendril of connection snap, and the last of his energy leave him. It took considerable power to cut off a Pack member. It usually took the Alpha or Heir to do it, but Jasper was just strong enough to pull it off.

Camille screamed in pain, writhing on the ground. The demon sighed, lifted her, and threw her over his shoulder, fading from sight as he was a ghost.

Another howl split the air. This time a Redwood. The Centrals were retreating. For now.

He sat up and pulled Willow with him. "Come on. Let's go see the mess and try to figure out what we are going to do."

Willow kissed him softly, somehow making his hurts fade away. "I love you."

"I love you, too."

REED WAS GONE. Not even a blood trail. Willow could only guess that the demon had taken him the same way he did Camille. She prayed he was still alive. He had to be. What would her new family do if they lost him? Willow shuddered to think.

It was all her fault. Reed was gone, possibly dead, because he'd sacrificed himself for her.

Jasper kissed her softly. "Stop thinking what you're thinking."

"You don't read minds." But he always seemed to know anyway.

"I don't need to. Your thoughts are all over your face." He held her close. She inhaled his scent and calmed. "Baby, whatever happened to Reed, it wasn't your fault."

She took an achy breath. "It sure feels that way."

She sank into his hold, taking whatever comfort she could. At least they were alive. She felt horrible even thinking it, but in the grand scheme of things, Jasper was her rock. Without him, she'd break.

Willow looked around the block, the faint smell of ash and fire tickling her nose. Buildings were ruined, crumbling to the ground. Children were crying, clinging onto their mothers. It looked like a war zone.

Her heart clenched, sorrow sweeping over her.

It *was* a war zone.

North and Pat had set up a triage station in front of her bakery. Most of the wounds were small, and those that weren't would heal relatively fast because of their werewolf abilities. The children would take a bit longer to heal, but all of them were wolves. But some people were witches. They would heal faster than humans but were still more fragile than a werewolf.

"Momma? Daddy?" A young girl around three toddled over the broken path, unhurt but crying.

Where were her mother and father?

Willow ran to her and enveloped the girl in her arms. The girl wrapped her arms around Willow's neck and held on for dear life.

"Shh, it's okay. What's your name, hon?" Willow held her close, feeling the little girl's heart beat slow against her. At least she was calming down. It felt good to be the one to offer comfort.

"Emily." She rasped. "Momma? Daddy?"

Willow looked over Emily's head toward Jasper, who knew the list of casualties. He shook his head, pain in his eyes. Willow's heart broke. Oh, poor Emily.

A single tear fell down her cheek. She didn't have much left as it was. The injustice of it all was too much to take. *Was it worth it, Centrals? All of this death and destruction?* Was whatever power they thought they held worth Emily's pain? To know that in the morning when she woke, her mom and dad wouldn't be there. They wouldn't watch her grow up, finish school, get a job, get married. They would miss all the moments in Emily's life because of the greediness of a Pack. Was it worth it?

She wanted to yell all this. Scream and shout. But what would it accomplish besides scare the little girl crying in her arms, begging for her momma and daddy. Her momma and daddy who wouldn't answer her. They had to fight against this evil. Crush it. She couldn't let another fate like Emily's come to pass.

"Emily!"

A woman ran toward Willow and Emily, tears running down her face, arms outstretched.

"Aunt Beth!" Emily screamed and wiggled out of Willow's hold. The girl ran toward her aunt, and Beth took her in her arms.

Relief, however little it might be, spread though her. Emily wasn't alone in the world. But it still didn't make the loss hurt any less.

Twenty-six. They'd loss twenty-six wolves. They'd also killed over forty enemy wolves. But that retribution didn't make it any better.

"Thank you. Thank you for finding her," Beth said.

Willow nodded.

The other woman's eyes held pain and recognition. She knew her sister or brother wouldn't be coming for Emily, that her life was now forever changed as Emily became her responsibility.

Beth squared her shoulders, nodded once, and carried Emily off, leaving Willow standing alone on the corner, not knowing what to do next. She rested her palm on her belly, cradling her child. Would this little one's fate be the same as Emily's?

Sandalwood enveloped her as Jasper wrapped his arms around her waist, placing his hand over hers, over their child.

"We will find Reed, Willow. We will have our vengeance. For Emily and everyone one else who lost someone today," Jasper vowed, his breath ticking her ear.

Willow shook her head.

"But at what cost, Jasper? Will it be enough? Vengeance won't bring those people back. Vengeance won't help us find Reed. But stopping them will. Stopping the Centrals from doing worse. That will bring something back, something lost."

Jasper nodded and held her closer. She leaned back into her mate and closed her eyes. Would it be enough? Was she strong enough?

———

"JASPER, you can't come with me," Adam grumbled.

Jasper clenched his fists and tried not to hit his own brother. They'd left the town square and reconvened at his parents' house to discuss what they would do about patrols, funerals, family, and Reed. His body ached from the fighting, his strength depleted and his heart heavy from loss, but right now, he fed on his anger.

"You want to go alone to find Reed?" Jasper asked.

"No, I don't *want* to go alone. But what other choice do I have?" Adam growled.

"Then I'll go with you."

"And what? Leave the family alone? Leave your pregnant wife to fend for yourself?" Adam retorted.

"Kade, North, and Maddox are here."

"And it will take all of you and more to rebuild our home while protecting it. And you can't leave Willow. You know that."

Jasper sighed. Dammed wolf was right. That didn't mean he had to like it.

"I don't like you going off alone," Jasper grumbled.

"It needs to be done. There is magic blocking Reed's location. We don't know where they took him, so I'll need to search. Alone, I can be more secretive. But we can still feel Reed, Jasper. We know he's alive."

Thank God.

Jasper exhaled and nodded. "Find our brother Adam. We can't lose him."

A solemn look passed over Adam's face. He must be thinking about Anna and the baby. They were too late that time, but they couldn't be again. They wouldn't survive if they were.

Jesus, his family had been through too much already.

Jasper pulled Adam into a hug and held him close. Going on the Central's land would be no walk in the park. There was a good chance he'd lose both of his brothers in this debacle, but he couldn't think about that.

He released Adam, and watched him walk out the door. He prayed this wouldn't be the last time he'd see him.

Please, let him bring home Reed. Alive.

Reed was the center of their family, the funny one who pulled them together. Without him, what would they do?

Jasper didn't want to find out.

CHAPTER TWENTY-FOUR

W illow winced as Jasper washed out her cut with saline –
again. They'd gotten home a half hour ago, and the man
had cleaned her arm four times. Her arm was already
healing due to her awesome werewolf powers. However, the adorable
look of concentration on his face melted her heart.

"Jasper, it's clean. I'm fine. It's only a scratch. Really," she whispered
and brushed away the lock that loved to fall out of place into his eyes.

Her mate exhaled and rested his forehead on her shoulder, rubbing
circles on her wrist with the pad of his thumb. Tiny tingles of something warm and needy raced up her arm, wrapping around not just her
heart but also her womb.

Jesus, she loved this man. Needed his man.

She ran her hand down his back and tucked her fingers under his
shirt, loving the heat of his skin. He lifted his head and rubbed his
nose on her cheek before he trailed kisses along her jawline, behind
her ear, and to her lips. She opened her mouth, welcoming him. His
tongue massaged hers, languid and slow.

Jasper pulled back and bit her lip. "Let's take a shower. I need to
wash the day away."

They stood, and she lifted her arms. Waiting. Jasper leaned down and kissed her again, fisting his hands in the bottom of her shirt. After releasing her lips, he slowly pulled it over her head. He ran his palm down her stomach, hovering over her still flat belly, and unbuttoned her jeans. He crouched and peeled them from her legs, kissing the spot that held their child. She loved the way his whiskers scraped her skin.

She wiggled her hips, and he laughed.

"I love you, baby," Jasper whispered.

Willow sighed. "I love you, too."

He stripped off her panties and bra. Her breasts fell heavy, aching, needy for his palms. He seemed to read her mind and cupped them, rubbing her nipples with the pads of his fingers.

Man, he had talented fingers. Whether it be his talent for wood working or his loving of her body, Jasper knew what to do with his hands. Lucky her.

"I thought you wanted a shower," she rasped.

Wait? Why am I stopping him?

Jasper laughed. "Yes, I did. But we can do both at the same time." He stood up and raised his hands like she had, causing her to giggle.

She stripped him of his shirt, pausing to caress his abs.

Seriously, who outside a romance novel has an eight pack?

He removed his pants and his boxer briefs in one move. Damn, she loved the way his cock sprang forth, tapping his stomach.

Yum.

Jasper took her hand and led her to the shower. He turned on the water to a warm, not-too-hot, not-too-cold temperature then stood in front of the spray, shielding her eyes.

Caring was her werewolf.

He turned, allowing the water to run down her body. It felt warm, refreshing after such a long day of heart-wrenching turmoil. She jumped when Jasper first touched her with his soapy hand. He used the soap on his palms to clean her body in slow, core-clenching circles. She returned the favor, washing away the dirt and blood from his battles.

Her warrior werewolf.

They rinsed themselves, and she wrapped her arms around his waist, his erection hard against her belly. He leaned down and captured her lips for a kiss, gently lifting her up against the wall. She wrapped her legs around his waist, and he slid inside. She gasped. So smooth and wet, no need for preparation.

The water beat down on his back and her arms as he stood there, savoring the moment She kissed him back, loving his taste, and he began to move. Slowly. Surely. They kept their eyes open, hardly blinking, their gazes connected. With each thrust, she felt his love, his determination to protect her. Water slid down their skin, pooling where they connected, trailing down his powerful legs that kept them both steady.

They came together in a slow rise of passion, their gazes never breaking. She watched as his pupils dilated, the green rim of color growing small under a rim of glowing gold as he came.

They stood there together, him still hard in her, until the water grew cold.

She yelped at the sudden temperature change.

"I guess we've been in here for a bit." He gave her a sheepish smile and pulled out, lowering her legs to the floor. He quickly turned off the water.

Willow reached out for a towel to dry him, but he took it from her with a shake of his head. He dried her with soft pats and kisses then dried himself.

God, she was so tired. Sore. Sad. But the love-making helped.

That is what your mate it for. To be there in times of need, to help you in any way he can.

Willow agreed with her wolf, loving the way Jasper cared for her.

Once dry, Jasper put the towel back on the rack and picked her up, cradled her to his chest.

"Ready for bed?" Jasper kissed the crown of her head, and she snuggled closer.

She nodded, and he carried her, naked, to bed.

He laid her down and covered her with the comforter, sliding in behind to spoon her.

"I wouldn't want you to get cold," he rumbled.

Willow sighed. "I like it." She wiggled her butt and felt his hardness against the crease. *Gotta love werewolf stamina.* "I'm tired but not." She laughed. "I think I'm going crazy."

Jasper nipped her earlobe, sending shivers down her spine. "Makes perfect sense to me."

Taking the initiative, she turned around and lifted to straddle his waist.

Jasper smiled a purely sinful smile. "Are you ready for me?"

"Always," she whispered.

She leaned down and kissed him, licking the seam of his lips and playing with his tongue. She lifted slightly, and he slid inside her core. She sat up and smiled, loving the feel of control from being on top, watching her all-too-masculine mate lying beneath her. Locking her feet under his thighs, she lifted up his length and fell back down again. He gripped her hips and she lifted up and down, over and over again, riding him. Her breasts bounced, and she laughed. A werewolf cowgirl in all her glory. He moved his hands, trailing up to take a breast in hand, the other rubbing circles around her clit. Again, they came together, his seed warming her from the inside out.

She lay on top of him, feeling his heartbeat beneath her cheek. Thank God he walked in the door of her bakery. Even through it all, she wouldn't change it. She had Jasper and the baby in her belly. They were worth all the pain and anguish. She had a family now.

Willow held Jasper closer. She'd never let go. He was hers. Now and forever.

———

JASPER SAT IN HIS PARENTS' house the next day, waiting for their dinner to begin. Willow sat beside him in his arms, his hand protectively on her stomach. She wasn't showing yet, but she would. He couldn't wait to see her grow round with his child. He might be Beta of the Redwoods, but he was Alpha in that respect.

He nuzzled her temple and kissed it softly. "Are you ready for the mating ceremony in a few days?"

She grinned. "Of course. Though it seems odd now to have one since I already have your last name and think of you as my husband and mate."

Pride filled him as he took her lips in a deep kiss. "We've done all of this, I know, but I want to give you a day that's all yours."

"Ours," she countered.

"Ours." He pulled her closer and gazed around the room.

Cailin paced in front of the fireplace, anger pouring out of her in waves. But honestly, that always seemed to be the case lately. Maddox sat in his usual corner, close to his family, but not touching. His mother cheeks held tear streaks, but she was strong. Steady. The wife of the Alpha had to be. And his mother was more Alpha than most of the men in the Pack. Mel stood and rocked baby Finn, keeping him quiet. Edward stood on the other side of the room with North and Kade, discussing how to better protect the Den. Jasper could hear what they had to say, and would speak up if needed, but he liked where he was, sitting with his mate.

This was his family. But not all of it. They weren't whole – not without Reed. No without Adam.

His mother's quiet voice interrupted. "Dinner is ready."

As a group, they ventured to the dining room, eating their roast and mashed potatoes, but not tasting. They were werewolves, they needed the fuel and nutrients. But the absence of Reed and Adam was the elephant in the room. Their absence was the rip in their structure, creating a vacuum, sucking the warmth and joy of a family gathering.

The Centrals had come onto their land and tried to break them. And almost succeeded.

Once they got Reed back, they would be better. But the Centrals needed to pay – dearly.

Willow snuggled into his side. "I love you."

He bent down and kissed her. "I love you, too."

Jasper was so thankful he had walked into that bakery that day and scented her sweet cinnamon. He loved the way his mate tasted. He always would. He couldn't believe the steps they'd walked, but he was grateful for where they had lead. He had his Willow, his child to be. He had his growing family. He'd do anything to protect them.

They were his.

EPILOGUE

"Well, my Corbin, everything worked out," Camille purred next to him. "We broke them, and we have a Redwood prince. I call this a good day."

Corbin smiled and then slit her throat.

The pawn in his plan slid to the floor, her lifeless body heavy against his legs, her glassy eyes wide with shock.

But really, how could the bitch have been so surprised?

Corbin shook his head. No, Camille wasn't his mate. There was only one, but she was long gone. She'd left before he'd even made this plan, before he'd met Willow to play with. But that was neither here nor there.

His footsteps echoed as he walked through the dungeon, a smile on his face. His demon, Caym, walked behind him. Such a good expense, this demon. What was the life of two family members when he had a demon that could take his Pack and him to greater power?

His captive lay on the ground, shackled to the wall. Reed Jamenson. The Alpha's son.

Corbin shook his head. *Stupid wolf. Trying to save that bitch Willow. Was it worth it?*

Caym rubbed his shoulder. Comfort swelled. The demon was right.

No use getting frustrated over the actions of cannon fodder. He'd kill the wolf soon. Fun.

The door opened behind him, and his father walked in.

"I see you've taken care of Camille. Good. She annoyed me. But have someone take care of the body. I'm not in the mood for the stench." Hector turned to Caym. "And good job capturing that wolf. The Jamensons might pay for him or at least put up a good fight. If they don't do anything about it, then Corbin has a plaything for a bit. No harm, no foul."

Excitement shot through him. Oh yes, that sounded like a plan.

The demon smiled coldly at them both. A shiver of evil and pain slid down his skin, arousing him.

Nice.

Reed lifted his head, and Corbin smiled.

"You will bring us greatness, Reed," his father said. "I hope it's through your death."

Reed just smiled with blood on his lips. "Bring it."

Anger coursed through him. *Fucking Redwood ego.*

A whimper sounded from the corner.

Ah, the witch.

"Watch what you say," Hector warned. "Or we'll hurt the girl. An enjoy it."

Reed stiffened and looked toward the witch, need evident on his face.

Interesting.

The Jamensons would know who they messed with. The stupid Jamensons would call for their lost son, and the Centrals would rule. With Caym by his side, he could do no wrong. They would win, and the world would bleed. And Corbin would rejoice.

TRINITY BOUND

Redwood Pack Book 3

By
Carrie Ann Ryan

TRINITY BOUND

Hannah Lewis, a rare earth witch, is taken from the only life she's ever known. Held at her will by a sadistic wolf, she almost gives up hope that she'd ever see her real life again. But as her fellow captive, a werewolf named Reed, tries to calm her fears, she begins to feel a spark of something she never thought she'd feel – love. But is Reed, alone, enough to get her out of this dark basement so she can move on with her life?

Reed Jamenson, the artist of a werewolf Pack of Alpha males, knows instinctually that Hannah is his mate. Thus, despite their imprisonment, he will do all to protect her and then worry about their hearts. But is he strong enough to find a way for both of them to escape? And why does he feel as though something else is missing?

Josh Kolb, an ex-military human, stumbles upon Reed and Hannah and finds he must trust this new world of supernatural beings to survive. But that desire will lead the three to a triangle of attraction that will test the boundaries they all possess and its consequences in defeating the enemy. Can they all trust one another to save themselves and life as they know it? Even at the cost of their own hearts?

PROLOGUE

The sweet coppery scent of freshly spilled blood tingled Corbin's nose as he inhaled deeply. His sister, Ellie, struggled against the restraints digging into her arms and legs, but she didn't make a sound.

Much to his disappointment.

He supposed he must play a bit harder to get his desired results. Yes, that would be quite nice. She was draped in his favorite sundress, bright yellow and white daisies smiling at him from a creamy ivory background. So cheerful to look at, and even better, the blood stains marked it vividly. And, of course, his Ellie needed to look pretty for her brother, even if he'd had to force her into the damn thing.

There was no use looking like a fucking Redwood without class if you were a Central.

His palm stung as he slapped her face then moved to hit her body, over and over again. The stinging increased with each brutal hit, and he sighed. Yes, this would help his headache and aid his thinking. Her skin began to redden from the contact as he beat harder. Laughter burbled from his throat as he continued. This was true contentment.

"Hit me all you want, big brother. But you won't break me. You can't break me." Ellie's voice was steady, without a hint of strain. One would think they were on a leisurely walk and not in a dungeon where he beat her. Corbin slapped her across the face, the sound of flesh against flesh echoing against the walls.

Bitch.

Fury pulsed in his blood and raced up his spine. He bit his lip and relished the tangy taste of blood. He couldn't kill her. Not yet.

It was her fault he was in this situation in the first place. If she hadn't healed that stupid woman, Willow, in the circle after he'd gutted the bitch, this never would have happened. But no, Ellie had to go and help the bitch. So Corbin was forced to save face. He'd stormed the Redwoods' den and attacked. Yes, he may have lost a few wolves to the enemy, but they were useless anyway. There were plenty of other men to die for him in any case.

"I may not break you now, little sister," Corbin snarled, "but I will eventually. Plus, the real fun comes from the play. The longer you stay your typical brazen self, the longer I can try and bleed that from you." He shrugged. "I really don't give a fuck. But you need to learn your place."

"They'll come for him, you know." A thin line of blood trickled from her mouth. He needed to stop soon so her internal bleeding could begin to heal before he started again. The next time he might take out his sharper toys. He smiled at the thought.

"Oh, they'll come. This is, after all, their weakling, their *artist*." He spat the word. Art. This Reed was an egotistical loser without a designated title in his Pack. He was just one son of the many, nothing like Corbin, the only son and Heir to the Central Pack. He cursed under his breath as he hit Ellie again. They'd gone into the Redwood den with a purpose—to find Jasper, the Redwood's Beta, and take him. But, instead, they got Reed.

They'd kidnapped the wrong wolf, but it would be okay. If Reed's family didn't come for him, Corbin would just kill him—slowly. It was no skin off his back. He hit Ellie again, and this time a slight whimper escaped her.

Ah, progress.

Though the whole wolf debacle grated on him, what really bothered him was the witch. He needed to know more about Hannah.

What made her tick? What were her powers? Why did the demon, Caym, tell him she was important? Damn it. He hit Ellie square in the face, harder than he'd planned, and she passed out cold.

Fucking temper.

He missed his other sister, Ellie's twin. But she was dead by his father's hands so they could bring Caym to this world. That sister would have at least screamed for him and moaned in pain. But no, Corbin was stuck with Ellie. Always perfect fucking Ellie, the one who wouldn't join in their father's plans.

Ah, Father.

Hector was getting on his last nerve. The old man didn't have the vision Corbin did. No, his father only saw the small picture. Ruling the wolves and killing some humans. Corbin saw it clearer, but as Heir, Corbin had to stand back and let his father have the power. That would have to change soon. He smiled at that promising thought. His jaw tightened as he clenched his teeth together and fisted his hands.

Caym prowled into his chamber and smiled at him. The demon's dark looks reminded Corbin of a fallen angel. Yet there was nothing angelic about the being in front of him. Midnight black locks of hair framed his chiseled, pale face. His black eyes had a rim of deep red around the iris, enhancing his darkness.

Simply beautiful.

"I see you've let Ellie sleep for a bit." Caym's smooth voice washed over him like liquid silk.

Corbin smiled. "Yes, I'm such a giving wolf." They both laughed.

"They have the video feed finally ready, if you'd like to join me." Caym slid his hand up Corbin's bare arm, causing shivers to race up his spine. Warmth tingled in his icy chest and his pulse raced.

"I'll just leave dear sister here. When she wakes up, she can think about what she's done."

"That sounds reasonable." Caym danced his fingers across Corbin's chin before turning to leave the room.

Intriguing.

He followed the demon out, watching him glide with each step. Caym really was a handsome man. Though Corbin liked to torture and play with women, he preferred men for his bedroom activities. And if the subtle, or rather not so subtle, touches that just occurred were any indication, Caym might prefer him as well.

Interesting.

They entered the viewing room. Two video screens hung on the wall, with buttons and knobs on a control panel beneath them. The demon sat back in a black leather chair, arms cradled behind his head. Lean muscles bunched as he stretched.

Nice.

Corbin strolled past and turned on one of the viewing screens. He walked to a chair, took a seat, and sat back as Caym rested his hand on Corbin's. The image came on the screen, bringing a smile to his lips. His two prisoners lay on the cement floor, chained to stone walls.

Very picturesque.

The male, Reed, clad only in his jeans, pulled at his chains. Silly wolf, those chains were reinforced and not easily broken. He knew from experience. Chills of need racked his body at the memories. The woman, Hannah, slept on the floor, just out of reach of Reed's hands. Perfect. Reed would try and help the girl but wouldn't be able to. It would only hurt and entice his wolf more. Corbin licked his lips in anticipation. He couldn't wait to get his hands on them both, if his father let him.

His fingers ached to see what would happen to the two in his chamber. They would give him information, no matter what it took. He hoped the process would drag on. He loved the prolonged screams of agony, the blood and pain like a cherry on his sundae. How he longed to play. And when he was through with them, he would kill them. There was no use, beyond his own pleasure, for a low-level wolf and a witch with no coven.

Caym squeezed Corbin's hand then brushed his fingers up his arm before standing and taking a step toward the screen.

"I can imagine what you and I could do with the pair of them." The demon's voice sank into his pores. His eyelids closed as his arousal peaked. "But," Caym continued, "we need to get rid of some...obstacles."

"Obstacles." Namely his father, Hector. The Alpha.

"Yes, once we achieve that, you and I could have a great partnership." He paused. "In more ways than one." He smiled, his angelic face taking on an evil light.

Corbin panted in need. "I agree."

"The two of us could strive for even greater progress together. We can call forth the whole of the demons and control them."

They both laughed with insatiable hunger. Yes, this would be a partnership made in hell. Literally.

CHAPTER ONE

Cold spread from a pinprick of sensation as a droplet of water hit Hannah Lewis's cheek. It trailed down to her eye, forcing her to open them to blink it away. Stone walls surrounded her, and the frayed edges on the cement floor dug into her skin. The only means of escape seemed to be a lone rusty metal door in the stone wall. No windows illuminated the room. Cut off from the outside world, she couldn't feel the earth.

As an earth witch, she needed the sensation of soil beneath her feet, the air dancing across her face and through her hair. But cut off, she drifted without an anchor. Hannah slowly sat up, and her muscles ached from her stay.

She snorted. *Stay*. Right.

That sounded like she was happy to be here. No, the bruises and cuts from her *captivity* hurt. But she thanked the goddess she wasn't hurt any more than she was.

The man sharing her room moaned in his sleep. No, not a man, a *werewolf*. By the shouts of their captors, she knew him to be Reed, a wolf of the Redwood Pack, son of the Alpha. They'd brought him in three nights before. At least she thought it was three nights. She couldn't be sure anymore. He seemed to hurt more than she. They had chained him to the wall, same as her, but far enough apart they couldn't touch. And if they were to speak to each other, the guards came in and beat Reed. Never her though. It was almost like a cruel joke to have someone share her burden but be allowed no contact. Her gut twisted, and bile filled her mouth.

Her fingers ached to touch his smooth skin and heal his pains as the healer she was. But she couldn't get close enough to him to do so. Another cruelty. She couldn't bear to see him hurt.

Reed shifted, then snapped open his eyes. She gave him an encouraging smile, the best she could come up with under these conditions. He smiled back, that small gesture almost lighting up his face. Maybe in another time, another place, when they weren't being held in the Central's basement, with no clue whether they would live or die, they would have met and gone on a date. She smiled again at the thought. Yes, that would have been nice. Her smiled faded. But that was not the case. And by the looks of this place, it would never be. Sadness filled her at the loss of something she didn't know she wanted.

Reed reached out and spread his fingers toward her, careful of the cameras watching their every move. Hannah did the same, longing to feel contact. To remember who she was.

The metal door scraped open, the screeching sound echoing in the dank room. They both pulled their arms back as she began to shake in fear. She cursed herself for her cowardliness. But it had been too long since she held hope. She didn't want to die. Not here. Not now.

The Central Alpha's son, Corbin, walked into the room with his smooth glide and a snarl on his lips. Hannah hid the shudders fighting to rack her body at the sight of him. His eyes were dark orbs with no light of goodness hiding within. Whatever was on his mind reeked of evil, an evil she wanted no part of, but it looked as though she had no choice.

The man strode to her, nodding to his two accompanying guards. The guards walked toward her and unshackled her arms and legs. Pain tingled in her fingers and toes as the blood rushed through them from being cut off from good circulation for so long. *Oh goddess. What is he going to do with me?* The guards lifted her to her feet, their grips digging into her arms, hurting her further.

"Let go of her. Take me," Reed's growled from his place on the floor, his voice gravelly.

Oh, how she wished she could just be with this stranger and not go where Corbin wanted. But she couldn't let him be hurt either. She didn't know why, other than the fact she hated to see anyone harmed. It pained her to think about him in her position. He might be a were-wolf and be able to heal at a faster rate, but she could take what Corbin brought. She had to.

Corbin laughed at Reed and took a previously unseen whip to her companion's back. Reed groaned in pain at the contact of the whip flaying his flesh. Hannah whimpered at the sight of his blood leaking to the floor. The guards pulled her toward Corbin, her feet trailing the ground as she fought their hold. They merely shook her violently for her to comply. The Alpha's son grabbed her from them and forced her against him. Bile rose in her throat at the oily feel of his skin, his aura.

She looked back over her shoulder at Reed. He lay bleeding, glaring at the guards and Corbin, still struggling against his chains to reach her. Why did she feel such a connection to a man she'd never met outside these stone walls? And, by the look on Reed's face, he might feel the same. Corbin dug his fingers into her arm and shook her, forcing her back to her cold reality.

As the man pulled her to the door, she fought against his hold. His hand came across her face, the sting radiating in her cheek, bringing tears to her eyes. Reed's shouts and pleas followed her out the door until the men closed it with a slam, along with the hope she would get out of this alive. A sinking feeling bottomed out in her stomach. This might be the end.

Corbin dragged her down the hall, and she pulled against at his grip, struggling to get free. She screamed at the guards for help. Surely, there was at least one person out there who could help her. *Dear goddess.* Her captor's hand, again, contacted her face, bringing stars to her eyes and a thin warm trickle of what must be blood down her chin.

At the end of the hall, a door with natural light spilling out along the cracks on the side and bottom, tingled that last spark of hope. Could she escape? She fought to release herself from Corbin's hold. If she got out, she could get help and come back for Reed. She didn't know when she'd started to think of not only herself, but Reed, but she didn't care. Her foot came down on Corbin's instep. She used the surprise to kick him in the groin and twisted free. The evil man yelled, as she ran toward the light. She panted and prayed she could make it. Corbin's hand shot out and grabbed her again. The spark of hope dulled to a slight numbing light. He took her arm in an unforgiving grip and threw her against the wall. Her head cracked against the stone, but she was thankful he hadn't used the whole of his strength.

"Don't you fucking try that again, girl. Or I won't kill you when I'm done with you," he snarled. His torment promised pain and suffering if the reward was death. She held onto the whimper that threatened to escape her throat. She refused to give him the satisfaction.

Corbin lifted her up and carried her to another room off the hall. Before she could pull her mind out of the fuzziness caused by his strikes, he had her strapped down onto a cool metal table, the leather straps digging into her arms and legs and around her stomach. He tightened the straps with a bruising force. The one on her stomach cut into her skin, a thin line of blood forming.

Oh goddess.

Fear crawled on her skin like thousands of tiny bugs searching for a home.

What was he going to do?

Hannah took deep breaths, trying to calm herself. If she panicked and lost her focus, she might lose a chance of escape. She almost laughed at that. Escape? She wasn't some alpha heroine in a romance novel. No, she was just a witch who needed her earth and missed a guy who shared a cell with her. She must be crazy.

The strong scent of lemony citrus invaded her nose when she inhaled again. She almost coughed at the pungent aroma. She looked around at the sickly sterile environment and shivered at the cold practicality of Corbin's torture chamber. The scent was harsh to her senses. Though not as strong as a werewolf's, her sense of smell was more attentive than a normal human's.

Corbin moved above her, blocking her view of the room, a gleeful look in his eyes. Like a kid on Christmas morning waiting to open his enormous amounts of presents and stocking stuffers. She swallowed down the vomit threatening to rise. This was going to hurt. Badly.

The evil wolf carried a cat-o'-nine tails in one hand and a whip in another.

He never stopped smiling as he hit her five times with the tails then five times with the whip. She cried out with each hit, each stroke. She might have been strong in some respects, but the blinding pain racking her body and her blood soaking the floor was too much for her to handle. Tears leaked from her eyes as he hit and hit.

"Tell me, Hannah, what is your power? Why are you so damn important?" Corbin sneered the words, looking engrossed in his flaying.

Powers? That was what this was all about? She was just an earth witch, a rare one due to her healing. But that couldn't be what he wanted. Right?

Corbin hit her again, her vision going black, as the door opened. Hector, the Alpha, Corbin's father, walked in.

"Enough, Corbin." Hector's voice radiated power and demanded respect.

Corbin stopped but looked like he was about to revolt. He took a deep breath, glared at Hannah, and then painstakingly placed the tools of his trade on their bench. With one last smirk in her direction, he stomped away like an insolent puppy.

Hector stepped purposely toward her.

She braced for his fist or hand, too pained to do anything but take it.

But the strike never came.

"Hannah, why won't you use your powers?"

She couldn't, not without the earth. But she wouldn't tell them that. No, she couldn't tell them anything. Once she did, they wouldn't need her anymore. Then they would kill her. And maybe Reed.

CHAPTER TWO

Reed Jamenson watched as Corbin dragged Reed's mate out of the dungeon against her will. He growled and pulled at his chains again as fury boiled in his veins. Hannah, sweet Hannah, with her curly brown hair and plump lips, dragged like a marionette doll whose strings were pulled too tight. Her screams seeped through the metal door, and he pulled at his chains, willing all of the strength a werewolf like him could possess. Blood seeped beneath the manacles as he struggled to no avail.

Typical. He wasn't strong enough to protect a mate he'd just met. Wasn't even strong enough to protect himself. Shame dimmed his fury. That's how he'd ended up in the Central's clutches to begin with. Too weak to escape capture. He might have sacrificed himself to save his brother's mate, but he could have done more. The Centrals had come to their den and attacked, killing countless Pack members. His brothers had fought valiantly, purposely. Yet, Reed, only an artist who thought he could fight, had lost.

They'd knocked him unconscious, thrown him in their truck, and taken him away. Three nights or so had passed, yet his family hadn't come. Did they want to? When the Centrals had taken Willow, his sister-in-law, she'd been gone for only a day at most. Their family had chased after Anna, his other sister-in-law, but they were too late for her. Grief warred with his other emotions. What group would he land in? Or would they come for him at all? He was the fourth of six sons and one daughter. He held no power in the Pack, no purpose. He was just a man who liked to paint and fancied himself an artist. A nobody. Yeah, he was a werewolf and could kill a man with his bare hands, but he still felt inadequate sometimes.

His arms and legs were a mottled collection of bruises and cuts spliced together in a macabre pattern that almost appealed to his artist senses. Almost. Every time they came in and he tried to help Hannah in any way, they beat him. His back and side were sore to the touch. No doubt he had bruised, if not broken, rib or two. They kept away from his face oddly enough. But Corbin and his cronies didn't stray from Hannah's. And Reed couldn't protect her. Rage bubbled up from deep inside him.

Reed shook his head to rid himself of those melancholy thoughts and took deep calming breaths. Acting irrational wouldn't help; it could only harm in this situation. And frankly, he needed to get out of here and save Hannah. Even if he had to do it himself. They'd dragged her out of here and he could do nothing but watch and pull at his chains.

The thought of her honey and bitter apple scent made his mouth salivate. Her corkscrew curls lay flat against her face when they let her walk or when she shook her head. His fingers ached to pull at one gently and see if it would spring back. He wanted to paint her angelic face, her chestnut hair. That's what he did when he found a subject he found desirable. But Hannah was no normal subject. Her wide gray eyes stared at him with a glimmer of hope, and he prayed he could deliver. Though he was in a dark, gloomy dungeon, his cock still hardened at the thought of what she would taste like when he licked her skin. Or lower.

"I'm sure you can find out hot stuff, once you actually get our mate out of here."

Reed's wolf practically snickered at him. But that was par for the course. Fucking wolf never took anything too seriously, but still wanted to protect in his own way.

"We'll save her. We have to."

Reed could only agree.

The metal door creaked open, and the demon walked in, a limp form in his arms. Reed bit back a moan. *Hannah.*

The smell of blood, her blood, reached his nostrils before he saw the thin trails on her stomach, arms, and legs. He was going to fucking kill whoever had touched her. Corbin, the demon, the random guard who looked at her wrong, he didn't care. They would die. Painfully.

Her spilled blood enraged him. Muscles bulging, he pulled at his chains and tried to take a swipe at the demon. His hand turned to a claw as his wolf tried to take control, which was a departure from his wolf's usual jovial self.

The demon merely laughed at his attempt and stood back. With a nod to the camera, the chains attached to the collar around his neck tightened and pulled, blocking his oxygen. He still fought his chains, not caring if he passed out. The demon gave another nod. The two goons who'd taken Hannah out the door before came back and locked her to the wall again. She slumped to the floor unconscious, and he growled in pain for her.

The demon smirked and walked out of the room, the goons on his heels like strays begging for scraps. Reed's collar loosened, and he gasped for breath. As his body absorbed sweet oxygen, he took a closer look at Hannah. For some, most likely sadistic, reason, they'd placed her closer to him. He didn't care to think of the whys yet, but now he could touch her, hold her, care for her. Though he wasn't like North, his brother the doctor, he would do his best to heal her as well.

He scooted on the stone floor, flicking pebbles of the broken wall away from her so she could be comfortable. Well, at least as comfortable as possible. She looked like a broken doll with her eyes closed and chocolate curls surrounding her pale face. He brushed a curl away, the soft hair like silk on his cut-up skin, and saw a large bruise forming on her face. A slight nick on her lip had already begun clotting, and Reed had to hold back a growl of anger. He didn't want to scare her. Only kill that slimy fuck, Corbin.

Long gashes ran up her torso, arms, and legs. The thought of the whip or whatever the fucker had used made him want to vomit then go back and use the damn weapon on Corbin. Yeah, that sounded nice. Maybe he'd give it to Hannah when she woke up so she could have a go and take vengeance on the man. That thought was almost enough to perk him up.

Reed leaned over her, careful of her injuries and whispered her name.

"Hannah," he whispered again, caressing the unbruised side of her face. Despite the coldness of the room and the loss of blood, warmth radiated from her skin. He inhaled her honey and bitter apple scent again, this time detecting a faint earthy scent.

Interesting.

His mate was a witch. He liked the idea she already knew of the supernatural. Once they got out of this, he wouldn't have to explain everything to her like Jasper had with Willow and Kade had with Melanie. It was nice at least something was going his way.

"Hannah."

She mumbled something incoherent and turned into his palm, nuzzling him. His heart swelled at the unfamiliar touch of a mate leaning closer. Was this what his brothers felt every time their mates walked into the room? He liked it already.

Even bruised, bleeding, and beaten, his mate was cute.

Her lips parted and Reed felt the very inappropriate urge to kiss her. He shook his head. *Seriously man, not the right time.* And frankly his mind was too befuddled to think about any aspects of mating besides the big picture.

Reed looked around for something to clean Hannah with, but in the moldy dungeon, not much was available. Desperate to at least clean up the dried blood, he tore strips off his shirt that lay on the ground next to where he was chained, the sounds of ripping fabric echoing off the stone walls. He took the strips of cotton and placed them against the wall, collecting the droplets and small streams of water along the stone. Now damp with whatever moisture he could get, he took the strips and carefully cleaned around her wounds. Only small gashes rose along her skin, thankfully. For the most part, there only seemed to be bruising and angry red lash marks. The bastard had only cut her skin in some places.

His scent mingled with hers, crisp apples and wolf. He liked it. And by the growling contentment he heard from his wolf, he did too. He could get used to this. But something still nagged at him. Something was missing. Was it because of where they were? Because they hadn't completed the mating? This was his first time meeting a potential mate. He didn't know quite what to feel—what was right. Not all things could come back to instinct.

That missing feeling crept up on him. Was this how Kade felt with Tracy? He had met another potential before he met Melanie, and it hadn't worked out. Did Kade also feel this missing element? Something lacking? Was Hannah really the right one for him?

Reed shook it off. This was not the time to think about such things. He needed to heal Hannah.

He traced her face again with the tips of his fingers, reveling in her beauty even with the swelling around her bruises.

Hannah opened her eyes and screamed.

"Hannah, shh," Reed gently whispered. "It's okay. It's me, Reed. I won't let him hurt you again. I promise."

Reed stared into her dove gray eyes, pleading for her to believe him, even though he knew some things might be out of his control.

Hannah took a deep breath and then sank into his arms. Her warm weight felt like heaven. Like home. He held her to his chest, careful of her hurts, and whispered reassurances in her ear.

"Hannah, don't panic, baby. We have to be quiet. The cameras are still on, and they can hear us." He kissed her temple, too weak not to relish her sweet taste. "I don't know why they put us so close together this time, but we can use it to our advantage. We can try to formulate a plan and get out of here. I'll protect you. I promise."

"I'm not incapable." Hannah's soft voice reached his ears. "I can help to."

Reed let out a dry chuckle. "Good, because we may need it."

She let out a surprised laugh then cringed in pain. Reed stiffened and his heart sped up.

"What hurts, Hannah? Tell me and I can help. I don't know much, but I'll do what I can."

He couldn't let go of her completely, but he did survey her body to check her cuts. Okay, he also looked because her curves were damned delicious. Bitable for sure.

He tore more off his shirt, noticing the way Hannah's gaze never strayed far from his naked chest. Reed almost preened for her but caught himself, finding that slightly inappropriate. As he cleaned up the rest of the dried blood, she cuddled into him, and he bit his lip not to groan at the contact. Definitely not the time to be thinking about pounding into her soft curves.

He stroked her face again, staring into her eyes. He could get lost in those eyes.

"Really, Reed? How cliché can you get?"

Reed held in a laugh at his wolf. Yeah, that pretty much summed up his thoughts for the moment.

"Dammit, I hate my powers sometimes," Hannah grumbled.

Startled at the curse coming out of her seemingly sweet mouth, it Reed took a moment to comprehend what she'd said.

"Huh?" *Smooth.*

"My powers. I'm a healer. But I can only heal others. Not myself." She bit her lip in what he thought was annoyance and looked damn cute.

"You're a healer?"

"Uh huh. So I can heal you, if you don't mind me touching you." Again, her teeth bit into her plump lip.

His eyes widened, and he told himself to remember the thing about touching for later. Their Pack was missing a true Healer. One who could heal by the touch of their hand and would strengthen the Pack. North, his brother, was their doctor. But it wasn't the same. Could this be fate giving him a nudge?

"Um, you can heal me. I don't mind." He felt his ears warm, and he knew he must be blushing like a school boy. *Oh, yes, that would show her how perfect I am for her. Act like a virgin in the back of my mom's Buick.*

"Okay, this won't hurt. But it might tingle."

She placed her warm hands on his chest and ribs. They both gasped at the contact. Did she feel something too? He didn't think witches had clear mates like werewolves did, but he couldn't be sure. His body tingled where her skin touched his. He felt the muscles and ribs knitting together, blood pulsating in his veins. Who knew healing could be so erotic? He growled at the thought of her hands on another male while she healed them. Did they feel this good too?

Hannah quickly lifted her hands. Reed felt lost at the loss of her touch.

"I'm sorry. Did I hurt you?" she said, panting a bit, but still sounding worried.

"What? No. It felt good actually." Again, he felt his face heat up.

"Oh, but you growled." She scrunched her brows, utterly confused and very cute.

"No, I was just thinking about something else. I didn't mean to scare you."

"Oh you didn't scare me. I don't think you could ever scare me." She ducked her head, but not before Reed caught a shy smile on her face.

He didn't know what to feel about that. Did that mean she didn't think he could protect her? Or did she feel safe around him? He hoped it was the latter.

She smiled then settled into his arms, careful of her wounds. Hannah felt incredible next to him. Right. But still, something was missing. Something important. He just didn't know what. And even though they fit together quite perfectly, he didn't tell her they were mates. This wasn't the right time, and frankly, he had no idea how to bring it up. They needed to get out of the basement first. Then he needed to kill some sadistic ass.

CHAPTER THREE

J osh Kolb rubbed the back of his neck, the tension of the day ebbing through his nerve endings, screeching at him to take a break. Right, like that would happen. Weary exhaustion crept through his body. He was getting too damn old for this shit. He'd been working for his buddy's security company for five long years since he'd got out of the SEALs.

He'd just got off a job he was sure was slowly sucking the life out of him. Mrs. Carnoski, an elderly woman who in no way resembled a nice grandmother type, was an ice queen with a stick up her ass. No matter how many times he showed the woman how to set the alarm and work the system, she still needed his "help." And by help, he meant she needed to press her Botox body against him and flirt endlessly with innuendos no one could mistake. Josh cringed at the thought of her touching him. Not even on his weakest days would he ever want that bag of bones.

Still fuming and a little uncomfortable, he walked to the hot dog stand and ordered a reindeer dog. He loved Jim's. Homemade sausage from reindeer, boar, elk, or anything the man could hunt for himself. Jim would grill it once it was ordered then add caramelized onions and cream cheese. Add a bag of chips and a Coke and Josh had himself a delicious meal for five bucks. Not too shabby.

Josh strode to the nearest bench and relaxed against the cool metal backing. He took a deep breath of the crisp mountain air. Snow was on its way. In the mountainous outskirts of Seattle, most were used to seeing rain, but the winter months were finally leading to snowfall. Josh shrugged. It didn't really matter what the weather was, nothing about his daily routine would change. He'd eat, sleep, watch TV, and work out—alone. Then he'd go to work and wish he were alone. What was a little snow?

He was off the job for the day but didn't know what he was going to do. He could go home, but why? Nothing was waiting for him there. Just a shabby apartment with bare walls devoid of personal touches. Josh swallowed the last of his dog, licking the cream cheese off his fingers before washing it down with the rest of his Coke. Fuck, he was lonely. And not happy about the fact he cared that he was lonely. He was a SEAL, for fuck's sake. He shouldn't care one way or the other. But here he was, at the onset of winter, sitting on a park bench, alone and pissy, and apparently a pussy about it as well. Josh shook his head.

Letting out a deep breath, Josh closed his eyes, and opened up his senses to his surroundings. The wind brushed his face, cooling the melancholy temper heating his cheeks. Murmurs of conversations from passersby, customers and townspeople quickly shopping and mingling before the coming storm drifted through on the wind. He turned his head toward voices, most likely two teens, both low, almost a whisper but with such a hint of excitement and dread, it carried to his ears on the wind.

"Did you hear?" one of the boys asked, fear on his tongue. "One of the Jamenson sons was taken after the fight. Reed, I think."

"Reed? Which one was he?" the other boy asked.

"The artist. No real title, but still the Alpha's son."

"Crap, what are they doing about it?"

"I don't know. But you know the Centrals are about to get their asses kicked. You can't just steal the son of an Alpha and think it's okay. No matter how crazy you are."

"No shit."

"I just hope they find him."

"Yeah. But it's weird, ya know."

"What?"

"Reed being taken so soon after that witch was. Remember that?"

"Huh?"

"That witch who owned the herbal shop in Callensbury. Some guys came in, roughed up the shop, killed her mom, and then took her."

"Really?"

"Yeah. I wonder if it's connected somehow."

"Well, if it is, I'm sure the Jamensons will find out. That's what they do."

"But they can't find them. It's been what...three days or so?"

"They will. They have to. The Jamensons are like gods. They'll do it."

"Sure."

Both boys walked off, leaving Josh to ponder their words.

Someone had kidnapped the Alpha's son? Interesting. As a human, he shouldn't know about werewolves, witches, and whatever else went bump in the night. But being on some of those more risky missions put him right in the path of nightmares better left unknown.

Not to mention Josh was a Finder.

One look at the person's face and he could close his eyes, open his senses, and Find them anywhere in the world. Not a bad talent to have in the SEALs. But he didn't want to use it in his new life. Too many memories. Too many people lost and never Found. Because no matter how hard he tried, he couldn't Find someone across the veil of death.

Flashes of chestnut hair and gray eyes merged with sandy blond hair and forest green eyes. What the hell? He'd never laid eyes on these two souls, but he could see every definition of them clear as day. Memories of their daily lives passed too quickly for him to discern any real significance other than the fact he felt as though he knew these people. Or needed to know them down to the very essence of his heart.

The images molded into fights, shouts, and scrapes. Men came for each of them, stealing them from their homes. Their lives. In that moment, he knew who he was looking at.

Reed and the witch.

How could he see their pasts? That wasn't something he normally did. No, he could only Find their present.

Josh closed his eyes, ignoring the first fall of snowflakes brushing his cheeks and eyelashes. He opened his senses the way his grand-mother had taught him before she passed long ago. Tunneling through the webs of souls he'd met, through the threads of destiny and paths less taken, he searched for the two he'd never met. He needed to Find them.

There.

The sandy-haired wolf, Reed, sat next to the curly-haired beauty, the witch. He wished he knew her name. Darkness surrounded them, creating an almost hazy interpretation of what he should be seeing, as though something was trying to block him. But he could still pull on that thin, but strong thread of connection between the three of them. Yes, for whatever reason, there was a connection, clear as day. What to do with that would have to be shelved for now and dealt with at a later date.

Josh concentrated harder, grasping at their location. *Ahh.* Reed and the witch were in a basement of some sort, deep in the forest. He looked harder and around the dilapidated building, searching for land-marks so he could get to them.

Wait. Go to them? Since when was he mounting a rescue mission for two people he hadn't met? He wasn't in the SEALs anymore. His internal military objective slapped him upside the head. *Once a SEAL always a SEAL.* That wasn't just for those pesky Marines. He would try to rescue them for the clear reason that it was his duty, not only because he felt that tenuous connection between the three of them.

No, definitely not.

Josh opened his eyes, looking at the slight accumulation of snowfall that promised to be a monster of a storm in the coming day. Fewer people lingered on the streets, and the temperature had slowly dropped. But Josh wasn't thinking about the people in his line of vision. No, the owners of those green eyes and then those gray eyes firmly held his attention.

No matter how hard he tried to deny it, it was there. But what was so special about this duo? Why did he have to be on this bench at this time to hear about the kidnapping from those two kids? Fucking fate and all that shit.

Josh closed his eyes again, remembering the looks on their faces in their captivity. Pain radiated in his head at the thought. Why was he so close to this? Why did it hurt *him* so much that they were out of his reach and in dire need of help?

What was Josh going to do? Could he talk to someone and let them handle it so he could run away? No, not run away; let someone closer to the situation and the captives deal with it.

Josh snorted. *Yeah, just throw away the responsibility. That sounds like a plan.*

He was ex-military. A human. He wasn't supposed to even know about the existence of another world. The supernatural. If he went to the Redwoods and asked them for help or gave them the information he knew, would they believe him? Or laugh at his face and tell him to go away? Or worse, would they believe him and kill him if they thought he was part of the plot of involving the loss of their loved ones?

Too complicated and strenuous by far. Fuck. He'd have to go in alone and get evidence. More evidence than just the fact he'd seen them in his head. Yeah, because that didn't sound crazy. His parents and other kids sure had thought so. But this wasn't about him. Two people who, for some reason he could Find in a way he could with no one else, were in trouble. They needed his help.

That settled it. Josh would go to them, to that old building with its dark basement and hazy surroundings, most likely due to some highly dangerous magic he had no defense for. He would get them out right then if he could, see what he was able to do. But if that didn't work, he'd get evidence of where they were and find a way to get it to the Redwoods. They were strong werewolves after all. Some of the strong-est. Surely they could rescue Reed and the witch if they had help.

Yes, that sounded like a reasonable plan.

Josh stood up and stretched his aching back. *Fuck*. He rubbed the back of his neck in frustration. He was most likely running to his death. But he couldn't leave them out there, alone but for each other. No, not when he was an able body who could maybe help. And frankly, it wasn't like he had anything else to go back to if he didn't make it. These two were important to him for some reason; he just had to save them and find out why.

CHAPTER FOUR

Hannah shivered in Reed's arms and he held tighter, trying to keep her warm. The temperature outside had dropped dramatically and slowly seeped into the small room. Her little body refused to stay heated in the dank basement. Her cold curves snuggled up to him, as he tried to infuse his warmth into her. His body temperature might be higher than a normal human's, but no matter what he did, she just couldn't stay warm.

Hannah sneezed in her sleep, jerking herself awake. Reed laughed at how damn cute she was. Seriously, who sneezed themselves awake?

"That wasn't funny, jerk." Her small smile and delicate blush belied any harshness in her tone. "Reed, don't laugh at me. This isn't any time to laugh." Her mouth curved a bit more, and she gave him a look like she was trying to hold back her own laughter. Reed wanted to lick the curve of her lips, taste them to see if she carried that honey and bitter apple scent in her pores.

"I'm sorry, dear Hannah." He tried to put on his best solemn face but barely refrained from laughing. Even though they were stuffed and locked in a basement, he couldn't help but relish the fact he held her in his arms. The only thing to make it better would be getting out of there. Oh, and if they were naked. But that was just a given.

"You better be. It's not nice to make fun of a sleeping person." She sobered. "But thank you for making me want to laugh, even though there really isn't anything to laugh about here."

Oh how he wanted to make everything better with a flick of his wrist, to be able to save and protect her. But he couldn't; there was nothing for him to do. The walls were too enforced, too many of the guards held strength that rivaled his own. Plus, Corbin held weapons no honorable werewolf should hold. If he didn't have to protect and shield Hannah, he might have been able to do it. But with his mind distracted by the fact he'd found his mate and still felt as though he was missing something, he didn't feel comfortable risking her life. Reed shook his head. He needed to find a new topic, something that would get their minds off their captivity. The only thing that came to mind and piqued his interest was sitting in his lap, rubbing her bitable bottom on his erection every time she moved, whether she knew it or not.

"Tell me about yourself, Hannah." If he hadn't been holding her, he wouldn't have noticed the almost indecipherable stiffness in her body, but he continued. He needed to hear more about her, and if her reaction was any indication, she needed to let out her tension and share. "What are you like outside of these four walls?"

Hannah took a deep breath, her breasts rubbing against his arm as she did so. Reed held back a groan. This wasn't the time to bend her over and mount her.

"I disagree on that."

Reed ignored his wolf. He was pretty sure the animal thought about sex more than he did. And that was saying something since he'd been pretty deprived recently.

"I shouldn't be telling you anything about me." Hannah's face scrunched up in confusion.

Reed felt a pang of hurt at her words, but reminded himself she didn't know they were mates. His fault, he knew, but it was still the right choice, for now.

"I won't share what you say here. But I want to know more about you. Who are you, Hannah?"

Hannah let out a deep breath and bit her lip.

"I'm an earth witch. I control the soils and can call on other parts of nature if I need to. But I'm only moderately functional with that stuff. My real talents are in the healing."

Reed nodded, urging her to continue.

Hannah held out her hand, absentmindedly playing with the hair on his arms. Goosebumps raised on his flesh at her soft touch.

"I owned a potions and herb shop with my mother." Her voice broke at that last part. Tears fell down her cheeks.

"Hannah, baby, I'm sorry. I didn't mean to upset you. We don't have to talk about this anymore."

She bit her lip in her delectable way and shook her head.

"No, I need to tell you. I want to tell you." She stared off into space, her mind on whatever memory haunted her dreams. "When Corbin's men took me, they destroyed the shop. My mom and I were working that day. It wasn't too busy so she told me to go in the back and mix up some more lotion for dry skin. She said she'd take care of the register and customers. If it got busier, or if someone needed me, she'd get me. I didn't hear the door open from where I sat. I was too engrossed in what I was doing. It takes a lot of concentration to make a good potion and herb remedy. So I didn't hear anything until I heard her scream."

Reed held her closer, her heartbeat fast against his as tears ran faster down her face.

"I ran to the front, not thinking of something that could hurt me. I just had to get to my mom. You know?"

Reed knew. That's how he'd gotten here too.

"And then..." Her voice broke again, and Reed rubbed small circles on her back, trying to offer soothing comfort where there was none to give. "I didn't see her, only a shadow, and a puddle of blood. But I knew. She was gone. And I had been in the back, not paying attention to what was going on."

"Hannah, it wasn't your fault."

"But I could have helped her."

"Hannah, they went there for a purpose." Shit, wrong thing to say.

"Yeah, to find me. And they killed my mom for it." Anger and despair swirled in her eyes.

Reed was at a loss of what to say—an uncommon occurrence for him. Usually, he was the one people came to for cheering up. He was the one with the words and pleasantries. Yet with his mate in his arms, he felt inadequate.

"It's not your fault. It's Corbin's and Hector's fault. They were the one who had those men come for you. They were the ones who took your mom away from you. There was nothing you could do." She must have felt a hundred times more helpless than he felt at the moment.

"I know that. But it still doesn't make it right. When I came out of the back room, I saw her and screamed. I didn't use my powers. Shock, I guess. But I should have. Maybe then I would have gotten out of there. But no. They came for me and knocked me out. I don't remember what happened after that. I woke up here, and then a couple of weeks or so later, you came too."

Reed held her to his chest, trying to give her the strength she needed, knowing he was lacking. She stopped crying, exhausted emotionally as well as physically. A salty trail of tears remained on her cheeks. Reed wiped away their evidence with the pad of his thumb, taking in the softness of her skin.

"No matter what happens, I will find a way to kill him." Reed's voice deepened with a promise of vengeance. He sounded cold and calculating, unlike his normal self. But maybe like he was worth something.

"You'll have to take a number and stand behind me. Because I plan on killing those bastards and dancing on their graves."

His Hannah was a force to be reckoned with. Sexy. He nuzzled her hair, inhaling her honey and crisp apple scent.

"Reed?" Her soft voice tickled the faint hairs on his chest.

"Yes, baby?"

"Why do they want us?"

That was the question, wasn't it? One he'd been contemplating since he woke here next to, but not touching, the sweet witch in his arms.

"I think they took you because you are a rare healing earth witch. You might be able to aid them somehow."

"That's what I thought. Odd to think a man so bent on pain would want a healer."

"I'd try not to think about that too much," Reed whispered as shivers racked Hannah's body.

"But what about you?"

"I'm not really worth anything. I'm just a plain werewolf. It must just be for ransom. They could have taken any of my brothers and had their powers on hand. But no, they took me." A nobody artist with no title. Just the blood of the Alpha running in his veins.

"Hey, that's not true. You are worth something. You are powerful. I've seen you. Don't count yourself short." Her indignation at his self-deprecation was nothing short of cute. Wrong, but cute.

"I'm only an artist, Hannah. I'm the son of the Alpha, but I don't have a title. I'm not really Alpha enough to be useful to the Centrals or even part of the Jamensons frankly. My brothers are so much more."

"Reed Jamenson, this isn't the time for a pity party." She scowled at him, her bottom lip puffing out.

He looked at the stone walls with their chains and lack of light.

"Hannah, baby? This is the *perfect* time for a pity party."

Their laughter mingled, boarding close to hysterical. Shit, they really needed to get out of here. Fast.

The metal door screeched open, bringing their laughter to a frightening halt. Without a word, Hector strode in, lifted his arm, and shot at the two of them.

A slight trickle of light bounced off the barrel of the gun a split second before Reed threw himself over Hannah. The deafening sound of a bullet leaving the chamber echoed off the walls. Reed flinched as the lead bullet tore through his flesh. He grunted but didn't scream. No, Hannah was doing enough of that for both of them.

Hector shot again, the burning smell of acrid flesh as another bullet penetrated his skin stung his nostrils. Hannah called his name, but he bit his lip, holding back a groan of pain. He mustn't show weakness. The bitter taste of blood filled his mouth as he bit his tongue to stop from reacting.

Two more shots. Two more ringing after effects that made him want to vomit. Two more lead bullets mutilating his back. If it were

Hannah in his place, she'd surely be dead. But he was a werewolf; he could withstand this. Hopefully.

Hector laughed, and Reed forced himself to turn to the evil sound.

The man lifted the gun and blew at the tip, as if smoke would resonate from it like in the olden days.

Sick bastard.

Blood trailed down his back and seeped into his jeans and onto Hannah's peasant skirt. He looked at his mate below him, wide-eyed but silent. She bit her lip but remained calm in his hold, giving him the strength to persevere and take whatever punishment Hector dealt from his whim of fancy.

"That was just a warning. I grew tired of the two of you mooning over each other. Fools. You really think you will live past this to quench those desires. No, you will not fuck each other like the crude instruments of fate you are. This is not a vacation or a honeymoon. You are my captives. I will cut you and beat you as I wish. And if I feel like it, I will rape the witch and make you watch."

Hannah shuddered in his hold, and despite the blood loss, he did not relent his grip. That fucker wasn't going to lay a paw on her.

"Your family will come for you, young Reed. They always come for those we take from them. Funny how they think they are the strongest and the best of the wolves. Arrogant pricks. They haven't stopped us yet. They are too cowardly to truly embrace their power, and now they grow weak from it. Gluttoned and bloated on their own self-worth, they will die by my hand."

Reed bit off a growl. He would enjoy slicing that vile tongue out of the bastard's mouth.

"We may have gotten the wrong brother, but you will prove your worth to me. Or if not, it's no worry. You will still be some form of entertainment. I will rape and then kill the witch in front of you. Then I will kill you. Slowly. It's no matter."

Hector pulled the gun up and shot Reed in the back once more. This time Hannah and he both let out a whimper. *Fuck that hurt.*

"Just for good measure. You know the drill."

With a nod at the guards, the bastard walked out of the room, head held high.

As soon as the door slammed shut, Hannah pushed him off her. Reed groaned in pain at the contact.

Hannah knelt over him, pale and wide-eyed. Crimson blood painted her hands in a cruel landscape, and Reed felt horrible she had to witness and touch his weakness.

Her chestnut corkscrew hair cascaded around her face, her dove gray eyes imploring. She'd be a treasure to paint. A blank canvas promising a beauty of strokes and colors.

Okay, I might be reacting to the blood loss. Just saying.

He was getting a little loopy. But she was just so pretty. He could stare at her forever.

Hannah smiled down at him and caressed his cheek.

"You're quite handsome yourself."

Shit, he hadn't realized he'd spoken out loud. Oh well, she was beautiful, no use in keeping in those thoughts.

Hannah bit her lip then turned him over to his stomach. He sucked in a breath, but held back a wince. He didn't want to show any more weakness than he already had in front of his mate. The cool cement floor felt nice on his heated skin.

She took a shaky breath and placed her palms over the wounds on his back and chanted a calming melody. His skin stretched, and his wounds knitted together.

Warmth seeped through the pain, a tingling sensation more pronounced than when she'd healed his ribs before.

After a few minutes, she sighed, and Reed stole a look at her. Exhaustion crept over her features and her eyes drooped.

"Hannah, you need to stop. You're hurting yourself."

"I'm sorry, Reed. I'm just too far from the earth. You'll need to heal the rest of it yourself." She stroked his cheek. "Change."

"You shouldn't have shown the fullness of your powers. They'll know now." He nodded to the cameras.

Hannah lowered her head, and whispered, "You're worth it."

Humbled. Yes, that was the feeling warming his soul at the moment.

She laughed a sad laugh, then continued, "Plus, you lost so much blood, and if you died, the smell would've gotten to me eventually."

He laughed then grunted in pain at the sickly holes in his flesh.

Hannah pulled him to a sitting position then went to the clasp of his jeans to help.

His cock hardened at her touch, and they both blushed. Well, as much as he could blush with the amount of blood he'd lost.

Neither of them said a word at his reaction, but he did smell a faint hint of her arousal.

Interesting.

Together, they stripped him of his jeans and boxer briefs. Though he could tell she tried not to, her gaze dropped to his cock.

Her cheeks reddened. She was embarrassed, aroused, and fucking sexy.

He crouched and looked into her gray eyes and changed.

Muscles tearing and forming, bones breaking and rearranging. He wanted to grunt in pain. Because of his numerous wounds, this was not the usual peaceful change. No, this was excruciating. At least the chains attached to his limbs and neck magically enhanced, to shrink and stretch, accommodating his new form.

As fur sprouted from his skin, covering his body, he also felt the wounds knit together, healing. And yes, that hurt just as well.

Once he became his wolf, he sat on his haunches, panting from exertion. Hannah scooted toward him, a calm expression on her face. *Thank God, she isn't scared.* He wasn't sure he could take his mate's fear of him on top of everything else. Hesitantly, she brought her hand to his head, petting his fur. If he were a cat, he surely would be purring in contentment right about now. She moved her hand in gentle circles, and he leaned into her touch. She quirked up a lip in a half smile, and he licked her palm, mostly because he wanted to see her smile more, but also because now, as a wolf, that honey and crisp apple smell was damn enticing.

Hannah giggled at the feel of his tongue, and she batted him on the nose.

"Bad, Reed."

He tilted his head in innocence.

She just laughed again and petted him some more.

Eventually, they both grew tired, and Reed lay down on his stomach. Gently, he used his teeth to pull her sleeve toward him. Thankfully, she got the hint and used his warm body as a pillow. Her delicious curves wiggled into his side while she got comfortable. Oh yes, when he became a man again, they would have to do something about their budding sexual tension. Naked.

"Goodnight, Reed."

He shifted his head in a nod. Her breaths soon deepened and steadied in a peaceful sleep.

"I could get used to this."

Reed agreed with his wolf. But could this intelligent, witty, and beautiful woman really want an artist and not an Alpha?

That was something to deal with later. They just needed to get out of here. Preferably alive.

CHAPTER FIVE

Snowflakes stuck to Josh's eyelashes, and he batted them away. A strong gust blew past him, the cold chilling his bones. He surveyed his surroundings, taking a silent step through the undergrowth. Tall trees reached to the sky, blocking whatever sunlight filtered through the dreary storm clouds. Their limbs, heavy with leaves and the extra weight of collecting snow, drooped down. Snow bundles dropped on his shoulder and, in one unfortunate incident, his face. If only he could have Found these two in the nice spring or cool fall months. No, he had to search for them at the onset of winter and the beginning of what looked to be a deadly snowstorm. Lucky guy.

When he left his bench on Main Street, he had quickly gone home to fetch some of his equipment. He dressed to stay warm, grabbed a pack with extra clothes for Reed and the witch, some food and water, and weapons. Lots of weapons. Knives and blades of various shapes and sizes adorned his body. He had his SIG strapped to his side, with extra ammo in his belt. Sadly, he didn't have any silver, but lead would at least slow the beasts down if they came after him.

And they would. He knew it because, as he'd followed the trail in his mind to this remote bunker, his sense of unease swelled to a staggering sensation. *Shit, I might not make it this time.* He was but one man, one human at that. But looking down at the lair that held two people he *needed* to Find, he set aside those worries and the creeps it gave off. And if anyone truly knew him, they would know that it was fucking hard to give Josh the creeps.

They were more important—for some unknown reason.

Those two boys in the alley had mentioned they thought the two disappearances were connected. Well, Josh knew for sure they were. He was also damn sure it was the Centrals too. If his memory served, Josh now stood on Central Pack land. Not a good thing for a human— especially one who despised the rumored brutality of this particular Pack.

These guys were werewolves and could kill him in a blink of an eye with their bare hands. Josh might be strong, pretty damn strong for a human if he had to brag, but not strong enough for the supernaturals. Hence, the overabundance of blades attached to various places on his body. He could reach them all in a split second. That might not be quick enough, but they were a security blanket for him nonetheless.

If there was any doubt the man in his visions was Reed, he'd had an eyeful when he tried to Find them again, because he found himself watching a naked man, an injured naked man, twisting and curving into a werewolf. He'd heard them speaking in hushed tones to each other when he focused. Reed said the woman, Hannah, had healed him before he changed, so she must be the witch.

Hannah. Reed. He liked those names.

What he didn't like was the reaction to Reed's nude body. Josh's cock had filled and his body had hummed. But that wasn't something he wanted to dwell on.

Josh adjusted the erection that hadn't subsided since seeing Hannah and Reed's faces the first time. Damn inconvenient.

What made them so special? Why could he Find them yet had never met them? He had to know. The slow desire welling up inside of him at the thought of the two had nothing to do with his decisions. Nothing.

Right.

Sure, they were attractive. Hannah was a curvy, sexy goddess, and he was man enough to admit Reed was damn sexy. That, though, didn't seem like a good enough reason to risk his life. But he'd do it. He couldn't let them die.

Josh crouched down below a copse of trees, searching for movement from the enemy. He might not know the Centrals personally, but their cruel and sadist ways made them that nonetheless. He closed his eyes, opened his senses and used his Finding. In his mind's eye, both of them sat huddled together. In human form, Reed held Hannah close to his chest, an overwhelming sign of protection. Josh didn't know why both a surge of disappointment and hope flooded his system in a wave of emotion. It made no sense.

The stone dwelling had no discernible features but a few doors guarded by cameras and a few electronics and a couple of closed windows, high above the ground.

Ah ha.

There.

He saw small window too high from the ground for anyone to care about. But it was far enough from the cameras that Josh could use his jammer on the electronics to cut the feed and show only static, scale the wall, and squeeze through the window undetected. Hopefully.

With one last survey of the grounds, he made it to the building, jammed the signal, scaled up the wall, and crawled through the window in under thirty seconds. Nice display of talent, if he didn't say so himself. Of course, he didn't say so, as that would be bragging. And SEALs, even ex-SEALs, never did that. Much.

Thankfully, or perhaps stupidly on the Central's part, no guards stood in the hall where Josh dropped to his feet. Still, he hid in the shadows, taking in his location. A long hallway stretched to the end of the building, doors branching off the corridor in a nonsymmetrical pattern. Dim lights hung overhead, illuminating the hall in an eerie glow.

Again, Josh used his Finding to follow the path to the two people crowding his mind in an unrelenting fashion. As he walked quietly towards the pair, no guards stood by or stopped him. That creepy feeling came back, making the hairs on the back of his neck bristle, but he shook it off. He couldn't think about what wasn't there, only what he needed to do to get out of there.

Just as he thought that, footsteps echoed. *Fuck.* Josh slid into a corner, fading beneath the shadows—something he was quite good at. He could hide from anything if he felt the desire. No one expected him to be there so who could possibly find him?

The guard in a black uniform and combat boots walked past Josh's corner and had no idea it would be his last patrol. Too bad for him. With a swift flick of his wrists around the guard's neck, the guard fell, and Josh pulled him into the shadows. Josh didn't want to leave the evidence, but he needed the key haphazardly dangling on a chain around the dead man's neck. It was a risk, but by the time someone found him there, Reed, Hannah, and he would be long gone. Safe from the oily clutches of the Centrals. At least he hoped so.

He slipped the key off the guard's neck, and walked towards the metal door from his vision. With a look over both shoulders to make sure he was still alone, he slipped the key into the lock. It clicked open as he turned the key, mercifully quiet and Josh let out a breath of relief.

When he opened the door, it made a loud screech, forcing a curse under his breath. So much for being quiet and stealthy. Fucking door hinges. How much did it cost for fucking oil? Then again, this wasn't the *Wizard of Oz*, and the door wasn't the Tin Man. They probably loved making that creepy sound every time they opened the door. Added to the spine-chilling torture feel of the room.

At the sound of the door, both heads turned toward him. Hannah, with her luscious brown curls and dove gray eyes. Reed, with his sandy blond hair and jade green eyes. Even bruised and bloody, they made quite a pair.

Reed let out a gasp when he looked Josh in the eyes.

But not a surprised one. No. This one held hope and awe. What the fuck?

Josh put a finger to his lips, urging them to be quiet. The jammer might block the camera signal for a bit, putting it on an automatic loop, but Josh couldn't be too sure with magic and werewolves in the mix. They both gave him a nod, Hannah wide-eyed but silent, Reed more curious than anything. Could the wolf smell Josh was different? Shit. Not something he should be thinking about. He needed to get them out of here.

Josh hurried over to them and checked for serious injuries. Reed seemed to be mostly healed, if not just a bit scraped up. Hannah had numerous lacerations and bruises, more than Reed, but looked okay. She was only a witch, not a wolf, so it made sense she would heal slower. How quickly a day could change things. He was human for fuck's sake, and now he was thinking about the healing times for different species. Talk about a game changer.

The locks on their chains and collars, luckily enough looked like the one on the metal door. How cocky were these bastards? He slid the key in, and with a snap, the locks opened, and the chains fell to the floor. Both rubbed their wrists as Josh moved quickly and efficiently to the collars at their neck. Fucking animals. Who the hell *collared* people?

Hannah put her hand on his arm, a jolt of electricity flashing between the two. She gasped, and he held back the urge to do so. She gave him a smile, and he desperately wanted to brush the curls from her face, soothing the bruises that couldn't hide her radiant beauty. Reed crouched behind her, still protective. He too was beautiful; with his chiseled cheekbones pronounced against the shadowed, healing bruises.

Dear God. He could understand thinking sexy thoughts about Hannah, but since when did he think males were attractive in any way? Either that weird connection confused him, or he really was falling for Reed. He didn't know which one, if either, he wanted to be true.

Reed bent over Hannah to whisper to them both. "Camera."

"Don't worry about them now. We have about ten more minutes and then we'd have to worry."

They both looked curious with a similar tilt of their heads but didn't say anything, merely nodding.

"Who are you?" Reed whispered, leaning closer.

"Josh." Why the hell had he said his name? He was never a name, just a presence, on any other mission. Why did he want them to know his name? Know him? "I'm no one. Just a friend."

"You're human." Hannah's surprised gasp was still whispered.

Exhaustion overwhelmed her features, and Josh couldn't take it anymore. He picked her up and cradled her to his chest when he stood.

She felt warm in his hold. Right. An instant heat flooded his system as desire rocked him. That annoying connection flared, but he tamped it down. So not the time.

Reed let out a soft growl, pulling Josh to a stop.

Shit, she's his mate. And here he was holding her to his chest and liking it.

Josh cleared his throat. "Sorry, man, I'll let go of her soon. But we need to leave, and since you're stronger than me, I thought you'd be better at the front, protecting her." And he really liked the feel of her curves, even if this was the first and last time.

Reed look perplexed. Huh?

Josh didn't know what to think, but he still felt that connection to both of them. What the hell? He nodded at the other man, and they both left the room cautiously, Hannah still barefoot in Josh's arms. They hurried down the empty hall, past the shadowed corner where the unlucky guard lay dead, and to the window without a hitch. Reed pulled himself up and out of the small gap in the cement walls, and Josh lifted Hannah through. She looked back with a small smile, and his cock hardened again. Fuck, he was going to need therapy once he left these two. Hannah jumped into Reed's arms as Josh pulled himself through right behind them. With a possessive nod, Reed handed her back to Josh, and they all started walking quickly to the surrounding forest.

The hair on the back of Josh's neck rose at how easy it all had been. Something wasn't right, but he couldn't worry about everything all at once. He needed to get the two lovebirds out of here and away from him. That way he didn't have to think about the two ever again.

Right.

Josh could practically taste their nervousness as they reached the tree line. Barefoot and shirtless, Reed had to be cold as hell, but they didn't have time to get him properly dressed. They needed to get the fuck out of here.

A howl spilt the night, freezing them in place.

Oh hell.

Reed looked around, his nose on the wind.

"Josh, take care of Hannah; I'll watch our backs." Reed's deep voice resonated calmness. Not what Josh thought he'd hear from the man.

Hannah cleared her throat and elbowed Josh in the gut. Ouch.

"I can take care of myself. I'm a witch, you know. An earth witch at that. I'm in my element."

Josh let her slide down his body to the ground.

"I hope so," Reed said unenthusiastically. "Because we're surrounded."

CHAPTER SIX

Hannah could feel the vibrations from the earth beneath her bare feet. The soil tickled the skin between her toes. She inhaled the woodsy scent, relishing the fact she was now connected to nature, not the stone walls holding her in. Relief spread through her at being part of the earth again. She'd spent too much time behind walls in chains. Her body was weakened, but soon, after time and fuel, she'd be at her peak. A true witch. She could smell the wolf scent of Reed, the human male scent of Josh. Wetness seeped from her core at the thought of both.

Hannah shook her head. Not quite the time to be drooling over two prime specimens of man. Well, wolf and "special" man. But whatever.

She took a deep breath and struggled to find her strength. They might die here, fighting together. But for some reason she had never felt as safe as she did right now, surrounded by these two men. Reed, who'd protected her with his body against the onslaught of lead bullets and held her through the night for warmth. Josh, the stranger who'd risked his life for two prisoners. He wasn't completely human; he held something else along the ridges of his aura, but she couldn't discern what.

But it wasn't just that they both protected her. No, usually she could accomplish that herself because she hated feeling weak. No, for some reason, an unknown force pulled her toward the two men, who at the moment stood on either side of her, blocking her from an outside enemy. There was a tingling sensation, a connection between her and each of the men.

Oh goddess.

What kind of person wanted two men at the same time? Two strangers at that. Not to mention the fact that who knew how many dangerous werewolves were about to attack them? Not the greatest of timing.

Reed let out a growl. "They're coming. Try to get away and be safe." He looked into her eyes, pleading, before doing the same to Josh.

Reed planted his feet, his fists clenched. Josh did the same on the other side of her, yet with a gun in one hand and a blade in another. As a human, he would need all the protection he could get. A gun wouldn't necessarily kill the beasts, but it would slow them down. And frankly, he looked damn sexy all armored up. Reed looked sexy, too, with his natural charisma and powerful werewolf body.

And, this was totally not the time again to let her thoughts wander.

But what a place they would go.

Hannah gave a nod and closed her eyes, calling to the earth. She might be a healer, but she could still go on the offensive with the earth and kick ass if she had too. Well, at least she hoped he could. She'd trained with her mother—Hannah held back the sharp pain of loss at the thought—but she really hadn't used it. Plus the last few days and her tiredness caused her bones to ache.

Another wolf's howl echoed in the not-too-far-distance. Hannah concentrated and moved her arms like an orchestra conductor to take a large pile of soil, rocks, and roots in her hold. The resulting mass looked like a crested wave and slammed into the wolves trying to come from behind in a sneak attack.

Power surged through her as she lifted up the dirt and felt the connection to the earth deep in her tissues and tendons. When she used this power she always felt like she was on top of the world and could stop anything. The rough wave looked like a cresting peak of control that she alone had the knowledge and capability of. It smelled of earth, nature, and home—everything she held dear. As wave hit the wolves, her power fluctuated back and shocked her body. Hurting any living thing forced her to pay a price, but in this case it was worth it.

Stupid wolves. Didn't they know she could feel them when they trampled too heavy-footed on her earth?

Josh and Reed each granted her a look of pleasant surprise then a sexy smile.

They'd underestimated her. They wouldn't do it again.

But she was glad they approved of her. She wasn't some weakling needing help, however soft she might be inside and out. And she certainly didn't need a strong man to hold on to, though it couldn't hurt. And if there were *two* strong men...

And going away from that subject.

Josh fired into the mass of fur and flesh coming down on him. A sharp cry followed. Good, he'd hit one. The smell of seared flesh hit her nose, and she was grateful for Josh's weaponry.

Reed stood by her side, apparently determined not to leave her. Rather than changing into a wolf, he fought as a man, hand to paw. An ugly gray wolf jumped toward his face, and he crushed its skull. With his bare hands. *Geez.* She figured he was fighting as a man because the lack of food had cost him some energy. But apparently he wasn't lacking in strength. And Reed thought he wasn't Alpha enough. He was plenty for her. And then some.

His slender, lithe body packed heat and strength. Lickable.

And enough of that.

She sent another wave of earth towards a group of wolves. With a flick of her wrist, she buried another wolf and it yelped in pain. She balled her hand into a fist and grabbed a large rock with her powers and hurled it at another wolf, leaving it in a furry mass on the dirt floor. With another movement of her arms, a mound of soil fell on two more wolves. They yelped a bit louder than before. Apparently the sexual tension from her and the men increased the force of her magic. Interesting.

More wolves came from every direction. She concentrated and used the roots of the trees around her to trip them up by reaching out and grabbing their paws and tails. But she could only use a few trees. She wasn't strong enough to do more than that. Out of the corner of her eye, she saw Josh throw his empty gun to the ground as a wolf jumped on him. He pivoted, took out another blade and stabbed his opponent in the flank.

She pulled deep within for more power, knowing she would need rest and food once they made it out of here. If they made it out of here.

Over her other shoulder, she saw that Reed continued to fight, though blood seeped out of various nicks and claw marks. He growled before pulling the fur of another wolf to use for leverage as he broke its neck. The crack barely made a sound over the loud, vicious sounds of the battle at hand. Blood and fur littered the ground in an abstract pattern, mingling with the soils and snow.

Both men's backs were turned from her, and her attention lay on the two wolves coming for her. She braced herself for their attack, arms ready to pull at her magic to bury them in earth. Her concentration was focused on them so intensely she didn't hear the footsteps behind her until it was too late.

A hand gripped her hair and pulled her backwards. The wolves that crouched in front of her turned their backs, shielding her from Josh and Reed. The man that held her turned her toward him.

Caym.

The demon.

He fisted one hand in her curls, and the other came to stroke her face.

Shudders racked her body, and fear took hold. This was it. She'd die by his hand. If she were lucky. Bile rose in her throat at the thought of what else he could do.

"Hannah!" Reed shouted behind her, trying to reach her. But then he grunted, and she could only guess something had stopped him.

She looked into the demon's dark, fathomless eyes.

Pure evil. But not callous like Corbin. Who was the true master? And why did she care?

"Get your hands off of her." Josh's fist connected with the demon's face, forcing Caym's head to snap back.

The demon laughed.

He laughed. What kind of evil was he?

Caym stopped stroking her face then shot out his arm in a blink of an eye to grab Josh's.

No.

Josh struggled to get free, but the demon smiled and bit into the meaty part of Josh's forearm.

Dear goddess.

Hannah screamed, but Josh didn't. He looked at the demon then punched him square in the face, before ripping his arm from the demon's sharpened teeth. Caym gave an odd smile then, after, letting Hannah drop to the ground, walked away.

They reached for each other, and Josh helped Hannah to her feet. She bent down, tearing a piece of fabric off her skirt to try and stop the bleeding. Jagged tears surrounded the bite. Blood flowed freely down his arm, and tears filled Hannah's eyes. The wound looked horrible. And what did a demon bite do? Did it turn him into one? Would it infect him and make him sick? Or kill him? Shudders slid down her spine.

Oh goddess.

Hannah looked up into Josh's face. He'd gone pale, with a sickly green hue. She needed to clean the wound then try and heal him. But she didn't know the consequences of that. And there were always consequences working with something a witch didn't know. Not to mention they were in the middle of a fight.

Though she suddenly realized it'd gone quiet. Hannah looked over her shoulder, surprised to see Reed killing the last wolf. A mound of dead fur and flesh surrounded him, but he didn't seem to care. Bloodied and sweaty, he walked towards them, determination on his face.

Everyone who didn't lie in the pile of death seemed to have vanished. What on earth? Was this all a joke to them? Why had the others left? And why had the demon bitten Josh?

Something didn't add up, but pinged on her memory. She buried it back though; she had to think about Josh and Reed. And herself.

Reed finally made it to them and placed one hand on her cheek and the other on Josh's shoulder. With her hand still on Josh's arm, the three of them gasped. A spark of electricity, magic, or just a simple connection flowed through them. Josh grunted and swayed against her body. Reed widened his eyes and gave a small smile, while she bit her lip in confusion. The three of them glanced at each other but didn't speak.

Reed lowered his hands while they all looked at each other for answers. *What was that? Are we going to talk about it?*

"We need to find some place to go," Josh whispered as he looked up toward the sky.

Apparently they were going to ignore the spark. Hannah grumbled inwardly.

She followed Josh's gaze. *Oh crap.* A blizzard. Just what they needed. Dark clouds moved in overhead and the wind picked up, howling through the trees. Fat snowflakes began to fall from the sky, quickly accumulating on the forest floor. With each gust of wind, the temperature dropped another couple of degrees, chilling her to the bone.

Reed went to Josh's side and put the other man's arm around his shoulders. Then he, because Reed was smaller than Josh, leaned in and wrapped his arm around Josh's waist to lift him slightly off the ground.

"I can walk myself," was Josh's disgruntled response.

"I'm sure you can. But we need to get out of here quickly. Let us help you." Reed's smooth voice held a hint of nervousness but a calming undertone.

They ran together through the forest. Well, they ran as best as they could with two barefoot people half-carrying an injured human. The snow began to fall around them about twenty minutes into their escape. Hannah panted heavy breaths, praying they would find somewhere to ride out the storm soon. From the looks on both men's faces, their thoughts ran along the same paths.

But other thoughts threatening to edge out the panic and hope for shelter worried her. What would they do when they got there?

And what would they do about each other? Was she really thinking about a ménage with these two men just because they panted for each other in a few brief moments? How will each of them react? How should she react?

316

Even as the cold surrounded her, her body warmed to the thought of being loved and touched by these two men. Tingles shot up her body and she didn't bother to suppress them. They kept the cold from seeping into her bones more than it already had and made her think of a future that she didn't have before. A future with two men. Could it really work? Did she want it to?

CHAPTER SEVEN

Jesus, his chest hurt. Reed shook off the burning pain of newly healed tissues and even newer slices and bruises and heaved Josh a bit farther into the forest. He didn't know why the surviving wolves had left, but Reed thanked whatever the reason. Though he might have been stronger than the wolves that leapt at him with their gleaming teeth and sharp claws, he couldn't have lasted much longer.

Hannah's breath came out in fast pants on the other side of Josh. They needed to get to shelter soon. But Reed couldn't help but remember the way she'd stood and fought by their sides. *Dear Lord, she was amazing.* He'd never seen magic like that, hadn't even known earth witches possessed that type of power. Add into the fact she was a rare healer and his Hannah was a force to be reckoned with. And damn sexy when she did it.

And Josh. For a human, his fighting and perseverance rivaled most Alpha's. When he'd run out of ammunition, he'd gone for his blades and hand to hand without even looking like he was thinking. Thank God for his training, whatever that was. The human that didn't smell quite human was a mystery to him.

A damn sexy mystery.

Reed lifted Josh a bit more, trailing the human's feet in the snow. Whatever the demon had done to him, it didn't look good. Josh leaned heavily against Reed and groaned with each stumble and time they had to climb over a large hill or rock. His skin had paled enough that Reed didn't even think he had any blood at all. And scariest of all, though it was freezing, Josh's body warmed Reed's side like a furnace.

Snow fell in earnest around them, beauty in an evil nightmare. The trees parted farther up their makeshift path, revealing a hopeful shadow.

Please don't let me be hallucinating like a man dying of thirst in a desert.

"I think I see a cabin up ahead. The lights are out so I don't think anyone's home. But at least it has a roof." Relief spread through him as he told the others.

"Where? I don't see it." Hannah couldn't hold back her hope; it reflected in her voice.

"Me neither." Josh's voice was weak, filled with pain.

"It's there; I can just see farther than you. But it's there. Believe me."

They both nodded. Again, relief filled his chest at the thought of their trust.

They walked a bit farther until the cabin came into view for every-one. With a grunt of relief, they reached the door. Reed let Josh sway on his own two feet, leaning against Hannah, as he went to the door. Locked. Reed took about two seconds to search for the key before shouldering the door open. The lock busted with an audible snap, and he ushered them both in.

Hannah flicked the light switch to find no electricity. Josh looked lost on his feet, so Reed moved to help him stand, while Hannah found a lantern and matches. The soft glow illuminated what appeared to be a hunting cabin. The floor plan was larger than most hunting cabins he'd seen. A small living room with a hallway off to the side led to most likely a bedroom. A table and chairs stood off to the side in a makeshift dining room and there was a doorway to what must be the kitchen. Fur skins littered the wooden floors, insulating whatever heat it could. Stuffed dear, bear, and wolf heads adorned the walls.

Reed gulped. He *really* hoped those were all normal animals and not werewolves. Not something to think about.

Luckily, during their trek to this abandoned cabin, they'd left Central land and now stood on neutral land. No Pack held deed so Reed was safe from meeting another Pack and be called out for trespassing. But they weren't on Redwood land either. No, they were further away then when they started. They'd had to go in the opposite direction of his Pack because they wouldn't be able to reach the Redwood land without crossing the Central land unless they made a wide circle. It sucked but couldn't have been avoided. They were sheltered, maybe would even be fed soon. And they were away from the Centrals, at least for the time being. Things could be worse.

The feel of Josh's weight against him reminded Reed of where he was. *Oh yeah, things were worse.* They needed to take a look at that bite.

Reed shifted slightly and inhaled Josh's scent. He smelled of ponderosa pine, a sweet wood. Odd, since that tree was typically found in the southwest, but that really wasn't the point.

Reed cursed under his breath, startling Josh. He shouldn't be sniffing this man, no. He had Hannah. And Josh was most likely a narrowly straight man.

But hell. Reed's wolf knew.

"He's our mate, too."

Shit.

When Josh had first walked through that metal door to rescue him and Hannah, Reed had gasped. The human had stood tall, with a powerful body that demanded attention—and maybe Reed's tongue. He had brown hair that stood up in long spikes that begged for Reed's hands and blue eyes that saw into Reed's soul. When the connection set in and his wolf growled in contentment, Reed knew he was done for. His cock, already hard from Hannah's presence, had throbbed and ached for release.

How fucked up was fate anyway?

How could he have *two* mates at the *same time*? Was he supposed to choose? Could he have them both?

What if they both walked away?

Holy shit.

This was why he didn't really want a mate to begin with. All decisions went out the door and choices right along with them, and the world revolved around another person who may or may not even return their love. And if they weren't a werewolf, they couldn't feel the mating heat. It was just a simple attraction to them.

Fuck.

Again, Reed shook out his thoughts. He didn't have time to worry about the inevitable. No, he needed to get Josh resting and try to figure out what to do with a fucking demon bite. Not to mention, he still had the overwhelming need to protect Hannah, to protect them both, because, even if they both walked away from him once he told them they were his mates, they were still his mates. He protected what was his.

Huh. Who knew he had such Alpha tendencies?

"Reed, get Josh to the couch," Hannah ordered in a soft voice. "I'll set the wards."

Reed merely lifted a brow at her stern, yet, sexy tone while Josh whistled in appreciation.

Their mate was full of surprises.

Wait, their?

So, not going there. He couldn't. It was taboo. But he still smiled at the thought. Could it work?

Reed walked Josh to one of the plush brown couches and set him down carefully.

Josh winced in pain.

"Shit, did I hurt you? How can I help?" Because at this moment, he'd do just about anything to save him. Anything.

"No, you didn't do anything." Josh heaved a breath as Reed pushed him onto his back and covered him with the blanket from the back of the couch. "My arm just hurts like hell. What was that thing, and why did it bite me?"

Reed let out a breath. He could almost forget Josh was human until he'd ask a question like that.

"It was a demon."

Josh's eyebrows rose. "That's a new one."

Reed would've asked what he meant by that, but then he got a good look at the wound on Josh's forearm.

It looked as if a ravaging beast had taken hold of the flesh and tugged and torn until a mess of ligaments, muscles, and flesh swam in a pool of blood. He was pretty sure he could see bone fragments floating in the open wound, as well one of the bones in the forearm, though he didn't know if it was the radius or ulna.

The man must have been in an incredible amount of pain. Yet, except for the green hue of his skin and occasional moan or grunt, Josh struggled through it like a pro. What atrocities had the man seen if he was able to withstand this with only minor complaint and remain conscious?

Reed went to the kitchen, and thankfully, the water still worked. He filled a bowl and found some towels. On the way back, he noticed food stores and thanked whatever hunter had left there them for a rainy day because the three of them sure needed it.

Carefully, Reed cleaned the drying blood around the wound, doing his best not to aggravate it further. Josh sucked in a breath through his teeth when Reed got too close to the edges.

"Sorry, man."

"It's okay. It needs to be done. It just hurts like a bitch, you know?" Josh smiled at him, and Reed could feel his face heat to the tips of his ears.

Damn, the man was sexy.

Dark brown hair, cut close in the back, but slightly longer in the front, so it spiked up just a bit. Pale, scarred skin on a slightly bulkier and taller body than his own. Ocean blue eyes that seemed to change to a foamy blue in the light.

Like before with Hannah, Reed felt the urge to pick up a brush and paint.

Trying to get a closer look at the wound, Reed placed his arm on Josh's bare skin. The man gasped at his touch.

Reed pulled back, but not before he saw a wave of desire flash across Josh's face. The other man's pupils dilated and his lips parted, a flush rising to his pale skin.

Interesting.

322

Was Josh gay? No, bi maybe, like him. He'd seen the way Josh looked at Hannah. The expression was probably a mirror image of his own face, but for some reason, he didn't feel a twinge of jealousy, only a feeling of rightness. In fact, the idea of the three of them felt even more right than the idea of just him and Hannah alone. Weird.

"The wards are set; we're as safe as we can be, considering. How's our patient?" Hannah's brisk steps broke whatever heat had passed between the two men, but Reed didn't care too much. He was too busy looking at the rosy-cheeked beauty walking towards them.

Still barefoot, she'd wrapped herself in one of the furs on the mantel and looked like a sexy cavewoman with her curly hair going every which way.

Reed rubbed the back of his neck, trying to release some of the sexual tension piling onto the tension from their imprisonment. His cock rubbed against the zipper of his jeans, threatening to leave a permanent scar. Tingles shot up his arms as her bitter apple and honey scent floated on the air to him, mixing with Josh's ponderosa pine and he held back a groan. These two would be the death of him.

"I cleaned his wound, but I didn't try and bandage it. I thought you'd look at it first."

She blushed. "Okay."

Reed moved back but didn't get out of her way completely. He wanted to see her work, to smell her honey and crisp apple scent. She put her small hands around the wound, her teeth biting her bottom lip and tears forming in her eyes. They both gasped as Reed felt the energy in the room shift. The sexual tension calmed as the energy swayed and ebbed before funneling through Hannah and into Josh. He watched as parts of Josh's arm knitted back together, ligaments winding against the muscle and tissue and his skin fusing together.

Really cool, but still kind of gross. He could totally do a project with some acrylics on canvas.

"Oh, darn it," Hannah cursed under her breath.

Reed gave a look to Josh. *Yeah, she was really cute when she tried to curse.*

"What is it?" Josh sounded worried.

Not surprising because Reed was worried too.

"It won't close all the way. I was worried to even attempt this in the first place since I've never healed a demon bite before, but it looked so bad I couldn't *not* do it. You know?" She bit into her lip. She was gonna draw blood soon if she didn't quit doing that.

"It's okay, Hannah. You tried. Thank you." Josh placed his hand on hers and gave it a squeeze.

Reed had the sudden urge to join them but held back.

The wound indeed looked better but was not healed per se. It still looked red and angry around the bite mark, and he was sure that, unless Hannah could use some herbs, it would be infected soon. Plus, they still had to contend with the whole bitten-by-a-demon thing and its repercussions.

All three looked at each other. The underlying current of unease at the unknown infection and the connections between them lay heavy.

"Reed, let me heal those bites from the wolves; that way you are at full strength."

Though he really wanted her hands on him, he shook his head. "I don't want you to use up all your energy; I'll heal."

"No, really, it's okay. As long as I can go outside at some point and recharge and get some food and sleep, I'll be fine. Please, let me help you."

He gave Josh a look, who smiled back at him. "Okay."

She placed her cool hands on his overheated chest, and he felt the warmth and tingles that came from her healing. He could only imagine those precious hands on other parts of his anatomy. Coincidently, said part started to rise in attention at her touch.

This is looking to be a hard night. Hard being the operative word.

When she finished, Reed cleared his throat again. *I really need to stop doing that.* "Let's get Josh to one of the beds and light a fire in there and out here. The couch can't be comfortable."

"It's okay." Josh gave a pained laugh.

"That settles it then. We'll light the fires, try to get something to eat and maybe some sleep. I can hear anything coming at us for a mile or so since we're so isolated. What about your wards?"

"I set them about that far, as well, so I'll know. We'll be prepared, but I don't want to stay here too long."

324

"I agree," Josh mumbled, fading into sleep. "Just don't leave me alone too long and don't go too far. I like you guys close." Josh fell asleep as soon as they laid him in the large queen-sized bed in the room with the other fireplace.

Wow, the guy must really be out of it if he was spouting his thoughts like that. Reed kind of liked it.

Reed smiled down at the human. "Don't worry, I'll protect you."

Josh smiled in his sleep, and Reed let him be, walking out of the room towards his other mate. He took her hand, leading her to the couch. She sat with a vacant expression on her face.

"Hannah, what can I do for you? I'm going look around the cabin and get you some shoes, but what else?"

She smiled at him and shook her head. "I don't know; everything's different. What they did back there..." Her voice broke, cutting off her sentence.

Reed placed an arm around her shoulders, pulling her into his side. He didn't want to think about what had gone on in that stone basement. The blood, the pain, the loss. It was too much.

"Shh, it'll be okay. You're tough. I've seen you. We'll figure it out. Together." At least he hoped.

"I'm just so tired, but I don't want to sleep." Her eyes held horrors he knew would take time to get over, if she ever did.

"Okay, just lie down on the couch and rest. You don't need to sleep. I'm going to go in Josh's room, get the fire set, and do the same in here. We need to find a way to contact someone. If we can't then we'll get out of here soon and get help. I'll look for some clothes for us, then some food. How does that sound?" Telling her his plans made him feel better, like he might actually accomplish something. If she knew he wanted to care for her and Josh, maybe she'd relax enough to sleep.

"Let me help." She made motions of getting up, but Reed stopped her.

"No, not now. Let me get everything but the food. I think you may need to help me with that part." He blushed a bit. "I'm not a great cook, so that might be your job. But you rest."

"I'm better with potions than food, but I can do my best."

"That's all I ask." He gave her a smile, fought the urge to kiss her goodnight, and went to do his chores. At least doing something productive would help his rising fears—and rising erection.

"Once Josh sleeps a bit," Hannah said when Reed came back from Josh's room, "he'll hopefully be able to move. I don't like staying here. Away from everyone." That haunted look came back in her eyes.

Reed would have done anything to sweep that look away.

He looked around the cabin, noting the lack of phones or radios. Well crap. It looked as though they'd have to wait out their growing strength before they made it home. Wherever home was for his two mates. Reed couldn't be so lucky to think their home would be his.

"There are no phones, are there?" Hannah whispered.

Reed shook his head. "No, but when we get rested, we can go to my Pack, the Redwoods. They'll take care of us. Protect us." He held his breath, waiting for her response.

Hannah nodded. "Okay." A sad look came into her eyes. "I don't have anywhere else to go."

Reed felt for her. How horrible would it be to be Packless? Have no connections? No family?

"I'll take care of you," he promised.

She batted his arm. "I said I can take care of myself."

Reed smiled. "Then you can take care of me, too."

She smiled back. "Sounds like a plan."

They paused as the heat grew between them. Reed shifted, his arousal increasing as he inhaled her luscious scent.

Hannah's breaths came in shallow pants. Her cheeks reddened as she lowered her eyes, her eyelashes dusting the tops of those rosy cheeks.

"I think I'll try and get some sleep in the room across from Josh's, the heat reaches there."

She stood up quickly, and practically ran to the room like a frightened rabbit.

Too bad Reed was a wolf and liked to chase.

"Sounds good to me. Let's go."

Reed ignored his wolf. He looked down the hall where his two potential mates lay across the expanse of the hallway from each other. No, this wouldn't be complicated at all. *Right.*

CHAPTER EIGHT

J osh cracked open his eyes, straining at the glow of the roaring fire by his bedside. He quickly shut them again against the raging headache currently doing an Irish jig on his temples. Crap, where was he? Images of wolves and sharp teeth, curly brown hair, then green eyes flooded his mind. Oh yeah, Reed and Hannah.

He'd saved them. Well, he got them out; they seemed fit enough to save themselves. Another image, this time of the man—no demon— with deep black eyes and sharp teeth impaling his flesh. He flinched at the memory, causing pain to lash up his arm.

Fuck.

When he opened his eyes again, he surveyed his surroundings. The large wooden sleigh bed he slept in took up most of the room. Dark, musty drapes covered the windows so he couldn't tell if it was day or night. But cold seemed to slip through the slits, letting him know the storm was either just starting fully or in the middle of its downpour.

On the side wall, a large brick fireplace stood out, heating the room. Josh guessed that either Reed or Hannah had lit it for him, not wanting him to be cold. For some reason that warmed him from the inside out.

Josh tried to swallow, but it caught on his tongue. It felt as though he'd eaten dried rags and then chased them down with cotton. He needed water or something to sooth his aching throat, but couldn't call out for help or find the energy to get out of bed and get to Hannah and Reed. How was he supposed to leave the cabin and go for help if he couldn't even get out of bed?

He shook his head, trying to clear it of sleep as flashes of his dreams came back. Memories of demons with forked tongues, fire burning flesh, and screams made him want to shudder in fear. But he didn't. He couldn't be weak. Not when others needed him.

But those weren't the only dreams bugging his subconscious. No, they mingled with images of a gray-eyed beauty and her green-eyed companion. Reed and Hannah had loved and kissed and sexed him throughout his fantasy. Panting, moaning, and thrusting interplayed with chanting and proclamations of forever and love.

Josh didn't know which of the two dreams frightened him more. Painful death by fire and demons or the love of two supernaturals.

Not to mention the fact he'd never known he was attracted to men. But, damn, Reed was sexy as hell. And by the gasps and heated looks on the other man's face, Reed thought the same of Josh. What was he going to do with that?

And hell, Reed and Hannah were mates. They might not have fully connected, or whatever the hell werewolves did in a mating, but they were for each other. Josh was the odd man out. Again.

Some part of him, though, couldn't forget the energy that shot through them when they all touched at the same time. There was a link there, better left ignored in his opinion. He'd wanted to make sure they were alive, not impede on their ogling love and some shit.

Josh let out a sigh. *Keep telling yourself that, man.*

Straining almost every muscle he had, Josh slid himself out of bed, his feet flinching at the feel of the cool wood beneath him. Sometime during his sleep, someone had taken off his shirt, boots, and socks.

Josh felts his skin heat at the thought of Reed or Hannah—or both —touching his bare skin.

Enough of that.

He pulled himself to a standing position, releasing a groan.

Dear God, every joint in his body hurt like that of an elderly man.

Josh looked toward the end of the bed to find his shirt laid out. It was still dirty, with soil and bloodstains, but didn't smell that bad, so he shrugged it on, exhaling an oath when he did. *Yeah, this is going to be a long day.*

The cotton slipped over his arm, and he gasped out in pain.

The demon bite.

If only he could forget.

Josh looked down at the offending wound. Though Hannah had helped it along some in the healing process, it was nowhere near where it needed to be. Red, angry lashes spread out from the bite like a sadistic web. He hated to think it, but it looked like an infection that was spreading. But he didn't want to think about that. Apparently he didn't want to think about a lot of things lately.

He pulled his socks and boots on, grateful to whoever had put them near the fireplace. They were nice and toasty on his cold feet. Sucking in a deep breath and gathering his strength, he left the warmth of the bedroom and ventured out to the living room. The resulting image made him smile and his cock harden.

Hannah sat before the fireplace, legs crossed in a position that promised more aerobic activities in his mind.

Her corkscrew curls circled her face, making it look like she'd just rolled out of bed after a long night of passion. Damn, had she and Reed done anything when he'd been asleep? So not his business, but the image that ran across his mind made him want to groan with need.

Hannah bit her lip in concentration, a delectable habit of hers, while chanting something he couldn't quite make out. From the looks of it, she was meditating and doing a damn sexy job of it.

The front door opened, letting in the chill from the outside. Josh immediately pivoted towards the intruder, blocking Hannah from their path. He cringed at the sharp pain digging into his side from his fast movement but ignored it.

Reed stood in the doorway, red-cheeked and wide-eyed. He gave Josh a worried look then quickly covered it up with a smile.

Damn that smile could stop a train in its tracks.

Reed shut the door behind him, shook off the snow that had collected on his hair and shoulders, and came farther into the room.

"Good to see you up, Josh." Reed looked him over, his gaze leaving scorch marks as it passed.

"Yes, Josh, how are you feeling?"

Josh spun around to Hannah, who'd opened her eyes and smiled warmly at both of them.

Reed and he both started toward her to help her to a standing position, but she waved them off, gracefully straightening her legs and stretching her back like a cat.

Like a fucking sexy ballerina. Damn.

Josh coughed to cover his staring. "I'm feeling a bit groggy and could use some water. But the sleep helped."

"Oh, I'll go get you some." Hannah stretched one last time and ran to get him a glass before Josh could even open his mouth to say he could do it.

"Let her help you; you scared her. Me too." Reed smiled again and led him to the couch where they both sat.

Hannah hurried back in as they were getting comfortable.

"Here you go; I hope this helps." She smiled again and Josh almost fell in love right there.

Not something he should be doing.

Reed and Josh left enough space on the couch for her to sit in the middle. She snuggled up between them, reminding him of a very vivid dream with the three of them. Josh shifted a bit to relieve the pressure against his zipper.

His thought from before repeated like a loop in his brain. *Gonna be a long day.*

"We need to get out of here. I don't feel comfortable staying in a cabin we don't know, stealing from them, hiding from someone—or something—trying to kill us." Josh was adamant on this. Fear crawled up his spine at the thought of what hunted them.

"We know," Reed said. "The snow's getting pretty bad out there though. I don't know if we can hoof our way out of here. Plus, we needed to make sure we were all ready for the journey."

Reed paused, and Josh felt his stomach fall. They'd waited because of him. He hated being the weak one—the human.

"I can't get a hold of the Pack at the moment," Reed continued. "We're essentially cut off, but at least we have each other."

Josh liked the sound of that.

"Okay, I understand. What about our defenses?" Something he was good at.

Hannah spoke up. "Well, between my wards and Reed's senses, we should be able to get fair warning. It's the best we can hope for the time being."

Josh was at a loss. Did they even need him? He didn't know how he felt about that.

"Josh, I need to know something." Reed looked serious, almost as if he didn't want to know the answer.

"Okay."

"How did you find us? Why did you help us?"

Josh looked at both of them sitting stock still on the couch, as if waiting for him to tell them he was in on the Central's deal. He couldn't blame them for their worry, but it still stung just a bit.

"I'm a Finder."

Silence.

Okay, apparently I need to explain exactly what that is.

Josh rubbed the back of his neck, suddenly nervous about what they would think of him.

Hannah's soft voice urged him to continue. "What's a Finder, Josh?"

"I can Find anyone I've met before. Anywhere and anytime. I just need to see their face personally, and then I can concentrate on the memory and Find them."

"That's remarkable," Hannah whispered.

"I agree, but you've never met me. I'd remember." Reed quirked a brow.

Did they not believe him?

"I know. I've never seen either of you before. But when some kids mentioned you, flashes of your lives and who you were came to me. I had to Find you."

Hannah brought her hand to her mouth, trembling. "Thank you."

Josh held her other hand. "You're welcome. I don't know why the two of you are so special, and why things worked the way they did. But I'm not unhappy about it. I'm glad I Found you."

Reed nodded and something flashed across his green eyes.

Huh?

Relief spread through him at their acceptances, but he didn't know why he'd told them exactly. He'd never told another soul outside his family about his gift—if it could be called that. But it felt good—complete even—to do so with them.

"I knew I smelled something different about you," Reed murmured.

"Are you saying I smell?" Josh fought the urge to sniff his dirty shirt and sat back slightly offended.

"No, no." Reed waved his hands. "I'm a wolf, remember? I have a better sense of smell, and while your scent was definitely human, it held a trace of something different. Now I know why."

"Oh." Josh shrugged, feeling slightly better.

"Were you always this way?" Hannah wondered aloud.

Josh nodded. "I don't remember *not* having this ability, so yes. And no, it wasn't some military experiment or anything."

All three laughed, the tension of their conversation dissolving away.

On an offhand thought, Josh closed his eyes and tried to Find Corbin, just to see if the bastard was close. But his vision grew hazy, almost at a disconnect.

What the hell?

He rubbed his temples as a headache set in.

"What's wrong, Josh?" Hannah asked.

"I just tried to Find Corbin. But I think the wards or something is messing it up. Don't worry; I'm sure it's nothing." The bite mark on his arm tingled, but Josh tried not to connect the two incidents. No, it was just the wards. It had to be. His Finding would come back, and everything would be normal. He'd go home. Alone.

"You know, Josh, that's a very useful talent," Reed commented.

Ice settled in Josh's chest. "I won't be used by anyone for anything."

Hurt crossed Reed's face and Josh backed down. "That wasn't what I meant. I'm sorry. I was just complimenting your gift. Not everyone can say they are useful in the world. I would never use you for myself or my Pack. And if they go against their nature and even think about using you, then they'd have to deal with me." His eyes grew hard, threatening.

"Me too," Hannah added in, a fierce expression on her face.

Warmth filled his chest at their promise of protection and acceptance. He'd never thought he'd ever tell anyone what he was, let alone feel as though they understood and wanted to know more. It was interesting to say the least.

Josh let out a breath. "It's okay. I'm sorry for overreacting. It's just odd to have others know what I am, ya know?"

Reed and Hannah looked at each other before smiling at him.

Yeah, the wolf and the witch would know for sure.

Hannah reached out and grabbed both of their hands, warmth infusing into his bones.

He shouldn't get used to this. He *couldn't* get used to this.

The windows rattled as the wind howled outside. Cold seeped underneath the panes and doorways, cooling the room considerably, despite the roaring fire. His arm rocked with pain, but he didn't flinch because he didn't want to worry the others.

Reed went to the door, making sure it was secured. Hannah put another log on the fire, to keep the warmth from leeching to the outside. Josh looked through the windows to see the blizzard had come down on them. Fat snowflakes fell to the ground in a blur. The wind picked up, carrying snow-drifts and slamming them into the surrounding trees and walls of the cabin. The snow had already accumulated to what Josh estimated to be at least three feet—and counting.

Shit, it looked as though they'd be stuck here for a lot longer than they wanted.

Josh tried not to feel excited about sharing a small cabin with two people who drove up his sex drive faster than anything he'd ever felt, but he couldn't do it.

If he was going to be stuck with them indefinitely, he'd use it to his advantage. Even if it was going to kill him that much more to say goodbye when the time came.

Hannah came up from behind him, putting her hand in his. "Thank you again, Josh." He turned toward her. Tears filled her eyes, but they didn't fall. "I don't know what we would have done. The things they did to me were horrible. But I couldn't watch them hurt Reed anymore." A single tear fell, leaving a thin trail down her face.

Josh wiped the tear from her cheek, hating to see her in pain. "I'm so sorry you had to go through that. But I'd Find you again if I had to."

Hannah looked down at the bite mark on his arm that throbbed with his heartbeat.

"Yes, Hannah, I'd do *everything* again," Josh stressed.

"Thank you, Josh. For everything." Reed came up behind Hannah holding her shoulder.

Josh's stomach grumbled, and he blushed. *Well, that broke the moment.*

"Oh, you must be starving." Hannah bit her lip. Damn she was cute, but why was she nervous? "Reed and I ate some canned green beans and carrots, but we aren't really good cooks. There is a gas stove so we don't have to worry about electricity. Oh, and plenty of frozen meat, starches, and canned goods. We just can't put a meal together and not risk poisoning ourselves."

Reed shook his head, looking unrepentant. "What can I say? I'm good at bachelor food or going to one of my brothers' houses. Plus my brother Jasper just mated Willow, who's a baker. I'm in love with her cooking." A light went on in his eyes, like he was remembering good food and fond memories.

What would it be like to have a family that would feed you and give you such good memories? Josh just couldn't comprehend that.

"Well then, today's your lucky day. I'm a pretty decent cook. I'm not gourmet or anything, but I'll feed you."

Reed's face brightened. "Thank God. I may be a wolf, but there is only so much meat I can eat without missing side dishes."

Hannah smiled then bit her lip. "I know. I'm not a wolf, so anything you can make would put me in your debt forever."

Josh liked the sound of that.

"Oh," Hannah continued. "if you ever need a potion or herb concoction, then I'm your girl."

"I'll keep that in mind," Josh said.

"I can paint you a picture of our meal if you want, or something to add ambiance, but that's about it," Reed added in.

Josh quirked a brow as he went to the pantry to find some potatoes. "You paint?" He went to the ice box and got lucky and found some frozen vegetables.

Reed smiled. "I'm an artist."

"By that smile, I'd say you love it." Hannah sat on the counter, watching Josh cut potatoes into cubes.

Reed shrugged. "It's my life. I've been doing it awhile; I love it."

Josh turned toward him while he browned some stew meat in a large skillet on the gas stove. "How long is awhile?"

"About a century or so."

Hannah looked Reed up and down. "And you don't look a day over ninety."

They broke out into laughter, not at all ill at ease with Reed's age. What would it be like to be so long-lived?

Josh shook his head to clear his thoughts. "So, Reed, tell me about your family. I heard you mention some of them, but I don't remember them all."

"Oh, I have tons of family to go around." Reed explained. "I have five brothers and one sister."

Hannah and Josh stood wide-eyed.

"There are *seven* of you?" Josh asked.

"Yep, my poor mother."

They chuckled at Reed's answer.

"Kade is the eldest," Reed explained. "Then Jasper, Adam, me, the twins, Maddox and North, then our baby sister, Cailin."

"So many boys. How did your mom manage?" Hannah asked.

"I don't think the six of us were too bad. Cailin though is a troublemaker. She's just hitting her stride at twenty-three. I'm afraid to see what will happen when she gets older."

"Wait," Josh interrupted. "Cailin is the *baby* at twenty-three?"

"I told you I'm almost a century—ninety-eight actually. Cailin's still our baby sister. And with six older brothers she doesn't forget it." Reed gave a smile only a big brother bent on terrorizing his younger sister could give.

Or at least that's what Josh thought a look of terrorizing one's little sister would look like. He didn't have any siblings to really know.

"Wow, I'm only twenty-five. You must think I'm a toddler." Hannah looked troubled at this thought, but didn't bite her lip.

Reed reached out and held her hand. "It's not the same thing at all. Cailin and you are both adults. It's just Cailin's my sister, while you are definitely not." Reed smiled, and Josh felt as though he was intruding.

"And you're pretty close to my age—twenty-nine." Josh pointed to himself with a ladle.

"Well thank the goddess for that." Hannah said. "I guess we'll just have to be careful with the old man over here."

Reed looked on in mock-outrage. "Hey, you two whipper-snappers. When I was young we respected our elders. And I can always get us the senior discounts." Reed wiggled his eyebrows and Josh threw a dish towel at him.

It was nice to laugh and play around about something, and just for a moment, forget the dangers lurking outside.

Reed smiled. "So tell me about you, Josh. Any family?"

Hannah and Josh sobered. "No. I have no one."

"Since I lost my mom, I'm alone now too."

The kitchen fell silent except for the sound of the boiling stew on the stove.

"I'm sorry. I didn't mean to bring it up. But you aren't alone if you don't want to be." Reed spoke softly. "You can always go home with me to the Redwood Pack."

As good as that sounded to Josh, he didn't think he could think about the future. Not one that didn't include the two people in the kitchen with him.

Josh looked around the cabin, trying to break the sudden tension in the room. "I don't think we should use the bedroom tonight and waste the wood. It's gonna get real cold, real quick. So I think it'd be best if we all pile up in the living room in front of the fire and close to the nearest exits in case we are attacked. We may have to cuddle."

The tip of Reed's ears reddened and Hannah blushed. *Damn these two were cute as all hell.*

"Okay, but we'll take turns keeping watch," Reed agreed.

Josh and Hannah nodded, and he went back to the stove to check their meal. "Stew's ready. It won't be too bad, though it didn't have all day to simmer and we don't have bread, but it'll do."

"I don't care how it tastes. It smells divine." Hannah closed her eyes and inhaled. The look of pure ecstasy on her face made Josh want to bend her over the dining room table and fuck her until they both dropped to the floor in a sweaty pile.

He looked over to Reed and knew the man's thoughts were on the same page.

Fuck.

Reed checked the fire and Hannah set the table while Josh ladled stew in to the bowls. They sat down together, talking and eating a surprisingly decent meal. It almost felt like they were a family. It was nice. A little too nice. Because Josh couldn't allow himself to get used to this.

They'd leave him like everyone else always did.

A crimson hue flashed across his eyes. Blood and dark evil attacked his thoughts, and Josh held his forehead. Weariness spread over him.

What the hell was going on? He'd never had an attack like this before. This wasn't part of his Finding. No, this was something different. Was it because of the bite? It felt like something else was trying to take over his body and cloud his emotions.

Irrational anger seeped through his pores, anger at those that had left him. Anger at the two strangers sitting across from him who would fuck tonight and leave him alone and needing. He didn't want to feel needy. He wanted to be alone.

"Josh?" Hannah's soft voice intruded his increasingly violent thoughts.

"I'm getting a bit tired. You mind if I just crash on the couch? You can wake me when you're ready to go to sleep and I'll take the floor. Okay?"

Both of his dinner mates looked at him with worried expressions.

"Okay, try and get some rest. We'll do the dishes and try to be quiet," Reed answered.

Josh nodded, too afraid of what would come out of his mouth if he spoke. He left the two lovebirds at the table to talk about him behind his back. Yeah, fuck them.

He slung himself onto the couch, head aching. His arm pulsated to a staccato tempo, pissing him off. He glanced down and paled. His wound looked even redder than before but for some reason he didn't want to tell the others. What was going on with him? He needed to leave here soon, before he did something he might regret.

CHAPTER NINE

Hannah watched Josh walk out of the room, a painful expression on his face. She hated to see him in pain. The feeling was much like what she'd felt when Reed was hurt.

"He looks tired." Too tired for someone who'd just slept eight hours.

"I know," Reed agreed. "I don't like it. But when we get to the Pack, we'll try and figure it out. I think it may be the bite, but I don't want to say anything just yet."

"I know. I'm scared. I've never seen anything like that before."

"It's okay, Hannah. We will figure it out." Reed reached out and held her hand.

He was always doing things like that. Touching her hand, arms, kissing her forehead or cheeks. She loved it every time he did so and didn't want him to stop. She felt as though she'd known him for so much longer than just a handful of stolen days. How would she say goodbye? Did she have to?

Reed stood and cleared the table. Hannah grabbed what she could and followed him into the kitchen that stood off the living room. They started doing the dishes, and the cold water bit into her hands, stinging.

"Hey, why don't you do the drying? I don't want you to freeze your hands off since we don't have heated water at the moment. Should make showering interesting." Reed quirked a lip, and Hannah blushed.

Goddess, the image of him in the shower, water sliding down his naked skin.

Hannah gulped, knowing she was blushing like a school girl.

She dried the bowls using a towel she found in one of the drawers. That reminded her.

"How are we going to replace anything we use?"

Reed kept rinsing the bowls and gave her a smile. "I've thought about that. We'll leave a note."

Hannah exhaled in relief. "A note? That'll be enough?"

Reed nodded and bumped her with his hip. "We'll leave our information and pay them back. Don't worry; I'll take care of it. And you."

"I'd like that. But don't think I won't reciprocate." She smiled then froze. Had she really just said that aloud?

From the pleased look on his face, she thought she had.

What did that mean?

They finished the dishes, their arms and legs brushing and bumping together as they worked as a unit. She didn't know quite what was going on, but parts of her liked it. Parts of her *really* liked it. But then those same parts reacted whenever Josh touched her or looked into her eyes.

Her heart hurt at the choices she might have to make if what she saw in their eyes was true. She wanted both men. And if she was honest with herself—she was falling for them, too.

Did that make her a slut?

Because the fantasies rolling through her mind made her think of even sluttier thoughts. Really dirty, slutty thoughts.

They both went into the living room and sat on the love seat across the room from where Josh lay sleeping. He had his arm over his eyes, blocking out soft glow of the candles, so she couldn't see the bite. But she knew it was there. To her dismay, even though it was cold in the cabin and he needed the warmth, he'd kept his shirt on this time.

She remembered what it had felt like to strip that off and look at his lean muscles as he slept. She'd only done it to make him more comfortable. At least that's what she told herself. Sure.

Reed wrapped a blanket around them both as they snuggled to keep warm in the dropping temperatures. But she still felt on edge, because even though they felt safe in their forest oasis, werewolves lurked and hunted them.

Hannah shivered at the memory of that basement, and Reed held her closer then took her hand in his.

Tingles raced up her arms as he rubbed small circles in her palm with his thumb.

Dear goddess, the man is smooth.

And apparently none of them were going to talk about what was going on. Fine with her for now, but once they left the cabin, they would have to break the barrier. She didn't know what would come of their talk and it scared her.

"You two look comfy." Josh's voice sounded rough with sleep.

"Hey, do you feel better?" She refused to take her hand away from Reed's. Had she just make a choice?

"A little. I just can't sleep with those fuckers out there, ya know?"

"I know what you mean. But as soon as this storm lets up, we'll get out of here. We'll get somewhere safe." Reed smiled, but a cold gleam entered his eyes. "Then we'll make sure the Centrals know not to fuck with us."

The men looked at each other and seemed to come to an understanding.

They were so strong, just in different ways sometimes. But in this one case, she knew they would be on the same page.

Josh sat up and patted the seat next to him. "Come sit by me. The fire helps, but it's getting cold in here."

Reed shuffled to the couch, pulling her with him, and they sat down. Josh pulled the blankets around the three of them, cuddling close into her side. Her womb clenched at the feel of both men on either side of her, warming her from the inside out.

Dammit. Things couldn't go on like this.

Finding the shred of courage she possessed, she blurted, "What's going on? With us?"

Both men stopped the subtle stroking on her arms and froze. Their faces looked guilty, but slightly intrigued. That was a good sign. Right?

They removed their hands, and she immediately felt cold at the loss of contact.

Josh furrowed his brows and tilted his head. Reed took a deep breath.

What was going on? Hannah feared their answers.

"You are my mate," Reed finally answered, a look of pure joy and anticipation on his face. He smiled and looked into her eyes.

Happiness, unprecedented happiness, filled her. She knew about werewolves' mates. She was his fated destiny. His other half. Together they would live in love and faith because it was fate. She'd known there was a connection, but she'd never thought to even hope for this outcome.

A link. Between the two of them.

"Oh." She uttered that single word with a mix of joy and pain.

What about Josh? There would be no Josh. She was Reed's, as he was hers.

And Josh would be alone, without them.

Josh grunted, a hollow sound full of pain. Then his expression blanked and he stood. "I'm happy for the two of you, though I'd suspected it since we met in the basement. I'm going to leave the two of you alone for a bit to talk. I'm going to go back to the bedroom for a bit."

Reed's hand shot out, catching Josh by his uninjured forearm before he could leave the room.

"Don't go."

"Yes," Hannah added, "stay. Please don't go."

She looked into his ocean blue eyes full of pain.

Wait. Why did she feel such desire, desire that matched what she felt for Reed, if she was Reed's mate? Wasn't there like a wolf law against that or something?

"No, I need to go. You two are mates. I can't be here right now. Don't you understand?" Josh's eyes were hard. What could he be feeling?

Hannah's chest hurt. *Oh goddess.* Apparently her heart wanted two men, but why? Why did this have to happen now? Why did Reed have to say anything and make Josh go away? Why did Josh have to feel anything for her anyway? Even though she felt the same way. Damn it. He must hurt. It wasn't fair.

But life wasn't fair. Her mother's short life and her own captivity were proof positive of that.

Reed's voice broke into her thoughts. "Josh, you're my mate too. Our mate."

Wait. What did he say?

"Oh." What else could she say? What did this mean?

Josh's eyes widened and his face paled. "No way."

"Yes, way," Reed replied. "I feel it here." Reed put his hand over his heart. "My wolf also knows it. I know it's not what you expected, but it's true. You're both my mates." He looked between them, pleading in his eyes but strength in his features, as if preparing for rejection.

Josh shook his head. "Don't get me wrong. I find you both attractive, which by itself is odd. Not that you aren't hot, but the fact that I'm looking at a *man* that way..." Josh blushed. "But I'm straight, Reed. I've never wanted another man. I just don't know."

Reed gave a hollow laugh. "I've always been happy with men or women."

Hannah didn't like the sound of that. Why was he bringing up past relationships at a time like this? She didn't want to feel jealous, but seriously.

"Don't look like that, either of you," Reed interjected. "You two are the first two I've ever felt the mating heat with. Ever." Reed looked at them through smoldering eyes. "You're both my mates. Believe me."

Hannah took a deep breath. Two mates? Was that possible? She knew that wolves had potential mates, others out there that could be their other half. But some never found even one, let alone two in a long life time. Did this mean Reed would have to choose? Did he want Josh and not her? This was just too confusing and made her heart hurt.

Reed cleared his throat and rubbed his hands on his thighs. "I've never heard of this happening before. I mean, one of my brothers has had two potential mates. Kade met Tracy first, but that didn't work out." He let out a hollow laugh. "Thankfully, he met Melanie soon after and now they are mated. But it wasn't at the same time, and once he met Melanie, he wanted nothing to do with Tracy."

She didn't know exactly who these people were, but she needed to discuss the three of them in this room, not others.

"But," Reed continued, "this is about us. Not them. I don't want to make a callous decision. I don't think I *can* make a decision. I don't want to choose." Reed looked at them both, his heart in his eyes.

"This is a lot to take in, Reed," Hannah whispered.

"Don't worry. I don't want in." Josh's voice was cold, emotionless.

A part of her heart broke off, shattering into a thousand pieces.

She'd been wrong. She never had a choice. She never did. Josh didn't want her...them.

Her arms tingled as a hollow feeling spread through her. He'd walk away. Alone.

Hannah looked away from Josh. She couldn't bear to see the man she'd almost fallen for anymore if he didn't reciprocate those feelings. Her gaze landed on Reed. She saw a mirror of her emotions on his face before they faded away into resignation.

"I didn't mention all of this to let you walk away, Josh. Don't go. Let's just sit on this for a bit and talk it out. See where things go." Reed took a deep breath. "Please."

Hannah jumped in. "That sounds very reasonable. Please, Josh. Let's just wait a bit." Tears filled her eyes, but she blinked them away and forced a smile on her face. "I mean, we just escaped from a lunatic's prison and everything. Let's take a day or two to settle."

Josh clenched his jaw. "So let me get this straight. We just parade around here like Goldilocks in a fucking cabin we don't own, waiting for Reed to get off his ass and choose between us? That's rich. And how about the fact that I want you, Hannah? That I keep dreaming about you and me and forever? Reed is dreaming those same dreams. I already know whom he'd choose. Why should I just sit here and watch him choose you and not me?"

Embarrassment covered his features and he quickly shut his mouth.

Hannah was speechless.

Josh wanted Reed and her. All three of them wanted each other?

And to think, the week before she'd had no one. Now she had two of the sexiest men on Earth wanting her. Nice.

Reed stood and paced through the room.

"I don't know what's going on," Reed finally said. "I need to go home to my family. To the Pack. But I also don't want to leave you. I know I *can't* leave the two of you. Let's honestly see where this goes, with the three of us."

Wait. What?

"The three of us?" Hannah squeaked.

Josh cleared his throat, looking slightly embarrassed. Not at all like the tough military man he normally did. "You mean like the three of us together—at the same time?"

Reed gave a startled laugh. "The looks on your faces are priceless. Yes, I mean the three of us at the same time. But I don't mean like an orgy on the floor at this exact moment or anything."

They all paused for a moment. She pictured the sweaty, naked goodness that would come from an orgy on the floor, and by the looks on the men's faces, they were picturing the scene too.

"Okay, enough of that." Reed laughed again. "I mean we should at least acknowledge that there is an attraction between the *three* of us. Then we can work on it and getting home safe."

Josh scowled but nodded.

Hannah didn't say anything. A werewolf and a gifted human? Is this what her mom would have wanted for her? What would the other witches say? Did she even care?

What did *she* want? Did she want two men? Could she handle it? Well, it wasn't as if this one moment would decide her fate. Things could always change in the future. Right?

Taking a deep breath, Hannah nodded.

She'd already known her decision before Reed asked. Why did she even hesitate?

All three of them exhaled at her nod.

"Good," Josh interjected after a moment of silence. "Now what?"

Reed rubbed the back of his neck. "Well, I'd say we should shake on it, but I'll do one better. Let's kiss on it."

Josh let out a rusty laugh. "Okay, what the hell. It's been a day of revelations that's for sure."

Hannah nodded. Then bit her lip, not trusting her voice.

Both men took a step toward her.

What had she gotten herself into?

CHAPTER TEN

Reed's pulse raced at the thought of the Hannah and Josh. This was it. Everything he'd wanted and more.

Hannah stood in front of him, her teeth biting into her plump lip, like she did when she was nervous. Her chestnut hair curled in disarray around her face, emphasizing her curious, yet heated, slate eyes.

Josh stood on her other side, clenching his fists. Whether in frustration from this situation or from the sexual variety, Reed didn't know. But he hoped it was the latter. His normally spiky brown hair lay down on one side, looking like he'd just got out of bed. His blue eyes stared into Reed's soul.

Shit, Reed knew he had to be the luckiest guy on earth.

He couldn't believe they actually said they'd think about a three-some in real life—and not just in the bedroom. Happiness practically burst from every pore. Even though the situation they were in— kidnapping, bullets, basements, and borrowed cabins—made it seem inappropriate, he couldn't quite gather up the nerve to feel bad about it.

Reed watched Hannah bounce on the balls of her feet then lick her lips, anxiousness mixing with her nervousness for what was to come.

He looked over at Josh's forearms, the veins popping out of the muscles. Damn that human was strong. Reed could imagine Hannah using her tongue and teeth and Josh using that strength in other areas —particularly on Reed.

Hell, yeah.

Josh coughed. "Um, so how should we go about doing this?"

All three of them laughed.

"Oh, I can tell this is going to be fun." Reed smiled then walked to Hannah and framed her face in his hands.

Her pupils dilated, and her breath quickened.

He heard the rustle of clothing as Josh moved behind him. Reed's cock hardened almost to the point of pain at the thought of Josh and Hannah together, then both of them with him.

His gaze lowered to her lips as her tongue darted out and licked them. He inhaled her honey and crisp apple scent, the aroma rocking him to the bone.

"Kiss her then kiss him. This is it."

He couldn't agree more with his wolf. Reed bent and touched his lips to hers. A shock rushed through his system. Her taste. Dear God, her taste. She tasted just like her scent but more potent. Her soft lips slid against his, and he groaned. Her lips parted, and his wolf growled. Her hands roamed his back, hesitantly at first, then firmer as she got into the kiss more. He tilted his head, deepening the kiss, sucking on her tongue and drowning in her taste.

Knowing he only meant this to be an initial kiss, and not wanting to leave Josh out, he forced himself to lift his lips from hers. He panted and looked down at her pouty, swollen lips as her eyes slowly opened.

"Oh my." Her voice had deepened with sexual energy.

Sexy as hell.

He held her in his arms, watching her breathe rapidly. Josh came to their side and brushed a lock of hair out of Hannah's face. Hannah moved her gaze from him to Josh, her body pulsating in Reed's arms.

Surprisingly, Reed felt no jealousy watching Hannah's eyelids lower with desire as she looked at Josh. Reed himself wanted to groan at the look of pure promise and ecstasy on the man's face. With only a slight reluctance, in that he wanted to hold the both of them forever, he loosened his grip on Hannah as she pivoted fully into Josh's arms.

Hannah tilted her head up, and Reed watched as Josh lowered his face and kissed her. Both of his mates, together. Perfection. Josh bit her lip and growled.

Fuck, the human was damn sexy.

Josh kissed harder than he had. He seemed to put his whole body into the action, grinding against her and sucking her lips, then nibbling to take his fill. Hannah moaned and squirmed against him, much like she had with Reed.

Reed had to adjust himself as his erection pushed painfully into his zipper. This was going to be amazing—the three of them. An unknown feeling swept over him...completion? Suddenly, Reed knew he wanted this more than anything he'd ever known or seen. He'd never heard of threesomes as a fixture in daily life and not just in the bedroom in the Pack. Would they accept them? Did he care? This was fate. He couldn't argue with fate, nor could he argue with how he felt and how the three of them acted around one another. No, this was for real. The Pack would have to learn to adjust.

"Stop over thinking everything. It will work out. These two are keepers. Now, shut up and watch them go at it. Nice, isn't it?"

Reed smiled at his wolf. Yeah, they were keepers for sure.

Hannah gasped into Josh's mouth, and Reed groaned. *Fuck yeah.* They pulled apart, breathing heavily.

"I think I need to sit down." Hannah backed herself to the couch and sat down, out of breath.

He and Josh reached for her at the same time and the other man's hand ended up in his. Josh tried to pull away, but Reed wouldn't let him. The other man tensed, his hand freezing in his, but relaxed after a moment.

Hannah looked at them both then smiled. "I'm fine, really. I just had the two best kisses of my life." She let out a giggle. "They were different but so amazing. So perfect." Her gaze traveled down their bodies, leaving a trail of heat and desire, before landing on their joined hands. Her tongue reached out and licked her lips.

Reed looked at Josh, studying his strong features. His lips weren't as full as Hannah's or his, but still looked edible. He reached up with his other hand and brushed an unruly lock of hair from Josh's forehead. Why did he have such long hair up top if he was a military man? He'd have to ask that sometime.

"*Kiss him,*" his wolf growled.

"Have you ever kissed a man before?" Reed needed to know. Josh said he'd never found another man attractive so Reed guessed the answer. He just needed to hear it.

Josh let out a surprised laugh. "Can't say that I have."

Reed nodded, squeezing his hand. "I'm going to kiss you now."

Josh looked toward Hannah and gave her a small, sexy smile.

Hannah laughed. "If you two kiss each other the way you just kissed me, I may just die watching."

Josh knelt beside Hannah and in front of Reed. Josh smiled again. "I have a better idea. Why don't I kiss you?"

Reed widened his eyes as Josh pulled him by the back of his neck over Hannah's legs and crushed his mouth to his.

Sweet ponderosa pine burst on his tongue. Teeth clashed against teeth, as Josh thrust his tongue in and out of his mouth. Reed groaned as an overwhelming sexual fog took over, weakening his already weak resolve.

Dear God, I could live on Josh's and Hannah's taste alone.

He held onto Josh like a drowning man, playing an intricate game of war with their tongues and lips. Reed pulled back then bit into the fleshy part of Josh's lip. Hard. Then he soothed the sting as Josh's eyes widened.

Oh, they would have to see which of the two of them would be dominant. If either. It would be arousing as hell to take turns and then both take Hannah—together. He almost came in his jeans at the thought.

They pulled apart again, breathing heavily, much like they had with their kisses with Hannah. His wolf howled in utter bliss and contentment, and Reed wanted to join in.

All three of them looked at each other then burst out laughing, the tension from the unknown dissolving away. Tears leaked from their eyes as their laughter grew.

"I'm sorry," Hannah gasped through her laughter. "I don't want to laugh. But I was afraid it'd be awkward."

"It's not awkward. I thought it would be, but it was damn good," Josh added in.

"Hell, yeah. We should do it again," Reed agreed.

"Hey, it was totally worth it." Josh smiled, then got a wicked gleam in his eye. "Best guy kiss ever."

Reed punched him in the arm. Josh's eyes widened, as he rubbed the spot.

"You sure do pack a punch for a little guy," Josh practically leered.

"Uh, dude, I'm a werewolf. And only like an inch shorter than you."

Hannah giggled. "Yeah, this won't be complicated at all."

"Hey," Reed interjected, "we can do it. Fate's cool like that."

"Reed, man, you sound like an old man trying to use slang." Josh laughed.

"Hey, I *am* an old man."

All three dissolved into laughter.

This felt good. Like family. His family.

A soft crunching, like snow under a paw, reached Reed's ears, interrupting his peace. Hannah froze, her eyes wide.

"The wards. Someone's breached the wards."

Josh grunted, closing his eyes in pain, and grabbed his arm.

"Fuck, my Finding's back—I think."

All three jumped to their feet, ready to fight.

Their time in their forest oasis faded away. Back to reality and the dangers that hunted them.

CHAPTER ELEVEN

A howl broke through their uncomfortable silence. Shit, Josh didn't think their interlude from danger would end this fast. But he should have been expecting it, been prepared. Now instead of thinking about the aftereffects of kissing the two most important people in his life—and likening it—he had to fight. Maybe to the death.

He wanted—no, needed—to protect Hannah and Reed, no matter what. Though how he'd accomplish that, he didn't know. He was the weakest of the three of them by far. An uncomfortable and unfamiliar feeling settled in the pit of his stomach. He'd have to get used to it if they stayed in this odd three-way relationship.

Did they really need him for anything? Would they just walk away when they realized he had nothing really to give? And what would happen when Reed, and maybe even Hannah for all he knew of witches, stayed young forever, and Josh grew old? He knew humans could be turned into werewolves but he'd heard the horror stories of the change. Would he have to turn into a wolf?

Another howl, this time closer. Thoughts warred in his mind, but he shook them off. Not the time to be thinking about relationships.

He had to bear down and go back to his training. It was what he was good at.

Hannah stood beside him, with her palms held outward and fingers spread.

"Do you have enough, you know, juice, or whatever?" Wow, he really needed to brush up on his magical knowledge.

Hannah smiled, nervous tension evident in her eyes. "Yes, I have enough. I'm near the earth, and that's why I meditated before. Plus the kiss helped." She blushed and lowered her eyes.

Reed exhaled. "I'd heard that sex increases some witches' powers. Good to know."

Is that right? If so, we'll have to work on that.

Reed planted his feet, ready for battle. "Something just brushed along a tree outside."

"Shit," Josh cursed. "I don't want to be surrounded in this cabin; I think we need to go outside."

Reed nodded. "I agree. Let's go outside and take the fight to them."

Josh tilted his head, his focus on the two who called themselves his mates. "And if it's too much…" He let his voice fade, unable to voice the all-too-real possibility they would die once they crossed the threshold.

Reed met his gaze but didn't say anything. He didn't need to. Understanding lit his eyes. They'd run if there were too many, if there were no other options. At least they'd try to run through the snow drifts. They had too much to lose now.

Reed would protect him and Hannah at all costs. Josh didn't know why he was aware of these unexplored feelings at the moment, or why there was even a I, but there was something here worth swallowing some pride. They'd run and trek through the snow to save their lives and save each other. That was how it had to be. Though Reed might not need it, Josh would be by the wolf's side through thick and thin, protecting his ass as well.

Josh walked out the door first and onto the patio, crouched low to duck for cover if needed. Shit, with all the snow, they couldn't see anything. Hannah mumbled something under her breath and the snow moved in drifts and made pathways. Hannah fell in behind, sandwiched between him and Reed. He was a fucking idiot. Reed had wanted to go first, but Josh ignored all of his previous internal ramblings and went through the door first anyway. Stupid. What role did a mere human play in a war of supernaturals other than for cannon fodder and playing the role of the redshirt?

Cold wind lashed against his skin. Though it was daytime, the sun didn't peak through the clouds. It was light out, but still pretty dark. The blizzard warred in full force, causing limited visibility in the falling snow. Shit, if only he possessed Reed's eyes. Another reason he shouldn't have been a prideful prick and let him go first. *Dammit.*

Josh heard the growl a split second before Hannah pivoted and used her amazing powers to send a dirt-filled snow-drift smack into two wolves. They yelped and tried to dig themselves out. She buried them deeper.

That's my girl.

Josh looked behind him, squinting through the snow. Reed glanced around then cursed under his breath. The sexy man quickly rid himself of his clothes and stood naked in the middle of a fucking blizzard.

"I need to change; too many wolves." Reed shook his head but didn't blush, apparently either too cold or comfortable with his nudity.

And the man didn't have anything to be ashamed of. Lean, like a swimmer, and yet still muscular, Reed's golden skin formed a stark contrast to the white snow. Josh risked a glance and saw his dick.

Fuck.

Yep, no need to be ashamed there. Long and thick, maybe not as thick as his own, but they'd compare later. What would Reed do with that thing? There was no way it would fit. Okay, he really needed to get his mind out of the gutter.

Reed cleared his throat, and Josh looked up, feeling only slightly guilty. Out of the corner of his eye, he saw Hannah's with a guilty expression on her face. They were all goners.

Reed crouched down low and, before Josh's eyes, changed to a sandy-colored wolf with rust-colored streaks woven into his fur. The wolf opened his mouth in almost a yawn, showing off some long and dangerous looking teeth.

And all Josh had was an aluminum bat, since he was out of ammo and his knives were back at the compound. He'd lost most of them during the fight and after the demon had bitten him, he hadn't been in the right mind to remember to pick them up. Something he'd never do with a clear head.

In a tangle of fur and limbs, Reed jumped into the fray, taking down two opponents. Vicious growls erupted as blood seeped from wounds on both sides. Snow continued to fall, making it hard for Josh to see exactly what was going on and if Reed was okay.

Josh stood by Hannah's side, protecting her from wolves getting too close. She might be amazing with her magic, but if she missed just one wolf, she'd get hurt just as badly as a human. Josh couldn't take that. A muddy brown wolf leaped from the bushes toward Hannah, and Josh swung with the bat. The metal clanged against the side of its head, the sound of its skull crushing echoing in his ears. The vibrations from the connection of aluminum to flesh and fur ran up his arm, jarring the bite. Josh cursed under his breath at the pain.

"Josh, behind you!" Hannah yelled over the growls and wind.

He pivoted, hitting the gray wolf in the flank as Hannah used her power to bury another wolf. Shit, the wolves kept coming, with no end in sight. What should they do? Was it time to run?

Out of the corner of his eye, he checked on Reed. The sandy-haired wolf fought off two of the mangier wolves, growling and biting. Josh wanted to help, to see if he could hit the other wolves away, but he couldn't leave Hannah's side. Was this what it meant to be in a group of three? To constantly be in the middle, trying to choose between mates?

Reed twisted his head towards Josh, caught Josh checking on him and glared, before turning back to his fight. Okay, apparently Reed could handle himself.

A chocolate brown wolf with black ears and the left side of its face black, stared at him. His green eyes looked familiar to Josh, but he couldn't quite place why. Startled, Josh raised the bat, ready to swing at the wolf, but something tugged at his sleeve. He looked down at Reed's pleading eyes, as Reed shook his head.

What the fuck?

Wolf-Reed yelped at Josh then barked at the other wolf. They really needed to find a system to talk when Reed was in his wolf form. The other wolf gave a nod then turned his back to Josh, blocking him from the fight.

This stranger was going to protect them? How did Reed know him? Was he part of his Pack?

Josh looked toward Hannah, but she shared his confused look. Josh shrugged, no time to deal with it. He'd take any help he could get.

A growl sounded behind him. Josh turned quickly to see a wolf coming at his face, teeth bared. He slammed his bat into the wolf's side, and it let out a yelp. He pivoted, hitting it again with all his strength. The wolf went down and Hannah buried it in dirt and snow. Teamwork at its best.

Wolves came from all directions. Josh worked with Hannah in tandem, fighting them off, killing those who dared too close. Despite the freezing temperatures, sweat rolled down his back. His vision darkened as his arm throbbed. A wolf came from behind a bush and bared its teeth at Hannah, ready to pounce. Before he knew it, he was at her side, beating the fucking thing to a bloody pulp.

Josh looked around and exhaled. They seemed to be winning—for now. He took what he could get and grabbed Hannah's hand.

"We need to run. Now."

Hannah nodded, gripping him tightly. The other wolf, Reed's friend, stopped in front of them and beckoned them with a nod. Apparently they were following this stranger to a safer place. Anything sounded better than the debris of dead wolves and enemies they were currently facing.

They trailed the dark brown wolf as Josh looked for Reed, the man he'd kissed like his life was on the line less than an hour ago, followed with a slight limp and blood on his paws and flank.

Some fucker hurt Reed. Made him bleed.

Oh, Josh was gonna kick some ass. That was for sure.

Thank God, Hannah looked unharmed, though she was quiet and out of breath. It could have gone worse, and they weren't out of danger yet.

He pulled Hannah through the trenches, the snow up to his knees. A wolf howled over the blowing wind, and she tightened her hand around his. Reed and the other wolf had almost no problem navigating through the snow, and Josh was glad he only had to pull one person. Off in the distance, a tan SUV came into view. A godsend in the middle of an icy hell.

Cold had leached through his jeans, numbing his legs, but he held on, praying he'd make it before Hannah froze or the other wolves came back. Once they made it to the car, Josh wrenched opened the door, thanking God the other wolf had left it unlocked. Using whatever strength he had left, he set Hannah into the back seat and tossed the bat in behind her, careful not to hit her.

He looked at the two wolves at his feet and, after nod from Reed, got into the back, holding Hannah close to his side for whatever warmth they could find. Josh watched as both Reed and the other wolf change back into human forms. The other man looked a lot like Reed. Too cold and full of painful adrenaline to stare at any naked bodies now, he handed Reed the clothes that he had carried for him. Josh looked in the back of the SUV and found another set. He gave them to the stranger who helped save their lives.

"Josh, Hannah, this is my brother, Adam." Reed motioned to the stranger. Taller than Reed, and a bit bulkier, he had the same green eyes but had dark cropped hair. They could have been twins.

Adam pulled his brother into a deep embrace.

"It's good to see you, Reed, but let's get the fuck out of here before someone comes back for us," Adam grunted.

"Sounds good to me, this is Josh and Hannah." Reed nodded towards them sitting in the back seat.

Hannah squeezed his hands, tense like he was, waiting for Adam's reaction.

Before Reed could think or feel bad, Josh spoke up. "We're his mates. No need to be embarrassed. But it's fucking cold out there, and I'd like to get away from those maniacs out there and get somewhere warm."

Adam stood there a moment longer as a pained look flashed across his face. But as quickly as it came, he brushed it away, putting on a blank mask.

"Get in the car; we need to get moving." Adam grunted again and went around to the driver's side, keys in hand.

Reed leaned into the back seat and kissed Josh then Hannah, surprising them both—and Adam. He gave an apologetic look when he backed away and jumped into the passenger seat.

"It will be okay," Hannah whispered in his ear, even though the wolves would hear them. She took his face in her hands and kissed him softly.

Josh smiled and watched as they passed the trees outside of the Jeep's window as Adam hightailed it out of the forest. Away from their cabin and captivity.

And to think, only yesterday he'd been enjoying a reindeer hotdog with caramelized onions and cream cheese. He'd closed his eyes on a bench and heard two kids talking about people he didn't even know.

Now he had two people that might be his mates, one a beautiful woman with soft curves and the other a man who made him hard like no one before. A crazy Pack of werewolves were after him, bent on killing him and the two people he was falling for. He'd met a member of Reed's family with a pained look and was now on the way to meet another Pack to explain one of their sons might be in a three-way relationship with a man and a woman.

It was odd how things could take a turn so quickly. For the better or worse, Josh didn't know. But it didn't seem too complicated, right? *Fuck.*

CHAPTER TWELVE

T all trees blurred as they passed them as Hannah sagged against Josh's side. No one spoke, either too tired or finding it too awkward to deal with the emotions running through the air, which became so thick it lay heavy on her tongue.

Her body ached from all the magic she'd poured from her system, protecting herself and the men in her life.

The way Josh had introduced them to Adam as Reed's mates made her feel warm and soft inside. Whatever doubts he might have, he believed in at least something concerning them. Reed had said their names with such caring and affection, Adam would have known exactly who they were from his voice alone.

And Adam. Poor Adam. The look of pain in his eyes when Josh spoke had hurt her heart. Something bad had happened to Reed's brother, something no one should go through. What it was she could only guess, but she didn't know for sure. Hannah knew there would always be a barrier between them and Adam for that reason alone. And she didn't know if she could blame him for it.

"How did you find us, Adam?" Reed asked.

"I didn't really." Adam answered. "I sort of stumbled across you. I'd been looking since they took you, but I couldn't get onto the Central's land and find you. Then after I drove around to the other side of the territory to find another way in, I came across your scent." He took a deep breath and his hands tightened on the wheel. "I'd never been so relieved."

Reed squeezed his brother's shoulder, but didn't say anything.

Josh rubbed circles into her wrist, infusing warmth from just his touch. She leaned into him once more and kissed his stubbled cheek. With a deep breath, she leaned forward and placed her free hand on Reed's shoulder.

He gasped at the touch and looked over at her, warmth in his eyes.

"You're hurt," she said, her voice barely above a whisper. "Let me help."

Reed smiled. God how she loved that smile. "Okay."

She used most of the power she had left and healed the wounds on Reed's side and hands. It took more because she couldn't put her hands directly over the wounds. But she didn't want to wait any longer, not when she could still heal him.

Adam inhaled loudly beside her.

"You're a healer," Adam murmured, an odd mix of awe and resignation in his tone.

Confused, she glanced at Reed. But he only mouthed "later" and shook his head.

Okay, she could wait, but something was off.

But Hannah nodded and leaned back into Josh's arms, sighing when he held her close, kissing her forehead and temples.

Goddess, he felt like heaven.

As the drive continued on, no one spoke, all too tired to expend the energy. Hours passed, and Hannah reflected on the kiss the three of them had shared in the cabin before their time was cut short by the angry mob of wolves.

The kiss felt right. Good. But could she live in a threesome? Ignoring the fact that people would scoff and call them names better left unsaid, could she deal with the emotional aspect? Having one man seemed too much for some women. The attachment, the overwhelming intensity, the sex... Everything added up to an emotional toll. But multiply that times two and it seemed astronomical.

But the benefits and feelings of two men with her made Hannah want to ignore her misgivings and jump in head first.

The car slowed down as they passed an ivy covered stone archway guarded by two people she could only assume were wolves by their energies. The two guards nodded at the Jeep, and Adam continued up the drive.

Magnificent large trees covered the land. Between the trees, dark green grass was interspersed with a covering snow. She hoped the empty spaces of land would be filled with beautiful flowers come spring time. She was immediately sucked into the Redwood den. She loved it. The energy surrounding her pulsated and tugged on her, calling her home.

This was it. The missing piece clicked into place, and she knew it. She'd never want to leave. She'd stay here with Josh and Reed forever if they'd let her.

The Redwoods called to her.

Adam wound along the road, passing homes hidden among the brush. Frankly, it was a beautiful den. They pulled up to a home, nestled beneath a canopy of two large trees with branches reaching up to the sky. It was a two-story, older looking home with fresh paint and shutters.

"This is my home," Reed said simply.

Reed's home. Could it be hers and Josh's too?

Hannah shook her head. This was too much too soon. She tucked away those promising and somewhat nerve-wracking thoughts for later.

The front door to Reed's home opened and people filed out.

"Oh Reed! The sentries called to tell us you were coming." A short light brown haired woman with warm eyes ran to Reed and held him close.

"Hi, Mom. I've missed you," Reed choked out, holding his mom and rubbing his cheek on her hair.

Brothers, sisters, or sisters-in law, and his parents came at him, hugging, patting, and crying, reassuring themselves Reed was actually with them. That he was home.

With such an out pouring of love, Hannah felt out of place.

Goddess, she missed her Mother.

How would it feel to be part of such a family, to never be alone? It was what she thought she wanted with Josh and Reed. But could they achieve it?

Josh came from behind and held her hand. The feelings of reassurance and hope slid through her as he squeezed it. He understood. He was alone, just as she was. But it seemed like he had been alone longer. Would he want to give that freedom up and be a family? Their connection and the pulsating thread knitted between their three souls flared.

Please, let this work. Please, let us be a family.

"Come on, everyone. Get inside and get warm. I'll introduce everyone once we do." Reed ushered his family in, then stood back to take Hannah's hand and nod at Josh.

They walked into his home and found themselves in a cozy living room with a large L-shaped couch. She wanted to sink into the comfy cushions. Art covered the walls and framed pictures of family members dotted shelves layered with books. It looked like an artist's home.

Hannah fell a little bit more in love with him right then.

Reed's family talked above each other, eager to hear about his captivity. But they didn't outright ask who Hannah and Josh were, though she could tell by their not-so-casual looks they wanted to.

"Hannah, Josh, this is my family." Reed laughed under his breath. "From the top, this is my father, my Alpha, Edward. And my mother, Patricia." Reed pointed to a couple holding hands but looked to be Reed's age. Edward had darker hair, almost black, but still looked like Reed enough there was no mistaking the family resemblance.

Hannah waved.

What was she supposed to do in this situation? Talk about awkward.

"Over there is my eldest brother, Kade, and his wife, Melanie. She's holding their son, Finn." Kade looked a lot like Edward, only about an inch shorter and a soft blend of their mother's features mixed in. Melanie was a short blond beauty, smiling and rocking baby Finn to sleep.

"Next to them on the couch are Jasper and his wife, Willow." Jasper had even darker hair than Kade and seemed taller, about six and a half feet. Willow had light brown hair and had pixie features. She was slender except for one noticeable thing.

"And our soon-to-be baby." Willow gave a radiant smile and held her protruding belly.

A tug of maternal instincts Hannah didn't know she possessed startled her.

"I don't think we can forget that, Willow. You're a little hard to miss." Reed laughed.

Jasper growled. "Watch what you say about my mate, dear brother." But his eyes were filled with laughter when he said it.

Their family dynamics made her smile.

"You've already met Adam. So here are the twins, North and Maddox." The twins looked like wiry versions of Jamensons but with dark blond hair that obviously had come from their mother. They were practically identical but for the large scar running down the side of Maddox's face.

"And last, but not least, Cailin." Reed gestured toward the most beautiful woman Hannah had ever seen. She had long indigo-black hair with blunt bangs, big, green Jamenson eyes and full lips.

These brothers had a hell of a thing on their hands if they were typical big brothers and wanted to protect her from men and the outside world. And from the Alpha energy she felt swirling around the room, she would place money on it.

"Hi, it's nice to meet everyone." Hannah's voice was small. She didn't know what else to say.

"Yes, nice to meet you. Reed, can we get someone to look at Hannah? We haven't seen a doctor yet." Josh asked.

"Of course, sorry, I'm being an idiot. North? Can you help?" Reed asked the twin who must have been the doctor.

"Sure, let me take a look. I'm not a healer, but still a doctor." North stood and walked over to her, placing his hand on her arm in a comforting gesture.

Reed and Josh growled behind her at the touch. Talk about territorial, but she liked it. Who knew? Hannah noticed the looks passing between the family members but fought down the apology in her throat.

Were they judging her? She didn't want to be a burden to this family and she honestly didn't want to hurt Reed.

North walked back to the couch and opened his medical kit that he must have brought over when he heard Reed was home, and cleaned her visible scrapes and bruises. The lash marks on her stomach had healed overnight through the use of earth magic, thankfully.

"Son," Edward interrupted, "why are you two undamaged, but not Hannah? Why would you allow her to be hurt in your place? Or is there something else going on I need to know about?" He quirked a brow, waiting for his answer.

Hannah felt a wash of an age-old power. Alpha. Edward apparently wanted answers. Now.

Reed looked at Hannah with a question in his eyes. She nodded.

"Hannah's a healer. A witch."

The people in the room fell into silence. Even baby Finn seemed to know this meant something. What, she wasn't sure of. Yet. But Reed owed her answers. Both times he told someone she was a healer, they reacted strangely. Why?

Reed's mother put her hands over her mouth, and then smiled a watery smile. "We've been waiting for you."

Edward looked her up and down, assessing her with those beyond his years, wisdom-filled, green eyes. "Yes, Hannah, we have."

Hannah looked around the room; eyes filled with awe stared back at her.

"What are you talking about? What do you mean you were waiting for me?" Hannah asked, her voice rising in a squeak. *What is going on?*

"You're our Healer." Edwards placed emphases on the word, as if it meant more than her normal abilities.

"What is that?"

"Hannah, I was going to explain. Take a seat, baby." Reed looked at her and she knew something big was happening, but she still trusted him.

"Reed?"

"Every Pack has certain titles associated with the Alpha's family. Dad is the Alpha, the one in charge. Kade is the Heir, the first son. So he's in line to take over. Jasper is the Beta, meaning he deals with Pack business and takes care of us. Adam is the Enforcer; his job is to protect the Pack from outside forces. Maddox is the Omega; it's his job to protect and soothe the emotions of the Pack. And lastly, there is the Healer, the one who Heals the Pack physically. We've been without one since the last war with the Centrals a century ago. But Hannah, with you here, we aren't looking anymore. You're our Healer, Hannah." Reed held her hands, his eyes imploring her to believe. To accept.

"I don't know, Reed. This is a lot to take in. I can't think about this right now." Hannah shook her head. It was all too much.

"It's okay, don't worry. We can talk about it later. God knows we need rest." Reed leaned forward and kissed her forehead while Josh rubbed her back.

Reed told the story of his ordeal. Of Caym capturing him and putting him in the dungeon. Of meeting Hannah and not being able to help her. He didn't share everything, like her torture. That was something that she had the right to choose to share. He told of the demon's plans as he knew of, though that wasn't much. He spoke about the compound and wards and everything they could possibly think of to help his Pack. Then he spoke of Josh and how he rescued them, but Reed didn't mention Josh's special abilities. That was Josh's secret.

Josh.

"Crap. I almost forgot. My head's too crazy. We need to have someone look at Josh's arm." Hannah turned towards him and reached for his arm.

"What happened to your arm, son?" Edward asked.

"The damn demon bit me. Pardon my language." Josh rolled up his sleeve to show the still-healing bite.

Kade and Jasper growled and moved to stand in front of their wives.

"Hey, back off." Reed growled. "Josh is hurt. We don't know why the demon bit him, but he needs our help. Now."

His family's eyes grew wide, as if they were surprised at the aggressiveness in Reed's demand. Why would they be surprised that Reed had a backbone? Maybe that was why Reed felt inferior to his brothers' power and strength. She held back the urge to say something rude to them or kick their ass. Reed was protecting what he deemed his. Plus, Reed looked damn sexy when he acted all Alpha. She liked it.

"Reed, I don't want to cause a rift between you and your family," Josh whispered, his voice sad.

Hannah gasped and looked into Josh's eyes. Would any of them be okay if Josh walked away and out of their lives?

Reed fisted his hands, his eyes darkening like the coming of a deadly storm. "No, you can't leave. We need you here. And don't forget the Centrals are after you too. You risked your life for two strangers, and I won't let you risk it again because some *people* don't feel comfortable."

Kade growled and Melanie rubbed his arms.

"It's not that we're uncomfortable," Jasper reasoned, ever the Beta. "But we need to know more about what happened."

Adam narrowed his eyes. "Yes, Josh, tell us. How did you find them?"

Josh opened his mouth to reply, his eyes narrowed into slits.

Damn it, they are going to fight. This isn't going to end well.

"Adam, it's none of your fucking business." If looks could beat the crap out of someone, Reed's would have. "Josh found us. He's a good guy. And he's my mate. Hannah too. So back the fuck off."

The room went silent again.

"A trinity bond." Patricia whispered.

A trinity bond? What is that?

She didn't realize she'd spoken aloud until Patricia tried to answer. But Edward cleared his throat.

"It means," Edward said, "that there are three people in a mate bond. It was written long ago that a bond of such nature would come into our lives and into our Pack. But I'd thought it forgotten. I see I was mistaken." He raised an eyebrow, but didn't continue.

Hannah knew he was hiding something. She didn't know why, but Reed's father obviously refused to reveal everything he knew about this bond and what it would entail. Why wouldn't he tell them? It was between the three of them—Reed, Josh and her. Was it because she and Josh were strangers? Though it stung, she understood. They were new, and this was a time of a coming war. Why would they unveil all of their secrets to two people they'd just met? Maybe Edward would tell Reed; after all, he was his son.

Reed squeezed her hand. "I see. I'm sure there's more that you aren't saying, as always. But we need to rest and heal."

"While you do that, we'll regroup and talk about what we will do with the Centrals." Kade interjected. "This can't go on."

"Agreed," Edward said. "Come to our place and we will discuss this. The three of you can stay here and get some sleep. Talk. Get to know one another."

Pure anger passed over Reed's face. How could they just shut out their son like that? Hannah felt rage for him, and by the tension on Josh's face, he did too. Why didn't the Jamensons know Reed needed to be there?

"Fine." One word. One word filled with so much anger that Hannah thought she would have to hold Reed back.

"If it's all right," Adam interrupted, "I need to sit this one out. I need to leave for a while. I don't know when I'll be back."

The room fell silent—again.

"Adam, why? What's wrong?" Patricia asked.

"I just need some time away to think. I can't do it here."

Edward looked on his son, the Enforcer, then nodded. "I understand. We can handle well enough. But we will *always* be here for you."

Tears filled Hannah's eyes, but she refused to let them fall. Even with the tension and worries, they were still a supportive and loving family. And if it worked out, they could be hers if she mated Reed.

Adam walked toward his mother and kissed her wet cheek. "I love you, Mom."

His family went to him one by one, patting him on the back, and hugging him. Josh and Hannah stood back. She felt too much like an outsider to intrude on a clearly private and painful moment.

He kissed Finn's head and traced a finger down his cheek. Whatever else happened to Adam, Hannah knew at that moment Adam had lost a child and his mate. It was the only answer. Her heart hurt for them all.

On the way out the door, he paused and looked back toward where Josh and Hannah stood. "Take good care of him." His deep voice resonated in the room as he cast a dark look at the three of them. For some reason he was angry as all hell at whatever was happening between her, Reed, and Josh. Then he walked out of the house without another word, leaving a grieving family behind him.

Reed cleared his throat and went to stand between Hannah and Josh, showing a clear sign of the solidarity of their bond.

"Thank you for taking care of us, but we need to get some sleep now."

The Jameson men exchanged glances and nodded. Apparently they weren't going to talk about the fact that they had been thinking about kicking Josh out of the house. Well, then.

"Of course, we'll just get going." Patricia started forward and hugged and kissed them goodbye, the rest of the family following suit.

They soon found themselves alone in a large and cozy home, knowing they were part of a trinity bond. Reed turned a heated gaze on the two of them, leaving goose bumps in its trail along her too sensitive skin.

Oh crap.

CHAPTER THIRTEEN

R eed watched the chicken sizzle in the pan as Josh added
more oil to the beginnings of chicken cacciatori. He added
olive oil to the boiling water plus linguini pasta. Though
Josh was doing most of the cooking tonight, Reed wanted to feel
useful.

After his family had left, the three of them had stood in the living
room high on tension and low on energy. Josh suggested dinner, and
Hannah quickly agreed. Reed could have gone for food, sleep, or
frankly sex at this point but didn't argue. They took turns taking
showers and getting dressed while dinner cooked. Pat had come back
to the house soon after she left with a pile of clothes for them. Josh fit
in some of Kade's borrowed clothes and Hannah in some of Melanie's.

Hannah walked into the kitchen. "I feel so clean now. I hadn't realized how much I wanted a shower until I felt the hot water on my
skin." Both he and Josh groaned.

In borrowed clothes, she looked amazingly fresh, clean, and sexy.
That shower had done her well. Her skin looked soft and begged to be
nibbled by his teeth.

Damn.

"You look good; the shower helped me as well." Josh's voice grew deeper when he spoke, and Reed's cock hardened. Again.

"It smells good in here. I wish I could cook like you, Josh." Hannah grinned, and Reed felt just a bit more in love with her.

"I'll teach you." Josh went back to his cooking, unaware of the looks between Reed and Hannah.

Josh wanted to stay for at least a cooking lesson? What did that mean? Reed couldn't get his hopes up, but he wanted to anyway.

"Josh, do you think Reed can brave the stove long enough for me to clean your arm again?" Hannah asked.

Josh laughed. "I sure hope so, since at this point, he only needs to stir."

Reed held a clean wooden spoon across his chest and nodded solemnly. "I will do my best."

They all laughed as Hannah led Josh out to the living room to clean his wound. Reed's fear that something was wrong with the bite never quite left his system, though there were no outward appearances of a curse or such. Well, at least that's what he thought. He didn't know much about curses, but Josh could walk and act on his own free will and he wasn't violent. That had to count for something.

The two of them came back into the kitchen soon after, Josh sporting a new white bandage, and thankfully, Reed hadn't burned their dinner. The pasta decided to boil over at that thought, causing Reed to blush.

"Shit, sorry, guys." Reed moved quickly to the pasta, bumping into Josh on the way. A zing of pleasure and warmth traveled up his arm as Josh placed his hand on him to steady to them.

"It's okay, Reed," Josh said, desire evident in his eyes. "I left the lid on when I left. You didn't burn down the house. Yet."

Reed smiled, and they finished making dinner then plated up the cacciatori. Hannah had buttered the bread and placed it on the table.

"See? I helped." Hannah winked.

"Yes, babe, you did great." Josh leaned over and kissed her softly before sitting down.

"Better than I did." Reed kissed her as well then kissed Josh before finding his seat.

"Thank you for making dinner, Josh." Hannah beamed, before taking a bite and moaning.

Fuck, she's the hottest thing I've ever seen. Through the gleam in Josh's eyes just about tied Hannah for that honor.

They ate with little conversation, a sexual undercurrent dancing along the edges.

"We need them, Reed. Now."

Reed couldn't have agreed more with his wolf. Tonight the three of them would spend the night in the same house. He just hoped they were together in the same bed when they did it. Preferably naked and sweaty with lots of intimate touching.

After they put the dishes in the dishwasher, Reed felt at a loss as to what to do now.

"So, are you two tired?" Reed asked. "I know we've had a trying couple of days."

"Not really. I know I should be, but I'm kind of wired," Hannah answered.

"I agree. I have some pent-up energy." Josh's voice deepened, and Reed moaned.

"I know a way we can use that," Reed teased.

"Oh really? How, pray tell?" Hannah asked.

Reed didn't answer, but prowled toward her and pulled her into his arms, crushing his mouth to hers. The sweet taste of honey and bitter apples burst on his tongue. He licked the seam of her lips, begging her to open. When she did, Reed danced his tongue along hers, both of them gasping for breaths. He held her face in his hands, as hers roamed his back under his shirt. Her soft skin felt like smooth silk against his.

Josh came up behind Hannah and moved her thick, curly hair out of the way as he trailed kisses along her neck. She moaned in Reed's mouth, alternatively grinding between the two of them. Josh's hand brushed Reed's, and both men gasped at the fire burning at the touch.

Hannah pulled away, gasping for breath. "What's going on here?"

As if she didn't know.

Reed looked toward Josh, not surprised to see the heated desire there. But it was the slight alarm and worry mixing in that made Reed pause.

Do they not want this? Not want me?

An ache went through Reed's heart, but he held back the fear. They needed to talk, not make assumptions. That's what had gotten in the way of Jasper and Willow's mating for so long. He had sworn that would never happen to him.

"Hannah," Reed soothed, "I want to make love with you. Tonight."

Hannah stiffened, but he could smell her arousal. "What about Josh?"

"Josh does too." Josh nodded, and Hannah relaxed.

"But what about *Josh?*" Hannah asked again.

Reed looked at the man in question. "I want to make love to Josh as well, but I don't know if we are all ready for that. I want you first. You will always be first and center for me."

Josh rubbed small circles in both of their backs. "It's the same for me. You're the center. Always." He let out a rugged laugh. "Plus, I'm still a little too new to the whole guy-on-guy thing. I may need to take it slow there."

"I'll help you," Reed promised. "Don't worry."

Hannah let out a breath. "Okay, I understand. I want the both of you too. But we will have to promise always to talk, be open. Voice our concerns. I don't want to offend anyone. This will be complicated enough without hurt feelings."

"Agreed," both men said that the same time.

"Though tonight, I think we're done with talking." Reed took Hannah's hand, walking her to his bedroom.

Josh followed behind, turning off the lights as he went.

They walked into his bedroom and surveyed the large, dark cherry sleigh bed with cream and green linens. His room felt masculine and right for him, but Hannah might want to change something later. The thought of her—and Josh—adding personal touches made Reed grin.

"I want you both, I do." Hannah bit her lip, nervous about something.

"Okay." Reed was slightly scared about what else she may say.

"I'm not ready to complete the mating," Hannah whispered. At

Reed's widened eyes, she explained. "I'm a witch remember, I know some things about werewolves—like mating. I think we need to get to know one another first before we connect our souls that way."

"Wait? What is she talking about?" Josh asked. "I thought we were already mates. What is completing the mating? And what do our souls have to do with it."

Reed ignored the light sting in his heart that she didn't want to mate yet, though he shouldn't have been surprised. After all, they'd just met.

"Okay, take a seat, both of you." Reed led them to the bed, and they each sat on the edge.

"There are two parts to mating. Seed and marking. When I bite your fleshy part where your shoulders meet your neck, we will be bound through our wolves." Reed held up a hand when Josh wanted to interrupt. "I'll explain, don't worry. My wolf can be bound to you, even if you aren't a wolf yourself."

"But will we have to become wolves?" Josh asked.

Reed sighed, "I don't think Hannah will. I'll have to ask my mom. But once we are fully mated, the fact that she is a witch should tie her to my lifespan. Witches are paranormal just like werewolves. They live longer than humans as it is—but not as long as my family. When a witch is paired by fate to a werewolf, their life binds to the wolf in order to prolong their time together. But when I die—hopefully in the distance future—she will as well." Reed shrugged. "It's harsh, but most of us live well into our thousands. But you, Josh, would have to turn into a wolf if you decide to be immortal, or long lived, like us." Reed looked into the other man's eyes but couldn't see any emotion there. "I can't turn you into a witch, and since vampires—even the sparkly ones —don't exist, there is only that option. Or we'd have to watch you grow old and die. I don't think I could do that."

Josh nodded. "What's the other part of mating?" He didn't say anything about becoming a wolf, but Reed let it slide. The man would have to think for himself.

"The other is through sex." Reed laughed at the expression on Josh's face. "If I spill my seed in both of you, then our human souls will join, and we will be fully mated. I know when humans have sex their souls don't join, but since we're not human, we work differently. We may call them our human halves, but in reality, we aren't human at all. We will be able to feel each other at long distances. We don't get any cool powers like telepathy, but it's still pretty cool, so I hear."

Josh stared wide-eyed, but thankfully no disgust crossed his features. "This is more in depth than I thought."

Hannah reached for his hand, and Reed did the same.

"It's okay; we don't need to make any promises like that tonight. We can go to sleep and talk about it later, or I have another option." Reed stood and walked to his nightstand and pulled out an unopened package of condoms.

Hannah gave a squeak and Josh grunted. Reed didn't know what to think. He wanted them both but he didn't want to push them.

"I want us to be safe," Reed whispered. "But make no mistake—I do want you. Both of you."

He watched both of their faces as they panted with arousal. Nice.

"As long as I don't actually come inside you both, there will be no mating. That means we can still have sex; we just have to be sure that we're always careful."

Both nodded, and Reed relaxed.

Hannah bit her lip and looked upset.

"What's wrong, Hannah?" Josh asked, rubbing her shoulders.

"I know it's stupid, but I don't like the fact that he already had condoms here, even though he just met us." Hannah lowered her head, embarrassed.

"It's okay, Hannah. I'd be jealous, too." Reed went back to the bed and sat next to her, pulling her in his arms. "I haven't been with anyone in years, actually." At their outrageous looks, Reed laughed. "I just couldn't find anyone, and I really didn't care too much. I only have these because North always hands them out in case we find a human we like. We can't get diseases, and we can only impregnate our mates, but it's good to have them for the humans anyway. Try not to think of our pasts right now. We have plenty of time to talk about all of that. I know you won't stop thinking about it just because I ask, but at least try just for now. Only think about the future, because the two of you are it for me. Forever."

Hannah nodded, and Reed kissed her again, inhaling her sweet scent.

Josh cleared his throat, pulling the two of them out of their haze.

"Before we go too far and can't think, I thought I'd say something. Reed, I don't know how far I can go with you. I'm sorry, I'm just not ready." Josh lowered his gaze, as if he was afraid he'd hurt Reed.

But Reed understood. "I know, Josh. It's okay. If we go through with the mating, and I hope to God we do, then we have lifetimes to be together sexually."

Josh's eyes widened at that, and he was just too cute to resist, so Reed leaned over Hannah to kiss him. That sweet woodsy taste danced on his tongue, mingling with Hannah's to form a perfect symphony of pleasure. He pulled back then kissed Hannah again. Josh tugged off her skirt and top, leaving her clad in only her panties and bra. Reed growled at the sight of her pale flesh against her white lacy underthings.

Hannah sighed into his mouth and gripped his shoulders, grinding against his leg. *My little witch is eager. Good.*

Josh trailed his fingers up her sides and pulled her away from Reed. With a groan, Reed watched his two mates kiss and moan. He rubbed his erection, turned on as hell. He stood and quickly divested himself of his clothing, leaving him naked but for his boxer briefs. The two in front of him writhed against each other, clearly into what they were doing. Reed pulled off Hannah's bra, brushing the undersides of her breasts while he did so. Hannah gasped, and Josh looked on in appreciation.

"Dear God, baby, you're magnificent," Josh rasped.

Oh, and how she was. Reed had known she was curvy in all the right places, but damn. Her breasts were full and heavy—more than an overfilled handful, and he had large hands—with dark rosy nipples, already two little hard points of desire.

Dear God, he wanted her more than anything.

Josh lowered Hannah to the bed so they were both sitting and kissed her again. Reed slid back onto the bed to sit on the other side of his witch and lowered his head to pull Hannah's nipple through his teeth.

"Oh, goddess, Reed." The rest of what she would have said was swallowed by Josh's mouth as he kissed her harder.

Reed bit and suckled her nipple, twisting and pinching the other in his hand. Hannah leaned into his touch, begging for more. Reed could only oblige.

Josh pulled away to disrobe fully and sat back on the bed. Reed and Hannah paused to take in Josh's long and thick cock, fully erect with its mushroom head pulsating and a little bead of pre-cum at the tip.

Fuck.

Both men shifted so they sat facing Hannah and her eyes widened. Reed went back to her breasts, indulging in her firm mounds and sweet taste.

Josh massaged her arms, legs, and stomach, rubbing small circles, kissing and licking as he went along.

"Guys," Hannah gasped. "It's too much, and you're barely touching me. So many emotions and sensations. So many hands."

Both men gave hearty chuckles and continued their slow torture.

Reed leapt off the bed and took off his underwear, then slid Hannah's down. He stood back and took in his fill.

Dear God, she's beautiful.

Kneeling beside her, he reached down and traced her brown curly hair to her wet nether lips. He gulped and struggled for control, and then he gently separated her folds with two fingers. Her pink center pulsated and swelled with desire as she gasped at his touch.

Reed looked up at Josh who sat on the other side of their witch, his pupils dilating wide with a rim of ocean blue around them.

"Taste her, Reed," Josh rasped. "Tell me how good she is. I need to taste these rosy nipples; they're begging for my mouth."

The other man leaned over their mate and took her nipple into his mouth. Reed groaned when Hannah rocked her hips against his hand at Josh's touch.

He leaned over and ran his finger around her opening, skirting the edge of her clit, careful only to tease.

"Reed. Please. Touch me. Let me come. I can't take it!" Hannah screamed.

"Is that what you want? You want me to touch you? Here?" He kissed the inside of her thigh.

"No. I mean, yes, that's good, but please. Josh, that feels so good." Hannah arched into Josh when he pulled her nipple into his mouth.

"Please what, Hannah? Tell me," Reed demanded his voice husky.

"Reed. Please touch my clit. Please!"

"Well, since you asked."

Josh laughed. "I think I'm going to like playing with Hannah and you, Reed."

Reed smiled then lowered his mouth to her clit, her honey and bitter apple taste decadent on his taste buds. He flicked it with his tongue at the same time he shoved two fingers into her.

She bucked, and Josh held her down.

"How does she taste, Reed?" Josh asked.

"Let me show you."

Josh bent down as if to lick Hannah, but Reed caught his lips instead. Josh gasped into his mouth then kissed him back. Hard.

"Fuck," Reed muttered when they pulled back.

"Fuck is about right. She tastes fucking amazing on your tongue, but I want to taste from the source. Soon." Josh knelt, wide-eyed, near Hannah, who moaned at the two of them.

Reed sucked and licked, while curving his fingers just right to rub her g-spot.

"Reed...Josh..." Hannah breathed.

Reed groaned and bit down on her clit. She rocked against his face, her pussy closing on his fingers as she came, their names ripping from her throat.

"Jesus, Reed. Did you see how magnificent our girl looks when she comes?" Josh asked in wonder.

"The way her ivory skin blushes with arousal and how her nipples reddened to little pluckable cherries after our mouths feasted on them? Oh, I noticed."

Hannah opened her mouth to speak but only let out a soft moan.

Reed chuckled. "I suppose that means you liked it?"

Hannah nodded.

"Baby," Josh whispered, rubbing her ass as Reed sheathed himself in a condom. "Have you ever had a cock in your ass?"

She bit her lip and shook her head.

"Do you want to?" Reed asked, holding himself still while he waited for a response.

"I think so. I want to do everything with you both." Fear lurked in her eyes, but it was obvious she was also overcome by desire.

"We won't do it tonight, baby," Josh said. "But we will prepare you just a bit. I don't want to hurt you. So we will make sure you are loose and ready for us when one of us sinks our cock into your ass. And then, when you are fully there, I can be in your ass and Reed in your pussy. What do you think about that?"

Hannah nodded, needy. "Okay."

"I'd say fuck yes to that," Reed answered and laughed.

"What's next?" Hannah asked then giggled.

"Oh, I have an idea." Reed slid her to the end of the bed where he could stand and still reach her. "Josh, stand on the side where she can reach you."

Josh smiled with understanding, and Reed leaned over Hannah to take her lips again.

"You taste delicious, baby," Reed whispered.

"You're not so bad yourself."

Reed stood back and watched as Josh took Hannah's head and pulled her to his engorged cock.

"Swallow me, Hannah," Josh groaned.

Hannah opened her mouth wide, the cap of Josh's dick making a slight popping sound as he slid into her mouth. Josh held her in his hands, keeping her head still, and slowly worked his way in and out of her mouth. Reed almost came on the spot watching Hannah's throat work as she tried to take more of him with each stroke.

Reed rubbed her clit, watching her gasp around Josh's cock. She was already wet and flush, waiting for him to fill her. Reed didn't wait any longer. With his gaze on hers, he hooked a knee over his elbow and slowly entered her.

He paused, loving the feel of her around him and then he pounded into her, relishing in the sounds of flesh against sweaty flesh and the moans of all three when they hit the right spots. Josh grabbed his hand, and the three of them came together in a rush of pleasure and intensity.

"Dear Lord. How can you still be hard, Reed?" Hannah panted, heaving for breath.

"I'm a werewolf," Reed answered simply. "I have all sorts of talents."

Josh laughed. "And we're two of the luckiest people out there, right, Hannah?"

Reed skimmed his hands up both of their sides, and they shuddered. He lowered his hand and took Josh's cock, which hardened at the touch.

"Damn, I'm the lucky one. You have a quick recovery time for a human."

"All the better to please you with, my dear." Josh laughed.

"Hey, I thought I was the big bad wolf here." Reed pulled Josh by the cock and kissed him on the lips.

"Well, that was a new touch for me," Josh said.

"Good," Reed and Hannah agreed.

"Now, it seems to me that Reed has been monopolizing that pussy of yours. I think it's my turn." Josh smiled then moved to the edge of the bed before flipping Hannah to her hands and knees.

"Here" Reed handed him a condom then moved around to the other side of the bed to kneel in front of her. He shuddered when Hannah licked the bulging vein under his cock.

She licked up the side then put her mouth around him. He felt her throat muscles relax and she swallowed him whole.

"Jesus, she's tight." Josh groaned as he pushed inside her.

"I know. She's perfect," Reed agreed.

Hannah sucked and swallowed. Reed fucked her mouth while Josh fucked her pussy. Reed reached over and pulled out lube from his nightstand and coated his fingers. Bending over her with his cock still in her mouth, he slowly traced her puckered hole. Hannah stiffened but relaxed, waiting for his next move. He slowly worked one finger in, listening to her moan as he moved past the thin ring of muscles. Josh pulled her cheeks apart, aiding him. He worked his finger in and out until he felt comfortable adding a second, then a third.

When Hannah lifted a hand to cup and fondle his balls, he stiffened then his hot seed poured down her throat as he roared in approval. Josh groaned and followed soon behind. He couldn't wait fill her womb with his seed, completing the mating then, one day, watch her grow heavy and ripe with their young.

Both men pulled out slowly, careful not to hurt her. Josh set Hannah down on her side as she lay there boneless. Reed ran to the bathroom to grab a wet cloth. He cleaned them all up then got into bed, under the covers, holding Hannah against his chest, Josh nestled against her back.

"I'm falling in love with both of you," Hannah whispered. "But I don't understand it. I've only just met you; I don't even know you." She fell asleep snuggled between the two of them, all sweaty and glowing.

Reed looked over her head to Josh, who nodded.

"I'm feeling the same way, but I don't know what to think about it," Josh whispered.

Reed reached for Josh's hand, clasping it tightly. "We will work it out. Get some sleep. We need it."

They slept in a sweaty pile, limbs linked and tangled, and all Reed could think about was that this was the best time of his life.

CHAPTER FOURTEEN

J osh woke to a plump, curvy butt rubbing against his crotch. His dick woke up and pressed against the seam of her ass, probing for an entry. Her tousled curls lay haphazardly around her as she pillowed her head on his arm. His other arm wrapped around her, resting on Reed's side. This could be happiness. The happily-ever-after-hot-regular-sex-three-kids-cozy-fireplace kind of happiness.

But that wasn't for him.

This was just a phase. It had to be. They would grow tired of him, and then he'd leave. He'd be left with nothing, something he was used to. But this time it'd be harder. Much harder.

Reed shifted in his sleep, rubbing against the bite mark. A low tremor of pain radiated up his arm.

Damn.

Throughout the night, even through the amazing sex, his arm had throbbed. He'd tried to ignore it, but he knew something was wrong. Was he dying? Could someone turn into a demon from a bite? No one really had any answers for him.

Hannah's butt wiggled again, and Josh let out a long, guttural moan.

Reed's narrow fingers ran up along Josh's side in a smooth motion. He smiled at the sleepy man.

"Did you sleep okay?" Reed asked.

"Never better actually. The two of you feel amazing to sleep next to."

Reed practically beamed at him. "Good."

Shit, this was getting to feel too normal. Too perfect.

"I need to piss." His words rushed out.

He mentally slapped himself. *Great job, dude. Tough Navy SEAL can't just be content in bed. Has to ruin it by opening his big mouth.*

The bed shook slightly with Reed's laughter, then the other man bit his lip, presumably to try and not wake up Hannah.

"Go, you know where it is. I'll be up in a minute."

Naked, Josh slid out of bed while Reed hugged Hannah closer to his side when she whimpered at the loss of contact.

"Look in the top drawer for some pajama bottoms," Reed said. "They should fit you since we're about the same size except through the shoulders and torso. We can worry about getting you both some clothes and everything else you'll need from your places or the stores later." Josh stiffened and Reed sobered. "Even if you don't live here permanently, you can't go home yet. It's not safe. Let me at least make you comfortable. Please."

Josh nodded. "Okay, we can talk about it."

Hannah snuggled into Reed's side and touched his sandy-blond hair. The two of them molded together perfectly, as if they were made for each other. Josh snorted. Considering they were mates, that was likely the case. Josh yearned to jump back in bed and hold them close, but he didn't. He couldn't. He had to wean himself off the two of them.

Josh also couldn't rely on the Pack. He didn't want to be a burden. And at this point, as a mere human, that's exactly how he felt. He quickly took care of his business in the bathroom and looked at the bite mark. Still bruised and red in some places, the web of red marks didn't seem to have changed. They still stretched from his wrist to almost his elbow.

At least that was something.

With Reed and Hannah still in bed, he took the time to look

around the house. It looked like an affluent bachelor pad decorated with an artist's flair. Comfy furniture with a large screen TV and entertainment system appealed to the man in him. Reed's kitchen however left something to be desired. If Josh moved in, they'd have to change a few things to utilize the space better. And he was sure Hannah would want to add some feminine touches and colors. Not to mention the fact that they would need to add space somehow once they had kids.

Josh pulled himself up short.

What the fuck was he thinking about the future for? They didn't have one. Why was he going about trying to pick out fucking china patterns and thinking about green-eyed babies with curly brown hair? There wasn't a place for him here. He couldn't contribute. He was just a human in a paranormal world. And even though Reed said they were mates and Josh was honest enough to say he felt the connection between the three of them, a permanent threesome, or triad, would never work. It couldn't work. There would always be jealousy and hurt feelings. Especially since there was sexual tension between Reed and him.

Josh left the kitchen and went through a door he hadn't seen before. Art covered the walls. Canvas and paint supplies filled every surface. Reed's studio. Josh had known he was an artist, but they'd been so busy with fighting he hadn't really thought about the talent that lay in those narrow fingers. He groaned remembering how talented they were with that oh-so-soft touch last night. His dick hardened, tenting out his pajama bottoms, first at the thought of Reed and then remembering the feeling of being inside Hannah. Her soft warmth milking his shaft last night, even through a condom, was the most earth-shattering experience of his life.

"Hey, you found my room." Reed walked into the studio wearing only pajama bottoms, looking tousled but relatively awake.

Not to mention fucking sexy.

Reed padded over and kissed him gently, his sandalwood taste on his tongue. Josh wasn't sure if he'd ever get used to kissing a man and feeling the difference from when he kissed Hannah. But he liked both. A lot. He ran a hand down the other man's arm, noticing the goose bumps left in its wake. He'd never thought he'd like touching a man, but it didn't feel wrong. It felt right. And with the addition of Hannah, it felt more so.

Could he go further with Reed? Let them go down on each other? Then submit to him and let him take him? Or could he take Reed? He shuddered at the thought. He wasn't ready by any stretch for that, but he still got turned on. That was a good sign. Right?

Reed kissed him again, this time letting his tongue slide along the seam of his lips. Josh opened for him, allowing the man entry. They each fought for control, the kiss intensifying with each passing second.

Reed pulled back first, breathing heavily, as Josh shook his muddled brain.

"Good morning." Reed laughed.

"Yes, it is," Josh agreed.

Reed took his hand and Josh let him. *Huh, not too bad.*

"I have something I'm working on I want to show you."

"Okay, lead the way."

Reed went to the back corner and let go of Josh's hand long enough to pull the fabric off an easel.

Josh gasped.

A naked Willow knelt in a grassy grove, the angles and her hair covering the most essential parts. She looked towards the observer, her warm brown eyes glowing with hope and promise. Her hands rested on her protruding belly, cradling her and Jasper's child.

She looked magnificent. And Reed was beyond brilliant.

"Wow, Reed. This is remarkable."

Reed took a deep breath. "Thank God. I was worried. I loved it, but I wasn't sure. No one else has seen it."

Josh looked at him in surprise.

"It's a secret for Jasper. I didn't even let Willow sneak a peek. She only posed when I did the prelim sketches. I'm going to give it to them both after the baby shower. I just don't want Jasper to kick my ass for seeing his wife naked."

"I'll protect you." He grinned. "Plus she looks like an angel, and this will be something they will treasure always. She doesn't look nude. Honestly, she looks like a mother. It isn't pornographic; it's something for their family."

Reed hugged him hard, kissing his temple. "Thank you. That was the perfect thing to say."

Josh shrugged. "It's the truth."

"Well, thank you anyway."

"If it's a secret, why is it not hidden more?"

Reed laughed. "Well, since nobody is allowed in my studio without permission, and even that is rare, they don't have a chance to see it."

Josh blushed in embarrassment. "Shit, I'm sorry, man. I just barged right in and didn't even think about your privacy."

Reed touched his cheek. "It's okay, Josh. Really. You didn't know. And I didn't mean it that way. I'm sorry. Honestly, I'm not even too concerned by it. I want you to see everything I have, everything I am. Hannah too. And if I do need to paint something I don't feel is ready for others' eyes yet, I will let you know and do more to prevent accidental sharing. Don't worry."

Josh exhaled. "Okay, but let me know if I'm intruding. You've already done so much."

"Josh," Reed said, shaking his head, "I've done nothing. You saved me and Hannah. I want you here with me. Let me take care of you how I can."

Though it wasn't easy to do so, Josh nodded. If it made Reed feel better, he'd give in, but he knew this wouldn't last. Something would happen.

Was he ready for forever?

"Reed, I don't know about our future. I need time."

"Okay."

"But what we can do is talk about the Centrals. Do you have any idea of your father's plans?"

Reed sighed. "I'm not part of Dad's enforcers. And I'm not *the* Enforcer."

"What does that mean?"

"Adam is the Enforcer. Capital E. He is the one in charge of taking care of forces that want to hurt us, though he answers to Dad. And now that he's gone, even for a little while, I think that will go to Kade, since he's next in line for the throne. Dad also has men outside our family that act like guards. Neil, the husband of Melanie's friend

Larissa, is one of them. They help Adam and Dad. Kade and Jasper do a lot as well. I'm stuck in the middle. Not really useful."

"Reed, you're everything." Without thinking, he rubbed Reed's chin, liking the stubble across the pad of his thumb. "Look at the work you do here. You help out the Pack with their archives and paint their history. And you teach the children at school. I mean, that counts for something. You can do what others can't. I don't know why you feel inferior to your family. You shouldn't. Plus, you are a fighter. No matter what you think, I know this. I've seen you. You fought off twenty wolves single handedly, and only ended up with a few scratches. You are a strong wolf, believe in that."

Reed shook his head. "You understand so much, after such little time."

Josh smiled, not liking the sad look on Reed's face. "It's not that hard to take in, Reed. And when we finish getting ready, we can go over to your Dad's house and see what's going on. They can't just leave us out."

Reed laughed. "Yeah, they can. He's Alpha. He can pretty much do whatever he wants."

"Well, then we'll ask." *Forcefully*.

"Okay. It can't hurt."

"Reed, how did all of this happen?"

"What?" A cute, confused look appeared on his face.

"How could the Centrals take you? How could the Redwoods let this happen?" Josh winced at the way that had come out. Shit, he didn't want to offend anyone. He just needed to know how the Centrals got so powerful.

Reed sucked in a breath and clenched his fists, anger radiating off of him.

"Reed, I didn't mean..."

"No, Josh. It's okay. I'm not mad at you. It's just a fucked-up situation. You see, evil doesn't follow the same kind of rules we do. They don't have to worry about killing people with their powers. They relish it. They don't have to worry about crossing the lines of demonic nature and fucking with fate. They do what they want. And no matter what we do, the Centrals have the upper hand because we can't cross those boundaries. We fight back, and we do our best to keep the damage to a minimum, but until we can find a way to use magic and energy that doesn't cross into evil, we're always going to be behind."

Well, fuck.

"Reed, some things aren't black and white. There has to be a way."

"Sometimes even the gray isn't strong enough."

Reed closed his eyes, lines of tension on his face. Josh couldn't resist and brushed the lock of hair that fell across his brows away.

Damn, he wanted him.

Josh lowered his face and brushed his lips against Reed's. The other man pulled him closer, their rigid cocks sliding against one another, creating heated friction.

A polite cough made them pull apart, slowly.

Hannah stood in a pair of borrowed boxers and Josh's shirt, looking like a damned fuckable pixie.

"Good morning, boys. You look like you've been busy." She gave them an impish smile.

"A little," Josh rumbled.

She prowled over to them both, kissing Reed, then Josh, giving him the best good morning he'd ever had.

With Hannah in his arms, and Reed by his side, he could almost see a future. Pain pierced his temple as a sudden headache came on.

"Josh, what is it?" Hannah asked.

"Just a headache. I need some water." He strode away without a look back.

There was no future with them. He needed to stop thinking about shit like that. It led to nowhere. He was a loner. That was all he was.

Pain lanced up his arm, pulsating around the wound.

Great, that was all he needed.

CHAPTER FIFTEEN

"**A**re you ready to go?" Reed came up behind Hannah and held her close.

Hannah buttoned up the last button on her borrowed blouse and took a look in the mirror. She finally felt clean after four showers. The dirt and grime from the basement hell wasn't seeping into her pores anymore. Though she wasn't wearing her own skirt and top, it still fit well enough that she didn't look too bad.

Hannah shrugged. "Sure."

"You look beautiful."

A laugh escaped her. "You have to say that; you're sleeping with me."

"True." Reed grunted when her elbow came in contact with his stomach. "But you are beautiful. I'd say it anyway."

"He's telling the truth." Josh came in the room, freshly showered and looking quite edible. "Just saying."

"Okay, boys. Now that my ego is restored, I guess we can go."

"As long as you're happy, milady." Reed bowed extravagantly.

"Really, man? Milady? Did you say that back when you were a young man?" Josh laughed.

"Ha ha. Let's make fun of the old man. But remember, I can keep both of you busy and satisfied with my old man cock. So what do you say now?" Reed raised a brow.

"I'll take it for a ride?" Hannah asked, smiling.

Both men burst out laughing, and she joined them.

"Sounds good, babe." Josh held her close, brushing his lips against hers. "Let's go to the Alpha's. This should be fun."

"Don't worry. I'll protect you from the big bad Alpha." Hannah laughed.

Josh's eyes darkened. "I don't need you to protect me."

Okay. Touchy subject.

"I was just kidding. I'm sorry."

Josh shook his head. "Sorry, I knew you were. Apparently my headache is making me act like an ass."

Reed cupped Josh's cheek. "Do you need something for that? Can I help?"

Hannah cupped his other cheek. "I'm a witch, after all. I can make you something."

Josh quirked a lip. "I'm okay for now. If it gets any worse, I'll take you up on it. Thank you."

"Okay, then. I guess we're ready." Reed sighed.

He looked so nervous, but Hannah didn't really understand why. This was his family. But then again, they'd cut him out during the decisions last night. Reed said it was because he was just an artist. But she'd seen him fight to protect her and Josh. He was fierce and strong, despite what he thought of himself. He'd been kidnapped, tortured, and shot; yet his first thought was always her. Why couldn't his parents see that? Was it because he had two mates? Would that lower his status because he wasn't normal?

Since all of the Jamensons lived relatively close to one another in the den, it was just a quick walk to Edward and Pat's house. Along the way Hannah looked at the tall trees with snow on their branches and the snow covering the forest floor. Though winter was just starting, up in the mountains, it got colder quicker.

She inhaled the crisp mountain air. Even with the natural setting, the den felt like a home. Welcoming and warm despite the cooling temperatures, not to mention loving. Could it be her home? Could she get used to this?

Hannah sighed. Everything had changed so fast. But she didn't know if she resented it exactly. Last night had been amazing. She blushed just thinking about the movement of three bodies and their sweat while making love. She'd only been with a couple of men before Reed and Josh, and never in her lifetime would she have thought she'd be the girl sleeping with two men at once.

And liking it.

Okay, if she were honest with herself, *loving* it.

Geez. What must Reed's family think of her? She was a slut with even sluttier thoughts. She'd had the most amazing sex of her life with two men and didn't feel bad about it. Oh, she worried all right, but she'd do it again. Planned on it. She'd let them do things to her she'd never let another do, and she wanted more of it. When Reed had played with her bottom, she'd thought she'd come right on the spot. She held back a moan at the thought of Josh buried there, with Reed in her pussy.

Goddess. If his parents knew what had gone on in that bedroom with their son, Hannah and Josh would surely be on the next ride out of the den. She bit her lip and groaned in frustration.

Josh squeezed her hand. "It'll be all right."

At least she wasn't alone in this. Josh must be feeling the same as she was. More so. He was looking at his sexuality in a whole new light, crossing taboo boundaries and enjoying it. Thank the goddess they had each other, especially since they were about to go talk to the "in-laws" and she had to keep from blushing and bursting into flames on the spot.

They walked up to the large open house and Pat opened the door before they knocked. It must be nice to have werewolf senses sometimes.

"Oh, good. I'm so happy you're here. And you look so well rested." She winked and looked at the two men.

Oh. My. Goddess.

Mortified, and knowing she was as red as a tomato, she allowed herself to be hugged by Pat, while Reed and Josh barely held in their laughter.

"Now, you boys stop it with that look. I didn't mean anything by it. Get your minds out of the gutter." Pat fisted her hands on her hips with a not-so-serious scowl on her face.

It was such a mom pose that tears sprung in Hannah's eyes.

Oh my. I miss you, Mom.

It's had only been three weeks. Three little weeks since she'd heard her mom laugh, telling her to keep her head out of her potions and to find a nice young witch to settle down and make babies with. Three weeks since her mom had hugged her and told her she loved her. She'd known Reed even less since he'd come to the basement after her.

Sorrow crept over the ache in her heart, gripping and not letting go.

"Oh, baby." Pat pulled her into the foyer, out of the cold, and enveloped her in her arms.

Hannah sniffed. "I'm sorry. I'm just a mess right now."

"It's all right. That whole Centrals ordeal, meeting both of your mates, and losing your mom in such a short period of time would be too much for anyone. You just cry it out and let the Jamensons—and Josh—take care of you."

"Thank you, Pat."

"Oh, baby. When you're ready, you can call me Mom. But not before that. Your mother was such a nice woman. I'll miss her."

Hannah leaned back, startled at the news.

"You knew my mother?"

Pat smiled. "Yes dear. It was long ago, when you were just a baby. I held you in my arms and knew I wanted a girl. So I went back to Edward and said, after six boys, I wanted a baby. So two years later, after some wrangling with that Alpha, I got my baby girl, Cailin. And Edward is wrapped around that girl's finger like no other. If you hear him tell the story, it was his idea."

"I never knew that," Reed said, wide-eyed.

"You never asked." Pat shrugged. "But what a world we live in with fate as our guide. I got to see this baby again." She squeezed Hannah closer. "You look so much like your mother."

At that point, whatever resistance to sobbing Hannah had left, fell out the window.

Tears flowed down her cheeks. Josh pulled her from Pat's arms and kissed the top of her head.

"I'm so sorry, my Hannah," Josh whispered.

"Oh, Hannah. I'm sorry; I didn't mean to make you cry." Tears fell from the woman's eyes, and Reed held his mother close.

"It's okay, Pat. It's just hard to hear. But so, so nice. Thank you for that story."

Both women sniffed and pulled out of the men's arms, trying to compose themselves.

"It's just so good, seeing you three together," Pat said.

All three of them gave her awkward looks. What else could she do when the mother of one of the men she's sleeping with says the three of them look good together?

"I'm so happy another one of my babies found their mate. Well, mates in this case. After Adam..." Pat shuddered.

"Mom," Reed interjected.

"No, your mates need to know why Adam left. I saw the look he gave the three of you, and you need to know it's nothing you've done."

Josh held Hannah closer while Reed sidled up to them.

"Adam's mate, Anna, was taken by the Centrals. But unlike with you, we didn't get to her in time. They'd beaten, raped, and killed her. And the child she carried. Adam never recovered, and Maddox, who felt every emotion she felt, never did either. Our family was now just starting to heal, and then the Centrals came back."

Hannah's tears fell harder, leaving a salty trail of lost dreams in their wake.

"I think with Kade, then Jasper, and now you getting mated so soon after one another, Adam's feeling lonely. I just hope he finds what he needs. Because I don't know if he'll find what he needs here if, no, when, he comes back."

Pat let out a breath, visibly shaken and sad. "Okay, that's enough of that. Let's go into the living room." Pat led them though the hallway into the homey living room where Edward sat alone, reading something on his iPad.

Who knew older werewolves were so tech savvy?

"Ah, you're here." Edward set down the tablet and stood, walking to Hannah and giving her a hug.

Surprised, she hugged him back.

Edward let out a huge, booming laugh. "Sorry, we're wolves. Very affectionate. And you're family now. Get used to hugging."

As if to prove his point, he hugged Josh.

Josh just laughed faintly and did the whole man hug, pat on the back thing.

When Edward moved back from hugging Reed, they all sat down on the couch and waited for Edward to begin.

"Dad, are we early? Where is everyone?" Reed asked.

Edward sighed. "They've already left. We've had the meeting, son."

Reed lowered his brows and scowled. She held his hand, barely able to control her own fury. Josh reached over her and rubbed Reed's shoulder, tension rippling in both men.

How could they have decided everything without their participation? Weren't they the ones who had just been held prisoner?

Slowly, very softly, Reed spoke. "Why were we not involved?"

Edward raised a brow then glanced at her and Josh.

Oh. He doesn't trust us.

Hurt, Hannah bit her lip.

Reed growled. "My mates are trustworthy. You never had a problem with Willow or Melanie."

"And yet our Pack has been weakened by the traitors in our midst. I need more time before I share all of our secrets. I'm sorry Josh and Hannah, but more lives are involved than just those of us in this room. I need to be cautious."

She understood where he was coming from. As Alpha, he had more than his share of responsibility, but that didn't mean it didn't hurt to hear. Especially since he was the father of one of them men she was falling in love with.

Reed growled again.

Edward growled back, a magic she didn't understand washing over them. "Watch your tone, boy. I am still Alpha of this Pack. I don't know them, and frankly, I'm interested in just how Josh found the two of you. It's too coincidental for me."

Josh took a deep breath, rubbing his hand on her leg.

Hannah stayed silent, as if waiting for a fuse to be lit, for the bomb to explode.

"I'm a Finder," Josh explained.

Edward's eyes widened. "I see."

Josh cocked his head. "Do you?'

The Alpha sat back in his chair, rubbing his chin. "You are not the first I've met, but the first I've met in a long while." He nodded again, a thoughtful look on his face. "Good to know."

"He will not be used," Reed growled.

Edward actually laughed. "It's good to see you standing up for your mate. But I didn't say I would, did I? You are blessed in your mates. I will not use him. I only find it interesting."

Reed moved to stand. *This can't be good.*

Hannah jumped in. "Let's move on. Okay?"

Edward laughed again. "I like you, Hannah."

Hannah smiled while she squeezed Reed's hand.

The Alpha cleared his throat. "We tried to find you, Reed." Pain shot across his eyes. "But the Centrals used dark magic to cloud your presence. It was luck that Adam even found you."

The room sat in silence at the mention of Adam.

"We can fight," Edward continued. "Go to their territory, attack, and try and find retribution. But with the Central's dark magic, that dammed demon, and their witches..."

Hannah gasped.

The witches were working for their enemies?

Reed brushed her cheek with his finger. "Some are working for the Centrals. We've tasted their magic. But we don't know who. I'm sorry, Hannah."

She could only nod. What coven would align with that type of evil? Witches were white magic, though they didn't call it that. Goodness. The sort of thing Centrals did would only taint the inherent nature of witches.

"We will retaliate." Edward promised. "Mark my words. But we need to be strong. Find a way to use magic that doesn't cross our lines, one that is good. We need to know who exactly is there and how to fight the unknown."

Josh cleared his throat. "When I was in the SEALs, we came upon their den before." He paused, glancing at Reed and her. "I can give you the precise layout of what I know and any other info I may have."

"Impressive," Edward said.

Hannah smiled at Reed and Josh. Both of her men had such talents and hidden depths.

Wait. My men?

Huh.

She kind of liked that.

"Dad, you need to keep us in the loop. We will fight," Reed said.

"Yes," Hannah added. "All of us."

She looked at both her men, daring them to say anything against her.

Josh gazed into her eyes while Reed squeezed her hand, then they nodded as one. "Yes, all of us," they said together.

Edward nodded. "Okay then." Then he turned to her. "You are our Healer, Hannah."

"Oh, I don't know. I'm just a healer; I don't know if I'm *your* Healer."

"Hannah, I feel it. We all do."

Pat and Reed nodded in agreement.

"But..." She trailed off as a warm feeling of belonging settled over her.

She looked into Edward's eyes, and he smiled.

She *was* their Healer. She wasn't alone anymore.

Reed kissed her softly, then Josh did the same. She blushed in embarrassment.

"You feel okay?" Reed asked.

"I feel like I can Heal anything. You know?"

"Hannah," Edward interrupted, "once you are mated fully and become part of the Pack, you will feel every Pack member. If they are hurt, you will know. Maddox will help you in your training so you won't be overwhelmed."

She was overwhelmed as it was. How could she deal with all of these people? How many were there? The enormity of the situation hit her. She'd made her choice. She was Reed's mate. Part of the Redwoods now.

If she were already feeling like this now, how would she be when she felt the rest of the Pack? She needed to talk to Maddox. If he felt all the emotions, he'd be a total help.

"You will be an asset to the Pack; I can tell," Edward added. "I mean, look at what you've done to my son. Josh too. I've never seen Reed so happy and relaxed." He wiggled his eyebrows.

Again, Hannah blushed scarlet.

Do all werewolves talk about their kids' sex lives? Geesh.

"You are important. But remember, Hannah," Edward added, "you are not above others in the Pack. You are not more worthy than they are."

Reed let out a strangled cough.

"Is there something you'd like to add, son?" Edward asked.

"No, I'm fine."

"No, you aren't. Tell me."

Reed sighed. "Fine. I just don't believe you. You can't tell me that Kade or Jasper or anyone else in our family isn't more important the others. Yes, all Pack members are valued. But they are critical to our survival."

Edward looked at him with confusion.

"Reed, you are just as important."

Reed gave a hollow laugh.

"You are the one who paints our culture, our history. Since you were a pup, you've been keeping records and remembering those who would've been forgotten. Without you, our Pack would not have that backbone. Our future pups would not know their history by art. You are just as important as all my children."

Reed stayed silent, and Hannah eyes filled with tears at the pain and sense of loss on his face.

"Reed, we were coming for you. Never doubt that. No matter what, we would have found you. I felt you here." He placed his hand over his heart. "But we couldn't find you."

Then the tough Alpha of the fiercest Pack of werewolves in the nation, grabbed his son in a backbreaking hug with tears in his eyes.

Pat stood up and joined her family, crying with them. Then she stood back and pulled Josh and Hannah in the hug.

This was her new family if fate allowed it. Warmth infused her bones.

Pat patted both her and Josh's cheeks. "You may not have completed the mating, but you are our family now. We don't let go of what is ours. So you're stuck with us regardless."

Neither she nor Josh said anything, merely nodding.

Edward pulled back first, clearing his throat and unsuccessfully trying to put on his stern Alpha-mask.

"Go home. Get to know one another. When I know more, I will tell you."

"Thank you, Dad." Reed nodded.

They all hugged goodbye, then the three of them walked out of the house, hand in hand. They had accepted her into Reed's family. Just like that. Warmth spread through her. Things were happening so fast, but she could wait to see what would happen next.

CHAPTER SIXTEEN

After lunch the next day, Reed stood in his old storage room, staring at the skylights and hoping it would allow enough light in to room for Hannah. He bent and lifted a few old paintings he'd finished but never quite liked and just stuck in this room, forgotten.

"Reed, don't do this. I don't want to take up your space," Hannah argued.

"Baby, I've been wanting to put these in an actual storage unit for years. I want you to feel comfortable here. This way you can do your potions and grow an herb garden. I know you've been itching to do it. Don't lie. Let me do this for you." He needed to do something to show he wanted her here permanently. And if giving her this room was only a small token, he'd do it without regret.

"But what if you need more studio space?" Hannah bit her lip in that sexy way of hers.

"Then I'll build on," Reed said simply. He had the money he'd accumulated from his paintings over his long life, and the space on the land around his home. Plus, Kade was an amazing architect and Jasper an equally amazing contractor who could whip something up for Reed in a heartbeat. It paid to have talent like that in the family.

"That does make it sound permanent," Josh said quietly, an odd look on his face.

"I hope so," Reed whispered. He didn't dare say anything else.

He thought he saw something dark flash across Josh's eyes, but it went away as fast as it appeared. Maybe a trick of the light? He shrugged it off. He was probably just seeing things.

Together, the three of them cleared away the rest of the canvases and paints, leaving a room with benches and pretty good natural light. They'd only need to add some paint to the walls, sand down the wooden benches and tables, and then add in whatever garden supplies Hannah needed to start up her workspace. Once the spring came, she'd be able to start one outside too. Maybe he'd talk to Kade about building a greenhouse.

"Where do you want these?" Josh asked.

He held a bag of soil over one shoulder and some cuttings from Reed's mother in his other hand. They'd gone to the town center in the den earlier and bought at least the beginnings of what Hannah would need. Plus they'd visited Willow's bakery and eaten some of her cinnamon rolls. *Yum.*

"Here, let me help." Reed walked toward him, but Josh shook his head.

"No, I got it, just tell me where."

Hannah pointed, and Reed watched the man's muscles bunch and flex under the weight of the bag with every step.

Dear God, that man is fucking sexy as hell.

Reed bit back a grown and went back to sanding the benches and tables.

"We should just mate them already. They are perfect for us. They want us. Why are we waiting?"

Reed could only agree with his wolf, but he still had to wait for the two of them to actually say they wanted forever. He was damned sure, but he saw the hesitancy on both their faces.

Reed shook his head and walked over to Hannah, who stood frozen looking at her new room.

"What do you need? What can I get you?"

She looked up at him, tears in her eyes. "Nothing." She paused. "Everything."

Her head came up, and Reed saw fear underlying the weariness.

What could be so wrong to make her look like that?

She let out a breath. "I'm afraid if I give in and hope for more, it'll crush me once everything falls to pieces and I lose everything."

Josh came up behind her and pulled her in his arms. "Don't think about that; it will only make your head hurt. I know because mine already does."

Reed kissed her softly. "Live for now. Find your way. We can still be together. Forever. Don't think about the unknown and what could happen when we don't even know what *is* happening."

Hannah nodded and wiped away the tears before they fell. "I've been such a cry baby lately. I hate it." She sniffed, and they laughed.

"What do you need?" Reed asked again.

She gave a half smile. "I want to feel the soil."

"Sounds reasonable. Go for it. I'm going to paint this wall, if that's okay. You said you wanted a landscape, right?" At her nod, he smiled.

Just as her fingers itched to plant and feel the earth, his did to paint and share his talent with his mates.

"Let me help, Hannah." Josh went and opened the bags for her, listening as she explained exactly what she was doing.

Reed's heart warmed at the thought of the three of them sharing the same space, working together as one. It was just a small step, but it meant so much.

Josh let out a big laugh. "I have a black thumb. I'll let you get to the planting. But I can sand these shelves and get these benches and tables ready."

Josh got busy, and all three of them worked silently on their goals to make Hannah's room hers.

Hannah moaned, and Reed looked over to see her arms above her head and her body stretched like a cat.

Fuck me.

He went on alert, hard as a rock, and out of the corner of his eye, he saw Josh do the same.

"What?" She batted her eyes playfully, knowing damn well what she

400

was doing. "It's been two hours. I need a break. Any ideas how to work the kinks out of my back?"

"Two hours?" Reed groaned. "I'm sure I can help you with your back. Come here."

She shook her head, smiling.

"Okay, then. Why don't you come here?" Josh teased.

She bit her lip and shook her head again. "Nuh uh. You come to me." Then she darted out of the room, leaving Josh and him looking on in astonishment.

"First one who catchers her gets to taste her?" Josh asked.

"Deal."

They both made it to the couch in the living room at the same time and stopped dead in their tracks.

Hannah lay on her back on the white couch, which was big enough for three to lie down. Naked. Her hand circled her nipple, and the other trailed down to her damp curls.

"Dear God," Josh rasped.

Reed growled, too turned on to speak.

Both men stripped quickly, and Reed pounced on her.

Sometimes it's nice to have werewolf speed.

Hannah gasped and smiled. "Caught me."

"Oh, I'll catch you again. And again," Reed growled. Then he crushed his mouth to hers, drowning in her honey and bitter apple taste. He fisted his hand in her hair, pulling her head to the side so he could go deeper with his tongue. His cock lay in the valley between her thighs, sliding in her juices, teasing.

Then Josh surprised the hell out of him by wrapping his strong arms around Reed's waist, kissing a trail up his spine. Reed pulled is mouth off Hannah, letting out a gut-wrenching moan. Josh continued until he gently nibbled his neck then leaned over and kissed Hannah, forcing a startled groan out of her. He could feel Josh's erect cock sliding against the crease of his ass, and he growled in need.

"Josh, damn, that feels good," Reed grunted.

"Well, you did reach Hannah first so you get a taste. But I never said anything about not tasting your skin." Josh bit his neck then licked the mark. Reed shuddered.

Hannah laughed. "Hey, don't I get a say in this?" She wiggled beneath him, her slick folds rubbing along Reed's cock.

"Well, I was going to lick up that sweet cream of yours, but I think it's Josh's turn. But I will let you swallow my cock. What do you say?" Reed licked her neck and plucked her nipples as he asked.

Hannah shivered and moaned. "Anything. Just touch me. Someone. Both of you. I don't care. Please."

Josh pulled Reed off Hannah, kissed him fully on the mouth, and grabbed his cock. Reed moaned and rocked into the man's firm hand.

Damn, this man turned him on like no other. Being near Josh and Hannah gave Reed a perceptual hard-on and was starting to give him a permanent limp.

Josh released him and nudged him towards Hannah's pouty mouth. Well, if he couldn't have Josh's hand, he'd be happy for that warm mouth of hers.

He was one lucky wolf.

Josh knelt between her legs and feasted like a starving man. Hannah buckled and moaned, fisting her hand in the man's dark mane.

Reed ran his hand up and down his dick, rubbing in the bead of pre-cum at the tip. He could come just watching the two of them.

"Reed, get here. Now."

He loved when his Hannah got demanding.

He moved so he stood in front of her and tapped her plump lips with his erection. She opened, and he slid into her, pumping in and out of her mouth while she licked, sucked, and used her teeth on the way out.

"Geez." He groaned when she swallowed him and he hit the back of her throat. She hollowed her mouth then screamed as she came against Josh's face, Reed following right afterward.

"Damn, hold on. I'll be right back." Josh lifted himself from the couch and ran naked to the back of the house. He returned quickly with a wicked smile on his face and condoms in his hand.

Though it hurt to think about the fact they didn't want a true mating yet, he ignored it. They were getting closer, moving in together, at least for the time being. He'd take what he could get.

Josh pulled Hannah in his arms and kissed her. "Reed," he said between breaths, "Lie down on your back."

Intrigued, Reed lay down, still hard, and watched the two he loved kiss and fondle each other. Josh lifted his head then turned Hannah around so she stood bent over Reed's cock, her ass against Josh's groin.

"Suck him off again," Josh demanded. "Make him want your pussy."

"Oh, I already want her, but I won't say no." Reed laughed then almost choked on his tongue when Hannah took his balls in her mouth.

Well then.

She sucked them and then licked his cock like an ice cream cone. Reed wanted to close his eyes in bliss but held himself still, fighting for control.

Josh pounded into Hannah from behind, gripping her hips. His knuckles were white against her skin, and his veins popped out along his forearms as he rammed into her.

Fuck, they were both so sexy.

Hannah's nose brushed his pubic hair as she took him down the back of her throat, and he couldn't take it anymore.

He came in a rush, holding her hair as she swallowed every drop.

She lifted her head and screamed both of their names as she came, Josh following them both with a roar.

He loved his two mates.

Now he just had to get them to stay for good.

Josh lifted Hannah up and onto Reed's lap.

"Still hard?" Josh asked.

"Fuck yes, give me that pussy, baby," Reed rasped.

"I don't know if I can take another one," Hannah whimpered.

Both men froze.

"Are you hurting? What can we do?" Reed tried to get up, but she clamped her thighs around him.

"I'm not sore; I just feel so good. But I want you. Please."

Josh handed her a condom, and she wrapped it around his length. Slowly. Then she slid down him, equally as slow.

Hannah used her abs muscles and moved herself up and down his cock, milking him. Her pussy fluttered around him, and he gripped her hips, slamming upwards into her core, rubbing against her g-spot.

"Did you forget about me?" Josh asked, running his hand along his freshly hardened length.

Hannah continued to ride him like a gorgeous buckle-bunny, and Reed turned his head.

"Come here."

Josh took a deep breath and shifted to face them both.

"Will you let me touch you?" Reed asked.

Please God, I need to taste this man.

"Just tell me what to do," Josh said, looking lost.

"You've done this before. I'm no different from Hannah."

Hannah laughed. "Well, maybe a little different, but let him lick you, Josh. His tongue is so talented."

Her breasts bounced as the rode him, and he tilted his hips to go deeper. She moaned and picked up the pace.

Josh moved closer, and Reed released one hand from Hannah's hip to grab the other man's dick and lick the tip.

Josh groaned. "Do that again."

Reed complied then took it one step further and put the whole thing in his mouth.

"Fuck."

Josh rubbed Hannah's clit while she worked Reed's cock. Reed swallowed Josh and fondled his balls. The three of them worked together in a frenzied pace, panting, sweating, and moaning. Reed's balls drew up tight, and he exploded in the condom. His only regret was that he couldn't spill his seed in her womb. But that would come. It had to.

Josh shouted then released down Reed's throat. Reed swallowed every drop, loving the heady taste.

Hannah collapsed, utterly spent, across Reed's chest. She laughed and squirmed at their joining. He had no energy to move, he figured he'd slip out eventually.

Josh's body shook, but he kissed them both then took the condom off Reed.

Damn, even that was sexy.

"I'll take care of this but make room for me." Josh ran out. Well, more like stumbled quickly.

He came back soon after and cuddled into Reed's side after throwing an afghan on top of them.

Sighing, Reed held them close.

"I could get used to more afternoons like this one." Hannah nibbled on Reed's ear, and he squeezed them both.

Yeah, so could he.

CHAPTER SEVENTEEN

"So, you're sure it's okay if we come with you?" Hannah asked Reed, looking quite delectable in her leggings and knit dress.

Reed looked down at her and smiled.

He loved this woman.

In the prior two weeks, they'd gone back to both Josh's and Hannah's homes and retrieved what they could. The Centrals had destroyed Hannah and her mother's place. She could only save a few keepsakes and her photo albums. But most of it was a lost cause. They'd shopped for clothes for her and anything else she might need. But Reed could tell she was still hurting over the additional loss of things that reminded her of where she'd come from. Josh's apartment startled Reed in its starkness. The ex-SEAL had no connections to the outside world, no family. He could just disappear, and prior to meeting Reed and Hannah, no one would know he was gone or even miss him.

Well, that would change now. Josh was his. He'd make sure the man knew it.

When they weren't getting to know one another, they'd been looking into Josh's bite. They'd scoured the old texts and literature to see what they could find, but so far had come up short. Reed wouldn't give up though, he couldn't give up.

"Yes, you can come. I want you there," Reed finally answered.

"Are you sure?"

Reed pulled her into his arms and kissed her. She looked so damn cute bundled up. Though winter had taken over the den, it hadn't snowed since that horrible blizzard. No, the weather was oddly dry, too dry in Reed's opinion. Something felt off, but he couldn't place it.

"Yes, I'm sure. Why not? It's a hunt. I'm going to be a wolf, and you two can hang out with me. It's not like I go out and chase a deer or anything. I mean, some of the younger wolves like to get in touch with their wolf sides to enhance their tracking and hunting skills, but I don't like to do it. I train with my brothers, but I don't need to kill a deer to be strong." Reed smiled, and Hannah wiggled in his arms.

"Don't I know it."

"I want you both there, please?" Reed asked.

Josh came into the living room and hugged them both. "I want to see what happens, so I'm in."

Ever since Josh had let Reed touch him, Josh had been doing that more often. Slight touches and caresses. But they still hadn't had sex fully. Reed was okay with that. He knew Josh was new to the whole thing, and he'd give him time. That didn't mean he couldn't appreciate the military man package though.

"Then it's settled. I will go wolf, and you two can hang out with me. Sounds like a date."

"A hairy one," Hannah added.

Reed put his hands over his heart. "Ouch."

"Well, it's true," Josh said. "Before we go though, can you tell me about wolves?"

"What do you mean?" Reed asked.

"Where do werewolves come from?"

Reed sighed. "It's only a legend, but it's said werewolves were formed from the Moon Goddess. I don't know what exact mythology she comes from, or even if she exists, but I feel her here." Reed put his hand over his heart. "She was saddened by the atrocities of man and the weakening of their souls, and the Moon Goddess stepped down from her ivory crescent throne and walked among the dense forests and rivers."

Hannah nodded. "I remember this story. My mom told it to me."

"There she found a hunter deep in the brush, searching for his next kill. The Goddess knew this man must eat and provide for his family, but she was disheartened at the depravity of the souls she watched over. The act of free will was not unknown to her so she stood back and waited for the decisions the hunter made."

"Sounds kind of creepy," Josh teased.

Hannah hit him in the stomach. "Shut up. Sorry, Reed, go on."

"So the hunter found his prey and wounded a wolf, not killing it. The Moon Goddess walked toward the hunter and asked what the hunter wanted to do. Startled by the Goddess presence, the hunter bowed yet stood protective over his kill. The Goddess told him man needed to understand the connection between earth and man. The man, confused and shocked, wasn't prepared for the magic pulsating through his system when the Goddess bent and touched her palms to his heart and the wolf's.

"That night she created the first werewolf. Not man, nor beast, but a medley of the two. Man would dominate and walk the world, yet the wolf would be internal always—challenging man's wants and desires. During times of the full moon, the Moon Goddess's pull is immense, a tactile entity and man will change into the beast he hunted and killed, running through the forest of earth on four paws rather than two feet. Though in times of great stress and need, man can choose to be wolf."

Reed blushed. "That's the legend, not my words."

"No, it sounded amazing. I wish I had a history like that," Josh said wistfully.

"You could, you know." Reed snapped his mouth closed and his body tensed.

Dammit, he didn't want to pressure him. Josh needed to take his time and decide if he wanted to be mates and become a werewolf. The other man didn't need Reed breathing down his neck.

"I know," Josh whispered. "Just give me more time."

Hannah patted both of their hands. "Come on, no sadness. This will be fun. We're going to see another side of Reed. That's the whole point of us staying here. To get to know one another before we decide if we want to commit to eternity. Oh, and the sex. I'm staying for that too."

Both men burst out laughing.

They needed each other more than he thought. They balanced one another, kept them on their toes. They were perfect.

They walked out to the backyard, and Reed inhaled the crisp cool air. The moon pulled at him. As werewolves, they hunted at night. He didn't want to endanger his mates by going outside in the dark, but he couldn't leave them alone and unprotected either. The full moon lit up the forest so even a human could see their way. Though it was cold and should probably be snowing, the air felt dry, very odd for northern Washington. A tingling feeling went up his arms. Maybe it was because he needed to shift.

"So we're going to hunt together. My family will most likely be hunting with the rest of the Pack or not at all. We don't have to change at the full moon if we don't want to."

"Is Willow going to change?" Hannah asked.

"She can, changing into a wolf doesn't hurt the baby, but she won't most likely," Reed said. "Melanie wants to go out tonight with Kade, so Finn will be hanging out with Jasper and Wil."

"Are they okay with you not joining them?" Josh asked.

Reed shrugged. "We don't have to go out as a Pack. It's nice, but since you two aren't wolves, it might be dangerous."

"Would they hurt us? I thought wolves retained their humanity, even after the change." Josh sounded worried.

Reed shook his head. "You have to remember, at three years old, pups can start to change. So there are toddlers and adolescents out there who are still learning their control. They are never alone, which makes it safer, but I don't want there to be an accident."

Hannah wrapped her arms around him and kissed under his chin. "Okay. Now get naked."

A discreet cough over Reed's shoulder stopped him from laughing. Damned wolf was too good at hiding and he hadn't sensed him until now.

"Hello, Maddox," Reed grunted.

"Don't sound so happy to see me or anything, big brother." Maddox casually strolled into the backyard and said hello to Hannah and Josh, but there was nothing casual about his little brother. Energy and tension rolled off him, something Reed was used to. The power that Maddox held would kill a smaller man. Since he could feel every emotion in the Pack, Maddox always had to have a higher control than anyone else.

"Sorry, Maddox, I was just surprised to see you here."

Maddox shrugged. "I thought I'd hang out with you guys for a while then go off on my own."

Something the Omega does well.

"Plus, I thought if Hannah had any questions about being part of the Pack in a position as the Healer, she could ask me. Or at least know I'm here if she needs me."

"Oh." Hannah bit her lip. "I don't have any right now. I don't feel any different. I guess it's because I'm not part of the Pack yet."

Maddox shrugged again, looking out in the forest at something Reed couldn't see. If there was even anything there. "Okay. Just let me know." He turned to Reed. "Is it okay if I join you then?"

"That's fine with me as long as it doesn't bother Hannah or Josh."

Hannah nodded.

"Sure, man," Josh put in. "I don't see why not. Plus, I'd like to see another wolf change, if that's okay."

Maddox nodded but didn't smile. His brother never seemed to smile these days.

"Fine, but don't be showing off your junk to my mates," Reed joked.

Well, it wasn't that much of a joke.

Maddox raised a brow. "Worried?"

Reed's only response was a growl.

Hannah laughed then looked Maddox over. "He is kind of cute."

She squealed when Reed threw her over his shoulder and carried her to the other side of the lawn.

"And you?" Maddox asked Josh. Reed could hear the humor in his tone.

Josh just laughed and held out his hands. "Not interested, man. Sorry."

Maddox just stared. "Didn't think you were."

The skin on Reed's arm rippled.

Damn, he needed to change. Soon.

"Reed, are you okay?" Hannah whispered.

Reed looked down at her wide-eyed face. "Yeah, I just need to change soon. But it doesn't hurt; don't worry. The moon's pulling at my wolf. I haven't changed in the two weeks you've been here. Not since the cabin."

"You shouldn't hide your wolf." Maddox stared at him.

Reed looked at Maddox and swore. He could never hide anything from the dammed wolf.

"I've been preoccupied. But I haven't hid anything. My wolf understands," Reed said quickly.

His wolf didn't respond. Shit.

"You shouldn't deny your nature," Maddox argued.

Hannah jumped in. "Hey, don't fight. Reed's doing great. He doesn't deny anything. He's never hidden that he's a werewolf or anything like that from us." She paused and turned toward him. "Right? Have you?"

"I hope you haven't," Josh added. "Not because of us."

"I'm fine. Don't worry. I've just been doing other things," Reed sputtered. "I'm going to change now."

Hannah poked him in the chest. "You better. Because I love that you're a werewolf. I think you're cute."

Maddox coughed.

Bastard.

"And," Josh continued, "I like you as a wolf. You need to show me this side of you. Plus eventually I might turn. If you don't show me how it is, how am I ever going to know if this is right? I need to know everything and you can't deny who you are any more than Hannah can deny that she's a witch. Change," Josh ordered.

Happiness filled Reed. Josh was thinking about the future and was actually considering becoming a wolf. *Thank God.* Why the hell was he hiding from them? He hadn't changed over the past two weeks because he hadn't wanted to scare them. Hadn't wanted to remind them of the inherent danger that came with being mated to a werewolf. But why?

Reed shook his head. He was an idiot.

"Okay," Reed replied. "I'll show you."

"Touching," Maddox deadpanned.

For a guy so in tune with everyone else's emotions, he sure was an ass.

Josh pulled Hannah into his arms and smiled. "Go for it."

Reed kissed them both then stripped down. Hannah whistled and he shook his ass.

"Dude. Never. Do. That. Again." Maddox rubbed his eyes. "I think I'm blind."

Whoops, forgot he was there. Whatever.

Maddox took off his shirt, and Reed growled. "Hey, what did I say about your junk?"

"You just whipped yours around. I'm going to bend so they can't see. Geez. Get over it. If they want to live with the Pack and go on hunts, they better get used to nudity."

Hannah laughed. "Oh, I'm fine with it. Continue, Maddox." She yelped when Josh bit her neck.

"I will deal with you later," Reed growled playfully.

"I'll count on it," Hannah purred.

That's great. Get an erection right when you have to change in front of your brother. Not awkward at all.

Thankfully Maddox was already in the throes of his change so he couldn't remark about Reed sporting wood. Reed bent down and pulled on his magic. His skin rippled again, fur sprouting. His muscles and bones stretched, broke, and rearranged.

Soon he sat on his haunches as a wolf, breathing in the mountain air that seemed crisper to his new scenes. Hannah walked toward him and kneeled by his side. She kissed his muzzle then petted his flank and rubbed behind his ears. He leaned into her touch. If he were a cat, he'd be purring by now.

Josh slowly stepped forward and crouched near Hannah.

"You okay?" he asked.

Reed gave a slight nod, and Josh rubbed his back. He sighed inwardly. Both his mates felt so good and understood who he was. This was perfect.

Maddox grunted behind him and nipped at his heels. Reed turned and looked at the gray and tan wolf with green eyes. So, he wanted to play? He loved fighting with his brothers, but Maddox usually stayed away. This should be fun.

Reed let out a short bark and tilted his head at Josh and Hannah.

"Go," Josh said. "I can track you. We'll find you. Have fun with your brother."

"But be safe," Hannah added.

Maddox and Reed took off into the forest. His paws beat down on the dirt floor, and the wind rustled his fur. Why did he deny himself this? This was part of him. He was a werewolf.

"It's about time. I've missed this too, you know."

Reed sighed at his wolf. Yeah, he'd fucked up.

"It's okay. I understand why you did it. But we need to mate with Josh and Hannah already, then everything can go forward."

Reed wanted to laugh. If only it were that easy.

A gray ball of fur slammed into his side as Maddox came out of nowhere.

Shit, he really needed to pay attention.

Both of them yipped and growled, biting but not using too much force. They fought and rolled through the brush until finally Maddox pinned him.

He always won. Stupid brother.

Maddox bit into Reed's scruff, growled, then released him. Sometimes Reed could best one of his brothers, but Maddox always knew what Reed's next move was. Eerie.

His brother inclined his head then shot off into the distance, most likely going home. Maddox always stayed alone unless someone needed him. He might be an ass, but if someone needed him for something, he'd be there in a moment's notice. Being the Pack's Omega wasn't a job for him but a duty. A calling.

He heard footsteps on the dead leaves behind him. Hannah and Josh.

"Found you." Hannah laughed.

Reed batted her hand with his head so she would pet him. He leaned into her side when she gave in.

"Needy, aren't you?"

Reed merely looked up at her and blinked.

See how cute I am? Pet me.

Both his mates let out a laugh.

Josh picked up a stick and waved it at him. "Want to play fetch?"

Reed lifted a lip to show off his elongated canine.

Seriously?

Josh threw the stick, and Reed refused to follow its trail. He wasn't a dog for fuck's sake.

"I don't know, man. What do wolves do? Do you want to go find a rabbit or something?" Josh asked.

"No. Not Thumper," Hannah said.

Josh boomed out a laugh. "Not every bunny is Thumper, babe. But seriously, Reed, what do you want to do?"

"Well, not play fetch. I was surprised Reed didn't bite you. How about a game of chase?" Hannah asked.

Reed perked up. Hell yeah. With Hannah as the prize, he'd totally hunt and chase for her.

Hannah smiled and grabbed Josh. With a look over her shoulder she laughed. "Come and get us."

Reed let them get a head start. He could scent them and would find them easily, but it was more about the chase. And odd feeling crept up his spine, tangling his fur. He inhaled, trying to figure out what it was but could only scent Josh, Hannah, and the land. What was it? He listened for what it could be and only heard a deer run away in the distance.

Odd. He shook it off. He needed to get to his mates and that would make him feel better. That must be it.

Reed ran on all fours through the undergrowth and found Josh first. The human wasn't trying to hide but stood near a tree, looking the other way, shaking his head. Reed made no noise as he crept up behind him. Josh, the SEAL that he was, turned quickly and tackled him. Reed rolled with him until Josh lay pinned beneath. He licked the other man's face.

"Hey, not nice." Josh laughed.

Reed quirked his head.

"Hannah? This is so odd, by the way. She went off that way." He lifted his head. "She didn't go too far; she just wanted to give you more of a chase."

Reed let Josh stand then bumped his hand. Josh scratched behind his ears, stroking his fur. He could get used to this.

They followed her honey and bitter apple trail until the scent of sulfur hit his nose.

Shit.

Smoke filled the trees, and Josh coughed.

Fire.

A scream sounded in the distance.

Hannah.

CHAPTER EIGHTEEN

Hannah coughed and sputtered as the smoke burned her nose and throat, filling her lungs.

Dammit, why did she leave Josh and Reed to play? It wasn't safe. Yet she'd forgotten that in the heat of the moment and run off alone.

The fire grew closer, and Hannah didn't know where to go. A rock face was the only thing she could see that wasn't burning around her. The fire had come up so fast; she didn't even see where it started.

The air grew thick, dry. She'd known it felt drier than normal all day, and that fact scared her. Between the lack of moisture in the air and the decade's worth of undergrowth, the fire would spread fast, not only potentially killing her but endangering the entire Redwood den. With most of the Pack on the hunt, this would be the perfect time for the enemy to attack them. It only made sense that this was at the hands of the Centrals or another enemy, and not something natural.

The earth screamed in pain around her. Her magic wanted to heal, to save the dying plants and animals. But she couldn't. She only healed humans. And she couldn't even save herself, let alone something else.

The fire urged its way closer, dancing in the moonlight. Hannah ran to the rock face and looked up to the cliff. There was no way she could climb it. She coughed again. All other paths were blocked by the fire or debris. She was trapped. What would she do?

"Reed! Josh!" she screamed, but she didn't think they'd hear her. Dammit. She felt more alone now than she ever had before. She'd had but a taste of what life could offer, and now it would be wrenched away from her.

She used her powers to pull the dirt and soil on top of the fire, trying to bat them down. But every time she did, the flames came back harsher, higher. She couldn't manipulate fire or even water. She could only heal and play with dirt. Her powers were to heal and aid, not destroy. What use was that now?

A wolf howled in the distance.

Reed.

At least she prayed it was.

"Reed!" she called again but choked on smoke.

Reed jumped through the flames but didn't make it to her side of the flaming wall as he hit an unknown barrier. She could smell burning fur in the air, and she bit back a sob. What was he doing? He was going to kill himself. There was no way out. He needed to leave, save himself.

"Reed, you need to go you can't save me. Go, run fast. It's too late for me."

He growled, jumped again through the flames, this time making it passed that unknown barrier and threw himself over her as the flames licked higher, hotter. It raged out of control, faster and louder than she thought possible without any aid. This wasn't normal fire. Reed licked her face and covered her with his body when the flames reached them.

Her brain grew dizzy. So much smoke.

Reed growled again and licked her face, covering her body more when she pulled her legs up.

"We need to get out of here. Please. We need to get to Josh." Hannah coughed, and he licked her chin.

She shifted from under his body and stood up. They began to move, but the fire grew. Fire shaped like arms reached for them. No, this was demon fire aided by witches, magic so dark and evil she didn't even know if there was a counter spell against it. They weren't going to make it.

Reed used his teeth and pulled on the sleeve of her burned dress, careful not to touch the slight burns on her arms. She stood on shaky legs, followed him to the rocks, and found a small alcove.

"We'll still burn here."

He growled, pushed her to the ground and covered her body with his. The flames licked around him, hunting them, and Reed groaned in pain.

She screamed. He was dying in her arms, and there wasn't a thing she could do about it.

He howled in pain again and shifted to human.

"No! What are you doing?" Hannah screamed.

"I can't shift. No magic," Reed rasped. Burns marked his skin and his flesh boiled in some spots.

Tears ran down both of their faces as she coughed.

Why hadn't she mated with him fully before? What was holding her back? She'd been ready. *Dear goddess, please let us live. Spare us.*

She framed his face with her hands. "I love you."

Reed closed his eyes, strained agony on his face. "I love you, too."

He held her closer as she sobbed.

A figure in the flames caught her eye, and she froze. Was it the demon? Only they could walk through demon fire. Was he here to kill them or prolong their torture?

The man walked out of the flames into her field of vision, and she gasped.

Josh.

The bite mark. The demon had bitten him, and now he could walk through flames. Oh goddess. What did this mean?

"Hannah! Reed!" he called. "I'm coming. Hold on."

Despite the oncoming fire, he ran to them and picked Hannah up, cradling her to his body. "Let's move."

Reed stood, naked, on shaky legs, and coughed. "You carry Hannah; I'll be by your side. She can Heal me, but no one can heal her."

Josh kissed him. "Stay close."

Hannah looked into Josh's eyes and saw darkness. Despite the flames, a chill raced down her spine. His pupils had dilated three times their normal size and his body rippled with unspent energy. What did this mean? What did the demon do to him?

"Aren't you hurt?" Hannah rasped.

Josh shook his head and started walking into the fire. "No, the fire doesn't hurt me. It feels warm. Good. I can't explain it, but I don't want to think about it right now. I just want to get the two of you out of here. Come on."

The fire screamed in fury as they ran through it. Reed buried himself against Josh's side, though he was about the same height. They ran and because she was in Josh's arms, the fire didn't hurt. What on earth?

They ran and ran until they made it out of the ring of fire. They coughed and gasped, as Josh dropped to his knees still holding her to his chest. Reed lay on the ground, bleeding, with third degree burns covering his body. His arms and legs were covered in burns that made her want to cry just looking at them. Angry welts dotted his chest and groin.

Dear goddess.

She sobbed and pulled every last ounce of energy she possessed and poured it into Reed, Healing his wounds. Warmth and connection filled her, different from her usual Healing. Her palms glowed as she watched Reed's flesh knit together in front her. Reed moaned and relaxed on the dirty leaf-covered ground.

"Pack magic," she breathed.

That had to be it. Her powers were so much stronger now than they had been before. There was only one explanation. She had accepted Reed and told him she loved him. Though they hadn't fully mated, she was Pack. She knew it. Taking a deep breath, she pulled more, liking the new warm sensation that came with this form of Healing. Her old healing had a slight tingling, but nothing like this. Finally, all the wounds had been healed and closed and Reed only had freshly healed, pink skin.

Before Reed could say anything, she turned to Josh and placed her palms on his chest. He gasped as she Healed his lungs from the smoke, though his body had no burns.

Thank the goddess.

She leaned back and fell on her bottom, tears running down her cheeks.

"That was close," Reed rasped.

"Too close," Josh added.

Hannah couldn't hold back anymore and sobbed, for the dying earth at their feet, for Reed's pain, and for whatever Josh might become. She hated crying. She wasn't a weak person, yet with every battle and every painful incident, she seemed to fold into herself and cry. She could fight her way out of most things and use her magic, but in the end, her emotions would be too much and the tears would fall. She wouldn't give up, but she'd still cry. It was too much, but unlike before she knew now what she wanted.

Josh and Reed. Together. In their trinity bond. Forever. She wanted the whole package. The marriage, the kisses, the children, the late night-feedings. Everything.

The fire died down around them, leaving only ash and smoke in its wake. Their enemies had lost this round, but she knew it wouldn't be their last attempt.

Reed coughed. "You used Pack magic, Hannah."

She gave a small smile. "I know."

"Thank God, you have that power," Josh whispered. "I know your usual healing is amazing, but I don't think it would have been enough this time. I don't know what we would have done. I know Reed heals fast, but without you, it might not have been enough."

Her heart lurched. "I'm Pack. I'm yours. I'm Reed's too." Hannah whispered.

Josh's black eyes didn't blink. He shook his head. "No, I can't be. Didn't you see what I just did? I walked through *fire* and I don't have a mark on me. There's something wrong with me. Don't you get that? I need to go. I don't know what is happening, but I can't stay here. I can't put you two or the rest of the Pack in danger."

Reed shook his head and coughed again. "No, you need to stay here. You can't go. We'll figure it out. We've already been researching, we won't give up. I won't let you hurt anyone." The men stared at each other, and Hannah knew Reed wouldn't let Josh leave no matter what.

Finally, Josh nodded. "I need your word, Reed. Kill me if you have to, but don't let me hurt anyone."

Hannah gasped and her heart ached. No.

Reed's eyes filled. "I promise."

Josh was too much a man to let himself become a danger. But she'd be dammed if she allowed Reed to put him down. No, she'd find a way to save him. Josh was her mate after all.

Hannah shook her head. "All I could think about when the fire came at us was that I should have made love to you both and mated you fully. I'm ready."

Reed inhaled. "Really?"

Josh gave a hollow laugh. "That's all I could think about too. Well, other than the ability to walk around in fire and not get burned, but we can talk about that later."

Hannah laughed. "All I can think about is the two of you. I love you, Josh."

His eyes widened, and he smiled. Really smiled. "I love you too, Hannah."

Reed coughed and sat up, healed. "I love you, Josh. I know you aren't ready to hear it yet, but I don't want to go further in this war and in our lives without saying it."

Josh traced Reed's brow. "I love you, too."

Hannah laughed. "Apparently all it took was a fire and a few new abilities for us to come clean about our feelings, huh?"

Josh laughed. "So how exactly does the full mating thing work?"

Reed smiled. "It's fate. You and I will make love to Hannah and not use condoms. Our seed will make the mating happen. As for you and me, it's the same way, but we don't have to do it all at once. I guess it's a little different for a trinity bond than others, since there are three of us. But as long as I do the *mounting*," they all laughed, "then we will be mated. Make sense?"

"Wait," Josh interjected. "Why is it only you? Why does it have to be your *seed*?"

"Because I'm the werewolf and the one whose species needs the mating this way. We can always have you *mount* me just in case we want to make sure the mating sticks." Reed smiled.

Josh laughed. "In other words, we need to have sex in as many ways and as many times as possible."

Reed joined in his laughter. "Not a bad deal." Reed sobered. "There is also the marking. That will bind my wolf to you, not just my human half. But I want to do that later, once we know what going on with you. I don't want it to hurt you."

Josh nodded. "I understand."

"Okay," Hannah cut in. "Let's get to it then."

Both men looked at her.

"What? Come on, Reed's already naked. Strip, Josh."

"Here?" Josh asked.

"Now?" Reed asked.

"Yes, here. Now. We need to reaffirm our existence and love. Plus, we are outdoors; I can feel the earth calling to me. Make love to me. Make me yours."

CHAPTER NINETEEN

Hannah watched as both men shifted to rest on their knees. Reed, freshly healed and looking almost pain-free, kneeled, naked, watching her. His sandy blond hair, slightly crispy on the ends, stood in a disarrayed halo around his beautiful artistic face. Josh knelt by him, strong and not quite as beautiful, but equally as handsome.

Josh took a deep breath and lifted the shirt above his head. Hannah caught her breath as she watched his biceps and abs flex with the movement. She swallowed and tried not to gasp.

Damn, they were both specimens of male perfection. Washboard abs, long, lean muscles. She ached to trace her fingers along every inch of them. They had that pretty little line at their hips that made such lickable trails to their, ahem, groins.

Hannah bit her lip and looked down. Reed, already naked, was hard and ready, his balls low and filled. His cock was long, longer than Josh's, and wide. Josh shucked his shoes and pants. The military man was commando. Hannah grew achy and wet. She quickly rid herself of her clothes as she stared at Josh's cock, long, and wide, wider than Reed's. Together they would fill her and hit every right spot. They were just different enough that she'd known who was in her in the throes of passion and she loved them both.

Hannah got on her hands and knees and crawled to Josh. She knew she looked like a desperate woman, but she didn't care. These two were hers. And after they made love, they'd be hers forever. She batted her eyes at Josh then wrapped her lips around the head of his penis. His sweet, woodsy taste seeped on her tongue just like when she tasted Reed's sandalwood flavor. She swallowed, forcing his cock farther down her throat. Josh tugged at her hair.

"God, I love your mouth," he grunted.

Reed went behind her and danced his fingers down her spine. She shivered in need. He traced his fingers over her sex and through her folds, until he slid one finger in to the knuckle.

"You're wet," Reed rasped.

She let go of Josh's cock with a pop. "Always. Just for you two." She licked up Josh's balls then took him in her mouth again.

Reed pinched her clit, and she jumped.

Oh. My. Goddess.

He scraped her clit with his fingernail, and her pussy fluttered.

Stop teasing.

But she couldn't say it because Josh was fucking her mouth. Hard. And she loved it.

Who knew she could be such a naughty girl? Maybe Reed and Josh just brought it out of her.

Josh played with her nipples while Reed entered another finger, then another, until she was filled with four of them as he worked her channel. She was about to come, just riding that crescent where she begged for stars, but both men backed off.

She lifted her head from Josh, her lips swollen. "Don't stop, please."

Reed chuckled and teased her folds with the tip of his cock, and she wiggled back, begging. "Oh, I like to hear you say please. But I don't want you to come until I'm in you. I want to feel your pussy clench around me, milking me."

She shuddered, almost coming at his words alone.

"Dammit, Reed, fuck her," Josh grunted. "Shove that fat cock into her, because I'm about to go just listening to you."

"Yes, what he said." Hannah agreed. Goddess, she wanted them both. Loved them both.

Reed slowly entered her, inch by agonizing inch.

Oh. My.

"That's it, baby, take me." Reed groaned. "Do you know how good you feel around me, bare? I never want to be in you again with a condom. I want to feel you. I want to fill you. Fill you with my seed and watch it take root. I want to you grow round and ripe with our child. With Josh's child. A child belonging to the three of us."

With each promise he reamed her. Goddess, she wanted everything he said and more. She wanted them. And she had them.

"I can't wait to feel what you feel, Reed," Josh breathed as he plucked her nipples and fucked her mouth.

Reed pounded into her, Josh too, until she found the crest of that wave again and fell. Stars shattered behind her eyelids, and her body rocked with emotions, feelings, connections. Everything. She could feel Reed's soul intertwine with hers. She could feel his every desire, want, hope. All centered around her and Josh. As she felt his warm seed pulsate in her womb, she bonded. She was Reed's, as he was hers. Forever.

"Oh my God," Reed whispered. "I didn't know. They said...but I didn't know."

Oh, she knew.

She lay on the ground, in Reed's arms, and felt his being.

"Josh, I want you." She needed him. Needed this feeling. She didn't want to lose him. She needed this last part of the puzzle to be whole. Josh.

"I want to come in you," Josh said. "I want you to look at me like you're looking at Reed. I see it. The link. Like a physical entity that I can feel, taste. I want it with both of you. Please don't deny me." Lines of strained tension covered his face, and she reached out to him.

"Please."

Reed rolled over, leaving Hannah on the grassy floor. Through the canopy, sunlight peaked through the trees, and a burned amber scent drifted along the air. Josh lay between her legs and positioned himself.

He twined his fingers with hers, looked directly into her eyes, then slowly, oh so slowly, entered her, filled her.

"Mine," Josh murmured.

"Yours," Hannah agreed.

"Ours," Reed added.

"Ours," Josh and Hannah whispered.

"Josh, please. Harder." She ached. She angled her pelvis, inviting him deeper. Josh was always the harder of the two, more demanding. She loved it, craved it.

"As you wish." Josh smiled a truly feral smile then slammed into her, pushing against her womb.

He did it again and again, crashing into her. Loving her.

———

WITH HANNAH WRAPPED AROUND HIM, Josh knew he was in heaven. Nothing could change it, not any amount of demons, torrents of fire, or whatever the fuck he was turning into.

Reed knelt behind them and reached over Josh to skim his hand between Hannah and him.

"Reed, touch her." Josh groaned.

"Oh, I will, then I'll touch you," Reed promised.

Oh shit.

He knew Reed would be topping first. That was the way it would be done. He trusted Reed and knew he could do it. He wanted to feel that long cock in his ass. It didn't scare him anymore. The connection between Reed and Hannah didn't scare him anymore either. He wanted that too, with both of them. And he wanted to feel Reed around his cock in the future.

Fuck. He almost came on the spot just thinking about it. But he had to maintain control. He didn't want to come in Hannah until Reed did what he wanted to do. He had only a few good shots in him since he was human. He envied the hell out his Energizer Bunny of a mate. Reed could stay hard for hours, days even. Josh might have a quick turn around, but Reed was fucking amazing.

Speaking of fucking...

Hannah reached up and cupped his face.

Tears in her eyes, gasps on her breath, she mouthed, "I love you." And he almost lost it again.

Like a curvy goddess, his mate lay below him, her heavy breasts bouncing with every thrust.

"I love you, too," he rasped, and she smiled.

God, that smile.

Hannah closed her eyes and moaned. Josh looked over his shoulder and saw Reed playing with her hole, and she bit her lip.

"Like that, do you?" Reed asked.

"Yes. You know I do," she answered.

"Oh, we'll both fill you at the same time. Just not tonight. Tonight, I'm going to fill our mate. What do you think about that?" Reed asked.

Both Josh and Hannah groaned.

Yes, please.

Reed took Hannah's juices and covered Josh's puckered hole.

He froze mid-thrust.

He'd never let Reed play back there before, but oh, how he wanted that.

"Lube," he forced out.

Reed licked his neck. "I don't have any. I wasn't planning on this. But I do have Hannah and me. It will be enough. I won't hurt you."

Josh shook his head. "No."

Reed stood back. "Oh."

"No, that's not what I mean. Lube," he rasped and had to pull out of Hannah to think. She whimpered and he leaned over to kiss her. "I have lube in my jeans pocket."

Hannah laughed.

Reed lifted a brow. "Boy Scout, are you? Always prepared?"

Josh blushed then grunted and slid his dick through Hannah's folds and back out again. "Actually, yes, but that's not why I brought it. I was planning on seducing Hannah in the woods before the fire." Josh shrugged and rocked against Hannah, loving the way she moaned.

Reed smiled full out, white teeth and everything. "Thank God."

The sexy man scooted to Josh's jeans and pullout out a fresh bottle of Liquid Silk.

"Nice." Reed laughed. "Now where was I?"

Josh wiggled his butt, and Hannah laughed. "I think you were right about here." He wiggled again.

"Sounds good to me," Reed grunted.

Reed bent and licked between Josh's cheeks and he squirmed with the new and not-unpleasant sensation. In fact, it was a fucking fantastic sensation.

Reed worked the lube, coating him, then slowly entered a finger. Josh froze. The tight, filled feeling sent shivers down his spine.

Jesus.

Reed rubbed the finger on a sensitive bundle of nerves, and Josh almost came again.

"How does it feel?" Hannah asked, a knowing smile on her face.

He leaned down and kissed her, loving the mix of her sweet taste and the sensation of Reed adding another finger.

"Like manna."

Hannah laughed, her pussy clenching around his shaft.

"Don't laugh; I'm fighting for control as it is," he groaned.

She pouted. "Oh poor baby. Is it too hard for you to be in me and Reed to play with you at the same time?" She gasped and shut her eyes when he slammed into her.

"If you're coherent enough to be teasing me, I'm not doing my job right."

"And," Reed added, "if you're coherent enough to be teasing her, I can add another finger."

Josh buckled when Reed added a third lube-coated finger, then a fourth.

Oh, sweet Jesus.

"That's more like it." Reed laughed. "I think you're ready for me."

Josh tensed.

"Hey." He slapped Josh's ass in one quick motion, and Josh moaned at the sting. "Don't tense up on me. I like you nice and loose."

"Okay, I trust you," he breathed.

Josh felt the touch of the head of Reed's penis at his entrance, and he forced himself to relax. He looked down at Hannah and saw the love in her eyes. He smiled. He could do this. He wanted this.

Reed pushed past the tight ring of muscles, and Josh stiffened at the invasion, but forced himself to relax. He felt overfull and loved, deep inside Hannah and Reed deep inside him. It was the three of them. It was always about the three of them. Forever.

Reed slid in inch by agonizing inch, pulled back, then slid in again until Josh felt the other man's balls against his ass.

Oh God, he felt so full. So wanted.

"Oh, fuck me. You feel so good. So tight," Reed said, straining. Then he worked back out then in again.

Again and again. With each motion, Josh mimicked it in Hannah, the three of them working up a rhythm of flesh, sweat, and heat. Josh felt his balls tighten, then he screamed their names and emptied himself into her. He felt Hannah tighten around him, and Reed fill his ass. Together they rose up then crashed down.

He felt Hannah's and Reed's souls intertwine with his, and he knew he'd never be alone again. Wherever he went, they'd always be with him.

Their trinity bond, and all that came with it, settled in, previously unknown but freshly hatched, waiting for its discoveries to be revealed.

CHAPTER TWENTY

They walked through the forest, past the trees that should have been burned to a crisp, but stood proud and strong. Reed shook his head. What the hell had happened? It was so weird. The fire had come, burned, and almost killed them. Yet no sign of it remained, no trace but a faint whiff of burned amber on the air.

The hunt had taken them farther than they'd thought, driven by fire. They finally trekked back to his home, no, *their* home and Reed smiled. He could feel Hannah's and Josh's souls tangling with his. Kade and Jasper had told him the connection was deeper than the bond with the Pack. More tactile, leaving one feeling naked. But he hadn't truly understood until he bonded himself to his mates. No wonder looks of joy that passed over his brothers' faces whenever their mates walked toward them. Kade said he felt it with Finn, too, to a lesser degree, and that their children would also be bound to them like a web. And as their children aged and moved apart, developing their own lives, the connection would fade.

He could only feel sorrow for Adam. When Adam had lost Anna and their baby, Reed grieved with him and had helped pick up the pieces and glue them together in an oddly connected jumble that was their brother. But the loss also scarred Adam more than the scar that ran along Maddox's face from a fight. Reed still didn't know the story behind it.

"Come on," Reed said when he spotted the house. "Let's get inside and get dressed." Still naked, the cold was starting to tingle certain bits better left unexposed.

They got inside and immediately Reed warmed.

"I'm going to jump in the shower. Is that okay?" Hannah asked.

Images of droplets of water running between her breasts, dusting her nipples, then carving a trail down to her sex filled his brain.

Josh let out a booming laugh. "Go for it, baby. Reed needs to get his mind out of the gutter." He gave a pointed look at Reed's crotch.

Reed blushed. Yeah, thinking about his woman nude and in the shower, while he himself was naked and couldn't hide his growing erection, might not be such a great idea. *Whoops.* Well, who could blame him?

He walked to their room and took out a new set of clothes. He pulled them on then shook out the kinks in his back. His newly healed flesh felt a bit tight. Watching Hannah using her Healing powers on him had been a revelation. She was the true Healer and part of his Pack. Incredible.

Josh laughed. "You're thinking about her again."

Reed joined in his laughter and shrugged, not ashamed in the least. "She's hot. And she's ours. At least I'm wearing pants this time. And as much as I'd like to make love to both of you again, I need to call my father."

The phone rang, and both men burst out laughing again.

"Do you hear the music to the *Twilight Zone?*" Josh asked.

"No, just my nosy Alpha of a Father who knows everything," Reed answered then walked to the phone and picked it up.

"Son." His father's voice sounded relieved and edgy all at once.

"Speak of the devil," Reed joked.

Something dark came and went in Josh's eyes, worrying him. The other man's pupil's dilated then went back to normal. A chill raced up Reed's arms and his heart sped up. He took a shuddering breath and held it in. *Please, don't let anything bad happen to Josh, not when I just found him.*

"It's good to hear your voice, son," his father quietly said.

"It's good to hear you too, Dad," Reed choked out. Okay, stop being a sissy.

"I felt you, your connection to the Pack," his father added. "So I knew you weren't gone. But that fire out there scared the crap out of us. We didn't know exactly what was going on. And when Maddox came to us screaming that the place he'd left you was now consumed in fire, I about died. Reed, I almost had to knock Maddox unconscious to keep him from going back for you. He would have and would have died."

Neither spoke. He knew his brother loved him, but he hadn't realized it was that deep. Damn, his family humbled him.

"Did it come at you, too?" Reed finally asked.

"No, we were safe. The den is protected by more magic than that fire could hope to destroy. But the land you were on, though it might be Redwood land, isn't protected by the same wards. I'm going to try and fix that, but it takes too much power. Your little Hannah may be of assistance there." His father made it sound more like a quiet order than a question. But he knew Hannah would do all in her power to protect her new Pack, her family.

"I'll let her know."

"Good."

"It scared the hell out of us, Dad."

"No kidding. How did you get out?"

"Josh."

Should he tell him anymore? He couldn't keep secrets from his Alpha. But what would happen if he revealed the source of Josh's new power? Would they lock him up and throw away the key? Or worse?

Josh came up from behind and held him. "Tell him. He needs to know," he whispered.

"Josh saved us," he repeated to his father. "Hannah and I were trapped, the fire coming at us, and Josh walked through the flames to get us. Dad, the fire didn't touch him."

He heard an intake of breath and a quiet curse.

"We will find the source of this. Josh is my son now. I know he can hear me, so Josh, you are mine. Mine to protect. You are a Redwood

432

and a Jamenson, even if you don't take the name. I won't let what that bastard did to you taint you. You got that?"

Josh stood rod straight and nodded.

"He says yes, Dad." Jesus, his dad was a great man, a noble man. A man who didn't care that his son was bisexual and loved both a man and a woman. Not many men, especially the Alpha of a werewolf pack, would be as accepting.

"Reed, I won't let you lose your mate. Not like Adam."

Reed released a shuddering breath. "I know, Dad. I know. We'll figure this out."

"Damn straight."

They all let out a ragged, tension-filled laugh.

If only it were that easy. But nothing seemed easy anymore, if it ever had been.

"Get dressed and come over. I felt it when Hannah and Josh came into the Pack. I'm sure the others with the power have too." Meaning Kade, Jasper, Maddox, and Adam. "Your Mother wants you here. She's already cooking up a storm and invited the rest of the family. Consider it a pre-wedding and thank-God-you're-alive party."

Reed laughed. "Great! I'm starving. I'm sure Josh and Hannah would love it."

Josh nodded, a smile on his lips.

"Good. See you soon. I love you, son. All three of you," his father gruffly let out, then hung up before Reed could speak.

"I love you, too," Reed answered to the dial tone.

Hannah came out of the bathroom, looking fresh and damned cute.

"I heard the last part. So we're going to dinner? Good, I'm starved."

"Yep, I'm going to go jump in the shower and wash off the smoke," Reed answered.

"I'll go jump in the other shower and meet you here in ten." Josh raised a brow. "Separate showers. We need to meet your parents."

Yep, loved them.

———

THEY WALKED INTO HIS PARENTS' home to the sound of a large family gathering. Finn screamed in glee as North took him around the house, playing airplane. Reed smiled, thinking of the children they'd soon have if he had anything to say about it, of all the children that would fill the house. Willow was due any day now, and Kade made whisperings of wanting another soon. They were growing up. Even though they'd long since reached adulthood, they were now moving on. It seemed like yesterday they themselves were six rowdy pups making too much noise and stress for their mother. He'd been close to eighty when Cailin was born. She hadn't grown up with them in the same fashion, but she was still his baby sister.

"Oh, my, Reed. It's so good to see you here." His mom came at him with her arms outstretched but bee-lined to Hannah, enveloping his bonded mate—that was great to say—in her arms. Well, he knew where he stood now.

"Hi, Pat. We're happy to be here as well." Hannah hugged his mother back, and just for one moment, he could forget all their troubles and tribulations.

His mom kissed all three of them and ushered them into the living room. There, the rest of the family hugged and kissed them. Tears fell on the women's cheeks. Damn, he hated he had scared his family so much. But thank God they were okay. He only prayed that, wherever the hell Adam was, he was the same.

Maddox was the last to join them and stood still, watching. He walked slowly toward them, and everyone quieted down.

"I never should have left you there." Maddox whispered.

"Bullshit," Hannah said.

Maddox laughed. Laughed. The room stood stunned. When was the last time they'd heard his brother laugh? Before the loss of Anna that had hardened him as much as Adam? Before the scar?

His little brother wiped the tears from his eyes. "That word coming out of that little mouth just sounds wrong."

Hannah didn't laugh. She stood with her fists on her hips and scowled. "If you were out there, you could be dead. I'm glad you were away. I don't know what we would have done if we'd have lost you. You're part of this family just as much as anyone else in this room. So

swallow that pride of yours and that self-pity. We are fine. We all are."
She lifted her chin, daring them to say anything.

Reed loved this feisty side of her.

"Now," she continued, "I think your mom has made us an amazing
dinner. Let's go and eat it. Shall we?"

The toughest male werewolves in the country, maybe even the
world, scurried to the table in the dining room and sat.

His mother wrapped an arm around Hannah and laughed. Willow
and Mel joined in.

"Well, my dear you are officially a Jamenson. As you can tell, it's the
women who control the family. They just need to remember that every
once in a while."

"Darn straight," Mel added, Finn now in her arms.

"Oh, this is going to be fun." Willow laughed.

The women joined them at the table, and Reed spoke up. "The fire
came out of nowhere. Literally. It hunted, tried to kill us. It didn't react
like a normal fire and then disappeared as quickly as it came."

"It was demon fire," Hannah whispered.

His dad cursed again, muttering an apology to Finn.

"Demon fire. Darn Centrals. They think it's okay to come onto our
land and use demon fire?" Edward rumbled.

"What is demon fire?" Willow asked, her arm wrapped protectively
around her swollen belly.

"May I?" Hannah asked. With a nod from his dad, she continued.
"Demon fire is just what it sounds like. Fire made from the depths of
hell and summoned by a demon. It also takes a witch with immense
power and an affinity toward fire to control it. I don't know of a way to
counter it. I don't even know if there is a way." She shuddered, and
Reed held her close.

"We can't allow this to happen," Cailin said.

"I agree," his father said.

His mom uncovered the dishes on the table and was about to serve
when North interrupted. "Josh, before we actually eat, I want to look
at that bite mark."

Everyone at the table froze.

"You told them," Reed said to his father.

"Yes, it needed to be done. For his safety, not only ours."

Josh rubbed his shoulder. "It's okay. I want them to know. Secrets only hurt people. Plus they only want to help." He stood up and walked with North to the back room.

Reed wanted to get up and join them, to scream and curse God, or at least ask how this could have happened. But he didn't. Josh needed to feel normal, and that couldn't happen with Reed hovering over him.

"We'll find out what happened. It'll be fine." His mother's voice was cool.

His mom might love to knit and cook, and she cried at the drop of a hat, but if someone endangered her pups, she'd kill them without breaking a nail or a smile. Bloodthirsty, thy name is Momma Wolf.

"Reed," Jasper cut in, "you said the fire disappeared. Are there any remnants?"

He shook his head. "No, just the smell. That acrid, smoky flavor that settles on your tongue. No damage."

"Yes," Hannah added, "but it felt like fire, and it damaged anything it touched at the time. The earth screamed in pain. I felt it."

She shuddered, and Reed wrapped an arm around her shoulders. The smell of fear and pain wafted off her skin. He couldn't imagine what it felt like to have his soul so irrevocably entwined with nature to feel it breathe and gasp. His Hannah was such a caring person to begin with, but add in the fact that she needed to Heal in order to feel calm, and it was all too much. Reed shook his head.

"We can't get into the Centrals' den," Kade said. "It's cloaked with some kind of magic. The stuff they're using to do it isn't anything we've seen before. They're touching dark magic. We don't have anything to fight against that—yet."

Reed nodded. They'd already discussed the magic the Centrals possessed. That didn't make it any fucking less futile.

"We'll have to go on lock-down," Jasper added. "No outside visitors, and people can only leave if they're in pairs, and even then, only if they truly need it." He rubbed the bridge of his nose. "I know it sucks and sounds like we're a cult or something, but I can't think of another way of keeping our people safe."

Reed nodded. "Okay, we'll go on the defense. Like we have been, but more alert. And we'll look for the magic that can be our offense."

"There has to be a balance," Hannah added. "That type of dark can't exist without some type of light to balance it. That's the way of magic. We just need to find it."

"Easier said than done," Maddox grumbled.

Cailin sighed. "It'd be easier if we just went dark."

The room went silent. Reed swore he could have heard a pin drop.

"No," his father said coolly.

One word, spoken as the Alpha, and that was it. No discussion. But they really wouldn't have discussed it anyway. No matter what, the Jamensons wouldn't go evil. That wasn't their way, their nature.

Cailin's eyes flashed, her back as stiff as a board. She turned to their father and lifted her chin. "I would *never* do that. You above all should know that. I was just saying it would be easier, not right."

"Then don't say it," Edward chided. "You are the daughter of the Alpha. You need to set an example and spouting off without thinking doesn't show that."

Cailin glared but didn't answer.

Reed had no idea what it meant to be in her position, the daughter of the Pack. He'd never really thought about it. Maybe he should have noticed her anger before. He took a deep breath. Complicated didn't even begin to describe his family.

His mother spoke up, breaking into the silence. "Enough you two. Come on, I don't want to let the food go cold. Eat."

He was so grateful for his mother. Something was going on with his little sister, but he didn't know what.

Willow rubbed her tiny hand on her heavily protruding stomach. "I'm so happy the three of you are mated."

Hannah blushed, her ears red. As a werewolf, Willow could smell the three of them all over each other and feel the bond slowly settling into place. Reed kissed Hannah's forehead and held her closer. "Thank you, Wil."

Mel leaned over beside Wil and rubbed the pregnant woman's stomach with one hand, holding Finn in the other. Mel was really becoming her own wolf in their Pack, someone they could look up to when she became the Alpha's wife, and not just the Heir's.

She laughed. "Yes, we needed more women. So welcome, Hannah."

"Hell, yeah," Cailin yelled, and pumped her fist.

Kade threw a roll her on the head. "Language."

"Kade," his mother scolded. "Don't throw food."

They broke out into laughter. This was his family. Dysfunction and all. Not too shabby.

"What's so funny?" Josh asked as he walked into the room, North on his heels.

They quieted again, but Reed just smiled, though his heart beat in his ears. "Cailin's potty mouth attacks again and Kade is the equivalent of a twelve-year-old in a cafeteria. Come on and sit; we're just about to eat."

Josh smiled. Man, how he loved that smile. He sat on the other side of Hannah and grabbed Reed's hand and squeezed. Hard. His mate might be putting on a brave face and masking his fear well for others, but he couldn't hide if from him. And by the way Hannah leaned over into him, Josh couldn't hide it from her either.

Josh kissed her temple, then leaned over and did the same to Reed. With a shake of his head, Reed leaned back into his chair.

North didn't know what to do with the demon bite. Damn it.

His father cleared his throat. "Since we are all here now, I'd like to formally welcome Josh and Hannah to our Pack."

His family smiled at his two mates.

"For most of my life, our Pack has been without a Healer. But now, in Hannah, we have one. A talented one by the way her power resonates off her." His dad smiled. His Alpha's strength washed over them, welcoming them into their fold. "And, we have a new enforcer to join our ranks."

Reed started. "What? Who?"

His dad threw back his head and laughed. "I mean your other new mate...Josh."

Reed looked over at Josh and saw a similar confused expression.

"Um...sir...I'm...I'm not sure I understand you," Josh stuttered.

His father lifted a brow. "Oh, I think you do, son. I need another guard. Someone to protect the Pack. And with your background and desire to help, I think you fit the bill. I know you've been looking for how to fit in and contribute, so here you go."

Josh furrowed his brows. Reed wondered what he was thinking.

"Don't look at me like that." His dad scowled. "I didn't make this job up for you. We really need you, and you'll be an asset. Don't let your fears of rejection and loss, cloud your judgment."

Josh gulped.

"But he's human," Hannah blurted out as a heavy blush filled her cheeks.

Josh laughed, Reed joining him.

"About that..." Edward interrupted. "Without the bite, you'd be human, and eventually, if you wanted to stay with Hannah and Reed for eternity, we would change you into a wolf. But with the bite, you may be turning into something else."

Hannah and Josh blanched while Reed's pulse quickened. Oh, Jesus, what had his dad found out? He couldn't lose Josh. Not now.

"I've talked to the elders." His father cursed, then shot an apologetic look to Finn. "They never like talking to anyone, and always talk in riddles, but that's their prerogative. They said that Josh might be stronger than humans now, long lived as well."

Hannah gasped, but the others in the room remained silent. Reed wouldn't lose Josh to old age?

"We'll have to wait and see," his father continued. "I can tell something is different, the way his power resonates. He may not need to change to a wolf to live in the bond the three of you hold."

The three of them relaxed somewhat.

Josh nodded. "Okay. I can do that. I'll be honored."

"Good." His dad smiled. "We need some new blood with good ideas to help protect the Pack. Kade's taking over Adam's job for as long it is needed, but I want you to help him."

"Okay," Josh answered.

Reed gripped Josh's hand harder and leaned into Hannah. His family trusted his mates. It was a far cry from when they weren't even allowed in the room during certain discussions. Things were coming together.

CHAPTER TWENTY-ONE

Blurry images filled with grays and blacks mingled with reds and crimsons flashed across Josh's vision. He squinted, focusing on the forms, trying to make sense of them. People milled around, moving past him. Josh tilted his head. Where was he?

He kept walking, past the stares of the people that had said they embraced him, sending flames into his back. The mummers of curiosity at his presence in their den stung like little pin pricks dancing along his skin. Why did he care what these strangers thought? He had nothing. No ties. Nothing to show for his efforts.

Deep, throaty laughter echoed along the forest's edge, calling him. He followed, the sound pulling him like a bull on a chain. A giggle broke through the masculine laughter, causing him to stumble.

His witch.

Hannah.

He changed directions, trailing after the voice that called to him.

The trees blurred, a smoky haze dulling his vision. He shook his head and stopped.

His Hannah stood in front of him naked, bare to the elements.

"Josh, I've missed you," his vixen whispered.

He strode towards her, intent solely on tasting her lips. She looked up, utter trust and pleasure in her gaze. Her skin felt soft under his trailing fingers as he led them to her neck.

And squeezed.

Her eyes bulged, a plea on her lips.

And he smiled.

———

JOSH SHOT up out of his dreams, panting heavily. He glanced down at his hands, thankfully they were not around his mate's neck. Swallowing hard, he looked down at Reed and Hannah, sleeping peacefully, curled into one another.

Dear God, what the hell had happened?

What kind of sick fuck would dream about squeezing the life out of the woman he loved? Shaken, he gulped and tried to calm his rapid heartbeat. The dream had started off peacefully as he walked through the den, but shadows cast doubt upon him, threatening to drown him in their forsaken promises.

Josh slid out of bed, careful not to wake his slumbering bedmates, and locked himself in the bathroom. He turned on the faucet and splashed his face with ice-cold water. He gripped the sink, swallowing the bile rising in his throat and looked at his reflection.

A flash of red passed over his eyes, and he bit back a scream.

Jesus, what was happening to him?

Was he in control?

He couldn't hurt Reed or Hannah. No. That would kill him quicker than a bullet searing his flesh. But what could he do about it? Leave?

"Josh?" Reed called quietly from their room.

"I'm okay. Go back to sleep; I'll be there in a minute," Josh promised.

"Are you sure?"

Josh shook his head again and walked back into the bedroom. He strode to the bed and kissed Reed softly on the lips. Oh, how he loved that now familiar sandalwood taste.

"I'm fine, just a nightmare." Just a horrific nightmare that threatened everything he had but didn't deserve.

Reed scrunched his brows. "Okay, get back in where it's warm." He lifted up the blanket, inviting him in.

Josh smiled then slid into bed, curling his body around Reed's naked form. He reached around and caressed Hannah, who lay sleeping in Reed's arms. He brushed a kiss on Reed's temple and settled in.

"Good night," he whispered.

"Dream well," Reed answered, half asleep.

Oh, if only he could.

———

LATER THAT DAY, Hannah and Josh were in her workshop getting a few things done. Water splashed on the sideboard, and Josh cursed. Dammit, his mind just wasn't on his actions today.

"Are you okay?" Hannah asked.

"Just clumsy." He smiled.

"Really, Mr. SEAL? Now why don't I believe that?"

He sighed. There was no hiding from this woman sometimes. Well, with most things. "I didn't sleep well, I guess." He shrugged and kissed her frown. "I'm fine. I got up in the middle of the night and splashed water on my face, and when I came back, I held the both of you. It helped."

Her smile could have melted glaciers. "I'm happy we could help, but I don't like that you can't sleep. Do you want me to make you something?"

Josh shook his head. He never did drugs—illegal or the herbal variety—they messed up his Finding, and he told her so.

"Maybe I can work with something. I mean, you have a psychic talent that must be related to magic in a way. If I dig deep enough, maybe I can find a way to help."

God, he loved this woman and her caring nature.

"Don't trouble yourself. I can work through it. I've been through worse." He shuddered, thinking back to his times on deployment when it was worse.

Hannah gripped his hands and ran her thumbs in soothing circles on his pulse. "I hate when I see that shadow in your eyes. I feel like I know you so well, but I hardly know anything about your past. Tell me, please?"

He looked down into her dove gray eyes and could have drowned in the warmth and worry. He'd never spoken about his family or where he'd come from before. Not to anyone, not even his buddies on his team. And those guys were the ones who he'd die for—and almost had. But he'd held himself back because there was a part of himself that he couldn't share. And now, in this weird three-way relationship, he was doing it again.

Josh sighed. He hated sharing his feelings, his thoughts. It wasn't something he did, something he could do. He was a SEAL, dammit. He'd die strong and in honor, and not by opening himself up.

"What do you want to know?" he asked after the silence stretched too long for him to get out of it.

"Anything, Josh." Hannah bit her lip, taking a steadying breath. "I'm not asking you to tell me all of your secrets. But frankly I don't know why you think you need to have any. We're bonded. Mates. I can feel you in my soul." She held her palm to her heart, fire in her eyes. "And even if we didn't have the paranormal connections we do, we're sleeping together and, in every way but on paper, married. I know *nothing* about you. How do you think that makes me feel, Josh? Like I'm not worthy. Like you don't care enough about me *or* Reed to share yourself with us. I know you are a SEAL. I know you are tough, and can protect us. But you're shielding yourself from us, Josh. It's like you take one step forward with our mating then take two steps back when you realize it's too much." She took a deep breath.

Dammit. His heart ached. He hated seeing what his inability to give a piece himself did to his mates. "Hannah—"

Hannah held up a hand, effectively shutting him up. "Wait. I know you're scared of what's going on with that bite and the Centrals. I get that. I'm scared out of my mind too. But we need to be able to get on with our lives while all this is going on. Because if we don't, then I don't know what to do. I don't know if I can take it anymore." Tears filled her eyes, threatening to spill over.

"Hannah." Josh pulled her into his arms, her shuddering body warm against his. "I'm so sorry, baby. I'm just not good at this. But I promise I'll do better."

She lifted her head, her gaze steady on his. "Tell me about your family."

Josh froze. Of all the things she could have asked, she'd gone there.

Hannah closed her eyes and exhaled, struggling to release herself from his grasp. He held her harder.

"I lived in Montana with my parents," Josh began.

Hannah quit moving; as if afraid he'd spook and quit speaking. Well, she wasn't too far off there. He'd better just get it all out now in one fell swoop to get it over with.

"We had a small ranch where we raised horses. It'd been in our family for generations. My father was good at his job, my mother great at being a homemaker. They had everything they wanted. A perfect normal life. Then I turned five and the little boy on a neighboring ranch wandered away from home."

Josh took a breath, bracing for the memories. The pain.

Hannah wrapped her arms around his waist, comforting him.

"I'd seen the kid before because our mothers had forced us to hang out together. So when my mom came in and told me the boy was lost, I closed my eyes and thought of him. It was a reflex. These images came at me of the boy walking out in the pasture after a stray cat and falling. I could see him clear as day, sitting beneath a tree with a bump on his head and tears down his cheeks. I thought the tree looked familiar, so I told my mom." Josh shrugged like it was no big deal

But it had been.

"Her eyes had widened, and she slapped me."

Hannah gasped, and he kissed the top of her head.

"Yeah, I know. It was like she knew what I was talking about, but didn't want it to be true. Took me years to figure that out. But anyway, my mom told me never to talk about that again, but I didn't under-stand. I just wanted to help the boy. So I told my dad. I don't remember exactly what happened after that, it's been awhile, but they found the boy eventually, exactly where I'd seen him."

"Was he okay?" She asked.

"Yeah, a gash on his head and sprained ankle, but he was okay. And so was the dammed cat he found." Josh let out a dry chuckle.

"The next day my mom took me to a shrink," he continued, trying to suppress the urge to vomit or flee. "Apparently this *affliction* wasn't a new thing for my mom. Her father had it and killed himself."

"Dear goddess, why?" Hannah's jaw dropped.

"I'm not sure, but my parents were religious fanatics, and apparently my grandfather was too. So maybe he thought it was cleansing. I just don't know. They put me in therapy and gave me a drug cocktail that fucked up my system. When that didn't work and I could still Find, they shaved my head and used shock therapy."

His body flinched at the thought of those electrodes and their pain.

"Oh, baby, I'm so sorry. What kind of evil human being does that to a child?" Hannah lifted to her tip-toes and kissed the bottom of his chin.

"They did that until I was ten, and then I guess they just gave up. Or maybe they couldn't hide the burn marks anymore. I don't really know, but I was fucking grateful."

"Me too. But what happened next? That couldn't be the end of it. And what about your dad?"

"My mom tried her own therapy while my dad looked the other way. She beat the shit out of me with the slightest indication I wasn't normal. She called me the devil's child, believing the only reason I was like this was because the devil put me in her womb. Doesn't make sense since it was her blood that made me the way I was in the first place, but that's how she rationalized it."

"Goddess. I really want to kill your mother, Josh."

"So did I. I stayed there until I was eighteen, and then I joined the military. I never looked back. I got some papers in the mail a couple years ago saying my dad had died from a heart attack and my mom had killed herself in grief. They gave the ranch to an uncle and left me out of the will. But I'm okay with that, honestly."

"I wish you would have been able to resolve some of the differences, but frankly, I don't know if you could have done that in this case."

Josh laughed. "Not so much. But I found another form of family in the SEALs. I used my Finding sparingly, only when I truly needed it. But I didn't tell anyone about it. I didn't trust anyone enough."

"Well, I'm glad you trust us enough."

Warmth spread over him at her words. They loved him. Truly. He wasn't alone. Didn't have to hide. He'd told Hannah his past, and she hadn't run away. Jesus, that felt good.

He looked down at her face, her big gray eyes, her pouty lips, and fell just that much more in love. He brushed a speck of dirt off her cheek then framed her face with his hands. This was it. His perfection. His future. Those dove gray eyes looked up at him with the unending love and support. Mix in the jade green from the man he loved and shared and Josh felt complete. He sighed. It was everything.

He leaned down and kissed her, the taste of bitter apples and honey melting on his tongue. He could drown in her taste and never get enough.

His body shuddered, and a graying darkness crept behind his eyes, pulling him deep, tearing at their bond. The bond trembled but stayed true. Josh lifted his head, curled his lip, and grabbed Hannah's ass, lifting her to the bench.

"Josh," she gasped.

He lowered his head and took her lips, shutting her up as he tore off their clothes. Lowering his mouth, he nibbled her jaw, her neck, then down her breastbone to her nipples. He bit down. Hard.

She buckled off the bench, lifting herself toward his face. He grabbed her and lifted, and she wrapped her legs around his waist, her core wet and hot against his dick. Josh kicked the clothes out of the way so he wouldn't trip and slammed her against the wall, not caring if he hurt her. Somewhere deep inside, he knew this was too hard, too brutal, but he didn't care. He only needed more of her. He took her bottom lip between his teeth and closed his eyes, too afraid they'd glow red like before and scare the shit out of her. Or worse, show her his secrets.

He positioned himself at her opening, her wetness telling him she was ready. In one thrust, he was inside, her pussy clenching around him.

"Josh," she screamed.

He reared back and slammed home again. And again. Her breasts bounced, and his balls clenched. He moved one hand up and brushed her clit. She came in a rush, her heat pulsating around his cock.

Josh lifted her, still deep inside, and pivoted, laying her on the table, knocking pots and dirt on the floor. He grunted, gripped her hips, and thrust. His body shook, his balls rising, ready for him to come. Hannah lay below him, eyes wide with passion, a rosy glow from her climax covering her skin, herbs and soil spreading on that milky flesh. He pistoned, grappling for that last shred of control before he lost it. She came again, a scream on her lips, and he followed right behind her.

He stood over her boneless form and took a deep breath.

What the hell had just happened?

Josh pulled out, his seed still spilling. Shaken, he reached for some towels and cleaned her. He didn't want to taint her with whatever he was. What if they made a child? Would it be like him? Maybe his mom had been right. Maybe he really was Satan's child.

He wiped her hips and cursed when he saw bruises clear as day in the shape of his hands. He was a monster, a fucking lowlife who didn't deserve the pixie in front of him.

Hannah looked up at him, her smile fading. "Josh? What's wrong?" She looked down and furrowed her brows. "It's okay. It's only a little bruise. I'll heal in a couple of hours. I liked it, really. I never knew you could be so powerful. You didn't hurt me."

Josh shook he head. "But I did."

"But I wanted it. Don't worry, Josh. I like how every time we make love it's new and different."

Happiness exuded from her, but he couldn't trust it. This time she'd been lucky he hadn't broken her. But what about the next time? What about when he couldn't control the beast inside of him?

CHAPTER TWENTY-TWO

The sun shone through the windows, warming Hannah's bare shoulders, her bruises long gone in the days since their love-making. But she still remembered them, felt them. She sat in Reed's studio, wearing only a sundress though it was winter, letting Reed sketch her. Her curly hair framed her face and tickled her back and shoulders.

She'd lied. Josh had scared her. Not the rough sex. No, that she'd liked. What had scared her was the way he'd turned into himself, like he wasn't really present. So internal, her Josh. He was doing his best not to be, but he still kept parts hidden, parts she feared would break out and destroy something she held dear. Not only their bond, but Josh himself.

Reed was so different from Josh. More open, more emotional. Yet he, too, hid a part of himself. This mate always had to be the smiling one—the happy one in his family. But he felt emotions so deep that it scared her and she was so happy he had her and Josh to lean on. With the amount of turmoil surrounding the Jamensons, Reed needed them because, if he leaned too far, he'd break. And she couldn't deal with that either.

"Hey, what do you guys want for dinner?" Josh asked, pulling her out of her increasingly depressing thoughts.

Reed smiled and laughed.

"What? Am I missing something?" Hannah asked. How on earth had that been funny?

"No, it's not funny; it's just that I'm happy." Reed shrugged, laughter still dancing in his eyes. "I love the fact the three of us are doing this. You know, the whole domestic bliss thing."

Josh shook his head, the edge of his mouth turned up in a slight smile. Hannah wanted to hold them both close to her and never let go.

"Well," Josh grumbled, "someone needs to cook. I'll die if I'm forced to live on a diet of cheese quesadillas and yogurt. I have no idea how the two of you have made it as long as you have. Reed especially."

Hannah rubbed her stomach. "Greek yogurt is manna. Yum."

"Sure," Josh answered. "I'll make rosemary pork chops then."

"Uh, Josh, what does that have to do with yogurt?" she asked.

"You could dip it in the yogurt," Reed answered, a pleased grin on his face.

Josh smacked him upside the head, a fake scowl on his face.

"No, that's gross. I want rosemary pork chops and the two of you aren't any help. No yogurt." Josh said.

"Hey, but what if I wanted yogurt?" Hannah whined, just to see the look on Josh's face.

He sighed and kissed her lips, lingering. "Fine, you can have it on the side. The things I do for love. Okay, I'll go take out the meat, then I need to head out to Kade's. He's going to train me on enforcer duties. I shouldn't be home too late. Kade said he wanted to be with Finn and Mel early."

He kissed them both and left.

"Okay, now quit moving," Reed said, and went back to his sketch.

Hannah watched, the graceful way his hands flew over the page. His talent amazed her. The utter beauty of his project and the way he immersed himself in every work he did just showed the breadth of his passion.

A passion that he'd used on both her and Josh last night.

"I don't know what I'm doing," she blurted out.

Reed paused. "With what?"

"With two men. This whole thing. I mean, this is so unlike me."

Her heart thudded in her chest, and her mouth went dry. But she couldn't take those words back, though she desperately wanted to. The thoughts and worries churning in her mind since she'd met the two of them struggled to get out. It wasn't that she didn't love them—she did. She couldn't, however, move on without talking about the fact they were a freaking threesome, something so taboo that only people in romance novels ever made it work. But this wasn't one of those—this was real life.

Reed set down his pad and pencil and walked toward her and cupped her face.

"We aren't just two men. We're your mates."

"I know, but it's so weird. I mean, not what we're feeling because that's incredible. But the idea of it just seems wrong. Everything's happened so fast."

Reed laughed. Okay. Not the ideal reaction. She bit her lip and fought the urge to hit him. How could he laugh at her feelings?

"You aren't the only one who's thought it, baby," Reed finally answered.

Wait. Was he regretting everything? Her heart pounded, and her eyes widened.

Reed held her close and shook his head against hers. "That isn't what I meant. It's just with the fire, the war, Adam, you, Josh, the demon..." Reed pulled back and shrugged. "Everything."

Reed leaned down, and she rested her forehead on his. "I know, I'm happy. Really." Wow, she seemed to be clarifying that a lot recently. "Any doubts I may have, I'm overcoming them. And I feel as though I know both of you so much better. But, Reed, you have so much history. I need to know more. You know?" Geez, first Josh, now Reed. She kept pulling and prying. Pretty soon she'd poke where she shouldn't, and she just might lose them. But she needed to know.

Hannah put her fingers on his lips when he tried to speak. She needed to get this out before she lost her nerve. "Not now. The three of us will get it over time. But I was a shop owner and a potion maker with my mom." Her voice caught, but she pushed down her pain. "I lived with my mom for most of my life. That's what I thought I would do. I would live a normal life span and maybe find a witch husband and grow old. I'm not sorry I didn't get that—I'm blessed. But I need to be more independent of the two of you and still be intertwined."

Reed kissed her softly. Heat pooled in her womb, but her mind whirled. "That's what a relationship is. Independence and connection. We will find the balance. Our bond is different because there are three of us and also because we aren't human. We are putting in three different types of people and melding them. Everything will calm down, at least with the three of us."

"And what about the outside world?" she asked.

Reed sighed. "Well, that's usually Adam's responsibility. But he's not here. Dad and the others say they can still feel him, so we know he's alive. But he's hurting. I hate that he's in this position, in so much pain."

"But there's nothing we can do about it," Hannah said softly. "We can only care for him when he gets back."

Reed choked, "I don't know how Adam can do it. I don't know what I'd do if I lost the two of you."

"I guess the best we can do is don't think about it. Submerse ourselves in the time we have and protect the Pack from what could come; it's all we can do."

"I love how wise my mate is."

"Well, it's true. I pretty much rock."

"That you do." He leaned down, kissed her nose, then trailed his lips on her cheek and found her mouth.

He tasted of sandalwood, wolf, and that special something she couldn't describe but was all Reed. She melted into his arms, worries and stresses of their conversation fluttering away as their kiss intensified.

Reed pulled back, his pupils dilated with passion. Goddess, she loved that smile. In it she could see their future, their love, and his nature, everything she never thought she'd wanted but everything she so desperately needed.

"Stay right there," Reed whispered. "I have plans for you."

Intrigued, she followed his path with her gaze as he carefully laid out a large drop cloth on the floor then went to a drawer and pulled out paint.

What was he doing? Weren't they going to make love? Why was he going to paint her? *Now?*

"Hey," he said, then kissed her softly. "Don't look like that. I told you I had plans for you." He picked her up and set her down on the cloth, then stripped her of her clothes, his fingertips tracing warm circles on her flesh as he did so.

Okay, this could be interesting.

He stood there, fully dressed, looking sexy as sin and undeniably hers.

"I love you, Hannah."

She didn't get a chance to respond because he crushed his mouth to hers, her nipples rubbing against the soft cotton of his shirt, sending tingles down her spine. He gripped her sides, rocking against her, then lowered them both to the ground. Kneeling, he stripped off his clothes quickly, then bent over to get a paintbrush.

Her breath quickened at the look on his face. His eyes had lowered and looked of molten heat.

"I've always wanted to paint you," he whispered.

"I thought that's why you sketched me."

"Oh, I'm going to paint your portrait, no doubt. But right now, I'm going to use these edible paints I bought and stroke you until you come. What do you say to that?"

She moaned. "Yes, please."

Reed smiled and picked up a brush and dipped into the blue. Her pulse raced as he slowly teased her stomach with the tip, and she shivered.

"It's cold."

"Let me warm you up then," he purred.

That was the response she was hoping for.

He leaned over and kissed her stomach, licking around the paint, nibbling her flesh. He raised his gaze, his long lashes utterly erotic surrounding his jade green eyes. Then he took one long lick in the paint, spreading it over her stomach.

Dear goddess.

"Tastes like sugar." He dipped the brush again, painting swirls and leaves along her torso, arms, and legs. Every time she wanted to move because he teased her so well, he tapped her with the end of the brush.

"Stop moving," he scolded. "I'm concentrating."

"But I want you. Please."

"You'll have me soon, I promise."

He changed brushes, this time using the silver paint. She bucked off the cloth when he bent and took her nipple in his mouth. He suckled and bit down, sending shockwaves of heat down to her core. When he released her, he trailed the tip of the brush around her areola, and she gasped.

She'd die if he did any more foreplay. She was burning up from the inside out, basking in her need of him.

But he didn't relent; he merely painted her other breast until she squirmed with need.

"There. My masterpiece is complete." Reed sat back on his haunches, looking like a cat with a big bowl of cream.

"Are you just going to look at me? Touch me. Please." Who was this girl begging for attention?

"Oh, I'll touch you. I'm going to lick every inch of you, then I'm going to take you," he promised.

"Can we skip the licking part? Not that that doesn't sound amazing, but I want you. Now." She moaned.

Reed gave a throaty chuckle, and she wanted to hit him. "Patience."

"Screw patience. Screw me."

He lifted a brow. "I like that mouth on you. I'd like it better on me. But that'll be later." Then he proceeded to lick every square inch of paint off her body like a starving man. She moaned and ached at every touch, every nibble, his touch sliding in every crevasse.

When he sucked her nipples into his mouth, she grabbed his hair to keep him there. Tendrils of heat curled around her body, soaking into her skin, bringing her closer and closer to climax. But every time she reached the edge, he pulled her back.

Damn frustrating man.

She closed her eyes, climbing to reach her peak, until she felt something blunt circle her lower lips and flick against her clit. She opened her eyes, wondering what it could be, and froze. Reed kneeled between her legs, a clean paintbrush in his hands and the rounded end without the brush playing with her pussy.

"These are clean, ready for you. I wanted to paint you, and I will," Reed growled.

She smiled and shook, then he dipped the end all the way in. The brush wasn't as wide as Reed or Josh, but felt so wonderful and smooth in her swollen channel. He slowly moved his wrist in a small circle, the edge of the brush rubbing against her g-spot. She almost came right there, but he pulled back, teasing.

"Please, Reed."

"Soon."

The brush rubbed again, but this time, he used another brush and painted her clit. She came hard against both, a scream ripping out of her throat. That had to be one of the hardest orgasms she'd ever had, and he hadn't even touched her with his hands—just his brushes. Talk about a new appreciation for art.

"Jesus, Hannah. The way you blush when you come, you're gorgeous." Reed leaned down and took her lips with his.

Her tongue danced against his, and she pulled him closer, wanting him inside. He cradled her face then moved his hands down to spread her thighs and slowly entered her.

Oh. My. Goddess.

How she loved this man.

She looked into his eyes, never breaking contact when he sank deep inside then pulled out and repeated it in a never-ending rhythm. With each pulse, she rose higher and higher, until she crashed down, falling into an abyss of pleasure, Reed following soon behind.

Breathing heavily, her mate collapsed on top of her, paint spilling around them. She held him close, soaking in his heat and scent.

"I love you," she said. "I never thought of playing with paint that way."

Reed growled in what could only be pure satisfaction. "I'm an artist; what can I say?"

CHAPTER TWENTY-THREE

Reed sighed. Dammit, that still wasn't the right color gray. No matter the blacks, whites, and silvers, nothing could blend together correctly. It looked drab. Boring. Not at all like the eyes of his mate that stared up at him with love and adoration. He growled in frustration, the sound echoing off the walls. No one was home to hear his annoyance, but it still felt good to release it.

It'd been a couple of days since their painting pleasure. Josh was out with Maddox, learning more about the Pack and what it meant to be an enforcer since Adam wasn't around. Josh had been gone most of the day, and Reed missed him. How silly was that? Like he was a teenage girl waiting by the phone for the quarterback of the football team to call. Josh worked hard at what he did, and according to his brothers was frankly a natural at it. He fit in to the Pack like he was born for it.

Hannah wasn't even here to watch him work or do her thing around the house. After their talk the other day, they'd decided she needed to do something on her own to feel like she was contributing to the Pack. Not to mention the fact that she needed to learn how to use her elevated Healing abilities. A friend of the family, Larissa's little girl, Gina, had a terrible cold that wouldn't go away, and Hannah had gone to help.

He shook his head. Since when did he need people in his house to keep him company? He'd spent nearly a century alone and lived just fine. Well, he had the numerous members of his family, but that wasn't the same. Despite himself, he missed that growly ex-SEAL and the curly haired gray-eyed beauty. They completed him.

Reed gagged.

He had *not* just quoted *Jerry Maguire*.

Okay, he needed to get back to painting.

Hannah's face stared at him from his canvas. Well, most of her face. He still couldn't get the gray right. The others hadn't seen it yet, and they wouldn't, not while it was still in the beginning stages. It felt too personal when it wasn't finished. Like he was a piece of a puzzle not fully formed, one that wouldn't match up with the others yet.

He added more silver to his mixture. At this point, it felt like a pointless waste. Could he even capture her spirit with a paintbrush? The way she laughed with a stroke of paint? The way she cried with a flick of the brush? The blush on her face with the blending of colors?

He'd painted others in his family, yet this was by far the hardest, the most personal. And Josh was next. Reed didn't even know where to begin with that one.

Reed shook his head. How on earth had he wound up with two mates?

He sat back on his stool and remembered another time he'd done the same thing, talking with Willow about her insecurities in mating Jasper. He'd told her he'd be happy with a man or a woman in his mating. Or even both. But he'd honestly never thought he'd actually be in a relationship with two other people.

The dynamics of the three of them were scary as hell. Not to mention the fact that his two mates had somehow secured jobs and positions in the Pack. But he hadn't.

He shook off his own insecurities.

What the hell? Talk about being a mess. He'd always felt a bit off kilter in his family, like he was lacking somehow. But it shouldn't make him feel like shit that his mates had found the place in the Pack when he couldn't.

How was this going to work?

God, how melodramatic could he get?

He was in a committed relationship with two people he loved. They were planning a future. Yet why did he feel so unraveled? So weird?

Maybe because Josh was acting weird. Those dark moments that Josh thought he hid so well were coming closer together now. The whole demon bite thing scared the shit out of Reed. He'd seen the bruises on Hannah's hips when he came home one day. She'd said she was okay with it, that the sex was consensual. But it scared him. And even though she denied it, he knew it had scared her too.

There were times during the day Reed found Josh standing in the middle of the room, clenching his fists, a hazy look in his eyes. Then the man would shake it off and smile like nothing happened. It chilled Reed to the bone.

He cursed. He'd kill the Centrals when he had a chance. Every last fucking one of them. They were only playing with his family because they could. He wasn't one of the violent ones in the family—no—that honor went to Adam and Kade. But he'd protect what was his.

———

HANNAH RUBBED HER HANDS TOGETHER, warming them. Was she ready for this? Cailin wiped Willow's brow as she squirmed. She'd only been the Healer for a few short weeks; now here she was, helping deliver a baby. Her skin grew cold and clammy, despite attempts at creating friction.

Okay, it wasn't a big deal. Just delivering a baby. Women did it every day. Not a big deal. Then why was she feeling light headed?

"Hannah, dear, do you need to sit?" Pat asked. "You're looking a bit pale."

"Here, let me help you." Mel came around the table and led Hannah to a chair.

She shook her head, clearing her thoughts. "No, no, I'm fine, really. I'm just new at this."

"Tell me about it." Willow laughed from her perch on the medical bed, her belly protruding and rippling in a contraction.

"Look at me, acting like an idiot, while you're over there taking this like a champ." Hannah mentally slapped herself. Talk about being selfish.

"I don't know about that." Worry flashed over her face, and Hannah ran to her side and gripped her hand.

"Hey, you're doing great."

"I'm so scared. I thought I'd be ready for this."

Pat and Mel laughed softly.

"Not so much, dear," Pat said. "I don't think I was ready for any of my boys. And I certainly wasn't ready for Cailin."

"You never are," Cailin said with a smirk.

"True, but you made it to adulthood. That's quite a feat."

Willow grunted and crunched up her face as another contraction hit her. "How did you go through this seven times, Mom? I mean, I don't think I can do it this once."

"Willow, it's a bit late for that now. Don't you think?" Hannah teased. She rubbed small circles on Willow's stomach, warming mom and the baby. Another contraction came, and she closed her eyes, concentrating on the pain wafting from Willow and syphoned it. This was her gift. She only hoped she did some good with it.

The door opened, and North walked in. Thank the goddess she wasn't alone in this.

"How are you doing, Wil? I hope these ladies are taking care of you. Everyone outside is thinking of you, hoping you're doing well." North smiled.

"That's our cue. Come on, Cailin, we'll go sit with the men. Now, Willow, baby, don't worry. North's delivered hundreds of babies, including his dear sister. He'll take care of you and my grandbaby." Pat kissed Willow and walked out the room with Cailin on her tail.

The Jamensons surprised Hannah with every turn. They were so close and at times were too much, but she loved them anyway. She had closed her eyes again and was concentrating on keeping Willow's pain down when Jasper walked through the door.

Okay, the amount of people coming and going was getting a bit distracting.

"I know, I know," Jasper said. "You said it might be too much for me to be here. But this isn't the eighteen hundreds. I need to be in here. I'll be good. I promise. I can take it"

North threw his head back and laughed. "Sure."

"What?" Hannah asked.

Mel shook her head, a smile on her lips as she held Willow's hand. "We kicked Kade out during Finn's birth. He growled a bit too much at every contraction. It's hard pushing a baby out while coddling a mate at the same time."

The room broke out in laughter, and Jasper hurried over to hold Willow's hand and give her a soft kiss.

Her eyes closed again, she pulled on her magic, infusing it into her patient with all her strength. Willow immediately stopped squirming and calmed.

"You're a marvel, Hannah. I wish you would've been here for Finn," Mel whispered in awe.

"I'll be here for the next baby."

"Uh, yeah. Give me a bit of time for that, okay?" Mel laughed.

"Hannah, you look like you have this under control," North said. "Do you want to do the actual delivery?"

Her eyes widened, and that faint feeling came back.

"I've never delivered a baby before, and I don't want to mess up. How about I just watch and help with the pain." *See, that didn't sound like a cop-out. I'm helping, right?*

"I trust you both." Willow gave a pained chuckle, and Hannah put more magic into her Healing. "Both of you just help me, okay?"

Jasper kissed her again, a pained smile on his face. "North knows what he's doing. He's an expert. Plus Hannah's our Healer; she'll help and learn"

Willow nodded. "Yes, for our next baby."

Her mate cringed. "Let's just get through this birth first, okay?"

Hannah smiled and leaned back during a pause in the contractions. She loved this family. Her hand came up on its own accord and rested on her flat stomach. She wasn't pregnant; she took herbs to make sure she wasn't. The three of them weren't ready yet. But they'd have babies in the future.

Her heart clenched. She'd have babies with two men. Two fathers. Totally remarkable and scary as hell.

Willow whimpered, and Hannah got back to her work. Peace flowed through her, magic filling the room and her patient. With one last cry from Willow, Hannah felt that little tendril of new life. A baby.

"It's a girl," North said, holding a bloody, wiggling infant. "Come and cut the cord, Jasper."

"She's okay? All ten toes and ten fingers?" Jasper asked.

"Count them yourself. Come and meet your daughter."

Tears filled her eyes as she massaged Willow's stomach to help with the healing.

"Brie," the new mom whispered in awe.

"Brie, baby. We have a daughter." Jasper cradled the little form and stared down.

"Jasper, let me clean her up and make sure she's okay," Hannah said. She wanted to make sure everything was perfect with baby Brie. After all, this was her first birth.

The new father nodded quickly and placed the newborn in her arms. She set Brie down on the padded counter and cleaned her off, staring into those beautiful blue eyes all babies seemed to have. Once cleaned, she set the baby in Willow's outstretched arms. Tears ran down everyone's cheeks. Hannah washed herself off and walked out of the room to see her boys.

Mel was already there, relaying the news of the new addition, but Hannah only had eyes for her two men. Her men. She fell into their arms, holding them close, inhaling their scent. This was everything she'd never dreamed of. This was her perfection.

CHAPTER TWENTY-FOUR

J osh looked around the empty house and sighed. After training all day, his muscles ached to the point that even his hair hurt to move. It was like training in the SEALs all over again. Yeah, because of the damn demon bite, his strength had increased, but those werewolves could kick serious ass. All he wanted to do when he got home was have a good meal then hold his mates close. So what if he sounded like a pansy? Frankly, there was no way he could have sex tonight. He was just too fucking tired.

Okay, he could probably have sex tonight. *If* his mates provided the temptation.

He chuckled. Okay, whom was he kidding? His mates *always* provided the temptation.

But they weren't here to do that. Reed was out at the elders' cottage doing some painting work for their scrolls. Whatever that meant. Hannah had decided to stay at Willow's tonight and help with the baby since Jasper needed to go out with the youths for a hunt.

Josh smiled at the thought of Brie in his arms. Such a small bundle of warmth. She was like a little person, all wrapped up in a pink blanket.

He snorted.

Yeah, she was a little person. Just like Finn. He'd never thought he'd hold a baby, let alone be contemplating having one of his own. But they would. The look in Hannah's eyes when she held that baby was a clear sign she wanted that.

Fatherhood.

For some reason, that didn't scare him as much as it should.

A sharp pain ran up his arm, over his shoulder, through his neck and cheek, then pierced his temple. He grunted then almost puked at the smell of rotten eggs overloading his sinuses. He ran to the bathroom and washed his face. His hands tightened in a firm grip around the sink edge, and he looked at himself in the mirror.

What the hell was going on?

If he didn't know any better, he would have thought he was having a seizure. But he didn't think so. No, this was because of that damn bite.

He splashed water on his face again then dried it off with one of the towels Hannah had bought to brighten up the room.

Like she planned on living here forever.

Something he desperately wanted to do, but it didn't look like it would happen. Not with whatever clawed beneath the surface of his skin, something he didn't want to think about.

A knock on the door startled him.

"Josh? Is everything okay?" Reed asked.

He put the towel back and tried to regain some composure.

"Yeah, I'll be out in a minute."

"Are you sure? I smelled your fear from the front door."

Fucking werewolf noses.

"I'm fine, really."

Reed sighed through the door. "Okay, I'm going to go and work on the deck while we still have some light. Do you want a beer?"

"Sure."

Off and on for the past few weeks, they'd been building a wraparound deck to add on to the one in the back yard. Jasper or Kade, who owned their own contracting business, could have done it in a pinch. But Reed and Josh wanted to do it themselves, use their own hands to build their home.

Plus, he liked watching Reed without his shirt on. Even in the dead of winter, Reed would peel off his sweaty shirt and work. Werewolves were damn hot. In every sense of the word.

He should know. He'd had Reed in his arms, against his chest the night before. He shook his head. Who'd have thought he'd be in a committed relationship? Not only with a loving, curly haired, curvy woman, but with a sexy male werewolf with a sensitive side. Talk about odd. But he loved it. Loved them.

His ears rang as his headache roared back.

Okay, enough thinking about that.

He gave his reflection one last look in the mirror and tried not to think of the flash of red that illuminated the dark.

Josh walked out of the bathroom, through the house and stopped in his tracks. Reed stood shirtless, resting against a pillar. His throat worked as he swallowed his beer, his lips wrapped around the bottle opening.

Damn.

Josh broke out in a sweat and tried to think of something to say.

Reed smirked and quirked a brow.

Yep, the man could read his mind.

He passed Josh a beer and winked. Damn arrogant wolf. He could have been thinking about Hannah, and that's why his erection tented his jeans, straining at the material. Though now that Josh thought about her and those pouty lips, the teeth of his zipper dug into his dick. Fuck, that'd leave a mark. He adjusted himself, then let the cold brew go down his throat. Hopefully that'd take an edge off the heat coursing through his system. Sure.

"You ready?"

Hell yeah. An image of Reed on his knees, sucking him off as he thrust down the man's throat made him groan.

Wait. Ready for what?

Reed laughed and tossed him a hammer, which he barely managed to catch in his current state of arousal.

"I meant to finish the deck. But if you want to hammer something else, I'm game." He raised a brow.

"Oh." He cleared his throat. "We need to finish this before we get another storm, but I'll take you up on that offer later."

"I'm sure you will."

With that, they got to work, laying down planks and hammering nails until their work resembled the deck they were going for.

"Shit," Reed growled.

Josh broke out in a laugh. "I thought werewolves had amazing reflexes. How the hell did you hit your thumb?"

The other man scowled and shook his hand. "It's not my fault. I was distracted."

"Oh really?"

"Yeah, you were bent over in front of me, shaking that ass of yours as you worked that last piece of wood. What do you expect?"

He swallowed hard. "You're gonna blame me for that?"

Reed shrugged. "Pretty much."

"Okay then." Deliberately, Josh turned around and bent over again, inspecting his work.

His mate groaned and walked up behind him, resting his hands on Josh's thighs, rubbing the worn denim. He wiggled his butt, something out of character for him. He was usually the dominant one, not the playful one. But being with Reed in this position sent shivers down his spine and made him want to submit to him.

"You know we haven't actually done this since the night in the forest," Josh said. They'd slept with Hannah and touched a bit, but they hadn't shared sex between the two of them. A fact that bugged Josh. Didn't Reed want him?

His lover leaned over and kissed his cheek. "I know. I didn't want to come on too strong and jump you every day. Though the thought did cross my mind."

"Are we done here?" he grumbled. "Let's get inside. I know you don't have neighbors, but the idea of giving anyone a show might be too much for me."

Reed laughed. "Come on, big boy." He slapped his ass and walked into the house.

Slightly offended, he rubbed the sting as he followed him. "Big boy?"

"Well, it's the truth. Ask Hannah." Reed frowned.

"What do you mean by that?"

He shrugged. "Maybe I want to know what it feels like. What Hannah feels."

Josh gulped. "You mean..."

"Yeah." Reed shook his head. "But don't worry. I mean, it's just a thought."

He blinked then brought the other man in close for a hug. God, to think this man needed reassurance that he loved and wanted him, floored him. That meant Josh wasn't doing his job. Yeah, his own identity shit took up most of his thoughts these days, not to mention the changes in him. But that didn't mean he had to neglect Reed.

He took the other man's chin in a firm grip. "Never, *ever*, think I don't want you."

Reed exhaled a shaky breath. "I know that, Josh."

"Do you?"

He laughed a hollow laugh. "God, I'm such a middle child."

Josh chuckled and kissed his forehead. "No, you just aren't the beat-your-chest-and-drag-your-mate-back-to-the-cave by their hair type of guy your brothers are."

They both laughed until tears leaked from the corners of their eyes.

"Besides," he continued, "I can do enough of that for the both of us."

"True."

He ran a hand through Reed's sandy blond hair "I do want you. In every way."

His mate growled and pushed him down on the couch. They shed their clothes, nibbling and licking at each other's skin. Josh could drown in that sandalwood scent. He twisted his body and crushed his mouth to his. The other man tasted of beer and that rich taste that was all Reed, so different from Hannah. But oh, when they both melded together in a medley of deliciousness, it was incredible.

Naked, he slid his hands up and down his lover's body, relishing the smooth contours of his body and the way the muscles on his stomach contracted and clenched when he trailed his calloused fingers up them. Reed lay beneath him, rubbing his hands down Josh's back and gripping his ass. Josh thrust in the same rhythm as Reed's rubbing, his cock sliding against his lover's. Thick tendrils of desire wrapped around his spine, and his balls grew heavy.

This was the first time it was only the two of them. No Hannah. He noticed the lack of her presence but had also wanted to know what it felt like to be with Reed alone.

"Damn," he grunted. "I want you."

"Then have me." Reed gripped his cock and pumped him.

Josh almost buckled of the couch and came. So different from Hannah. He loved her small hands on him, the way she twisted and worked him slowly. But with Reed, there wasn't any caution. Just pure passion and strength.

Jesus. He was one lucky man.

"You need to stop that," Josh choked. "I'm not like you; I don't have your kind of recovery time. I don't want to come until I'm inside you."

They both shivered at the thought.

"Then get inside me," Reed rasped.

"Oh, I will. But first I'm going to taste you."

"Fuck."

Josh knelt in front of Reed and took him in hand. He pumped his fist then slid slowly back down before rolling the other man's balls in his palm. Reed tilted his hips, and Josh licked the drop of pre-cum on the crown, letting the salty taste settle on his tongue before swallowing him whole.

They'd done this a few times before, but he still felt like he was learning how to please his lover and trying to find a rhythm both of them liked. That's what made this relationship feel real—the fact that they talked and tried to see what felt good. Josh relaxed his jaw and took him deeper, letting the other man's cock touch the back of his throat before he hollowed his cheeks and sucked. He lifted his head and released him then repeated the process until Reed panted with need, thrusting his hips.

"Shit, I'm gonna come."

Josh locked his hands around Reed's hips and swallowed that heady taste until he'd milked every last drop. He pulled back and let go of the man's still hard cock with a pop.

"I think I just died."

Josh licked his lips. "What a way to go."

Reed smiled then rolled over, putting his ass in Josh's face.

"Are you trying to tell me something?"

The other man laughed. "Well, I didn't mean to be that obvious. No, I was just reaching for the lube. Can you get it? It's in the drawer in the bottom of the side table. I'm too boneless."

Josh raised a brow and looked at the rock hard erection pressed between his lover and the couch.

"That's not what I meant."

"Oh, you aren't boneless at all, babe."

He laughed then dug around the drawer for the lube. His heart raced at the thought of what he was about to do. Such an unknown territory. Taboo to most. But, fuck, he wanted this.

"Uh, Reed, we may have to move the lube to a different room at some point. Not that I mind the fact that we are ready in every room in the house. But once Finn and Brie are big enough to walk around, that could get a little embarrassing."

Reed laughed. "Not to mention our children."

Josh smiled and ignored the headache forming then lowered his head to bite Reed's lip.

"Tell me what to do."

"Just rub me. Circle the rim with lube then put a finger in to stretch me out. Eventually you should be able to get three in. Okay?"

He took a deep breath and tried not to come just at the thought.

He dabbed his finger with the lube, then dribbled it on Reed's crease and his lover shuddered.

Nice.

He circled the rim, loving the way Reed clenched in response. Slowly, he entered a finger, and Reed clamped down.

"Shh, relax." Josh rubbed circles on his lover's back, and he calmed.

He played some more then added a second finger, finding that bundle of nerves that Reed played with on him then circled it.

"Yeah, right there, Josh."

He fucked him with his fingers, adding a third one when he was ready. Josh pulled out then stood behind him, positioning his cock at the entrance.

"Ready?"

"Always."

Josh pushed forward, the head of his cock disappearing into his lover's ass. Fuck. He'd never felt anything like it. So hot. So tight. So different from Hannah. But he wanted her too. Wanted them both. Fuck.

He pushed forward, pausing at intervals while Reed adjusted to him. Finally, his legs touched the back of his lover's. Josh paused, sinking into the feeling of the vise around his cock. Then he pulled back until just the head remained buried and slammed forward again.

"Josh."

"Reed."

He grunted then thrust over and over, panting, sweat dripping, until only the sounds of pounding flesh and groans filled the room. The couch shifted forward with each thrust, and Reed pushed backwards, wanting more contact.

Lightning shot up his back, tingling his arms and legs, ending in his balls, until he came with a shout, his body pumping his seed into his mate, Reed soon following. Josh collapsed on top of him, his cock still buried. They were both sweaty and he pulled out then rolled them to the floor, a tangle of limbs and heat.

"I love you," Reed whispered. "That was fucking amazing."

"I love you, too. And tell me about it."

Pain shot up his arm, and his head throbbed.

Reed got up on one elbow and ran his fingertips down Josh's temple. "What's wrong? Are you okay?"

"Never better," he answered through tight lips.

If only that were true.

CHAPTER TWENTY-FIVE

J osh scratched at the scab on his arm, frustrated the damn thing wouldn't heal fully. No matter what Hannah or North did, it still looked like a gaping wound. At least it didn't bleed anymore. But it was beyond annoying.

Pin-pricks of sensation danced along his skin, ending at his temples. Growling, he rubbed them. Why wouldn't this damn headache go away? It'd been acting up, getting progressively worse for the past week, since his interlude with Reed on the couch.

The three of them had made love every night, in various positions and couplings, and he felt closer to the both of them. Like they were a real family.

Blinding pain shot across his body, and he fought the urge to vomit. He let out a string of curses.

Hannah ran into the living room and held her hand out. "I felt your pain across the house. Let me help."

He stepped back, cradling his arm. "I'm fine," he bit out.

Her eyes widened, and Reed stepped into the room.

"What's going on?" he asked.

Josh shook his head. "I just have a headache and acted like an ass." He shifted closer to Hannah and kissed her softly. "I'm sorry, baby."

She smiled, but her eyes still look weary. "It's okay. Pain makes everyone nasty. But let me help." She held out her hands, and Josh shook his head.

"I'm fine, really." Something nagged at him, some reason not to let her touch him. He didn't know why, but she couldn't be allowed to Heal him.

She shrugged but still looked hurt. "Fine. But please let me know if something is wrong. I want to help. Okay?"

He didn't answer.

She brushed a lock of hair out of his eyes and reached up to place her lips on his. When the kissed ended, she walked back into the living room to look over a few of the Pack's medical books she'd brought over from North's clinic.

Josh looked over at Reed, who scowled at him.

"You're not fine," he growled.

"Back the fuck off. I just need a minute," Josh's voice raised with each word.

Why the hell was he yelling at him?

Reed growled again, this time his eyes glowing gold. "Watch it. Please."

"Reed, leave off," Hannah scolded. "Come and help me. Josh needs some space. I need your help placing names in this book with the faces I've seen."

"Always the mediator, our Hannah," Josh snarled.

What the fuck is going on?

"Josh, what's up your ass? Why are you acting like this?" Reed asked, both anger and sadness on his face.

I have no idea.

"What? I can't act like I want to? I can't speak my mind? I'm sorry if I don't want to act like the husband in this calamity of a relationship with the two of you. I'm not a sick fuck who needs this shit." His vision reddened. The fury of his lies and anger tasted metallic on his tongue, but urged him to stand tall.

Reed scowled, pain in his features.

Hannah paled, her breaths shallow. "Josh, why are you saying these things? What's wrong?"

"You're what's wrong. Everything about this. I don't want this. I just want to go back to what I had and not even think about the two of you and your fucking mind games."

"Josh." Reed lowered his voice to a guttural growl, his eyes shiny. "I love you. Hannah loves you. But you can't speak to us this way."

He screamed, his fury echoing off their walls. He stumbled forward and shoved everything off the counter. Hannah yelped, and Josh turned towards her.

Just like the dream. Her neck begged for his hands. Josh clenched his fists, his mouth salivating for the kill.

Reed jumped in front of Josh's prey, protecting her.

"I don't need this!" he screamed. "I don't need the two of you."

"Calm down, Josh," Reed soothed. "Let's just talk about this."

Hannah bit her lip, her eyes shiny. Why didn't his prey cry? Shouldn't she be sad? Her breaths grew shaky, her curly hair bouncing on her shoulders with each movement.

"Please, let us help," she whispered.

Josh screamed again, a red haze filling his vision. The room lit in an eerie red glow. Apparently it wasn't just his vision that was red, but his eyes as well. "I don't need your fucking witch and werewolf help. I was fine before I met you. And I don't need you now."

He picked up the clay sculpture of a curly-haired girl Reed had made for him and threw it into the wall. It shattered into a hundred pieces, and Josh reveled in it. He turned from them and ran out the house, destroying more as he went.

The cool air brushed his face as he left the porch.

Wait. Where was he going? Shit. Go Back. Find them. Apologize. Let Hannah Heal you. Anything to stop the pain. Not just his arm and head, but the bleeding in his heart.

A blinding pain came again, and he vomited in the bushes. Fuck. He needed to leave. Leave the Pack. Leave that sick filth behind him.

He didn't care where he ran; he just needed to go. A flash made him blink. Then he saw nothing.

———

471

HANNAH LET the tears fell from her eyes as the front door slammed. Her chest ached as she struggled to breathe.

Josh had left. He'd actually left. He'd just broken their things, said words he couldn't have meant, and walked out the door. Her heart quivered and she fought to remain standing. She'd thought everything was going well. The three of them were a family, and they'd been looking toward the future. They wanted babies.

She let out a sob.

"What was that, Reed?" she choked out.

"I don't know, baby."

She ran to his arms, sinking into his warmth. He sheltered her, holding her close and she inhaled that forest scent that came from his wolf.

"That wasn't him."

"I know. It was that damned fucking bite. We knew something was wrong but we pussy footed around about it. All we did was hope for the best and ask the elders. What the hell was that for, huh? I feel so useless. I'm a werewolf; I'm not supposed to be useless."

She took a steadying breath. "We can't just let him leave that that."

"I know, come on. He can't have gone far."

He held her hand and led her outside. He turned his face up to the wind and followed Josh's scent.

Oh, please let him be okay.

She didn't know what she'd do if she lost him. She loved Reed, but it was the three of them that made their bond work. Giving herself a mental slap, she shook her head. She couldn't think that way. They'd find him, restrain him however they could, and she'd Heal him. She'd use any power she could and find their Josh in the imposter that claimed him in fury.

Reed stopped and paled. Oh no.

"What?" she whispered. She bit her lip and looked around. She couldn't see their lost mate. Where had he gone?

"He's gone," he whispered.

"Gone?"

"He's gone. His trail ends here."

She looked around. Only trees and greenery surrounded her. Most

472

of the trees had lost their leaves before she moved in. Now in the dead of winter, their leaves lay like corpses on the ground.

"But there's nothing here."

"I know. It's like he disappeared." Reed gripped her hand and looked into her eyes.

"But what could do that?"

A pained look crossed his face, and he shook his head.

"Only one thing can do that, Hannah."

"A demon," she whispered and he nodded.

What had that demon done to Josh?

Reed pulled out his phone. "I need to call my dad. We'll find him."

Hannah let another tear fall down her cheek. Thoughts of what Josh's new ability could mean warred with what she knew of demons. She felt sick. "But what if we can't? What if the Pack won't let him stay because he might be a demon?

Reed moved the phone away from his ear as the person on the other end yelled. "Um, Dad heard that. Josh is Pack. We'll find him."

She wrapped her arms around her waist. They could only hope.

———

JOSH COULDN'T HEAR anything around him and didn't know where he was. He blinked and quickly shut his eyes again. That damned light that brought about the darkness hurt like hell.

Where was he? How had he gotten here? Wherever here was.

"I see you've made it."

He looked up. The demon, Caym, smiled.

Oh sweet Jesus.

He shook his head. "I don't know what's going on but take me back. Now."

Caym threw his head back and laughed. "You don't have any room to negotiate. But I didn't bring you here. You did."

His heart beat in his ears. "You mean I teleported here or something?"

The demon smirked. "Or something. You did it all on your own. But you won't be able to do it again. So don't try and go back to the

Redwoods. You aren't a full demon. When your powers came to fruition, you needed to find your maker. So you did." He shrugged, like telling a human he'd turned him into a partial demon was an everyday occurrence.

Maybe it was.

What the hell had happened? He needed to get back to Reed and Hannah. To apologize. To do something, anything, to get out of this new hell.

His head ached again at the thought of his mates, and he clenched his jaw.

Caym clucked his tongue. "Silly human. Stop thinking of them. That part of your life is over. You're not their mate, or whatever you thought you were, anymore. You're just like me. Something glorious. Every time you think of them, it will hurt. So stop."

Josh let out a hollow sound. Like it could be that easy. Like he could drop everything he wanted—no, needed—because a demon told him to.

Wait. What was it he wanted? His vision blurred and his memories grew hazy, like he couldn't quite reach that thought of happiness.

He knelt on the grassy ground and stared into the abyss. The demon brushed his fingertip along Josh's forehead, and he gasped. Ice cold skin left a fiery trail. He closed his eyes and let the demon's deep words resonate over his body. A sense of eerie peace settled over his rage and he calmed. Blackness swept over him and he slept.

———

"Wake up," a voice whispered at Josh.

He blinked. Dark eyes set in a tanned face stared at him.

He shot up and jumped away from her with a growl.

Dark hair in a tangle surrounded her face. she looked like she had curves, but was dressed in such baggy clothing he couldn't tell.

Who was this woman?

Anger crawled up his body and raged within him. Should he kill her?

"Stop fighting," she scolded, her hands on her hips. "My name is Ellie. I'll get you out of here."

He scrunched his brows. "But I don't want to leave."

A pained look passed over her face. "It's too late then."

"I don't understand. What's too late? I'm healed. I'm reborn."

She shook her head. "I'm so sorry. I was happy when you came and rescued your mates. At least someone should have their fairy tale ending. I thought it'd be over and you'd all move on. But I should have known. It's never over. Not with my family."

"Your family?" Now he was really confused. Why was she rambling about mates? He didn't have a mate. He only had Caym.

"I'm the daughter of the Alpha." She shrugged.

This seemed like it should be important, but he couldn't tell why. Bored with her, he turned away. He stood up, patiently waiting for his master to come and tell him what to do. Yes, that would be a good thing. He acted like a good soldier.

He'd prove his worth.

He hoped his task would be to kill the dark-eyed girl in front of him. He didn't like what she spoke of, because he'd never saved two people without the master telling him to. He didn't have mates. No, he had only himself and the demon who was his master. Pure satisfaction rolled over him.

The metal door to the room creaked open, and a man walked through, his master following. Josh stood at attention and waited for his orders.

The other man clapped his hands and leered. "Oh, this is wonderful. I love it. You've done well, Caym."

His master nodded regally. "Thank you, Hector," he purred.

Hector looked past Josh and scowled. "Ellie? What are you doing here? Leave. Go see Corbin. He wanted you earlier. And if I hear you disobeyed me and didn't go to him directly, I'll let him have you for two days straight."

Josh turned his head and watched Ellie shudder.

"Ah," Hector said with a sneer. "I see you remember the last time. Don't disappoint me more than you already do, child."

She ran out of the room, but she held her head high.

A strong soul in such a weak body.

"Well, Josh," he said. "I'm your Alpha. You will obey me."

Confusion swept through him. He thought Caym was his master. What was an Alpha?

Hector smacked him across the face with the back of his hand. Blood trickled from his lip, but he didn't move.

"Ah, Hector," Caym drawled, "he's a partial demon. He thinks he only answers to a demon. But if you punish him hard enough, he'll listen to you. It's part of his training."

Hector growled. Behind the Alpha, Caym gave a small nod.

Ah, his master wanted him to follow the Alpha. Okay.

Josh nodded toward Hector and didn't shout when the man's fist connected with his face. Nor did he when the man punched him in the ribs, the stomach, or any other part of his body. He took it. It was his due because that's what his master wanted. And he always did what his master wanted. No matter what.

CHAPTER TWENTY-SIX

R eed clenched his fists and scowled. He didn't want to be in this room, doing nothing but waiting. Josh had left. He'd walked out the door then vanished like a demon. Icy fear wrapped around his stomach and leveled him. Without a trail, they couldn't go after him. Couldn't find him. His mate, the other third of his heart. Gone. And turning into something Reed might not be strong enough to pull him out of.

Instead of running toward a goal that they didn't have a clear path to, he sat in his parents' home, talking about what they could do. Talk about futile. Hannah sat by his side, a broken expression on her face. She'd quit crying, almost like she'd given up. Utter failure washed through him. He'd let Josh walk away, now he let Hannah feel like there was no hope.

Reed glanced over at her and blinked. He was wrong. She sat like a stone, but not cold. Energy radiated off of her, like she was ready to pounce on any scrap of information that might lead to their mate.

He pulled her closer, her body melting into his. He'd mated a hidden warrior, a woman who'd find their mate by his side and kick ass while doing it. He couldn't ask for anything more. When Josh had spoken those venomous words, his heart had shattered. It took every ounce of strength not to hit back and demand the other man take them back, to pound on him until he was once again the man he'd fallen in love with. Not the monster lurking behind a red glow. But Reed had seen through the vicious words thrown at him to the man beneath struggling for control.

He sighed. He'd grown too complacent and fallen into a routine, practically sweeping their problems under the rug. The fault lay on his shoulders, a heavy burden if there ever was one.

"Hey." Hannah rubbed her palm on his knee, bringing him out of his thoughts. "Stop thinking that."

Reed lifted the side of his mouth. "How did you know what I was thinking?"

"It's all over your face." She frowned then bit her lip. "We did everything we could, but no one has seen this before. Josh is a first. There was nothing we could do. But that doesn't mean we can't do something now."

He nodded but didn't believe a word of it. There had to have been something he could have done to save him.

His arms tingled, adrenaline rising through him. He'd save Josh. There wasn't another option. He couldn't let his family lose another mate. Not like Anna.

The broken, dejected look on Adam's face filled his mind. The unfathomable anger his brother still carried after all this time had a tangible life of its own. Reed shuddered. He couldn't end up like that, and he refused to bring Hannah down too.

"We'll find him, son." His father gripped his shoulder, the familiar soothing of his Alpha's bond ebbed through him.

Reed shook it off. He didn't want to be fucking soothed.

"Really? And what then?" he shouted. "How can we save him? You didn't see him, Dad. You don't know. He's a fucking demon."

Reed panted and froze. Oh shit. Had he just yelled at his father? His Alpha? What the fuck was he thinking?

His father raised a brow. "You may be in pain, but I am your Alpha. You best remember that, son. But I'll let it slide this once."

He swallowed hard but didn't lower his gaze.

Hannah held on to his hand and squeezed. Calmness rippled through their bond, and he settled, finally showing proper respect.

His dad growled then shook his head. "I've never heard of what happened to Josh occuring before. But there may be a way to overcome it."

Alert, Reed slid to the edge of the couch. "What?"

Hannah tightened her grip.

His dad held up a hand, forcing Reed to calm. Dammit, he didn't want calm.

"Your bond," his father stated.

"What about our bond?" he gritted out. *Come on, speak faster. Josh might not have that much time.*

"The trinity bond is powerful."

"I remember you saying something about a trinity bond when we first mated, but I thought you meant because there were three of us in a bond."

His dad shook his head. "It's a powerful bond that has certain powers. The elders think it will bind a demon's power to this plane so he can't open another portal. Meaning that your bond can make the demon weaker and may give us an advantage in this war."

Reed stood up, anger pulsing in his veins. "Are you fucking kidding me? You've known about this the whole time? We could have done something before this. Why didn't you fucking tell us?"

"I didn't know until you called, Reed. I promise you that. The elders went into a deep trance and contacted the moon goddess."

"They can do that?"

"Apparently." His dad sighed. "It takes a lot of energy, but these are dark times."

"Okay, then let's use our bond to at least stop the demon."

"It's not that easy."

"Why?" His pulse pounded in his ears. The fact that they could bind the demon didn't help Josh, at least not directly. But it was something. Something worth moving toward and something that made him feel less helpless.

"We can't do it because I don't know if you actually have the bond."

"Huh? I don't get it. I thought you said we had the trinity bond." The vein on the side of his head began to beat harder. Reed rubbed it, trying not to attack his father for more information.

"Your bond whispers something different to me."

"What? I don't get it."

"It's not a normal bond. That's why I think it's the trinity bond. But it's not a full bond yet, so I don't know its truth or its strength." His father raised a brow and gave him a pointed look.

Reed cursed and paced around the room. "We aren't marked."

Fuck. Why did they wait? Oh yeah, because they didn't feel comfortable with the bite, because they wanted to wait until after the mating ceremony. They could've save Josh by marking each other. He was sure of it.

His body shook with rage and his arm shot out, his fist crashing through the plaster and dry wall. Pain ricocheted up his arm, but he welcomed it. It was a small price to pay for his stupidity.

"Reed!" His mother shouted. "That is not how you handle this. Go outside and punch something, fight your brothers, but do not attack our home. You don't know what marking would have done to Josh beforehand. He isn't a normal human anymore. We just didn't know. You took a risk either way, but at least this way you didn't potentially kill him. And it's not over. You can fix this. But not by breaking our home in the process."

Shamed, he pulled his hand out of the wall and stretched his bloody fingers. "I'm sorry, Mom."

Hannah grabbed his hand none too gently, and he winced. She clucked her tongue and didn't even look at him. "Stupid wolf," she muttered.

He brought his other hand up and brushed a wayward curl out of her eyes. "I'm sorry. I'm just frustrated that I was so stupid and reluctant."

She glared at him, a fire burning in her eyes, her curls swaying around her face. "You think you're the only one with the right to feel that way? Huh? I'm not marked either, Reed. Maybe that's why we've all been feeling on edge lately. Because we aren't truly mates with our supernatural halves—only our human halves. We've been denying it. And now its cost us Josh." Her voice broke at the last sentence, tears filled her eyes, but she shook it off.

They'd mated their human halves through their love making in the woods after the fire. He'd spilled his seed in both his mates, cementing the initial sparks of their bond. But without the marks on their shoulders, his wolf wasn't mated to them, something he needed to fix but had been too afraid.

He pulled her close, enveloping her in his arms. "I know we wanted to wait for our mating ceremony and for more information on Josh, but we can't wait any longer. As it is, we probably waited too long."

She nodded, her face pressing into his chest. "Now we need to find him."

"You might be able to through your bond, but it's tricky," his father said.

Reed's eyes widened. "I've never heard of that before."

"It's something that happens to some couples after a mating. Not all, but it's worth a shot."

"Then let's do it. Let's find him."

"We'll go with you," his father said. "But if he's where we think he is, we can't go through the boundaries protecting them. I can still feel Josh slightly through my Alpha bonds, but it feels oily—slick. I think, though, through your bond, you should be able to get through. The trinity bond should have enough power to do it."

"You think? All of this is just a guess?"

His father growled, but a sad look passed over his face. "It's the best you have."

Reed closed his eyes, praying for strength and whatever magic went into their bond. "Okay, let's go."

"Bring Jasper and North. We need to leave Kade and Maddox here to protect the Pack."

Reed nodded. No matter what, he'd bring Josh home. Demon or not.

———

JOSH HELD his stomach and groaned. Another wave of pain smashed through him and he threw up on the floor. His kidneys felt like mutilated raisins. He was sure his face resembled a black and blue likeness of his normal self. Bruises covered every inch of his body.

He took another breath and tried not to hurl again. As he did, he could feel his skin knit together, healing in soft bursts of warmth that itched.

Was this what it meant to be a partial demon?

He could apparently heal. His strength increased with each passing hour. He raged out more often than not. And he had flashed from one place to another with just a thought—once. The emptiness inside him spread.

He missed two people, but he couldn't think of whom. Flashes of gray and green, interspersed with laughter and heat filled his mind, but he couldn't remember who they were. His head pounded at the thought, and he promptly forgot.

The door opened, and Caym walked in. Josh bit his lip and pulled himself off the floor.

He must please his master.

"I like your obedience." Caym sneered.

Josh lowered his eyes. He wasn't worthy of looking at him.

"You've proven yourself to Hector by submitting to him. You will listen to him and follow his orders until I say otherwise. Do you understand?"

Josh nodded. Anything for his master.

"Your next mission will be to take back what has been lost."

He raised his head, keeping his gaze low. "Yes, master."

"I need the two that walked out of here by your hands. They are very important to me. They must die."

Josh nodded.

"You will bring them here, and I will drain them of their powers. And then you will have the pleasure of killing them."

"Yes, anything."

"The witch and the wolf will die by your hand. Good. Now take off your shirt." Caym raised the whip in his hand and grinned. "It's time for your training in obedience."

Josh quickly took off his shirt, not giving it a moment's thought. When the first blow came, he bit his lip but didn't cry out. He needed the training to kill the witch and the wolf. Anything for his master.

CHAPTER TWENTY-SEVEN

The Jeep hit a rut, and Hannah braced her hand against the door so she wouldn't hit her head. She gripped Reed's hand in a desperate attempt to keep her grounded. Her nerves frayed further as they moved closer to the Centrals' territory. She sat in the back seat huddled next to Reed, praying for the strength to get through this.

Because she had to. No other option remained Without Josh, they'd fracture and dissolve into the wind. He was their steady rock, the one that held them together, that melded Reed's outgoing personality to her hesitant and yet not-so-hesitant one, that took all of their strengths and weaknesses and made them better for it.

The car hit another bump, and Jasper cursed. "Sorry, guys, these back roads suck. But we're getting close." His knuckles whitened on the steering wheel, and another wash of sadness swept over her.

He'd left Willow and their new baby at home so he could be their backup for whatever danger lay ahead. North, in the passenger seat, rubbed his temples and looked just as stressed as Jasper.

The bond between her and Reed pulsed with each ragged breath. She could feel him in her soul. Not his pain, but his presence. That at least comforted her. But the bond between her and Josh felt like glass, like it could break at any moment, that any movement or breath would shatter it. She closed her eyes. Her teeth bit into her lip, and she concentrated.

Please, Josh. Be okay.

He had to be. She didn't know what she'd do without him. Or the man sitting next to her. But something from his conversation with his father churned her stomach.

"Reed?" Hannah asked. "Why didn't you mark me at your parents' house? Wouldn't it have been easier?"

North coughed up a laugh while Jasper snorted.

"What?" She looked at them both. "What did I say?"

Reed blushed. "Um, I wouldn't suggest that. The bite is an intimate thing."

"Oh, like it's personal? That makes sense."

North laughed again, and Reed kicked the back of his seat.

Okay, what's going on?

"No." Reed cleared his throat.

This could be bad.

Her mate smiled wanly. "Once I bite you, you'll orgasm."

"Oh." Her cheeks scalded, and she lowered her gaze from the brothers. *Talk about awkward.*

Jasper growled from the front of the Jeep, and Reed rubbed circles into her palm.

"What's wrong Jasper? Did I say something?" she asked.

North cracked up again. "I'm sorry. I'm not trying to be an ass. Really. Jasper gave Willow her mating mark in front of a bunch of us and most of the Centrals."

Oh geez. "So that means Willow..."

"Yes." Jasper growled louder this time.

Oh.

"Why would you do that Jasper?" Hannah had thought him a nice guy who cared for his mate with every breath he had. Why would he humiliate her like that?

"I didn't have a choice," he answered plainly, his grip on the steering wheel tighter. "They were going to kill her."

Damn Centrals. They messed everything up. Destroyed all of the precious moments.

Something else nagged at her.

"Reed," she said, "if we're going to mate Josh now, does that mean we'll have to... um...you know..."

Reed shifted in his seat. "I don't see a way around that."

"So Josh will, um...be really happy in front of everyone?"

He nodded in the fading light, but something flashed over his eyes. "What?"

He took a deep breath and shook his head. "To make sure the bond actually clicks and we can use whatever power comes with it, I'll have to mark you too."

She felt a blush rise up her cheeks. "You're telling me I'm going to have to come in front of whoever is in the room?"

Oh dear goddess. Talk about awkward.

Jasper cleared his throat. "If it makes you feel any better, North and I won't be in the room. We can't cross the barrier. So you won't have to do that in front of the family—like Willow did."

She had a whole new amount of respect for her Beta's mate now.

She closed her eyes and bit her lip. "Josh and I don't have to bite each other or you, right?"

Reed shook his head. "No, I'm the only wolf. You two can mark each other, but it won't add to the bond other than the emotional aspects."

She exhaled the breath she held. "Okay, then why can't the two of us just mark each other now?"

North snorted. "Please, not in the back seat."

Jasper shook his head.

Reed pulled her close, his calloused painter's fingers trailing goose bumps down her arms. He lowered his head, his lips pressing against hers, and she melted. She pulled back and panted.

"Oh my. I didn't mean while we were all still in the car."

North threw a wad of paper at the two of them, laugher dancing in his eyes above the nervous tension radiating in all of them.

Reed trailed his fingers down her cheek. "I just wanted to kiss you. I love you, Hannah. But I need to mark Josh first. Just in case."

His face shut down, and she couldn't read him. Couldn't feel him through their bond other than the faint wisp of his presence.

Her heart sped up and she looked into his iced eyes. "Just in case of what?"

He lowered his gaze then took a deep breath before meeting it again. "Just in case we're wrong and I can only mark one."

Her vision blurred, and her body shook. "You mean you might not be able to mark me afterwards. That the feelings we have are wrong and ugly? Is that what you mean, Reed?" How could he say that? They'd completed part of the mating that night in the forest. The three of them had made love and sent the tendrils of their souls through each other, anchoring them for all time. How could that be wrong?

"That's not what I'm saying at all, baby. But with the demon bite and everything attacking us at all sides, we can't be too careful. We are mates. I know it in my heart."

He held his fist to his heart, and she knew he desperately believed that. But what if they were wrong? The inkling of doubt spread through her and threatened to choke her.

"I trust you, baby. This just sucks." *What an inadequate word.*

Reed let out a hollow laugh. "Yeah, it does. No matter what, you and Josh are my mates. Mate marking be dammed."

She sank into his arms as dread filled her belly. What if it didn't work? What if all the powers of her Healing and the Pack couldn't save Josh?

The car lurched to a stop, and Jasper cut off the engine. "We're about a mile outside the Centrals' wards. I don't want to risk going any farther."

Hannah closed her eyes and felt her bond to Josh. Sadness swept over her. A small part of her had hoped he hadn't gone to the Centrals, that he'd be just fine and in a cabin somewhere, waiting for them. But no. She felt their fragile bond going into the dark abyss of the Centrals' den.

"I wish there was a way I could tell you to say here with my brothers and be safe," Reed whispered and kissed her temple.

"We're a team. Always."

———

JOSH TUGGED AT HIS CHAINS, and blood trickled down from the cuts created by the rivets from the handcuffs digging into his wrists. His muscles ached in their awkward position, but his legs barely had enough strength to lift himself off the floor so all his weight didn't pull on his arms and shoulders.

Where did the master go?

Shudders wracked his body, and his arm flared in pain. The bite mark had scabbed and scarred, though it now only ached for hours at a time with pain-free minutes in between. At least that was something.

Red light glowed in the darkness. According to his master, his transformation was almost complete, the rim around his irises almost completely red.

Good.

The metal door creaked open, and the daughter of the Alpha, Ellie, walked in. She held what must be his lunch in her hands but didn't look at him. Bruises covered her face, and her right eye was swollen shut. She walked with a limp, her left leg trailing behind her slightly, but she held her chin high.

"I have your lunch, Josh," she whispered.

He grunted. She wasn't the master. Why would he speak to her?

She shook her head. "Fine, don't say thank you."

He grunted again, and she put the tray on the floor before rigging the chains behind him so he could reach for his food but not reach for her. He grabbed his tray as soon as his chains loosened and shoved the roll and meat into his mouth. He barely chewed before he swallowed, then he slurped up the oatmeal in two gulps.

Ellie let out a disgusted snort but sighed. "Look at you. Look at what they've made you. An animal. Is this what you wanted to be? What you trained for?"

His vision reddened, and he swung his fist, connecting with Ellie's chest. She flew across the room with a whimper and crashed into the wall. A flash of pain and regret passed over him. What the hell was he doing?

"I..." He tried to talk, but nothing would come out.

She held up her hand and struggled to get up. He shoved the tray out of the way and tried to help her. Why was he trying to help her? She was just a girl. But when he tried to move forward, his chains held him back, just like the animal she compared him to.

"Don't bother." She whispered. "I shouldn't have antagonized you." She sighed and shook her head then winced. "I thought I saw something that clearly wasn't there."

What? He wasn't anything. Just the master's tool. Why would he be anything else? Maybe he should just kill...

A scent of honey and bitter apples mixed with sandalwood came to mind.

Home.

His body shuddered, and a fog cleared from his mind. Shit. Where was he? What did he do? Where were they? Hannah? Josh? Oh God, he'd hit her. How did he do that?

His thoughts jumbled together and his body convulsed as he took a deep breath.

"I'm sorry, Ellie," he whispered.

Her eyes widened, and she gave him a small smile.

"Fight it, Josh. I know it's not you who does these things. Fight it. Come back to them. We'll find them."

She took a step toward him, and the scents of home faded away.

"Find who?"

———

REED TOOK Hannah's hand and stepped lightly into the forest, on alert for any sign of the Centrals or their dark witch friends. An eerie silence enveloped him. But for their breathing, he couldn't hear a thing. Not even a bird or animal.

Not good.

Oily magic bore down on him, suffocating in its choke hold, as they continued toward the wards. Leaves brushed by his face and he flicked them away. His pulse beat in his ears, but he ignored the fast pace.

"We're getting there, Reed. We'll find him. We must. And we'll keep Hannah safe. Keep the faith."

Easy for his wolf to say. Reed shook his head. No, it wasn't. His wolf was hurting just as badly as he was. His wolf didn't have the mate mark and didn't feel the deep bond he so desperately desired. Reed had deprived his wolf half of that. More regrets piled on, adding to the ever-increasing pile of doubt and disgrace.

Reed growled. He needed to get out of his pity party. He could wallow later. Now he needed the strength to find his mate and keep his other mate safe. He was a fucking werewolf, dammit. A strong one at that. He could do this. Needed to do this.

He closed his eyes and lightly pulled at the thread that remained of their bond to Josh and followed its path to the barrier. When they finally reached it, they paused. Unlike the wards set at the Redwood den, the Centrals' didn't have the sense of peace surrounding it. That oily magic oozed through it and hazed its presence, shielding it completely from view. If it weren't for the bond, they wouldn't have been able to find it.

Hannah lifted to her toes and kissed his jaw. "Are you ready?"

"Ready to get him and get out. I love you, baby."

"Love you."

They closed their eyes and took a step through the barrier. Thousands of tiny pinpricks assaulted his skin. He fought the urge to scratch and howl, and he pulled Hannah closer to him until they found the edge. Immediately the sensation stopped and they gasped for fresh air. Reed looked around then pulled her toward a grouping of bushes and knelt behind them. He kissed the top of her head then shook his to clear it.

Though he wanted to stop and let Hannah take a break just to make sure she was all right, they couldn't. They were on Central ground now. For all he knew, the Centrals knew they were there. But they needed to find Josh. Now.

He looked down at his curly-haired mate and smiled. She absent-mindedly waved her fingers in the air, the earth around them moving in small cascading waves, mimicking her movements.

"Nervous?" he asked.

She jolted, her fingers stopped moving, and the earth fell quietly to the ground. "Yes, but I'm also making sure my powers are still charged after that sticky ward."

Reed's mind wandered to the time when Josh and he had charged her magic on the kitchen table, her body writing under him as she panted with need.

"I can always charge them for you." He grinned.

"Really, Reed?" she growled. "You're thinking about sex now?"

"I'm always thinking about sex. I'm a man." His smile fell, and he stood up straight. "But you're right. Let's get Josh out of here. Then we can have sex. That sounds like a plan."

She shook her head, her curls bouncing around her face. "Goddess. I don't understand the male species." She squared her shoulders and looked into his eyes, holding his hands "Let's go mark him and then you can mark me. Deal?"

God. The bravado in her voice broke his heart. He pulled her close and brushed his hand through her hair. "I love you, Hannah. This will work out. It has to."

She pulled back and bit her lip. "Sometimes I think you put a little too much in fate's hands."

He leaned down and kissed her softly, letting her honey and bitter apple taste dance on his tongue. "Fate brought me to you, didn't it?"

"And Josh."

"And Josh." The wind shifted, and he froze. "There. I think I can scent him. Dear Lord. It's him, but he smells different. I don't know how to explain it. But we need to find him. Be careful, baby."

Hannah nodded, hope flaring in her eyes. "I'm cloaking us somewhat. It's not the type of magic I'm strong in, but I'm trying. I don't know if the demon can see through it though."

He kissed her again, letting her know he had faith in her. "Then we'll see, shall we?"

———

HANNAH FOLLOWED Reed as he entered the stone building. It was a different one than the one where they'd met. Had it only been a few weeks ago that her life changed and she met her mates? Now their roles were reversed. Instead of Josh saving them, they had to save Josh. She only hoped she had the strength.

The earth pulsated around her, but it felt different here than it felt outside the wards. It was as if the earth was a prisoner as well, begging to be free of the chains the Centrals had placed on it. She needed to find her mate, but then she'd find a way to release the earth as well. It might not have been her initial duty, but her blood called for it. She needed it.

She looked around at the drab stone walls and sighed. She couldn't really feel where Josh was. He was here, but that was all she knew. Darn. If only she had a werewolf's nose. She couldn't scent anyone's trail, couldn't tell if anyone was around unless they walked on the soil. She only smelled the evil that possessed the pores of the compound.

Reed pulled her close, his heated skin warming her coolness. He tilted his head to the right then put a finger against his mouth.

Her heart sped up. They were getting close. Reed held her hand, and they crept down the hall, her body breaking out in goose bumps as they neared a metal door. Reed squeezed her hand, and the bond between them flared.

Josh was in there. Their mate.

Could she stand what she was about to see?

Did she have a choice?

Reed pushed against the door, and it creaked open, the sound echoing in the hall. Crap. Who'd heard that? Would they be coming for them? She didn't see any surveillance equipment like the one she was held in, but they could never be sure.

What she saw when she looked in the room made her blood freeze.

A bruised and bloodied woman ran from Josh as he growled and fought against chains. His muscles bulged, and his veins almost popped as he screamed in rage. He pulled at his bindings, and the metal broke.

The other woman stayed in the room, her wide eyes never leaving Josh.

Her shattered mate growled and bent to charge, and she did the first thing that came to mind. She threw herself in front of him, her palms raised and her gaze on his.

The rim around his irises were blood red, pulsating with a need that scared her. Tattoos of spiraled lines trailed up his arms and down his sides. His body lay thick with sweat, and his chest heaved with heavy breaths.

My goddess. What did they do to my Josh?

Josh growled and lifted his arm to swipe at her. Every ounce of love poured out of her through their bond, begging for something to hold. He didn't stop his violent movements, and she braced for impact.

A growl rumbled behind her, and Reed jumped and landed on Josh. Fists flew as Reed pushed Josh back, slamming both of their bodies against the wall with a crash. Josh screamed and clawed at Reed's arms, leaving layers of torn flesh, blood dripping from the wounds.

Hannah jumped when a small hand grabbed hers. The bruised woman squeezed and watched the door, presumably for anyone who could come in after hearing the loud noise of the fight between Hannah's two mates. She felt so useless. In the stark building, she was cut off from her magic. So she had nothing to pull on to separate the two loves of her life and protect them. She hated standing back. But without her magic, she'd be crushed like a bug between the two hulking strong masculine bodies.

The sounds of flesh slapping against flesh filled the room as the two men fought, and sweat poured from their bodies. Reed growled, his eyes glowing gold. Josh rasped out a curse, his glowing red. Blood seeped from cuts and gashes on both of them. Hannah instinctively reached for magic, but couldn't find any. Her soul ached, and dread filled her belly. She could lose them both.

Reed bent low and rammed Josh into the floor, pinning him. Hope started to make its uneasy pass through her. Could they beat Josh and save him? Josh struggled against Reed's strong hold and her wolf bent low, his fangs elongated on his still-human face, and bit into the fleshy part of Josh's shoulder where it met the neck. Josh screamed, and Hannah moved forward, a desperate need to protect them both from each other driving her, but the other woman shook her head and held her back. Hannah couldn't help. She could only sit back and watch and pray it worked. She hated being weak. Josh's body convulsed under Reed's powerful form. The bond rippled between the three of them, filling her womb with heat as energy pulsed in a rhythmic beat.

Tears fell down her cheeks, the salty taste burning her dry lips. Reed lifted his head, blood coating his lips, his eyes wet, and licked the wound shut. Josh heaved a breath and passed out. Reed held out a hand toward her, and she froze.

"Please. Now." A guttural growl.

The other woman released her hand. Hannah ran to them and knelt beside her two mates. She placed her hand over Josh's slow-moving chest. The heartbeat beneath her palm made her want to weep. Had they saved him? Reed brushed a bloody knuckle down her cheek then pulled her close, pressing his lips to hers. She could taste both men mixed with Josh's blood on her tongue. But it didn't gross her out; it was the only way to bring him back. With that taste, she could feel the hope of their bond growing and surviving. Reed pulled back, grabbed a fistful of her curls and leaned her head to the side, exposing her neck.

Please let this bond work. Don't let the mark be for nothing.

Reed bit into her shoulder, the piercing pain flashing through her and shocking her body. Was it supposed to feel like this? She thought it was supposed to bring her to pleasure. If it was this painful, did that mean she really wasn't their mate and she'd lose them?

And achy feeling of despair fought with the overwhelming pain in her shoulder, threatening to shatter her heart and soul. Just as she was about to give up hope, a viscous honey sensation slid through her body, coming to rest in her core. Her center thrummed, and she rocked against Reed, his erection brushing against her hip. He growled, the vibrations sending shivers down her body, and she came, shattering in her mate's arms.

Home.

Mates.

Trinity.

Forever.

Reed released her, and she slid down his body, resting her head on Josh's chest, his heartbeat steady against her cheek. Josh shifted, and she shot up. His eyes opened, a confused expression covering his face.

Her mind still foggy from the mate marking, she stared down at her clear eyed mate. His irises still had a rim of red but surrounded that clear, ocean-water blue she loved so much. Reed squeezed her shoulder and she fought the urge to throw herself on the two of them and cry.

"What did I do?" he rasped.

"Shh," she whispered. "It's okay."

Josh lifted his arm and held her face with his large, calloused hand before using his other to pull at Reed.

They'd done it. He was theirs. Thank the goddess.

A polite cough behind them pulled Hannah out of her thoughts.

The woman smiled. "I'm sorry. I know you guys are in the moment and everything, but we need to go."

She nodded and stood. No embarrassment filled her, though she'd just had an orgasm with an audience. She needed only to be with her men and get them the hell out of there.

CHAPTER TWENTY-EIGHT

Josh stood between his mates, his mind freeing itself from the fog that had threatened their mating. He'd been lost for so long, since the bite, but now he felt free, like he'd seen through the darkness and had come out on the other side. Not unscathed, but alive. Hannah, with her dark curls and gray eyes, stared up at him, and he could feel her soul wrapped around his, trying to ease his hurts. Reed fisted his hands as he looked around the room and through the door to make sure they were safe. With his new heightened senses, Josh knew it was safe. He could hear nothing outside the room coming for them.

He was home.

Well, at least on his way.

Josh pulled Hannah to him and kissed her fully on the lips, letting her honey and bitter apple taste settle on his tongue. It wasn't the time for it, but he needed it. Craved it. He let go of her and kissed Reed, letting their tongues clash in a harsher tone before he pulled back and took a good look at the other woman in the room.

A daughter of the Pack that had attacked him and the ones he loved. The Alpha's daughter in fact.

She was also the one who saved his life by keeping him grounded. She'd brought him food and talked to him when he would have rather screamed and fought. He owed her his life and would do anything to make sure she got a chance to live outside this hellhole.

"Hannah, Josh, this is Ellie. She kept me alive."

Ellie bowed her head and seemed to shrink into herself. What atrocities had she endured? He was responsible for some but not all.

"Ellie Reyes?" Reed asked, his eyes narrowing.

Ellie raised her head and met his gaze, defiance in her eyes. "Yes. The daughter of the Alpha. I won't waste my time defending myself by saying I'm not like my brother and father. It's not worth it."

Reed tilted his head and nodded.

"We'll get you out with us," Hannah promised. "Thank you for helping him."

Ellie nodded, her eyes wet with tears, but she didn't let them fall.

Josh grabbed Hannah's hand and led the way out the door with Ellie following and Reed taking up the rear. Nobody was in the hall, and they quietly wound their way through the deserted hall before they made it outside the building. The hairs on the back of his neck stood up, and Josh cursed.

Hector stood in their path, a cruel snarl on his face. "You think you can just leave, pet? No. I made you what you are. I ordered it. You are mine. And you'll do what you're told and kill those two. Now."

A wave of compulsion washed over him but didn't stick. He wasn't Hector's or Caym's pawn anymore. They'd lost. And Josh would make sure Hector wouldn't forget it.

"No," Josh growled.

Hector's brows rose, and confusion marred his face.

Oh, poor little Alpha. He just doesn't get it.

But he will.

Josh let go of Hannah's hand and leaped, his fist connecting with Hector's jaw before the other man had time to blink or defend himself.

Stupid wolf shouldn't have given him the strength. He'd pay.

The howls of other wolves reached his ears, but Josh had only one goal. Destroy his tormenter. At least one of them. Caym and Corbin would be dealt with later. Corbin may not have touched him, but the wolf had hurt his mates. Josh punched the Alpha with all his strength again, the feel of bone breaking and the sound of crunching a sweet symphony to his ears.

Out of the corner of his eye, he saw Ellie fighting another enemy, her nails digging into the flank of the opposing wolf. On his other side, Reed did the same with two other wolves, his hands forming claws and killing quickly and efficiently. Hannah pulled the soil and roots around them and buried anything that stood in their path.

"You shouldn't have given me the strength, Hector," Josh growled.

"You're still nothing, pathetic human," Hector spat, the veins in his neck bulging. The other man forced his hands to shift—a talent only the Alpha and a select few possessed—and swung his claws at Josh.

Josh howled in pain as the other man's claws gauged his arm and reopened his bite mark. Hannah screamed as a wolf jumped on top of her, knocking her down, its teeth bared. Reed grabbed the wolf by the scruff of this neck and took his other hand to break it then he flung the dead wolf against the wall.

Rage filled Josh at the site of his pale Hannah covered in dirt and blood, her eyes wide. He screamed, ducked another fist, then grabbed the bastard's neck and twisted. Hector's eyes widened, and with an echoing crack of his spine, his evil glare deadened. The Alpha's corpse fell to the ground with a plop.

No sense of retribution filled Josh, no feeling at all but the desire to go home and be with his mates.

―――――

REED EXHALED at the sheer daunting strength of Josh's hold.

Dear God. What had the Centrals done to him? It didn't matter though. He was theirs and Reed wouldn't let Josh go again.

Leaves crunched under feet as Caym and Corbin walked toward them.

"I see my charge has learned a new trick," Caym drawled.

Reed went on alert, putting Hannah behind him, Josh doing the same with Ellie. Caym and Corbin stood on top of a hill about two hundred feet ahead of them. A grouping of wolves in human and animal form stood between them.

"You're a traitor, dear sister." Corbin sneered.

Ellie stepped out from behind Josh and raised her chin. "I'd rather die than stay here with you."

"Good," Corbin growled. "Because I'm going to kill you slowly. After I play with you some more, my pet."

Ellie shivered but didn't move nor did she lower her gaze. Good girl.

"Your father is dead," Reed snarled. "We won't hesitate to kill you as well."

Corbin threw back his head and laughed. "Are you kidding me? You did me a favor. That bastard deserved to die. He didn't have the vision I have. Now I'm Alpha. I should be thanking you. But I think I'll kill you instead."

Josh growled on the other side of Hannah and clenched his fists, Ellie joining in with a growl of her own.

Oh, he already liked her. She was nothing like her family.

Hannah lifted her head, quirked a smile, and waved her fingers. A wall of dirt and rocks slammed into the wolves in front of them. Whimpers and growls echoed and Reed let out a yell.

It was on.

Corbin and the other wolves fell to the ground, the dirt burying them, but Caym stood tall and raised a brow, the magic not harming him.

Bastard.

The other wolves dug their way out of their dirt grave and ran towards the four of them, teeth bared, eyes glaring. Hannah hit them with another round of soil, but some broke through. Ellie charged, picking up a wolf and slamming him into the ground, Josh following with the same. Reed rushed forward, grabbed a wolf, and dug his claws into its pelt. It whimpered, and he snapped its neck and threw it across the field. More wolves came at them all. They tore at his skin, but he was stronger. They did the same to Ellie and Josh, but they pushed farther. Hannah stayed behind and used the earth to protect herself and the others as she went on the offensive.

Sexy as hell.

Hannah ran to Reed, grabbing his arm, and he pulled her toward Caym. Even though they'd fought against the attack, they needed to get close to the demon to use their bond. That much he knew. They needed to bind the fucker, though he didn't know how to do it. But being near him would help. It had to. Josh followed them, protecting Hannah's other side. They reached halfway up the hill where the demon stood with a smirk on his face then were thrown back. Reed landed with a crunch on the ground, pain radiating up his back. Hannah lay on her side, her body close to his.

"Hannah," He reached for her, and she shook her head.

"I'm okay. Just knocked the breath out of me. Josh?"

"I'm fine," Josh growled "But that fucker can't get away with this. We need to *do* something."

Reed grabbed both of their hands, their bond pulsating between the three of them. Hannah held on to Josh, and they all looked at each other. Dirt covered their faces. Blood splatter and cuts dotted them like a mosaic of carnage.

This was it. Their only chance.

Reed closed his eyes and pulled deeply on their bond. Warmth and energy pooled and resonated through them. As a unit they used this mass of energy and power and pushed it toward Caym. Reed's body shook as the power flowed through him. Immense heat made his body break out into a sweat, but it didn't hurt. White light erupted all around them and Hannah screamed. Josh grunted and Caym's eyes widened.

This was the trinity bond.

Caym screamed in pain, his body convulsing as a bright light surrounded him. Reed held onto both his mates' hands, not letting go for the world. Whatever magic their bond held, he didn't want to sever the connection. The demon writhed on the floor, the light dispersing, and his screams faded into a hiccupped pant.

"What have you done?" Caym panted.

The three of them let go of each other and released the power of their bond. Josh started to run up the hill, Reed and Hannah on his heels. This might be the only chance. If they could kill the demon now, it would be better for them all.

Caym screamed, and fire trailed out of his fingertips, cascading in waves around him and flicking against the trees.

Demon fire.

"Hannah, Josh, stop!" Reed yelled and pulled Hannah close as a flame came at her.

Josh fell back and pulled Hannah's other arm until the three of them were away from the fire. But it wasn't enough. The flames came closer, licking and burning anything in their path. Red and orange flames danced along the tree line, burning an unforgiving trail. Josh covered Hannah with his body as the fire didn't seem to hurt him. The heat radiated off the flames, searing Reed's hair on his arms. Smoke filled his lungs and he coughed. The corpses of the dead wolves burned to ash, and Corbin now stood near Caym, bleeding but still alive.

"We need to go. Now!" Reed yelled over the roaring flames.

Josh nodded then turned and ran toward a body on the ground. Shit. Ellie. Josh bent and picked her up just as a tree fell directly where she had lain. He ran toward where Hannah and Reed stood. It didn't look good, but Reed could see at least the rise and fall of Ellie's chest.

Thank God.

The fire surrounded them but for a small gap, and Josh ran toward it, the fallen wolf in his arms. Reed held Hannah's hand and followed Josh into the forest. The leaves crunched beneath their feet as smoke filled their lungs.

Josh stopped and looked behind him. "I don't know where I'm going, guys."

Fuck. Reed wondered where his mind had been. "Follow me."

He ran forward, practically pulling a tired Hannah in his wake. The fire roared behind them, coming too close for comfort. Hannah tripped over a root. Reed cursed and picked her up, cradling her to his chest. Why hadn't he held her closer before? She was a witch, not a wolf or whatever Josh now was. She didn't have their endurance.

They ran farther away, the fire losing ground behind them. Reed didn't have time to think about what happened, including the fact

Hector was dead, and Corbin, though hurt, was now the Alpha. He couldn't comprehend they'd actually bound a demon or the fact that he'd marked Hannah and Josh. Or that Josh wasn't the same as before, and they didn't know what the future held. Oh, and not to mention, they'd brought along the Centrals' princess, who looked like someone had thrown her into a wall then stomped on her.

No there wasn't time to think about any of that. He needed to get his new family and their new friend to safety. Then he could think about the consequences of their fight.

———

BLOOD RACED through Josh's veins as he huffed a breath. But at least he didn't have the haze in his vision that meant he wasn't himself. Their bond settled in like home and felt like honey, comforting him.

They'd found him.

They'd saved him.

He didn't know what he was now, but all that mattered at this point was going home. With his mates. They crested a ridge, and the Jeep came into his vision.

Thank God.

Ellie stirred in his arms. He felt a connection to the female wolf. Not a mate bond or anything near to what he felt with Hannah and Reed, but like a sister. He was also thankful that she was stronger than him, and he owed Ellie so much. He'd care for her and make sure the Redwoods accepted her. From the looks on Reed's and Hannah's faces, he'd have help in this possibly immense endeavor.

Ellie stirred again, and Josh held her close. "Hey, it's okay. I'm going to get you in the Jeep and get you away from here. Okay?"

She nodded and passed out again. One of the wolves must have knocked her unconscious. Or maybe she'd just lost all of her energy. She'd been fighting the battle longer than any of them knew.

Jasper and North ran from the forest behind the Jeep yet had a cautious look on their faces. He didn't blame them. He'd gone demon. He didn't know if he'd trust himself in their place.

"What happened?" Jasper asked.

Reed opened his mouth and coughed up a lungful of smoke. "Caym set demon fire behind the boundaries. It hasn't breached it, but it's bad in there."

Josh looked down and grimaced. Their clothes had burn holes and smelled of ash and smoke. Nice. He hadn't even noticed; he'd been too focused on getting out of there.

North walked toward him tentatively, a concerned look on his face. "Who's this?"

There was no reason to lie. They'd find out soon enough. "Ellie. Corbin's sister."

North's eyes widened and Jasper took a step forward.

"Is she safe?" Jasper growled.

"She saved my life," Josh said simply. "The things Corbin did to her..." He couldn't continue. They were Ellie's secrets told to him during his darkest moments, and were not his to divulge.

North nodded and took her from Josh's arms. He placed her gently on the back seat of the Jeep. Hannah walked up from behind Josh and wrapped her arms around his waist, burying her face in his chest. He held her close, relief pouring through her. His body shook, and he fought back tears.

"We should go," he rasped.

Reed leaned in and kissed both of their temples, lingering for a moment. "Come on."

Jasper got in the front, and Reed sat in the passenger seat. It wasn't a large Jeep, so North held Ellie in his lap and Josh sat with Hannah on his. The sickly feeling that plagued him since he'd flashed to the Centrals and knelt before Caym slowly ebbed away to be replaced by the warmth from the little witch on his lap currently rubbing against his cock and the wolf in front of him who turned to stare into his eyes.

They were his salvation. Now he just needed to feel like he earned it.

Jasper drove like a bat out of hell until they finally reached the den. The wards surrounding it melted over him as they passed through, calling him home. Ellie sat up abruptly and whimpered.

"Shh..." North whispered. "We're at the Redwood den."

Her eyes widened, fear wafting off her.

"You'll be safe here." North held her hand and brushed a long brown lock of hair out of her face. "We know what you did for Josh. We'll get you fixed up. I promise."

"Corbin?" she rasped.

Hannah gently placed her hand on the woman's and Ellie flinched, snatching her hand back.

Oh geez.

"He's still alive," Hannah said. "But he's hurt. Caym is alive too, but we bound him to this plane."

Ellie scrunched her face, the bruises stark against the caramel of her skin. "What?"

Reed turned around in his seat to face her. "According to the elders, he can't leave this plane. Nor can he bring any more demons to Earth. He's weakened, but still strong."

Relief poured over her face. "Oh."

The Jeep came to a stop in front of North's clinic, and Maddox practically ripped the door off its hinges. Maddox growled, and his eyes widened. Ellie gasped and shrank into North.

North merely raised a brow, and Maddox stepped back, allowing North to get out the car with Ellie in his arms. "I'm going to take Ellie to the clinic. Hannah, get your boys Healed and don't forget about yourself. When you have the energy and your magic's replenished, come on over and help."

North walked away, Ellie still in his arms. Josh helped Hannah out of the car and stared at Maddox. A stormy look crossed over the man's face, but it was so full of longing it made Josh shift away.

What the hell?

Maddox turned to him, his face now carefully composed. "Good to see you back," he grunted, and punched Josh in the arm. "Don't leave again."

"I'm not planning on it," Josh said.

"You better not," Jasper added.

Maddox and Jasper walked away, leaving Josh with his mates. Reed pulled him into a tight hug and kissed him hard. His mate's taste burst on his tongue as their teeth clashed together and Josh was hungry for more. They broke apart, both panting heavily.

Hannah slipped in between them and pressed her lips to his. Her sweet taste mingled with Reed's, and he fell into bliss.

He pulled back and tucked a curl behind her ear. "Let's go home." His voice was a rough, needy whisper on the wind.

Home. His heaven.

CHAPTER TWENTY-NINE

Hannah sighed as she stretched, her muscles aching from their fight. She couldn't heal herself, a drawback of her powers. But she'd heal eventually. She wasn't too bad. Her men were worse off. She pulled at her magic but felt depleted. Empty. Worn out. She looked in the mirror at her pale face, her brown curls framing the slight bruising, her gray eyes wide. She should go outside and lay on the soil to replenish, but she wanted to do it another way. A way she hadn't yet done before. A way the men in her life would appreciate. She grinned at her reflection.

When they got home, she'd Healed them then went back to North's clinic to check on Ellie. The other woman's bruises were already fading due to her werewolf powers, but Hannah had done more just in case. Just as she'd finished, Edward and Pat had walked in. A shiver had gone down her back at the look on the Alpha's face.

Pain at seeing his enemy's daughter? Or pain at the defeated look on her face that she couldn't quite cover up quick enough? Without thinking, Hannah had stood in front of Ellie, trying to protect her. But what good could she do? Ellie, however, moved out of the way and knelt on the floor in front of Edward, her throat bared.

Magic had pooled in the room, warm tingles tracing up her arms.

Pack magic wrapped its way around her body and held her close. It felt like summer and smelled like forest, rain, sunshine, and wolf.

"You are Pack," Edward whispered.

Ellie had broken down in gut-wrenching sobs and fallen into Pat's awaiting arms. Hannah knew what if felt like to be enveloped by the Pack. But by the way Ellie reacted, Hannah had no idea how it felt to be part of a Pack that hated. Hannah had left them at the clinic and come home, heavy thoughts on her mind. Though she'd healed the beautiful, exotic wolf, there were some things she couldn't touch. Some things ran deeper than a cut or bruise.

Maybe Maddox could help...

Hannah shook her head and brought herself to the present. She put on a black and red lacy number she'd bought to surprise her men before all of this. With a secret smile on her face, she walked out of the bathroom and into the bedroom. The two froze.

She looked at her two men, and tingles spread like syrup over her body. Reed with his sandy blond hair that was getting too long and almost reached his shoulders begging her fingers to grab hold, stared at her with a heated look on his face. The locks framed his face and his forest green eyes. Josh with his short brown hair, spiking slightly on top, flexed his newly tattooed arms, fisted his hands and breathed deeply. His deep blue eyes stared back at her with their rim of red, reminding her how close they'd been to losing him.

Goddess. I love them.

"When did you get that?" Reed asked, his voice deep with need.

Hannah walked into the room toward them, cocked her head to the side, and swiveled her hips. "What? This old thing? Do you like it?" She turned on her heel slowly, the heat of their gazes warming her up to a molten flame.

Josh growled, the vibrations sending shivers up her spine. "Come here."

Butterflies danced in her stomach and she turned then prowled towards her men, both panting with need, their chests rising and falling in heavy breaths. Reed took her in his arms and lowered his lips to hers. His heady male taste weakened her knees, but Josh was there to catch her. Oh the joys of having two men.

Reed pulled her closer and kissed her, his fingers playing with her nipples and caressing the underside of her breasts. Josh knelt between her legs and dragged the lace up her body, exposing the fact she was not wearing underwear. Both men inhaled a deep breath and Josh rubbed his face on her mound. She rocked against him, edging him closer. He put both hands on her ass and used his knee to spread her legs before he licked her clit.

Oh goddess.

Reed kissed her, dividing her attention between the two men. But did she care? No. She was happy just where she was, sandwiched between the two of them. Josh sucked harder, humming against her, and she closed her eyes in bliss. She trailed her hand down Reed's bare chest until she could blindly unsnap his jeans and grab his cock. Reed moaned in her mouth and flicked her nipple, making her moan right back. She twisted her wrist and stroked Reed, who took a minute to disrobe completely. She opened her eyes to see Josh doing the same, then he raised his face and smiled, her juices on his lips.

Damn.

He stood and lifted the lace above her head, leaving her naked before her two naked men. Did it get any better than this? Her fist tightened on Reed, and he groaned. She worked him harder, and he trailed kisses down her neck, her breasts, her lips. Josh licked and sucked until she couldn't hold on anymore and shattered against his face, Reed following right behind. Her knees turned to jelly, and she fell into Josh's embrace. Josh sat on the floor with her in his lap and kissed her, and she could taste herself.

"Oh goddess. Was it ever this good?" She moaned.

"It's always been good, but this was better." Josh smiled and winked.

"Hell yeah," Reed agreed.

Hannah grinned and wiggled off Josh's lap and knelt in front of him before licking the engorged head of his penis. He groaned and lifted his hips.

Oh, her boy wanted more. Okay, then.

She opened her mouth and swallowed him whole, the tip hitting the back of her throat. He worked his way in and out. She looked up at his and batted her eyelashes.

"Oh God, I love you, baby." Josh groaned and stroked Reed's cock.

She loved that the three of them could touch each other always. She hollowed her cheeks and wrapped her fingers around the base until Josh's balls drew up and he came down her throat with a guttural scream.

Still hard, Reed stood up, his cock bouncing against his stomach, and laid on the bed. Josh lifted her from the floor and carried her to the bed, her head cradled to his chest. Josh set her down, and she moved to straddle Reed. With a grin on her face, she slowly lowered herself on him, and they both released a strangled groan.

"Bend over him, Hannah," Josh ordered, and she heard him mess with something in the nightstand drawer.

She looked down at Reed and stared into his green eyes.

"You feel so good around me, baby," Reed moaned.

Josh got on the bed, the movement making her clit rub against Reed.

Yes.

Josh moved behind her and rubbed something cool between her cheeks. "You said you wanted to do this earlier. Are you sure, baby?"

She loved the way they both cared for her, but she wanted them both in her. Now.

"I'm ready, Josh. Please," she moaned.

He worked a finger in to the knuckle, and she froze. They'd done finger play before to prepare her, but the anticipation of what was to come sent tingles down her spine.

"Shh, Hannah." Josh groaned. "I won't go any farther. Just relax. You're tight, baby. You're gonna feel fucking amazing around my cock."

Hannah rocked on top of Reed, and he flicked her clit while Josh entered a second then third finger. She stretched and burned, but it was the good kind. Reed rocked against her, and she reached the edge of her crest but fell back once Josh removed his fingers.

She whimpered at the loss.

"It's okay, baby. I'm here. Are you ready for me?"

She nodded, lowered her chest farther, pressing to Reed, then wiggled her butt. She was past ready. Needy and achy.

Josh pressed the tip of his cock to her back entrance, and she moaned. He pressed forward, and her body burned and stretched, letting him in. He paused as she adjusted to his size because he was far greater in girth than just fingers. Reed held still, his cock in her pussy, as Josh seated himself fully in her ass.

So. Full.

They worked in tandem, filling her, and she sank deep into her bliss, only hearing them breathe and groan at the contact. Finally she reached her crest and came in an explosion of tingles, Josh and Reed following close behind. They all collapsed in a sweaty heap, limbs entangled and chests rising and falling.

Josh kissed her neck. "This may hurt." He pulled out, the burning increasing, but she felt too much like liquid honey to care.

"We need to do this more often." Josh laughed.

"I think you both killed me," Hannah said.

"Well," Reed added, "it is called the little death after all."

Josh grunted. "Who you calling little?"

They laughed and kissed, and Hannah snuggled in to their embrace.

Yeah, this was totally worth it.

———

A COUPLE OF WEEKS LATER, Reed leaned into Josh's side and watched North dance with their wife around the room, while she looked beautiful in her wedding dress. The strapless gown hugged her generous curves and flared out like a mermaid's fins. To him, she looked like a princess.

His princess.

Josh put an arm around his shoulders and hugged him closer. "She's pretty hot, isn't she?"

"We're two very lucky guys."

Josh sighed. "Tell me about it."

Reed took a deep breath. "I know we don't know everything that will happen, but the bond will hold us together. You're home."

Josh lifted his lips in a small smile. "Yeah, I know. And now that I'm an enforcer for your dad, I can actually do something with all this new-found strength."

"Well, I like your strength for other things too." Reed grinned.

Josh laughed and kissed his temple.

Ellie stormed past them, glaring, with Maddox trailing behind her.

"Maddox." Reed grabbed his brother's arm and stopped him. "What's going on?"

"Nothing. I just need to deal with something. Go on, enjoy your day." Maddox walked away, froze, shook his head, and turned in the opposite direction Ellie had gone.

Reed looked to Josh for a clue, but Josh just shook his head.

Whatever. This wasn't the time. This was their day. Well, Hannah's day. He and Josh were there to watch her. Nothing wrong with that.

The room quieted, and Reed stiffened at the newcomer to their reception. No one moved or dared to take a breath.

Adam.

His brother looked like hell. Dark circles smeared under his eyes, and he looked like he'd just come off a bender. Shit. What had happened?

"Adam?" his mother asked, taking a hesitant step toward him.

"Sorry it took me so long to come back," Adam grunted.

And yet for all the time he'd been gone, he looked even worse.

Hannah walked up to Reed and Josh, and they held her close. "Remember, we can't heal him if he doesn't want it, Reed. We'll just be here for him and wait."

He pulled her closer, and hugged Josh who leaned toward them both. Their trinity bond sparked between them, flaring with a heat that that would only extinguish in their bedroom. With their clothes off.

Though not all was bedroom activities.

The Centrals were out there watching. They'd lost their Alpha, but was that a good thing? Corbin's ruthless soul sunk into the depths of a dark morality. He might be an enemy far worse than the narcissistic

Hector. They'd bound the demon to their world. According to the elders, Caym couldn't bring his friends into this world. And hopefully they could kill him now. But was that enough? The odds against them seemed insurmountable.

Josh leaned over and kissed him, bringing him out of his thoughts.

"Hey, stop thinking," Josh admonished. "It's our mating ceremony."

Hannah kissed his jaw. "Everything will still be here tomorrow. Let's just take a day that's all for us."

"I could do that." Reed grinned.

Across the room, baby Brie squealed, and Finn giggled. Hannah sighed in Reed's arms.

"So," he whispered in her ear, "you wanna go start making one of those?"

Josh coughed. "Smooth."

Hannah smiled. "Okay, let's go."

Reed's eyes widened. "Really?"

Hannah hiked up her dress to her knees. "Come on. Let's go. Let's not waste any more time." She scurried through the throngs of people, and Josh laughed.

"I love that woman." Reed sighed.

"Oh, I know. I love her too." Josh agreed.

Reed quirked a brow. "Race ya to her."

"You're on."

They followed their curly-haired beauty, pointedly ignoring the laughter of his knowing family. Yeah, it was good to be a Jamenson.

EPILOGUE

Dammit!

Corbin flung the glass against the wall. The shattered pieces splattered over the floor.

Caym walked up from behind him and caressed his cheek. "Why are you so upset?"

"Why do you think? We lost them, and they bound you."

"Hush, we didn't need them. They took care of your father anyway."

Caym leaned down and brushed his lips across Corbin's. Tingles shot down his spine.

"Plus," Caym added, "I don't need to open another portal. I think I have our answers right here."

"What?"

"Another of my kind."

"What? Why didn't you tell me?"

"It just came to my attention. But don't worry. I think this one will be of help to us. Nothing that's happened will foil our plans."

Corbin sneered. He'd lost his father and sister, but now he was Alpha. He'd make the Redwoods pay for what they'd done. And with Caym and the other demon by his side, nothing could stop them.

The End

Next in the Redwood Pack Series:
A special bonus novella about Melanie and Kade called *A Night Away*
&
Adam finally finds his fate in *Enforcer's Redemption*.

A NOTE FROM CARRIE ANN

Thank you so much for reading **THE REDWOOD PACK BOX SET 1**. I do hope if you liked this story, that you would please leave a review. Not only does a review spread the word to other readers, they let us authors know if you'd like to see more stories like this from us. I love hearing from readers and talking to them when I can. If you want to make sure you know what's coming next from me, you can sign up for my newsletter at www.CarrieAnnRyan.com; follow me on twitter at @CarrieAnnRyan, or like my Facebook page. I also have a Facebook Fan Club where we have trivia, chats, and other goodies. You guys are the reason I get to do what I do and I thank you.

Make sure you're signed up for my MAILING LIST so you can know when the next releases are available as well as find giveaways and FREE READS.

The rest of the series is out now! I hope you enjoy Adam's story in ENFORCER'S REDEMPTION.

I'm also not leaving this world completely. You've met some of the Talons and because I fell for Gideon the first time he walked on the page to help the Redwoods, I knew I had to tell his story. I also knew I wanted to write some of the Redwood Pack children's stories. Rather than write two full series where I wasn't sure how they would work together, I'm doing one better. The Talon Pack series is also out now. It is set thirty years in the future and will revolve around the Talon Pack and how they are interacting in the world and with the Redwoods. Because it's set thirty years in the future, I get to write about a few of the Redwood Pack children finding their mates.

The first novel will be about the Talon Alpha Gideon and....Brie, Jasper and Willow's daughter thirty years from now. It's called *Tattered Loyalties*.

If you don't want to wait that long, I also have my Dante's Circle and Montgomery Ink series going in full swing now so there's always a Carrie Ann book on the horizon!

Redwood Pack Series:
    Book 1: An Alpha's Path
    Book 2: A Taste for a Mate
    Book 3: Trinity Bound
    Redwood Pack Box Set (Contains Books 1-3)
    Book 3.5: A Night Away
    Book 4: Enforcer's Redemption
    Book 4.5: Blurred Expectations
    Book 4.7: Forgiveness
    Book 5: Shattered Emotions
    Book 6: Hidden Destiny
    Book 6.5: A Beta's Haven
    Book 7: Fighting Fate
    Book 7.5 Loving the Omega
    Book 7.7: The Hunted Heart
    Book 8: Wicked Wolf

Want to keep up to date with the next Carrie Ann Ryan Release?
Receive Text Alerts easily!
Text CARRIE to 24587

ABOUT THE AUTHOR

Carrie Ann Ryan is the New York Times and USA Today bestselling author of contemporary, paranormal, and young adult romance. Her works include the Montgomery Ink, Redwood Pack, Fractured Connections, and Elements of Five series, which have sold over 3.0 million books worldwide. She started writing while in graduate school for her advanced degree in chemistry and hasn't stopped since. Carrie Ann has written over seventy-five novels and novellas with more in the works. When she's not losing herself in her emotional and action-packed worlds, she's reading as much as she can while wrangling her clowder of cats who have more followers than she does.

www.CarrieAnnRyan.com

ALSO FROM CARRIE ANN RYAN

The Montgomery Ink: Fort Collins Series:
Book 1: Inked Persuasion
Book 2: Inked Obsession
Book 3: Inked Devotion
Book 4: Inked Craving

The On My Own Series:
Book 1: My One Night
Book 2: My Rebound
Book 3: My Next Play
Book 4: My Bad Decisions

The Tattered Royals Series:
Book 1: Royal Line
Book 2: Enemy Heir

The Ravenwood Coven Series:
Book 1: Dawn Unearthed
Book 2: Dusk Unveiled
Book 3: Evernight Unleashed

Montgomery Ink:

Book 0.5: Ink Inspired
Book 0.6: Ink Reunited
Book 1: Delicate Ink
Book 1.5: Forever Ink
Book 2: Tempting Boundaries
Book 3: Harder than Words
Book 3.5: Finally Found You
Book 4: Written in Ink
Book 4.5: Hidden Ink
Book 5: Ink Enduring
Book 6: Ink Exposed
Book 6.5: Adoring Ink
Book 6.6: Love, Honor, & Ink
Book 7: Inked Expressions
Book 7.3: Dropout
Book 7.5: Executive Ink
Book 8: Inked Memories
Book 8.5: Inked Nights
Book 8.7: Second Chance Ink

Montgomery Ink: Colorado Springs

Book 1: Fallen Ink
Book 2: Restless Ink
Book 2.5: Ashes to Ink
Book 3: Jagged Ink
Book 3.5: Ink by Numbers

The Montgomery Ink: Boulder Series:

Book 1: Wrapped in Ink
Book 2: Sated in Ink
Book 3: Embraced in Ink
Book 4: Seduced in Ink
Book 4.5: Captured in Ink

The Gallagher Brothers Series:

Book 1: Love Restored
Book 2: Passion Restored
Book 3: Hope Restored

The Whiskey and Lies Series:
Book 1: Whiskey Secrets
Book 2: Whiskey Reveals
Book 3: Whiskey Undone

The Fractured Connections Series:
Book 1: Breaking Without You
Book 2: Shouldn't Have You
Book 3: Falling With You
Book 4: Taken With You

The Less Than Series:
Book 1: Breathless With Her
Book 2: Reckless With You
Book 3: Shameless With Him

The Promise Me Series:
Book 1: Forever Only Once
Book 2: From That Moment
Book 3: Far From Destined
Book 4: From Our First

Redwood Pack Series:
Book 1: An Alpha's Path
Book 2: A Taste for a Mate
Book 3: Trinity Bound
Book 3.5: A Night Away
Book 4: Enforcer's Redemption
Book 4.5: Blurred Expectations
Book 4.7: Forgiveness
Book 5: Shattered Emotions
Book 6: Hidden Destiny

Book 6.5: A Beta's Haven
Book 7: Fighting Fate
Book 7.5: Loving the Omega
Book 7.7: The Hunted Heart
Book 8: Wicked Wolf

The Talon Pack:
Book 1: Tattered Loyalties
Book 2: An Alpha's Choice
Book 3: Mated in Mist
Book 4: Wolf Betrayed
Book 5: Fractured Silence
Book 6: Destiny Disgraced
Book 7: Eternal Mourning
Book 8: Strength Enduring
Book 9: Forever Broken

The Elements of Five Series:
Book 1: From Breath and Ruin
Book 2: From Flame and Ash
Book 3: From Spirit and Binding
Book 4: From Shadow and Silence

The Branded Pack Series:
(Written with Alexandra Ivy)
Book 1: Stolen and Forgiven
Book 2: Abandoned and Unseen
Book 3: Buried and Shadowed

Dante's Circle Series:
Book 1: Dust of My Wings
Book 2: Her Warriors' Three Wishes
Book 3: An Unlucky Moon
Book 3.5: His Choice
Book 4: Tangled Innocence
Book 5: Fierce Enchantment

Book 6: An Immortal's Song
Book 7: Prowled Darkness
Book 8: Dante's Circle Reborn

Holiday, Montana Series:
Book 1: Charmed Spirits
Book 2: Santa's Executive
Book 3: Finding Abigail
Book 4: Her Lucky Love
Book 5: Dreams of Ivory

The Happy Ever After Series:
Flame and Ink
Ink Ever After

Made in the USA
Monee, IL
24 July 2021